LETTERS OF LIGHT & SHADOW

THE SHATTERING CHRONICLES BOOK 1

JENNIFER POLIWODA

Formatted by the author using Atticus.

Cover art and maps created by the author using original hand-drawn illustrations, refined with Krita and finalized in Canva.

CONTENT WARNINGS

☆ Explicit sexual content

☆ Religious indoctrination and dogmatic oppression

☆ Totalitarian regimes and state surveillance

☆ Gaslighting and emotional manipulation by authority figures

☆ Exploration of cult-like behavior and systemic propaganda

☆ Mental health deterioration and existential questioning

☆ Grief and loss of parents/family

☆ Implied and described war-related trauma

☆ Descriptions of magical harm or bodily consequences

☆ Public indoctrination ceremonies with psychological intensity

☆ Depictions of oppressive rituals and enforced obedience

☆ Uncomfortable age and power gaps with possible emotional grooming undertones

If any of the above themes are upsetting or triggering for you, please proceed with care. Your mental health matters more than any story.

If you find yourself overwhelmed, please prioritize your well-being. You can always pause, step away, or choose not to continue; that is valid, and respected.

You are not alone. You are important. Take care of you.

If you need support, consider reaching out to a mental health resource:
- U.S. National Suicide & Crisis Lifeline: Dial 988 or visit 988lifeline.org
- International readers: You can find local crisis lines via findahelpline.com

*For everyone who sees the world burning
and finds refuge in fiction's flame.*

*Most importantly, to my husband;
home is not a place, it's a feeling.*

Sacred Ley Lines
Weeping Trees
Velmourn
Black
Western Valleys
Umbriel
Relin Crest
Blackridge
Mountains
N
W
E
S
Breven's Pos
Shadow Grove

HOLLOW

ELEN'S CROSS

UMBRAXIS

SOLARA

THE VALE

AUREVERRA

KIRETH VALE

ST

ELITH

GLOSSARY OF TERMS

Vaeloria: The main continent, divided into two major regions: **Aureverra** and **Velmourn**.

Aureverra (Realm of Light)
Capital: *Solara* – A radiant city where Umbraxis Academy is located.
Ruler: *The Beacon of the Light* – Claims divine right from the god Light and governs by the divine verse.
Second in Command: *The Hand of Light* – Commands the Luminary Guards and coordinates with the Office of Enlightened Affairs; executes the will of the Beacon.

Umbraxis Academy (or the Academy)
Umbraxis is a general academy that educates students from early childhood through adolescence. At the age of sixteen, students choose their career path, either joining the Guard or the Order. This decision marks the beginning of their *first year* of specialized training.

Military - Light Battalion
Luminary Guards: Core military force under the Light, organized into four Watches, each with its own High Luminary.
Dawn Watch: Scouts, trackers, and border patrol.
Day Watch: Elite enforcers and keepers of public order.
Dusk Watch: Interrogators and hunters of dissent.
Night Watch: Silent operatives including assassins and spies.

Academia - Office of Enlightened Affairs

Light Warden: Headmaster of all Enlightened Orders.

Chancellor of Illumination: Oversees all academic functions.

Orders within the Office:

Order of Illuminants: Educators and scholars.

Order of Gilded Voice: Propagandists and artists who call themselves *Narrative Keepers*.

Order of the Veil: Ideological enforcers and inquisitors, often linked with the Dusk Watch.

Order of the Eternal Record: Historians and archivists who maintain Light's version of history; known as *Sealed Scribes*.

Order of the Sacred Flame: Spiritual leaders and divine casters. Perform rites and ceremonies; called *Verse-Keepers*.

Velmourn (Realm of Shadow)

Capital: *Umbriel* – A hidden city veiled in shadow and mystery.

Ruler: *The True King* – Revered but not obeyed. Leads through memory, pain, and vision.

Second in Command: *The Hand of the Hollow* – Guardian of instinct, clarity, and discipline. Leads the Hollow Guard.

Military - Hollow Guard

Cultural & Temporal Concepts

Luminday: First day of the week; reserved by educators as a "clearing day" for lesson planning and preparation.

Veriday, Pyreday, Kandreday: Core teaching days.

Sovinday, Umbreday, Vaelday: Rest days / the weekend.

Moon Cycles: Time is measured in lunar months; each moon cycle lasts approximately 28 days.

While this glossary includes many frequently referenced terms, it is not an exhaustive guide to the world's magic system or ceremonies. Numerous other concepts appear throughout the text but are defined contextually within the narrative itself. The entries above are provided for reference, as they represent terms that recur often and may benefit from additional clarity while reading.

THE SHATTERING

PROLOGUE

V AELORIA, ONCE A LAND of unity and brilliance, now lies fractured: a kingdom broken by faith and flame.

Before war, before gods, there was only Earth. She was ancient, endless, alone.

For ages, she governed in silence, her presence a quiet force felt in stone and sea, in root and sky. Over time, the weight of humanity, its cries, its hunger, its ceaseless striving, grew too great. Earth, weary of bearing these burdens alone, chose to step back, and in that surrender, she breathed out one final, divine breath from which her sons emerged: twins, born not of flesh but of essence.

Light and Shadow.

Shadow was the first. Born in stillness, he was vast and unseen. His power was drawn from within, deep and unknowable. He was not absence, but presence; a quiet, waiting vastness cradling what was not yet formed. Earth poured much of herself into him, and he held it all gently.

When she turned to create Light, she was nearly spent. What remained of her was fire and pressure, the last sparks of creation. She wove him from what little she had left: light from the sun, flame from her molten heart. His power was drawn not from within, but from without. It blazed brightly, but it was finite, borrowed, incomplete.

Still, the twins rose not to rule, but to guide. Earth had hoped that, together, they might bring balance to her creation, offering humanity power not for domination, but for unity.

For a time, they did just that. Light and Shadow moved together in harmony, their influence woven into every breath of the world. Shadow tempered Light's brilliance, and Light gave form to Shadow's depth.

One watched while the other acted. One remembered while the other reached.

They were worshipped as gods, not because they demanded it, but because their presence stirred something sacred in the hearts of mortals.

Though harmony does not always endure.

Like all siblings, they fought.

At first, their quarrels were harmless. Petty disputes, fleeting as wind through trees. Over centuries, their rivalry deepened. Light, impulsive and proud, bristled at Shadow's quiet certainty. Shadow, patient but distant, grew weary of Light's need to shine.

Seeing this discord, Earth stirred once more, briefly; just long enough to punish not only her sons, but also those who worshipped them.

With fleeting bits of her strength, she plunged the world into silence and darkness; not shadow, but absence: a void so complete that even the stars vanished from the sky.

The world changed.

In the absence, time itself faltered. Days no longer passed; only moments stretched, suspended and unmeasured. The crops failed first, withering under a sky that gave no warmth. Then the animals grew restless, untethered by the rhythms they had always known. Some fell into endless sleep.

Others turned wild, frenzied, tearing at one another as if trying to claw light from flesh.

But it was the people who suffered most.

Without the sun to anchor them, madness crept in like a silent tide, songs curdled into screams and temples became tombs. Families, unable to tell dawn from dusk, fell into despair. Fires were lit and relit in desperation, but no flame could banish what pressed in from all sides.

It was not darkness. It was nothing.

Dreams became indistinguishable from waking. Voices were heard where none stood. Some say Earth had opened her mouth and forgotten to close it, others believe she had simply turned away.

The only path was reconciliation. So the brothers made peace, if only to lift the darkness.

But in that silence, something had shifted.

Light, though outwardly contrite, harbored unease. The void had felt too much like Shadow. It was still, formless, and infinite.

He began to wonder whether Earth had favored his brother. Perhaps the punishment had been a gift.

And so, slowly, he began to twist the story: a whisper here, a doubt there. He told his followers it was Shadow who had brought the darkness in a fit of rage, and that it was he, Light, who had saved them.

Over generations, the lie grew roots.

Light became the hero. Shadow, the villain.

At first, Light knew what he was doing, but even he began to believe the story he had spun.

Light began to see his brother's stillness as something he lacked. Shadow moved with ease, his strength flowing from a deep and endless source. Light's power flickered; it had to be drawn, channeled, and fed. In that realization, jealousy bloomed. Fear followed.

What if his powers faded?

What if the people turned toward the dark, to the freedom Shadow offered?

So Light sought control.

He bound his power in laws: rigid, bright, unyielding. He declared that obedience would bring clarity, that purity was the key to divine favor. Those who faltered were cast out, those who questioned were marked as impure. Over time, his fire, once meant to guide, began to consume.

Shadow watched, but did not interfere. His gifts remained unbound. To receive them required no submission, only mastery. However, mastery came with its own dangers. Without discipline, his power could unravel the soul as surely as Light's could scorch it. Still, he trusted the people to find their way, even if it meant falling.

The twins turned away from each other again. The bond between them, once indivisible, broke.

With their parting, the land itself shattered.

From the wreckage rose two kingdoms, reflections of their creators. This wreckage, this parting, was known thereafter as the Shattering.

To the east lay Aureverra, the realm of Light.

There, the sun never falters, and the streets shine with golden stone. It is a kingdom of law and order, built on devotion and sacrifice. Its temples ring with sermons proclaiming divine unity. Its priests enforce purity with unwavering zeal. Doubt is considered disease; dissent is treated as decay. Aureverra claims to protect, but its brilliance blinds. It does not guide; it erases.

To the west, hidden in shadowed valleys and ancient forests, lies Velmourn, the refuge of Shadow.

It did not rise to conquer, but to remember. It shelters what was forgotten and what was cast aside: memory, instinct, freedom.

The people of Velmourn are labeled heretics, whispered of in Aureverran lore as monsters lurking in the dark. But they do not seek thrones. They seek only to endure, and to keep alive the truths that Light tried to burn away.

Yet even sanctuary is seen as rebellion, and so the war endures.

Generation after generation, it rages on, not only across battlefields, but in hearts, in choices, and in every moment one must choose between obedience and freedom, between brilliance and depth.

There is no end in sight, but even in the dark, something stirs.

SEEDS OF
LIGHT AND SHADOW
PRESENT TIME

From *Of Light, Shadow, and Kings; The Rule of Twin Flame*

The Chronicles of The Shattering

"And so the Crown broke — not by blade, but by belief.
The twin thrones were not emptied by death, but by division.
Light declared itself sovereign.
Shadow did not contest. It simply vanished."

This passage marks what historians now call the *Shattering*: the moment the unity between the divine twins collapsed, and with it, the last vestiges of harmony within the realm. Where once dual rule promised balance, only one voice remained, and it rang too loudly.

Not an Outsider

THE MORNING SUN FILTERS through my window, fractured by stained glass into shards of cold light that pool on the wooden floor like spilled water. It strikes my face, sharp and too bright.

The light clings to my skin with a familiarity I have not yet earned.

It is a sharp contrast to the muted greens I had grown up with, a lifetime spent beneath the forest canopy, where sunbeams fell in lazy shafts through layers of thick green boughs. There, light came softly and humbly, brushed with moss and shadow, filtered by nature's hand and never in a hurry.

The forest had been my sanctuary.

Trees older than cities stood in quiet congress, their branches high and interlaced like vaulted ceilings. Time moved slower there, measured not by the sun's rise and fall, but by the distant calls of migrating birds, the soft tread of deer hooves on fallen leaves, the cacophony of cicadas, and the slow crawl of the seasons. That was the rhythm I knew, one where the world did not watch you so closely.

Umbraxis Academy feels too bright, too exposed, too ordered.

Light bounces from every stained-glass window, refracting into kaleidoscopic brilliance on the marble floors. Golden railings gleam like weaponry: polished, perfect, purposeful. Yet, beneath all that radiance, there is a rigidity. A silence that is not peace, but pressure. Something unnatural. The light feels like surveillance; everything watches, judges, catalogs.

The academy's entire presence is as commanding and exacting as the Light it venerates. This is ironic, perhaps, because from a distance, Umbraxis looks cloaked in gloom. Its silhouette is a crown of shadowed spires piercing the sky like obsidian teeth. It looms over the city like a sentry, hunched and silent, as if guarding secrets no one dares name. The walls, built from black stone, shimmer like oil when sunlight strikes them. Ivy winds across their surface, pulsing faintly as though the building itself breathes. The air always smells of incense, chalk, and something older... deep magic, stale from long confinement.

The windows, tall and narrow, stretch like skeletal fingers toward the sky. Each pane burns with enchantments after sunset, becoming living murals of the Light's saints: their victories, their sacrifices, their dominion. The glass does not tell stories so much as enforce them, doctrine in stained light.

At night, Umbraxis whispers not in voices, but in a language older than speech; a language woven through policy, through architecture, through blood.

They say Umbraxis is a bastion of learning, the highest seat of knowledge in Aureverra. To me, it feels more like a fortress: ornate, beautiful, suffocating.

Despite the darkness, which comforts me in ways I dare not name, the light remains. It is plentiful but cold... a calculated brightness, less illumination, more warning.

Here, light does not simply reveal, it rules.

Every student at Umbraxis comes here for one purpose, to seek the Light. To be shaped by it, into servants, into swords.

They study its movements and laws. They learn to bend it to their will, to carve it into weapons and words. Those who master their magic are permitted to graduate. Their futures are bound to one of two paths: the Light Battalion or the Office of Enlightened Affairs.

Neither tolerates dissent, both are arms of the same blade.

With the pall of war stretching across the kingdom for the past nine years, mastery has become more than tradition, it is survival. The war hums beneath every lesson and every ritual. It is a quiet pulse, ever-present; a reminder that Light must remain unyielding, watchful, and vigilant.

Somewhere beyond these marble walls, in forests, in ruins, in memory, there are those who have turned toward Shadow. Each day, the divide widens.

Light demands loyalty, there is no room for doubt.

I personally never learned to wield Light. I never could. Still, here I am at Umbraxis, not as a student, but as an Educator, a member of the Order of Illumination. Today marks my first official day.

Classes will not begin for another week, but I am expected on campus early for onboarding. Today, I have a meeting with the Chancellor of Illumination and the Light Warden, along with a formal introduction to my classroom and office. A quiet beginning, all things considered.

For a first-year Educator, my schedule is not so bad.

The week begins with Luminday, a full day set aside for preparation. My Pa used to call it the clearing day. Clear your desk, your mind, and your intentions.

Then come the teaching days: Veriday, Pyreday, and Kandreday. Three in a row, each with its own cadence. I will teach four classes each day; an hour apiece, all Sacred Narratives, but tailored to students from second to fifth-year. Same subject, different depths; like telling the same story to four different rivers and watching how each carries it away.

On the second Veriday of every lunar cycle, the Office of Enlightened Affairs convenes, all five Orders attend. They call them Illumination Meetings, discussions on curriculum, students, behavior, adjustments, and things that need correcting or realigning.

After that, the rest days unfold: Sovinday, Umbreday, and Vaelday. Mine to shape. I do not yet know what they will become, possibly days filled with reading for pleasure, long mornings, and even longer silences.

Seven days, one rhythm.

The only interruption comes when the moon disappears. Those days belong to the Temple Hall and the Solis Rite.

It is not balance, but it might be enough.

I never saw the academy before division: when Light and Shadow walked these halls in uneasy peace, when curiosity was louder than reverence, when the old myths were just that. Myths, not marching orders. I never saw it before the Shattering, before Vaeloria cracked beneath the weight of prophecy and pride, before the breath of the gods shattered into warring winds.

Now, all we breathe is doctrine, dust, and ash.

Snapping back to the present, I blink against the sunbeams clawing their way through my window and sit up.

The day waits for no one.

I roll out of bed and shuffle toward the mirror, pausing for a breath before meeting my own gaze. A pale face stares back, framed by dark and unruly hair. The shadows beneath my eyes are faint but deep, bruises from too many late nights spent reading by candlelight. My cheekbones seem sharper in the unforgiving morning. My skin still holds the memory of forest wind and sun-dappled shade.

There is something wild in my expression still, some feral trace of the girl who whispered poetry to crows. I reach up and touch the side of my face, half-expecting it to vanish like fog.

I turn and make my way to the ancient claw-foot tub and twist the tap for hot water. It groans, then sputters to life. As the water rises, I move through my small cabin, tucking last-minute items I might need into my satchel.

The first is *The Star Thief*, its spine soft and edges curled. A children's book, yes, but layered with annotation. Every margin is a conversation with the girl I used to be. It is a tether to the forest, to my family, to the boy who gave it to me, a reminder of who I was meant to become.

I tuck it into my satchel along with a journal, ink, and quills.

When the bath is full, I ease in and let the heat untie the tension in my limbs. Steam curls along the windows.

I still cannot believe I am here.

Not long ago, I was a barefoot girl traipsing about the forest, collecting flora like they were secrets whispered by the earth: fern fronds tucked behind ears, wild violets cradled in my palms, pockets brimming with moss and wonder. The sun was a golden lantern above me, and every breeze felt like a story brushing past my skin. Back then, the world spoke softly, and I still knew how to listen.

Now, I am an Educator at the most prestigious academy in the kingdom. No one expected it, not even me.

I did not come through the traditional channels. I never followed the correct path: no formal schooling, no internships in the Sacred Flame, no purification rite before the Verse-Keepers, no Solis Rite attendance.

My education came through bark-bound books and questions whispered to trees. I chose the forest over politics. I ignored the whispers of war, opting to hear the whispers of the earth itself. I chose silence over ambition.

Rarely did I leave the safety of the forest, so I never quite understood all the changes happening in the world. In doing so, I missed the war creeping into every corner of the realm.

I was naive, but determined; stubborn and quietly bold. I submitted a thesis to the academy, and without warning, an invitation arrived.

There were whispers, of course. That I was some rare, raw, and untamed prodigy plucked from obscurity. That someone in the Luminary had plans for me.

Little did they know, I have no magic, no powers, not of Light or Shadow. I am untouched by the gods, never able to channel no matter how hard and long I tried. I do not know how that makes me an untamed prodigy.

I have stories and memory, that is powerful as well.

Lucien never confirmed anything, but I know my presence at the academy was his doing. Him being the Beacon of Light and current Light Warden.

When we first locked eyes across the Grand Hall, his expression was unreadable. Just the faintest flicker of recognition, or was it regret?

I still do not know why he vouched for me, but I accepted. Because something in me was tired of hiding, tired of wondering if I would ever be seen, tired of being alone.

When I rise from the bath, I wrap myself in a wool robe and sit by the mirror again. I braid my hair loosely, fingers deft and shaking just slightly. I weave in three small white blossoms collected during last night's walk.

They're a piece of the wild I will not let go of, my own quiet rebellion.

I pull on my dress, deep green sleeves fall to my wrists, the fabric brushing my skin like leaves. My dark loafers are polished, yet worn enough to feel like mine.

Today, I walk through the doors of Umbraxis for the first time. Not as an outsider, but as Sylvaine Nox, Educator; a bearer of stories and a keeper of the wild.

The campus is a vast constellation of buildings and bridges strung like pearls across the mountainside.

I chose to live in the cabin farthest from it, nestled at the edge of the tree line where the forest still remembers my name. It used to be a supply shed, but that didn't deter me.

The wild grounds me. The quiet helps.

As I make my way to the main campus, I savor the unusual calm before students return and fill the walkways with noise.

We gather for orientation in the courtyard, a quiet sanctum cradled by marble colonnades that gleam like bone in the tender light of morning. Sunlight filters through the arches in long, golden blades, catching on the pale stone and casting shifting halos across the ground. Beneath our feet lies an intricate mosaic, concentric rings of amber, gold, and pearl set into the marble, radiating outward in a sacred heliograph that mirrors the Light's ascent through the heavens.

At its heart rises a fountain shaped like a sunburst unfurling, its petals wide and solemn. The basin is dry this morning, strewn with wind-tossed leaves and faded flower offerings left by unseen hands.

A stillness clings to the air, laced with the faint scent of incense, old ash, and wild herbs from the mountains beyond. The blend is calming, ceremonial, and slightly bittersweet.

Staff and faculty mill about in stiff clusters. Robes in varying shades of white and cream trail along the stone, soft as whispers. Each hem bears the sigil of their Order: the sun flame of the Illumination, the copper quill of the Sealed Scribes, the twin masks of the Gilded Voice, and more; symbols stitched in glinting thread, easy to miss if you weren't looking.

I linger near the edge, silent and observing.

The academy itself is breathtaking, if a little chilling.

Ivy chokes its buildings in thick ropes, clinging with a hunger that feels almost sentient. It winds around pillars and spires, creeping along carved stone like it's trying to reclaim something lost. The stained-glass windows blaze with holy symbolism: halos and fire, sun-blades and blindfolded justice. Legends of glory rendered in colored glass, where the Light always triumphs, always prevails.

But none of the stories feel... full.

Each image is too clean, too one-sided.

There's no blood, no grief, only victory, gleaming and gold.

As the tour begins, I fall into step at the back of the group, quiet and watchful. Elowen, the Chancellor of Illumination, leads the way with a voice smoothed from years of public speaking. Her smile is practiced, but her eyes are sharp beneath the ceremonial circlet she wears. She guides us through arched corridors and sun-dappled courts, naming buildings as though reciting liturgy.

Her words drift over me like water: clear, constant, too much to hold. I try to listen, to anchor meaning to places and paths, but already the details blur, slipping from my grasp as quickly as they arrive.

Inside, the halls echo with my footsteps, a lonely rhythm. The ceilings arch like ribs high above us. Chandeliers shaped like radiant suns hang in long rows, shedding warm light over velvet banners that line the stone walls in solemn procession.

Each banner bears the crest of the Light, a stylized sunburst, its script once flowing and philosophical is now more rigid, more forceful. Beneath the old motto, *Obedience is Clarity. Clarity is Peace*, a second line has been stitched in, new and unmistakable:

The Shadow Corrupts. The Light Protects.

I blink. My stomach tightens.

We pass into the Main Hall and the scent shifts to old parchment, melted wax, and sun-warmed stone. It smells like history, and something less alive; like a library sealed too long, or a prayer spoken too often.

The tour ends in a wave of polite dispersal, murmured farewells and nods exchanged as the group begins to scatter like smoke through the marbled halls. Elowen clasps her hands and reminds the new Educators, softly, but with unmistakable weight, that each of us is to report alone to the Light Warden's chambers for final placement discussions. There is no schedule handed out, no list, only a name called at intervals, and silence in between.

I wait in a sunlit vestibule. The benches are carved from pale cedar, polished smooth by generations of anticipation. Light spills down from high windows in fractured beams, illuminating the motes of dust that drift in slow spirals, as if the very air here moves differently.

One by one, names are spoken by an unseen voice beyond the doors: soft, disembodied, yet absolute. Each name stirs a ripple of tension through the room.

I wait, back straight, hands folded in my lap, trying not to look nervous. I count the names and listen to the footsteps that follow. The doors open and close with a slow, echoing sigh.

When at last my name is called, it cuts through the silence like a thread pulled tight.

"Sylvaine."

I rise and walk toward the Light.

The doors to the Light Warden's chambers close softly behind me, the weight of the room immediately pressing down. Lucien, seated at the head of a polished oak table, looks up as I enter.

Lucien Corwell, the Beacon of Light and the Light Warden of Umbraxis Academy. My parents' former best friend. My reluctant mentor.

He's middle-aged, the same as my parents would be if they were still alive, but he wears the years like a polished mask. His features are symmetrical, classically handsome in a forgettable way, neither severe nor soft: dark blond hair perfectly combed back, beard trimmed just enough to suggest wisdom, not age.

His robes are immaculate, gold embroidery catching the light like thread spun from fire. He looks like someone a painter would use as the template for "righteous authority."

His brown eyes catch the light, giving them an almost molten quality. He smiles warmly, though there's a quiet assessment in his gaze, as if weighing me in ways that go beyond the casual familiarity we share.

Beside him, Elowen stands with her usual air of composed authority. Her robes, crisp and unyielding, shimmer faintly in the sunlight that filters through the tall windows. She is a sharp contrast to Lucien's relaxed posture. Her expression is more guarded, but her presence is no less commanding.

"Ah, Sylvaine," Lucien says, his voice smooth and warm, a smile playing at the corner of his lips. He rises to greet me with a look of unmistakable pleasure, his brown eyes glimmering with something more than polite interest.

"I've been looking forward to this moment. I am sure that if your parents were able to see you standing here today, they'd be proud as well." He adds, his tone light, almost teasing. "It's good to see you again."

He steps a little closer, his gaze steady and his words carrying a hint of something more playful. "Really good, in fact."

The words catch in my throat, and I offer a brief, polite nod. I don't respond immediately, instead holding the emotions his words stir in me at bay.

"I appreciate that," I manage, keeping my voice even and controlled.

Lucien tilts his head slightly, his expression thoughtful, but there's still that lingering warmth in his eyes. "I think you're going to do well here. The Light needs people who know its history, people who can understand what it represents. I'm glad you're here."

The weight of his gaze feels like it's testing me in some way, as though the conversation is only beginning and I'm already being sized up for something more.

At this, Elowen clears her throat, her gaze shifting between us with an unspoken command to move things along. She places a folder in front of her, the corners of her mouth tightening. "As much as I'm sure you're both eager to reminisce, Lucien, we do have business to attend to."

Lucien laughs softly, but it's clear he's more interested in the exchange than in rushing to the details. He gestures for me to take a seat, his eyes glinting with mischief.

"Of course, of course. Let's get to the task at hand," he says, all ease once more. "Sylvaine, we're all aware of your... heritage. Your parents' legacy is one of great significance. But let's talk about your role here, shall we?"

I sit, leaning slightly forward, feeling the weight of the moment settle in my chest. I had come here for this very reason, to begin a new chapter, but I hadn't quite expected the undercurrent of tension to feel so palpable.

"You'll be teaching the ancient myths and lore that you requested, of course," Lucien continues, his fingers lightly tapping on the table. "Sacred narratives that have shaped the foundation of this place, that have shaped us, our understanding of the Light. We need someone who can breathe life into these old stories, someone with a command of the material, and who isn't afraid to... make an impression."

His words stir something in me, a mixture of pride and anxiety. It's not the first time someone's told me I must take charge, but here in this room, with their expectations so clear, it feels different.

"Your role as an Educator in the Order is paramount," Elowen adds, her voice steady and clipped. "We expect you to guide our students through our stories, our truths, but also to maintain discipline in the classroom. We cannot afford to have any... misunderstandings."

I nod, swallowing the dry lump in my throat. "I understand. I'll do my best."

Lucien's smile widens, his gaze softening for a moment. "I have no doubt about that. But," he leans forward, voice low, almost playful, "you'll need to establish your authority in the classroom from the very start. Be strong. Command the room. The students will respect you more for it."

There's something in the way he says it that makes me pause, as if there's an unspoken implication I'm not entirely comfortable with. But I don't challenge it. Instead, I focus on the core of what he's saying.

The classroom is mine, the control is mine.

"I'll keep that in mind," I say, forcing a calmness into my voice.

Elowen, ever the pragmatist, speaks next, her gaze cutting sharply toward Lucien before turning back to me. "There's one more thing. The stories you teach must align with the truth we uphold here, our truth."

Her eyes flicker toward the heavy, gilded banners hanging in the chamber, the embroidered sunburst motif gleaming in the lazy afternoon sun. "Some myths, some narratives, can be... dangerous. We expect you to be cautious in what you choose to share. There's a fine line between teaching history and encouraging rebellion."

The weight of her words presses down on me. I nod again, though my pulse quickens. "I will be careful."

Lucien, who had been watching me with an almost too-intense focus, finally leans back in his chair, his smile returning to something warmer, more familiar. "I have no doubt you'll be fine, Sylvaine. Just remember, keep your distance from the darker myths. Don't let them cloud your teaching."

A flicker of discomfort stirs in me, but I bite my tongue.

Darker myths?

The ones that don't fit neatly into their narrative of the Light's unblemished victory?

"I'll teach as expected," I reply, the words tasting faintly of surrender.

"Good," Lucien says, standing and offering me a grin that feels just a touch too knowing. "We'll be watching, of course. Both of us." His eyes meet mine. There's an underlying intensity in them, a reminder of the history between us, something I don't know if I fully understand but have no choice but to accept.

Elowen, still standing, gestures towards the door, the sharpness of her movements makes the finality of the meeting clear. "We'll meet again soon to discuss your first lessons, Sylvaine. But for now, you're free to begin preparing. We have high expectations."

With that, the meeting concludes, the weight of their words lingering like a shadow at my back as I leave the chamber. The air feels colder now, thicker. I can't shake the feeling that something has shifted, something I might not fully comprehend yet.

My mind is spinning with new responsibilities, a sense of unease settling in. I've been handed the role of Educator, keeper of myth and truth, but at what cost?

How long before I find myself caught between the Light's glittering certainty and the stories I can no longer ignore?

After the tense meeting with Lucien and the Chancellor, I'm escorted to my office by a Scribe.

The corridor ahead stretches long and vaulted. Arched stone walls are lined with tapestries, their threads weaving the story of Light and Shadow.

A golden-helmed hero appears again and again, scattering cloaked figures into retreat. In one scene, a shadowed figure extends an open hand, peaceful, but in the next, that hand is pierced by a blade of pure Light.

My spine prickles. The figure cloaked in Shadow looks familiar... could almost be...

No, it's just the fabric playing tricks on me.

Yet something flickers within me, something too familiar to ignore. Memories of my childhood drift in like a quiet fog.

My parents never brought me to the city when they volunteered at the academy, and when they returned, they were always a little distant, their words clipped, as though something had been left behind, something they couldn't name. After their death, the forest became my refuge, holding me like a breath that refused to be exhaled. It kept me grounded, safe.

Alone, I turned inward: learning, surviving, clinging to memories of a boy with eyes like moonlight and a mind full of stars. We whispered of gods and ghosts beneath the trees, shaping our world in the silence of the woods.

We never spoke of war, not until it became impossible to ignore.

I was seventeen when the war became undeniable. Now, at twenty-six, I've outgrown the forest's protective silence. I left it behind, stepping into a world where Light rules and obedience is law.

Umbraxis wasn't always like this. But the questions I buried long ago are surfacing, unanswered, pulling at the edges of everything I thought I understood.

As I near my office, sunlight catches a panel of stained glass, sending brilliant colors spilling across the floor. The image shows a boy surrounded by Light soldiers. He is wielding Shadow not in fear, but as if it belongs to him. His stance is commanding, his jaw set in quiet strength.

I freeze. The glass flickers again, but I tell myself it was just a trick of the light.

But something stirs inside me again, a memory clawing its way up only to slip away before I can grasp it.

I turn my gaze away, my chest hollow.

I don't belong here, not in this city of ever-gleaming Light.

I make it to my office, it lies in a quiet wing of the eastern hall.

The door sticks slightly as I turn the key, creaking as it opens into the not-so-empty room. It's narrow, with high ceilings that arch, the windows soft with curling ivy. Shelves half-filled with dusty tomes line the walls. A modest desk anchors the center of the room, surrounded by an eclectic array of mismatched chairs scattered throughout the space.

It could be mine, it might never truly feel like it.

AN UNSETTLING START

THE SUN HAD BARELY risen when I left the quiet of my cabin and headed toward the academy. It is Veriday, the first day of classes. The campus stirs to life around me, a quiet contrast to the truth beneath it all: this is also the day with no moon, the Solis Rite.

Mandatory, always.

A tolling bell echoes through the courtyard as I enter: low, hollow, final. My heart sinks. The sound reverberates through me, marking the beginning of a new cycle, a reminder of the weight that presses upon us all.

The air in my small office is thickening with myrrh, the scent of ritual that permeates everything today. It never fails to feel anything less than suffocating.

I cross the room to the hook where my ceremonial robe hangs, waiting. They are white, embroidered with Light-bound sigils, with a golden sash that threads through the waist like a leash.

These robes are meant to erase us. All who wear them surrender their identity in favor of uniformity.

Descending into the Temple Hall is like sinking beneath the skin of the world.

The corridor narrows before it opens, the stone changing from black basalt to veined alabaster, a transformation that feels almost surgical, like bone exposed. Soft veins of living flame dance beneath crystal inlays that run along the walls, pulsing with gentle light, not bright, but constant. Sacred braziers line the path ahead, burning sun leaf, magnolia bark, sage, and root-glow, the rare plant said to bloom only on ground once touched by the breath of a god. The scent is layered and thick, a perfume of memory and mandate: sweet, sharp, purifying.

We move as one, hundreds of us, draped in the white ceremonial robes of devotion, each hem stitched with thread spun from sunrise. The silence falls like snowfall, soft, inevitable, and absolute, as we pass beneath the arched threshold and into the hall.

The ceiling vaults above, vast and starless, enchanted glass glowing with an internal radiance. At its center is a sacred mural: the origin of the Light, where golden beams slice through the heavens, splitting the world below into order and chaos.

That division is everything. It watches us as we enter, judges us.

The floor beneath our feet gleams with veins of gold, arranged in a sunburst, radiating outward from a central dais. The lines guide us, draw us forward, obedient feet to the center of all things.

At the heart stands one of the Verse-Keepers, a towering figure robed in ceremonial gold, face concealed behind a mask wrought in sun-metal: serene, inhuman, inscrutable. In his left hand is the Staff of Revelation, topped with a radiant crystal that catches the Light and splinters it into holy rainbows. In his right, the Scroll of First Flame, a relic said to contain the unaltered verses of divine law, transcribed before time had voice.

A silence deeper than reverence settles. It is not mere quiet, it is engineered, precise. A silence rehearsed like theater, like a threat. Then, without signal, the choir breathes. The hymn begins:

> *We rise in Light, from ash and flame,*
> *We speak one name, we hold one claim.*
> *O Light, who binds the stars above,*
> *Shine order on the ones You love.*
> *No Shadow dwells where You reside,*
> *No truth exists the dark can hide.*
> *We are the voice, the sword, the line,*
> *By Light we stand, by Light divine.*

The words bloom in the air like smoke catching fire, aching and beautiful. They rise like the morning sun over a battlefield, full of grief and glory. My lips shape them in perfect time with the others, but my voice feels distant, borrowed, like it's singing from somewhere else entirely.

The Verse-Keeper raises the staff.

A beam of pure golden light erupts from its tip, arcing upward to the domed ceiling. The chamber is bathed in brilliance so complete it silences even thought. From the far end of the dais, the Beacon of Light, Lucien, high servant of the Light god himself, rises, clad in robes so white they seem to glow. He joins the Verse-Keeper at the altar.

Together, they speak in unison, their voices echoing like metal on marble:

Let all who bear doubt cast it aside.
Let the Light be your thought, your
breath, your bond.
Let Shadow burn from within you, and
peace reign in its ashes.
Obedience is clarity. Clarity is peace.
The Shadow corrupts. The Light pro-
tects.

Candles are passed from hand to hand. A single spark, lit from the central flame of the altar, spreads like holy contagion; one acolyte, then another, a line of fire moving across rows of bowed heads. The heat rises around us. We are meant to feel purified, forged, but all I feel is... watched, held in place.

The Verse-Keeper lowers his staff. The music fades.

A gesture passes like a ripple through the crowd, and every robed form lowers in synchrony: heads bowed, knees bent, hands clasped over hearts.

A collective surrender.

I bow, too, but something pulls at me, a thread snagged on something unseen. I open my eyes just a sliver, and I see her.

Amid the ocean of bowed heads, one figure remains upright. She is still, quiet, and unshaken. An older woman.

Her robe is the same as ours, but it hangs differently, softer with age, like it remembers more than it should. Her skin is etched with deep, deliberate lines, each wrinkle an elegy. Her silver hair is braided down one shoulder like a snake at rest. But her eyes...

Her eyes hold me. They are kind, terribly kind and yet behind that gentleness, something older burns. Not defiance, not rebellion, something more elemental.

Memory, maybe.

She watches me as if she's waiting for me to become something I don't yet understand. My chest tightens, I drop my gaze fast, heart hammering.

Who is she?

Why was she looking at me?

And why did it feel like she knew me?

The final chant begins, *The Benediction of Flame.*

> *Light without limit. Flame without fear.*
> *May the path ahead burn bright and pure.*
> *Let your shadow fall behind you.*
> *Let your will bend toward the flame.*

I repeat the words, lips moving without will. My thoughts drift, untethered. I lift my eyes to the dome once more. The mural overhead burns gold and perfect, too perfect: a frozen moment, a story already chosen.

There is no mention of balance, no memory of Shadow as sacred: only sin, only silence.

But somewhere in me, something remembers differently. A time when Light did not erase, when it illuminated what it couldn't conquer. When Shadow was not opposition, but counterpart: breath to heartbeat, stillness to flame.

The final hymn ends. The candles are extinguished, one by one.

No one speaks, no one dares.

The Light has been fed and we are expected to feel whole.

I don't, not really, and the silence that follows feels heavier than faith.

Back in my office, I close the door with more force than necessary.

The air feels different, still heavy from the Rite, or maybe it's just me.

I glance toward the small desk by the arched window where a stack of untouched lesson plans sits like an accusation.

I'd hoped they'd come easier, that once I arrived here, once I accepted the position, it would all begin to make sense. But every time I sit to write, I feel like something's missing; something vital, something real, like a voice I've forgotten how to hear.

I sit for a moment, fingers brushing the worn edge of the desk. My eyes drift to the windowpane, where ivy traces delicate green veins across the glass. And then I see her again, in my mind.

The woman from the Rite, upright while the rest of us bowed.

Her face won't leave me. Her eyes, kind, ancient, and still somehow sharp, hold something I can't name; a knowing, like she saw me, not the robe, not the Educator, *me*.

Who was she?

Why wasn't she bowing?

And more importantly, why was she looking at me like she'd been waiting?

A knock at the door startles me, and I straighten, breath catching in my throat.

"Educator Sylvaine?"

I look up to find Lucien standing in the doorway, his presence filling the frame like he owns it, and in many ways, he does.

For a moment, I study him, my thoughts briefly derailed.

He has aged gracefully, the lines around his eyes deepening with experience, his expression still the same mix of confidence and warmth. A few more strands of silver have threaded through his light chestnut hair, but the effect only adds to his allure, making my cheeks flush before I can stop it. I didn't expect to see him here, not today.

After my parents' death, he was the first to come to me, and he continued to come. At first, I rarely let him in, wrapped too tightly in my grief to let anyone see me vulnerable. But his presence became constant, expected, like a shadow that followed me even when I wanted to be alone.

Eventually, I opened up. Slowly, at first.

At the time, I thought he was just careful, protective. Now, looking at him in the doorway, I'm not so sure.

The forest never let me leave with him: even when I wanted to, even when he said it was safer. But in the midst of war, he still visited, always. Sometimes after months, sometimes only a few days apart.

He always tried to get me to intern in the Order of the Sacred Flame, to attend my first Solis Rite, to come to Umbraxis, to learn to wield the Light, a way to find safety, a way to be useful.

I never let him know I tried to wield it, both Light and Shadow, but failed. It was as though the gods themselves had decided I was unworthy.

I never realized how much of my life had already been shaped by Lucien's decisions. So when the offer to teach at the academy came, I accepted without hesitation. He had guided me here, though I never fully understood the weight of it.

Lucien's eyes sweep the room, passing over the shelves, the unlit kettle, the papers scattered on my desk. His presence is warm, but something about it sends a shiver down my spine, like a draft slipping in unnoticed, unsettling the stillness.

"Nervous?" he asks, his voice smooth, leaning against the edge of my desk with a casual confidence that seems to say he belongs there, as much as he does anywhere.

I force myself to smile, though it feels strained. "I wasn't expecting to see you today."

"I always make myself available when it comes to you."

His words fall too easily into the room, like they've been rehearsed: familiar, practiced. I can almost feel them, like a net drawn taut around me, catching me just when I thought I could breathe.

He lingers, eyes drifting to the top sheet of the lesson plans. "What's the first unit?"

"Classic myths, my favorite," I reply. "We'll skim a few, but I want to start with *The Oresteia.*"

His brow lifts, faintly. "Dark choice."

"It's a story about justice and revenge, whether those things can coexist. It's supposed to get them thinking."

His smile is small but doesn't reach his eyes. "Just be careful what messages you send."

The knot in my chest tightens. I smile again, but it feels brittle.

He steps closer, resting one hand on the desk's corner, an old gesture, one he used to do in the forest when trying to reason with me. Reassuring, but never quite optional.

"Remember what we talked about," he says. "Control. Authority. These students will look to you for structure, discipline."

I hesitate. "I want them to think for themselves. Emotion isn't the enemy of reason."

The words slip out before I can stop them.

Lucien pauses. The silence stretches just a moment too long.

"Of course," he says softly. "But within the boundaries of truth, of Light."

He means it kindly and that's what unnerves me most. I nod.

Lucien studies me a moment longer, then turns, brushing a hand along the doorframe as he leaves. He carries with him a faint scent, incense and pine, as if the Light itself had been trapped in a bottle.

The door clicks closed behind him and I exhale a breath I didn't realize I was holding. The sound feels too loud in the quiet that follows.

Truth.

Light.

The words clang hollow in my ears.

Beneath all the layered smiles and soft commands, beneath the assurances of safety and structure, I feel the pull again.

That same strange weight I felt during the Rite. The old woman's eyes. The question she never spoke aloud. The feeling that something just beneath the surface is waiting to be found.

Or perhaps... remembered.

I move to the window, pressing my palm to the cool glass. In the courtyard below, posters flap in the breeze; white and gold, rigid block letters that scream:

Stand strong in the Light. Shadows corrupt. Obedience is peace.

Students pass them without looking, as if they've become part of the architecture.

My stomach turns.

When did we stop asking why?

I've learned the hard way that not all things born from the dark are evil. But then again, not all things born from the light are good either.

I shake it off.

Time to get to my first class.

THE FIRST LECTURE

M Y LOAFERS CLICK TOO loudly on the polished stone floor as I make my way through the eastern lecture wing. The sound ricochets off the marble walls, trailing behind me like a nervous echo I can't quite outpace.

The corridors here are bright; walls of deep black stone, polished to a mirror sheen are forced into brilliance by the cascade of sunlight through tall windows and the relentless glow of golden chandeliers. They're a kind of luxury that insists on being noticed.

Banners hang like verdicts overhead: suns, swords, and burning towers, stitched in fire-thread. Every emblem is an inheritance. Every emblem is a warning.

The portraits along the corridor regard me with the flat, superior calm of those who've never been corrected in public; immaculate robes, eyes rendered just shy of human. I nod to one... out of habit, not reverence.

Between each archway, the Luminary Guard stands immortal. Not real, of course, sculptures of them; stone robes swept in mid-motion, sword-hilts gripped with studied gentleness. Their carved faces glow faintly, just enough to catch the edge of your vision.

I hate that glow.

I reach the classroom door. My hand hovers over the handle, brass gone cool with shade.

The corridor hums with distant voices and footsteps on polished stone. But here, on this threshold, everything goes quiet. The kind of quiet that asks: *Are you ready to be seen?*

I breathe in, once.

I never saw my Pa teach, not once, but I've spent my whole life chasing the stories of it.

He used to guest lecture in these halls, sometimes right here in the eastern wing. He would tell me about how the students would sit spellbound as he spoke of old myths and forgotten rites, his voice rising like a prayer, like a spell.

I've been told he never used notes, that he didn't need to, that he spoke like he remembered the stories, not studied them, as if he'd lived them.

I try to picture it now, him at the front of the room, the hem of his coat dusted in chalk, turning to sketch myths across a slate board. He'd gesture with one hand, the other tucked behind his back, quoting forgotten lines of ancient tongues. His eyes would have been bright, alive.

And the room, this room, would've felt like a temple.

I swallow hard, the echo of him vivid in my mind. It was a life I was meant to inherit, or at least witness.

The war stole it from me, whether Shadow or Light I am still unsure. Now I'm the one standing on this side of the door, with no map, no flame, no myth to guide me but my own. I'm here and maybe that counts for something.

I press down on the handle and step inside.

The room yawns open around me, tiered like an amphitheater, the air soft with filtered light through stained glass windows. Carved beams cross the vaulted ceiling, casting long shadows on the pale stone floor. Along the walls, faint glyphs pulse with sanctioned warding magic; elegant and invisible until noticed, like most forms of control here.

Rows of students fill the semicircular benches, their desks gleaming with lacquered rune-wood, quills already poised. A few heads turn as I enter, then all of them.

They're older than I expected, mostly third and fourth years.

My gaze tracks slowly around the room. Sharp-cheeked, spine-straight scions of noble birth sit in robes that shimmer in the soft light, their family sigils stitched at the shoulders, wrists, and hems. Some wear their lineage loudly, others whisper it in gold and velvet.

Interspersed among them are students with stained sleeves and thread-bare collars, the scholarship few. Their eyes track faster, more hungry.

I spot a tall girl in the back with a crescent-moon tattoo just beneath her thumb. Her gaze meets mine and holds.

She nods once. I nod back.

I walk to the front, the click of my steps somehow louder here, more final.

The lectern is warm from the sun, my fingers rest on it. My throat feels hollow but my voice holds.

"Good morning."

A few nods, mostly stillness.

"I'm Educator Sylvaine," I say. "This is the Study of Sacred Narratives. It's exactly what it sounds like, if you're listening."

I leave a small pause to let the words settle.

"We'll be working through ancient texts: myths, parables, heresies, scriptures. Not just for what they say, but for why they say it, and who benefits from the saying."

Some heads tilt. A few students look down, already writing. One boy with expensive rings and no visible curiosity raises a brow like he's preparing to be disappointed.

"Before we begin," I say, stepping from the lectern, "I want to know who I'm teaching."

There's a beat of confusion.

"Names. One by one. You. First row."

The boy blinks, startled. "Me?"

"Yes," I say. "You're a person. Start there."

He shifts, clearly not used to being chosen. "Tomas. Fourth-year. Training for the Gilded Voice."

"Tell me one story you grew up believing. It doesn't have to be true, just something you believed."

He frowns, then shrugs. "That the Light always tells the truth."

A few chuckles. I nod. "Good. Next."

A girl with copper hair and a sharp voice. "Calyra. Third-year. Grew up thinking the moon was a god's eye. Watching."

I nod again. "Next."

And so it goes. Around the room, bits and pieces: a name, a belief, a thread of myth woven through childhood. Some are careful, some are ironic. A few hesitate, but they speak. That's the important part.

When it's the tall girl with the crescent-moon tattoo's turn, she just says, "Mirielle. I was taught that the Light devours what it can't control."

Silence.

I meet her gaze. "We'll come back to that."

A tall boy with hollowed cheeks and a pale blue sash raises his hand without waiting. "Educator? My name is Aric," he says, tasting the word like it's wine he doesn't trust, "will we be covering any heretical texts? Or is this a sanctioned syllabus?"

A few laughs, nervous, performative. I offer a slow, polite smile.

"All the texts I present have passed inspection, of course, but you're welcome to challenge them. Debate is not disobedience, at least not in this classroom."

The silence settles again, not resistance: tension.

Good. I can work with tension.

I walk to the lectern and write three names across the slate board:

Prometheus. Antigone. Eden.

"Let's begin with the myth of Prometheus," I say, turning back to them. "The Bringer of Fire. A thief punished for offering knowledge to mortals. Why might such a figure be revered, or reviled?"

A quiet girl in the second row raises her hand slowly, as if half-hoping I won't notice. "Because he disobeyed the Divine Order?"

"Exactly. And yet he's also seen as a hero, a rebel in the name of truth. He suffers not for evil, but for illumination."

I pace slowly. Light slants through the windows like falling blades.

"And what do we do with figures like that?"

A boy near the front mutters, "We burn them."

I freeze for a moment, but not because of his answer. At the back of the room, leaning casually against the stone wall like a statue that's always belonged is Lucien; not in uniform, but unmistakable. Arms crossed, silent, and observing. His presence slices through the air like a blade left on the table; not threatening, not overt, just there, waiting to be remembered. I don't acknowledge him, I move on.

We explore Antigone, moral law vs. state law.

Then Eden: the fruit, the fall, the cost of choice.

I watch the students closely. Some argue, some recite, some regurgitate the "correct" answers.

But a few, just a few, tilt their heads, frown at the text, squint at the contradictions. As if they sense the shape of something hidden behind the Light's polish.

Those are the ones I watch.

As class winds down, I pass out worn copies of *The Oresteia*, each marked with the Umbraxis crest like a brand. I return to the front, lifting my own battered copy, pages foxed and spine cracked.

"For your first assignment, we begin with the cycle of vengeance and justice. Orestes kills his mother to avenge his father. The Furies chase him to the edge of madness, until Athena intervenes, and creates the first court of law. Civilization triumphs over chaos."

I let the words settle. "At least, that's what the text says."

A few heads lift.

"But what if justice is more complicated? What if law simply replaces one kind of violence with another?"

Silence, thoughtful now.

"You'll write about that. Every week, you'll turn in a reflective letter; not just an essay, a letter, addressed to me, to yourselves, to a god, to a ghost. I want thought, not perfection. I will assign your letter topics on Veriday and I expect them to be turned in to me the following Kandreday. Question everything."

The girl with the moon tattoo, Mirielle, raises her hand again. "Even the Light?"

The room stills. I meet her eyes.

"Especially the Light. If it can't survive a question, it was never the truth."

Silence stretches, then releases, several students smile, scribble. A few nod to themselves like something just fell into place.

Before the final bell rings, I take a step closer to the front row. "One last thing," I say, softer now. "This course isn't just about ancient myths. It's about yours, too: your beliefs, your doubts, your stories. I want you to feel safe here: to speak your mind, to ask questions, to not know all of the answers."

I glance around the room.

"My office is always open. If you're struggling, come to me. I'll be holding weekly study sessions... Pyreday, in the evening, for anyone who needs it. No judgment, no expectations, just a place to think, or talk, or be quiet."

A quiet follows but it feels different now, less tension, more... reverence.

Then something strange brushes the edge of my senses. A flicker in the corner, not movement but a presence. A ripple in the shadows near the ceiling.

My skin tingles. I am hit with the smell of damp moss and wildflowers crushed underfoot. It smells like Pa, that same green, living scent from the woods behind our house. He used to tell me stories there, his voice low and sure under the trees. He'd be proud, I think, seeing me up here now, at the lectern, teaching myths.

The scent is gone, just as quickly.

The final bell tolls. Students begin to gather their things. Some offer polite nods, a few give sidelong glances, uncertain whether to admire or avoid. One boy leaves a folded note on my desk, I don't open it yet.

A girl with ink-stained fingers and star-shaped freckles lingers by the door. "Thank you," she says quietly, then slips away.

Lucien still hasn't moved.

"You're bold," he says, finally pushing off the wall. "Antigone? Really?"

I gather my notes without looking up. "It's a literary course, not a sermon."

His smile is faint, unreadable. "Be careful, Sylvaine. The Light doesn't always distinguish between metaphor and defiance."

He turns and walks out, only then do I let my breath go.

Outside the window, the sun dips low, casting the corridor in honey-colored light. I walk the length of the hallway, my reflection fracturing in every gilded pane: half in light, half in shadow. And somewhere between them, something watches, something waits. Far beyond the marble walls and the golden lies, I remember the hush of the forest, not silent but alive.

I had started to believe there was goodness in the Light. But... I wonder if what we call Light is just the safest shape of fire.

As I pass beneath a fluttering banner, a gust of wind catches a tapestry at the end of the hall, pulling it back just enough to reveal the stone behind it. Etched there, small but deliberate:

Truth hides.

I stop, stare. My pulse flutters like wings. Then I lift my chin, square my shoulders, and step into the fading gold of afternoon.

I don't yet know what I'll find at Umbraxis.

But I do know this; Light does not exist without Shadow, and I am beginning to feel both.

Strange Meetings

T HE BELL TOWER CHIMES softly in the distance, five past the hour.

Its echo filters through the ancient stone walls like a memory trying to return. The corridor outside my office lies cloaked in warm lamplight and the scent of aging parchment, dust, and old cedar. Silence stretches long here, dignified and patient, like the university itself. My door remains open, as I promised, always open on Pyredays.

A safe space, I'd said. No one's taken me up on it, not yet.

I sit alone at my desk, quill poised over a lesson plan for tomorrow. The ink dries slower tonight, as though reluctant to leave the nib. The words I've written feel heavier than usual, like they know more than I do. Outside, the wind shifts against the high windows, a quiet moan threading through the stonework.

From my door comes a knock, soft as moth wings.

I look up to see a figure standing in the doorway and I immediately recognize her shape. It's the woman from the Solis Rite, the one who didn't bow when the others did.

She appears older than she had in the half-light of the Temple Hall, yet she seems untouched by time in any meaningful way. Her presence is luminous in the stark glow of the lamp on my desk, as though carved from something older than bone. Her skin, dark and freckled, is worn like river stone, etched by decades, perhaps centuries, yet dignified. Her layered robes fall in soft waves of grey and dim silver, embroidered not with the sunbursts of the Order but with tiny constellations, patterns I almost recognize: the Lore Keeper, the Broken Crown.

Her eyes do not judge, they seem to remember.

"May I?" she asks. Her voice is a low, resonant hum, like wind through chimes made of glass.

I rise automatically, the legs of my chair scraping faintly against the old flooring. "Of course. Please."

She enters slowly, each step measured. She does not sit, but rests one long, ink-stained hand on the back of the nearest chair, more gesture than need. Her fingers are marked with faded quill-cuts and dark flecks of old ink, callused and sure, a scholar's hands.

"I'm called Educator Thaleia," she says, not proudly, but like one stating a truth that no longer needs defending. "Though few use my title anymore." She looks around the room, her gaze sweeping over the shelves, the half-drawn curtain. "I taught here once, Ancient Belief Systems. Before the war... before the Light burned too hot to cast a Shadow."

I falter. "I... I saw you. At the Rite."

Her lips curl into something almost but not quite a smile. "You saw me. Yes. And I saw you."

There's a pause. My throat feels dry, my pulse too loud in my ears. Something about her presence presses at the edge of my memory.

A scent?

A gesture?

A dream from childhood I can't name?

"Do we know each other?" I ask, cautious.

"We don't," she says, her gaze drifting to the high windows, where the fading sunlight gathers like dust. "Not truly. Once, long ago, I taught your parents, here at Umbraxis. Later... I was a friend of both."

My breath catches. The desk, the books, even the room itself feels farther away. "You knew them?"

"I remember them," Thaleia replies, her voice steady. "As they truly were, not as the Order chooses to recall."

She steps closer, and though her frame is slight, her presence deepens the shadows around us. She is rooted like an ancient tree and yet she could vanish in a blink. The room tilts around her.

"There are things you don't yet know, Sylvaine," she says, voice lower now, nearly a whisper. "Things buried. Things bent to fit the Light's story. But truth has a way of surviving, even when it's been rewritten."

In the corners of the office, the dark seems to breathe.

"You're remembering already, aren't you?" she asks. "Small things? Whispers? Half-dreams? Moments that don't belong to now? That's how it begins."

I say nothing, but something stirs in my chest: a tremor, a memory of a lullaby in a tongue I never learned.

"If you ever have questions," Thaleia continues, stepping back, "or if remembering becomes too heavy... come find me. My office is in the northern wing." Her expression shifts, the smile now wry, tired. "Or what's left of it, they don't tend to send students there anymore."

She turns, robes whispering with the motion. As she reaches the door, there are muffled voices that are both urgent and too close.

Thaleia pauses, the lines around her eyes tightening slightly. I follow her glance just beyond the open doorway to where three figures huddle too close to the corridor wall.

"Eavesdropping," I call, not sharply but with unmistakable authority, "is not considered scholarly behavior."

A beat of silence, a rustle of robes...

The trio emerges, caught in a moment that could be sheepishness or defiance, it seems like they're still deciding.

Aric, the noble boy with a house crest stitched in gold thread across his blue sash, straightens like a soldier at parade rest. His jaw is tense, posture impeccable.

Mirielle, the moon-tattooed girl with a shock of white-blonde hair and boots perpetually scuffed from garden shortcuts, shrugs as if this were inevitable. Her silver nose ring glints in the lamplight.

And Lina, freckled and soft-spoken, with a satchel overloaded with rune-maps, goes bright crimson under her curls.

Thaleia looks at each of them one by one with that quiet, almost amused disapproval only an elder scholar can wield. Then she turns, stepping through the doorway and vanishing into the corridor without another word. Her presence fades like mist drawn back into the stone.

The air feels thinner without her in the room.

Aric is the first to speak. "Who was that?"

Mirielle frowns, mouth pulling to one side. "She's not on the Educator register. I checked."

"She's not," I say. "But she used to be, long ago."

Lina glances down the hall, then back at me. "Do you... know her?"

I nod slowly. "She knew my parents. She taught with them before the war."

Mirielle exhales sharply. "She's kind of intense," she adds, "like... in a 'myth is real and it lives under your bed' kind of way."

"I like her," Lina murmurs. "She reminds me of my grandmother, but sharper. Like a blade that's been dulled and honed a thousand times."

A silence stretches, thoughtful now.

"You three were listening?" I ask again. My tone has softened.

Lina steps forward slightly, hands wringing the strap of her satchel. "We came for a study session. Together. We were going to knock, but then we heard voices, and…"

"We got curious," Mirielle finishes for her, unapologetic as ever.

Aric crosses his arms. "We weren't trying to spy. But if there's more going on here than sanctioned lectures and Light's truth, maybe we deserve to know."

My brow lifts. "You're very bold for someone who hasn't even finished their first assignment."

That earns me a grin from Mirielle, who flicks a braid over her shoulder. Even Aric's stern face softens at the corners.

I nod toward the chairs. "Sit, then. All of you."

They do. The scrape of wood against stone is oddly grounding. The lamplight above flickers slightly, humming with a quiet resonance. They settle in like students trying not to look like students: elbows on knees, fingers fiddling with book spines, trying not to be the first to speak.

"I meant what I said," I tell them. "This office is for questions. Conversation. If you need help with texts, translation, or gods forbid deconstructing the meaning of sacrifice in *The Oresteia,* I'm here. These are voluntary gatherings. No Light-mandated scripts, just discussion, and maybe tea, if I can convince the kitchens to give me more than one cup at a time."

"That sounds vaguely illegal," Mirielle says, clearly delighted.

"It's not illegal," I reply. "It's just… slightly unsanctioned."

Lina lowers her eyes to her hands, still stained with rune pigment. "You really don't think the Light is all there is, do you?"

The air sharpens. I meet her gaze.

"I think truth is always larger than the box we try to fit it in," I say. "And the Light... well. It's a lens, but it's not the whole sky."

A long pause.

Aric leans forward, the arrogance momentarily gone from his voice. "That woman, Thaleia. Do you think she'll come back?"

I glance toward the doorway, now empty. The wind slips through the window seams, cool and whispering.

"I think people like her show up exactly when they're meant to."

Mirielle taps a finger against the spine of her copy of *The Oresteia*. "Then I guess we're all in the right place."

Something settles in my chest, something quiet and real.

Then Aric clears his throat. "Well. If we're talking about questions... can someone please explain why Educator Corven's Light Theory lecture devolved into a fifteen-minute hymn and a group chant on 'purity of essence'? Is that... normal?"

Lina groans softly. "It's not just Corven. My runes class spent half the session translating praise hymns instead of actual spell work. I enrolled to understand construction glyphs, not sing devotionals to ancient glass towers."

"I think mine was worse," Mirielle says, pulling a folded parchment from her satchel. "We were supposed to practice casting the 'Trace Flame' illumination rune. Mine caught fire. The desk caught fire. Educator Vran said it was 'too much internal Shadow.' Whatever that means."

"That means they don't understand what caused it," Aric mutters, "so they blame you."

Mirielle smirks. "Then I must be very misunderstood."

"Runes are temperamental," I interject gently. "Especially when paired with Light incantations. The glyphs pull from your intent and intent is never as pure as the Order claims. That's not failure. It's... complexity."

Lina looks up sharply, "So we're not broken."

Aric leans back, arms folded again, though not in defiance this time. "I don't suppose you could look at my rune grid from class? I think I'm drawing the symmetry wrong. Vran wouldn't explain it twice."

I smile faintly. "I'd be happy to."

"But..." Lina hesitates, then blurts, "you don't, sorry, I just mean... you're not... I heard that you weren't blessed with the Light?"

Mirielle shoots her a look. "Lina!"

"It's fine," I say, holding up a hand. "No, I wasn't blessed by the gods. No magic. No divine Light. Just ink, parchment, and a lot of long nights with reference texts."

"So how do you know how to draw runes?" Aric asks, frowning. "Aren't they... inert without magic?"

"They are," I say. "But the structure still matters. Like architecture without tenants, if the frame is flawed, the whole thing collapses when the Light moves in. I can help you build the frame. Embedment, that's your burden."

Mirielle leans forward, curious now. "Wait, so you've never cast? Not once?"

I shake my head. "Not once. I've seen enough of what magic can do. That's different from needing to wield it."

Lina shifts her satchel onto her lap and pulls out a crumpled sheet of rune practice. "Then maybe you could help me with this curve here? I keep getting blowback when I try to channel into it."

I take the sheet, smoothing it flat with my palm. "That's because this loop is closing on itself, like a trap. The energy gets confused. You're bottling it instead of guiding it."

Her eyes go wide. "No one told me that. They just said I was 'resisting the Light's will.'"

I glance up. "You're not resisting, you're thinking. That's harder, but it's also the beginning of real knowledge."

Outside, the wind shifts again, whispering through the high arched windows like a promise.

Kandreday morning is quiet but not calm.

There's a restlessness in the air, the kind that settles in your bones before a storm or a reckoning. The students feel it too.

Today is their first submission day, and I can see the tension in their shoulders: the way their hands tighten on satchels, the glances they exchange when they think I'm not watching.

Aric arrives first, as always. His posture is straight as a drawn blade, his uniform crisp and precise. He nods to me, polite, reserved.

Lina and Calyra come in next, whispering in a language I suspect they invented just to keep secrets from their classmates.

Tomas lumbers in behind them. There's always dust on his boots from the outer courts, a stubborn echo of where he came from.

Mira follows, silent, a strand of hair is stuck to her cheek, as if she forgot she had a face.

Mirielle is last. She hums as she drops her bag with a theatrical sigh, taking her seat like she owns the room. She doesn't, not yet.

We spend the class discussing *The Oresteia*, its bloody logic, its careful resolutions. The students speak more than usual, their voices braver today. Something about knowing their thoughts are already on the page frees them to test them out loud.

When the bell chimes clear and resonant, I rise.

"Next week," I say, "I'll explain your assignment on Veriday, but don't worry about anything from me until then."

I pause to let the silence settle.

"Letters," I add. "Drop them on your way out. Face down. No spell-seals, no mimic wards. Just ink and thought."

They move slowly, like the weight of the parchment has increased with time. There's the soft rustle of paper, the sigh of hesitation, a few uneven heartbeats.

Some look away. Some meet my gaze with challenge.

Tomas's hand lingers on his page like it hurts to let it go.

Lina's is smudged at the corners with thumbprints. The ink is still damp. She hesitates in the doorway. "Did you mean it?" she asks. "About questioning everything?"

I meet her eyes. She's sharper than she lets on. "I don't say what I don't mean."

Her lips twitch, not quite a smile, but something close, then she's gone.

The stack of letters feels heavier than it should. I tuck them under one arm and close up the lecture hall behind me, heading to my office to grade.

The corridors are quieter by the third bell. I light the wall sconces with a match. It would be so much more convenient if I could produce thumb-fire. The hearth crackles. A storm is whispering somewhere in the distance, I can smell the copper tang of it through the cracked window.

I unroll the first letter.

A noble-born, Elswyn, clearly worships the Light. The submission is predictable, clean, and efficient.

Civilization is not a story of kindness. It is a story of control.

*The Furies, for all their passion, served only fear. Athena replaced that fear
with a system. With logic.*
*The Light does the same. It guides us. Elevates us. Replaces the old chaos with
righteous discipline.*
Orestes was an instrument of justice. Athena was the hand that steadied him.
May the Light never flicker.

There are a dozen lines I could mark for empty flattery, but I won't. Not
today. They're not writing to me, they're writing to be seen. I sift through
the stack and find Mirielle's next.

To the Furies, wherever You Are,
*I know I'm supposed to hate you. You scream too loudly. You bleed too easily.
But silence is how rot begins.*
*Athena's court is tidy, yes. But it was too clean. There's no room in it for real
grief. Only tidy endings.*
I don't think I believe in tidy endings anymore.

Clever girl, more than she lets on behind her smirks and scented oils.
Tomas's letter is ragged at the edge. He writes like the paper offended him.

To Orestes (Coward or Victim?),
I don't buy it.
*You say you acted in the name of justice, but the moment you killed her, the
world didn't get better.*
It got quieter. Not cleaner.
*Justice in this world is just another kind of violence with better robes. I've seen
it. In border towns, in burned villages.*

My fingers tighten around the edge of the letter. That last line echoes
too close. Calyra's is florid, as expected, but there's a wound beneath the
poetry.

To the One Who Waits in the Dark,
Clytemnestra was wrong. So was Agamemnon. So was Orestes.

But wrong in a human way. I understand that.

The Light asks us to be perfect. To rise above "base" emotions. But who decides what's base?

I think the Furies represent what we bury to survive under the Light.

Maybe survival isn't the same as healing.

That one I reread, twice. But Lina's... Lina's is different.

To the Light (If You're Listening),

I thought you were warmth. I thought you were clarity.

But now I wonder if you're just the strongest story. The one we're all afraid to contradict.

I don't hate you. I'm just... doubting. And I don't think I'm alone.

The Furies might be monsters, but at least they never asked to be worshipped.

A log splits in the hearth with a sharp *crack*, like punctuation.

I lean back, the stack of letters before me, the air suddenly colder. They're not just questioning *The Oresteia*, they're questioning the very frame it was handed to them in. Everyone knows that once the frame cracks... the painting never looks the same.

WHISPERS IN THE LIBRARY

T HE RHYTHMS OF TEACHING settle in quickly, like a familiar melody. Soon, I find myself moving in time with it, the cadence of it all becoming second nature.

I stand before the students with chalk-ridden hands and skeptical eyes, speaking of myth, of rite, of the sacred and the profane. Some listen with wide-eyed hunger, while others remain distant, the polished surface of their Light-born compliance unyielding.

I keep the note Rellington slipped me on the first day, tucked between the worn pages of *The Oresteia*:

What if the Light lies in its silence?

I haven't answered him, not directly, but I've begun, indirectly, in my own way; not with declarations, but with questions. They'll have to think for themselves, I'm not here to hand out answers like blessings.

So I ask questions, quiet ones, sharp ones, the kind that don't come wrapped in righteousness or ribboned in Light.

By midweek, the murmurs have begun. Sacred Narratives is strange, they whisper: unorthodox, dangerous.

There are whispers that students ask aloud if the Furies might've been right. They submit letters instead of essays: half ritual, half confession.

I see it in their eyes... fear, yes, but fascination too, and something else, longing.

After Thaleia's visit, her cryptic warning and the way she moved like a memory I'd misplaced, I find myself craving something I can't quite name. Her presence clings to the corners of my office. She told me she's here, if I need her, and for reasons I can't fully explain, I do. Not to speak, not yet, but to remember.

The days blur: repeated lectures, parchment-heavy mornings, names slipping through my hands like wet stones.

So when the week's final lecture ends, and the last of the letters have been read, graded, and tucked away, I don't turn toward the woods, I turn toward the library.

The library at Umbraxis is its own labyrinth, five floors of carved obsidian and soft-lit vaults, vast and winding, built more to contain than to reveal. It is a sanctum of silence. Its stained-glass skylight, even under clouded skies, spills fractured color across the marble like scattered jewels, as though the light itself has shattered to enter.

The upper levels are curated, manicured; stacks are aligned with precision. Students drift through their studies like ghosts in uniform. Catalogued texts line the shelves like obedient soldiers, each spine labeled, every volume scrubbed clean of controversy. A few Educators sit behind glass-paneled carrels, sipping steep leaf tea, cloaked in veils of rules and reverence. Their presence hums with a quiet vigilance.

I move like a ghost between them, unseen, unbothered, my steps soundless on the polished marble. I am not here for order. I am searching for something else.

I tell myself I am here gathering materials for next week's readings, *Inferno*, excerpts from the *Enchiridion*, a few passages from myth-cycles that had been deemed safe for devotional use. Acceptable texts: scrutinized, sanitized.

But that is a lie dressed in purpose, I am not collecting approved ideas. I am hunting something I can't name: a thread, a fracture, a truth hiding in the seams.

The main readings are complete, focusing on older literature that will help students question the realities they've grown up with and the morals that have been ingrained into their brains. My syllabi are airtight, my required reading is approved. A lot of the main texts I want to teach were questioned, but I promised to keep things "Light."

Still, I want to give my students something else: something smaller, something quieter, something real. A truth hidden between the lines.

Most students avoid the lower levels, even Educators hesitate before descending too far. Down there, the air shifts. The temperature drops. The shelves tangle like roots, thick and sprawling, books crammed into the crevices like forgotten teeth. Dust hangs like pollen. The light dimmed by degrees, until it no longer warms but watches.

It feels less like a library and more like a wound that had been bandaged too tightly, one that had started to fester.

Undeterred, I descend past the third floor, beyond sanctioned tomes and departmental barriers, following instinct more than reason. I reach an old iron gate, ribbed with rust, its hinges bowed like weary knees. It is meant to be locked but it isn't. A cracked sign swings lightly from its frame, the string frayed, the ink half-faded:

RESTRICTED: Archival Access by
Authorization Only.

The metal is cold beneath my palm, like it remembers every hand that had trespassed before mine. I hesitate, the silence thickens, and then I push the gate open. It groans like something roused from sleep, a deep, spine-rattling sound that echoed down the corridor beyond.

The sconces give only the faintest shimmer, their flames guttering as if reluctant to stay lit. The shadows press inward, slow and deliberate, like the held breath of something vast.

And yet... I am not afraid. The silence isn't empty, it is listening.

Here, between forgotten tomes on magical jurisprudence and lost treatises on pre-divine rites, I find a narrow shelf tucked into the alcove of a collapsed wall. It holds books with no spines, no titles; one charred, one split down the middle like a wound that hadn't healed right. Another had a crumpled note tucked beneath its flap:

The boy-king vanished. Some say he is in hiding with the Shadows.

I stare at the words, a chill running down my back.

Carefully, I reach for the most intact volume, its leather soft and dark, as if it has been handled often. The moment my fingers brush it, a jolt runs up my arm. It is not painful, but cold and familiar; the kind of familiar that doesn't come from memory, but from the bones.

I pull it free and open the first page.

Blank.

I turn to the next, also blank.

On the third, something scrawls itself as I watch, black ink rising from nowhere:

You are not lost. Only hidden.

My breath catches.

The words fade a moment later, as if they had never been there at all.

I flip the brittle pages again. The next few are filled with ink, faded in places, smudged at the edges, but what they say makes my pulse thrum.

Those born to Light are taught to shine—unyielding, absolute. Light demands clarity, obedience, absolution. And in return, it offers order. Certainty. The safety of a world where every question has a sanctioned answer, every doubt a sin to be purified.
Those born to Shadow are shaped differently. Shadow does not burn; it remembers. It turns inward—toward instinct, toward memory, toward the grief Light teaches us to silence. Shadow asks nothing but honesty. It carries what Light cannot hold.
Not a lesser path. Not a darker one.

I reread the passage.

My fingers hover above the page. In the margins, almost too faint to notice, another phrase curls like a vine between the lines:

Shadow remembers what Light forgets. Vaeloria was never meant to burn.

The candle beside me flickers violently. For a heartbeat, I am submerged in darkness; total and complete, like the book itself swallowed the light.

When the flame sputters back to life, I glance over my shoulder but see nothing.

I run my fingers across the text one more time. As I do, a strange clarity settles over me, like déjà vu folded into a dream. I've read this before: or dreamed it, or lived it. Memory or prophecy, I can't tell, only that it knows me.

I snap the book shut and turn, heart racing.

The corridor behind me is still empty, but the shadows pulse at the edges of my vision. The deeper truths I have stumbled upon don't want to be forgotten again.

I slip the book into my satchel and make my way back to the upper floors, legs trembling. The air lightens with every step toward the surface, but something clings to me... a feeling I can't shake, like I have disturbed something that had been sleeping.

The echoes of my footsteps chase me as I wind my way out of the library, past shadow-draped statues and arched doorways that seem to lean closer than they should.

Outside, the night air is brisk, slicing against my skin with more sharpness than it should for early autumn. The path to my cabin is quiet, winding like a black ribbon through the sloping hills of campus.

As the bells toll the seventh hour and the campus dims into a twilight glow, I pass the central courtyard. A new set of posters has gone up, freshly pasted over the older ones:

Shadow is Lie. Light is Law. Be Clean. Be Vigilant.

Students pass in silence. One or two tear corners off the posters, quickly, guiltily. Most simply look away.

A quiet fear has settled over campus this week, like an invisible smog. Even the ivy along the stones has grown still.

When I reach my cabin, dusk has swallowed the woods. While I fumble for my keys, I see a note half slipped beneath the door like a warning.

I bend to retrieve it, and my satchel tips; pages spill, books, the text from the library, my student's note from earlier, all skittering across the porch like leaves caught in the wind. I curse softly, scrambling to gather it all before the wind takes them.

I feel a breeze that is too warm, too knowing. It curls around my neck, lifts a strand of hair like a question: not threatening, not unkind, just... aware.

I freeze, and then think to myself, *you're just tired.*

I gather the last of the papers and finally snatch the note that was slipped under the door. I sigh, leaning my head against the frame for a moment before unlocking the door.

Still trembling, I enter my cabin.

Inside, the fire is out. My breath ghosts in front of me, the note still in hand, the strange book heavy in my bag.

Outside, the wind picks up, howling through the trees beyond campus. Inside, the shadows remain still, but I swear they shift when I'm not looking.

As evening settles in, I prepare the space, keeping the fireplace crackling softly, lighting a few extra candles. I steep a cup of chamomile and mint tea, then unfold the note from my student once more, as I have many times this week. I read it slowly, letting the words settle like seeds in soil.

What if the Light lies in its silence?

What if?

The question gnaws at me. I turn to my desk and begin to write, not a lesson plan, but a letter. Not addressed to any student, but to the person I used to be.

You do not need to be right. You need to be real.

Remember the trees. Remember the silence that listened back.

Remember that the wind never asked you to obey, only to breathe with it.

Don't forget what called you before they taught you fear.

I seal the letter and place it on the bottom shelf of my bookcase, behind the copy of *On the Balance of Powers*, one of the required texts I am supposed to be teaching this semester.

After writing my letter, I finally turn to the note that had been slid under my door. The seal is broken, unprofessional for something from the academy. Inside, the parchment bears only a few words, written in careful, practiced script:

Dinner. My study. Tomorrow night. – Lucien

Outside, the wind howls softly; not ominous, just wild, and for the first time in days, I breathe easier.

Tomorrow, I'll respond to Lucien.

ATTENTIONS

THE SHUTTERS FILTER THE early morning sun into quiet stripes across the wooden floor, dust motes drifting like tiny prayers between them. I let myself wake slowly, staying under the covers longer than usual: the blanket cocooned around me, the world beyond my bed reduced to a breathless hush.

Sovinday: no lectures, no students, no pretense.

I brew tea from dried melisse leaves, the scent citrus-sweet and grounding. The mug warms my palms as I curl into the small reading alcove by the window, a worn copy of *The Enchiridion* open across my lap. I underline a phrase with a soft-barked stylus, pause, then cross it out again. I repeat this a couple of times before giving up. Philosophy feels sterile on mornings like this: detached from the soil, the skin, the ache of living.

I set the book aside and step outside.

My garden is still more dream than reality at the moment. Just a crooked corner of dry land at the edge of the stone path behind my quarters, fenced in by an ivy-covered trellis and quiet intention. Autumn sunlight pools golden across the flagstones, warm despite the crisp edge to the breeze. The scent of drying leaves clings to the air: faint, brittle, familiar.

I kneel beside the soil, brushing it with my fingers like one might check a sleeping child's breath. It's cool, damp, and waiting.

A few brave shoots of frost-mint have already started to push through, their silvery-green leaves trembling in the light. The fever root I planted last week lies hidden still, curled deep beneath the surface. Nearby, a low row of cold-enduring marrow vine creeps along the edge of the garden bed, stubborn and silent.

I scatter a few more seeds: moon blossom, maybe, or dusk fennel. I mixed the satchels up weeks ago, and never bothered to untangle them. A handful of late-harvest sorrel joins them, and a few seeds from a forgotten pouch I suspect might be ice-bell or twilight radish. I press them into the soil with the heel of my hand, not knowing what will take, but giving them the chance.

I whisper a blessing; not one sanctioned by the Light, but older, wilder. It's a rhythm with no need for translation, just breath and hope and the memory of hands that once taught me the shape of the words.

The sun's rays warm my shoulders. A few bees still hum in the ivy, drunk on the last flowering sage. I let myself breathe.

By the time I reach Lucien's study, the sky stretches clear and pale above, the sunlight catching in the ivy that climbs the eastern wall of the academy. The cold air presses softly against my skin, and the stone steps beneath my feet hold the faint toastiness of the afternoon sun. I linger outside the door longer than I intend, fingers brushing the smooth wood as if seeking courage.

The invitation was simple.

Dinner. My study. Tomorrow night.

But simplicity often masks intent.

I knock once.

The door opens almost immediately; Lucien stands there, as if he's been waiting for me. He's dressed less formally than usual, his heavy outer robe loosened, gold-threaded cuffs undone and pushed back at his wrists. The scent of spiced wine and roasted root vegetables curls into the hallway, warm, earthy, inviting.

"Sylvaine," he says in that familiar velvet voice, equal parts amusement and expectation. "Come in."

"Thank you." I step over the threshold.

The room glows softly from a fire that hums rather than crackles, a Light-forged illusion that is steady and warm, but too still. The candles along the mantel flicker to life as I enter, flaring gently one by one, perfectly timed, as if reacting to my presence. The air shifts subtly, growing warmer than the hall just beyond.

Comfort tuned to mood, magic tuned to control.

A long oak table stands center, set carefully for two. There are no scrolls, no papers, no academic clutter, only candlelight, silverware, and us.

"You look well," he says quietly.

I glance down at my dress, simple dark crimson wool, belted at the waist, with a thin silver chain resting lightly around my throat. I hadn't thought when I chose it, but now it feels like a statement I wasn't ready to make.

He doesn't stare, but he notices. Lucien always notices.

A flick of his fingers, casual, practiced, and the fire brightens by half a shade. A warmth blooms across the floor like morning sunlight, not ostentatious, just... visible.

I say nothing, but I think: *magic doesn't have to be loud to be theatrical.*

Lucien has always known how to set a stage.

"You said it was just dinner," I murmur.

Lucien's faint smile holds a hint of something unspoken. "It is."

But his eyes don't leave me, lingering a little too long.

He steps beside me, pulls out my chair with a gentleman's grace, and waits until I sit before moving to his own. By the time I take my seat, the candles are all lit, the chill entirely banished, and the scent of citrus peel now mingles with the wine. None of it was done by hand.

He begins plating the food: roasted root vegetables dusted with rosemary, thick slices of crunchy bread, tender rabbit in a wine reduction. He pours us each a goblet of spiced wine with ease, filling the glasses halfway.

I hesitate before taking a bite, the rabbit sits heavily on the plate. It's not the taste, I've had it before, but the idea: the smallness of the creature, the softness of its death.

"You don't like it?" Lucien asks, noticing my pause.

"I don't prefer it," I answer, gently pushing the meat aside. "I was raised in the forest. Killing for food... felt like theft."

He hums thoughtfully, tearing a piece of bread. "Mercy is a rare trait in a scholar."

We shift into easier topics... literature mainly. He asks about my class, what myths we're covering, what the students are responding to.

"They're terrified to be wrong," I tell him. "It's why I've assigned personal letters instead of essays."

He arches a brow. "Why letters, why not journals, poems even?"

"Letters are a way for the students to write honestly, without the pressure of citation or canon, to get them to think and not be scared of being right or wrong." I respond, followed by a large sip of my wine.

He doesn't give a response, just a low grunt while he continues to shovel rabbit in his mouth. I grimace, I can't help myself.

"One of them slipped a question onto my desk, I still haven't answered."

"A question?"

"Not a literal one," I lie, swirling the wine in my glass. "Just... curiosity, veiled in metaphor."

His gaze sharpens. "Students must be careful with metaphors. It's a favorite hiding place for dissent."

My fork pauses midair, I force a smile. "Maybe that's what makes it valuable."

His lips curl upward, but the warmth doesn't reach his eyes. We eat in polite silence until the conversation wanders, but it never deepens.

It's all superficial: the upcoming lectures, a faculty gathering I hadn't heard about, his recent travels to the Guard Watches, checking on the war.

As he refills my glass, he glances at me with a thoughtful frown. "You look so much like your mother when you're guarded like that. Same silence. Same sharpness."

I blink. He rarely mentions them, almost no one does.

"I still miss their presence at the academy," he continues. "Your father's guest lectures on comparative rituals and myths were always the first to fill. And your mother, she challenged me more than anyone else ever dared to."

He gives a soft, almost disbelieving laugh. "You can imagine my shock at their sudden deaths. Just earlier that day I had seen them. I think they knew something, suspected something was going to happen. They slipped me a letter as they left. A contingency, apparently, asking me to watch over you."

The room shrinks suddenly, the weight of it pressing close. "They wrote to you? You think they knew something was about to happen?"

He nods, solemn. "It was brief but clear." He swirls the wine again, watching the slow spiral. "They trusted me with something precious."

I say nothing; there's no safe answer to that.

After a pause, I venture, "speaking of my parents, I met Educator Thaleia the other day. She said she knew them and that they were remarkable."

Lucien's expression tightens. "Thaleia..." He shrugs, voice cool. "The academy keeps her around out of respect. She devoted many years to teaching, but she's old, losing her mind. She confuses students for ghosts. It's sad, really."

I swallow the lump in my throat. "She seemed to be in good spirits when we talked."

"Then you're lucky, normally she is incoherent, spewing falsities and scaring people. It's best if you keep your distance." His words are final, dismissive.

"Sometimes loyalty is just another burden." He sinks into his chair. I sit gingerly across from him, still cautious.

After a pause, he tilts his head. "I do wonder... everything you know, you couldn't have learned that alone. I never..." He trails off, the implication sharp beneath his smooth voice. "Did your parents leave behind texts, journals, notes?"

I hesitate. "Not exactly."

His eyes narrow scantily, waiting.

"There was a boy," I say, my voice softening. "From The Vale near the forest's edge. I didn't know much about him other than the fact that we were both curious. He'd bring me books, and we'd stay up late working through old homework assignments. Sometimes he'd copy pages from the academy archives when no one was watching. He knew how to ask the right questions, and I... I liked answering them. We'd argue about meaning, about myth. We'd dream about what the world might be like outside the trees."

A faint smile touches my lips, unbidden. "He made it feel like it mattered, like learning was alive."

Lucien watches me for a long moment, expression unreadable. "It's impressive you made it this far."

I glance away. "Thank you."

"I saw something in you," he says, swirling his wine again. "Something rare."

I shift in my chair. "What's that?"

"A desire to belong. But also... the courage not to."

It's dangerously close to the truth, too close. So I give him a practiced nod, the one I wear when students overshare.

He leans forward, elbows on knees. "I want you to know, Sylvaine, that I'm invested in your success."

The way he says it makes my spine stiffen: not *the academy is invested,* just him.

He lifts his glass toward me. "To potential."

I echo the gesture, my voice quieter. "To potential."

Then, he touches my wrist... lightly, as if unsure whether the gesture is welcome.

I don't pull away.

It's not that I'm certain of what I want, only that I don't *not* want it.

There's a quiet kindness in him I have always recognized, especially after my parents' deaths, after Lysander left, when others turned solemn and silent. He stepped in, not to replace, but to steady.

He lets his fingers rest just along the line of my forearm: not possessive, not demanding, just there, present. I meet his eyes, and for a moment, neither of us speak.

When he leans forward, it's not with the certainty of a man expecting to be welcomed, it's hesitant, questioning. And when his lips brush mine, the touch is soft, tentative, careful.

I don't stop him but I don't rush forward either. My heart stirs in ways I haven't fully named yet. I close my eyes, and let the moment be what it is: a gentle, uncertain beginning I didn't expect.

He draws back slowly, as though afraid to have asked too much of me, and I realize, maybe he isn't sure either.

By the time I leave Lucien's study, night has fully settled over the academy. The halls are hushed, heavy with silence, and the air outside is crisp with the clean scent of damp stone and moss.

The stars are out, sharp and silver, scattered like spilled salt across the black velvet sky. I lift my face toward them, pausing at the edge of the path, letting the quiet wrap around me. They're beautiful tonight; clear, endless, the kind of sky that makes you feel ancient and small all at once.

My breath curls in the cold as I begin the long walk back to my cabin. My shoes crunch softly over the gravel, the lanterns were left unlit along this stretch, but I know the path well enough to walk it blind.

As I walk, I'm not thinking about the trees, or the stars, or even the wind pressing gently against my back. I'm thinking about Lucien; the way he touched my wrist, carefully, like someone handling something breakable, the way he kissed me, as though asking a question he wasn't sure I'd answer. I let him and I didn't hate it.

But there's a weight under my ribs, something unshaped and stirring, because the only other person who's ever kissed me was a boy with stars for eyes and a laugh like birdsong. A boy who brought me books wrapped in linen, who asked questions no one else dared to ask.

My friend, my first, Lysander. Everything with him felt like discovery, like promise.

And tonight, Lucien's kiss felt like memory colliding with the present. Two lives, two selves, brushing shoulders inside me.

I reach my door, fingers stiff as I unlatch the handle. Inside, the cabin is dark but familiar. The hearth is cold, the air inside holding the faint scent of herbs and paper.

I undress slowly, slipping out of the crimson wool and silver chain, folding them with quiet care. I slip beneath the quilt, body still warm from the wine and the firelight and the weight of too many thoughts.

Sleep comes slow.

Even with my eyes closed, I see the boy from the forest, and then Lucien's gaze, and somewhere between them, me: still choosing, still unsure.

A soft rap pulls me from sleep. It's not loud, just a steady, uncertain tap against the cabin door, the kind made by someone who doesn't want to intrude but hopes, still, to be welcomed.

The sky outside is grey, just past dawn. Mist curls along the windows like a breath held too long.

I sit up slowly, brushing sleep from my eyes. My quilt slips down my shoulder and cool air rushes in to greet my skin that is still warm from dreams.

Another knock.

I wrap myself in a shawl and pad barefoot across the floor, heart ticking faster than it should. For a moment, my mind jumps to Lucien but when I open the door, it isn't him.

It's Thaleia.

She stands bundled in a too-large coat, its buttons mismatched and fraying at the edges. A woolen hat tilts narrowly to one side, and in her hands she cradles a woven basket filled with small cloth sachets and what looks like scones, glazed with something pale and sweet, dusted with dried lavender.

"Good morning," she says, her voice soft, wind-chapped. "I wasn't sure if you'd be awake. I... wondered if I could come in."

For a heartbeat, I falter.

Lucien's voice rises like a low tide in my memory: *She's losing her mind, Sylvaine. The academy keeps her because they don't know what else to do. Be wary, be cautious.*

But then I think of Mama, her hands always busy, her heart always open. Offering kindness, always, even when the world didn't deserve it.

I step aside. "Of course. Come in."

Thaleia smiles, her eyes warming behind the fatigue that clings to her. She moves with care, as though she's lived a dozen lives and each one left its own bruise behind. She sets the basket on the table and shrugs off her coat.

Beneath it, she wears three different shawls, a linen blouse embroidered with curling ivy along the hem, and a skirt patched with sun-faded silk.

"Your cabin smells like cedar," she says, glancing around. "Like the old sanctuary halls."

"It used to be a storage lodge," I explain, offering a faint smile. "It was cleaned out when I requested it. The scent's stubborn."

"Stubborn can be good." She busies herself with the basket, unwrapping the contents like offerings. "I brought lavender-honey scones. And sachets for your drawers, moth's bane and sweet fern."

I run my fingers over the delicate linen pouches, the stitching is uneven but careful, initials embroidered in one corner: *T.E.*

My breath catches. I swallow hard, the room suddenly growing heavy around me. The initials are so familiar and I hadn't expected them here. For a moment, I forget to breathe.

I blink rapidly, trying to clear the sudden sting in my eyes. It feels like a cold gust of wind blowing through the door of a memory I'd thought was buried deep, locked away. The years between now and then seem to dissolve into the haze of time.

"T.E...." I whisper, almost to myself. "Thaleia..."

Her hands pause in the basket. She looks up at me, a slow, knowing smile playing at the corners of her lips, as if she recognizes the quiet recognition in my eyes.

"You remember, don't you?" she asks gently.

I nod, my throat tight. I can barely form words as the memories crash over me, flooding back with a force that makes my heart beat too fast. The scent of dried herbs, the soft rustle of cloth, the quiet, persistent presence of someone who had always been there, leaving packages for me long before I understood the kindness behind them, long before I realized the deep care woven into every tiny stitch of the parcels.

I was only a child then, too young to know where the food and supplies had come from. After my parents died, the forest had been my only home, but sometimes it was so cold, and the nights so dark. As if by magic, parcels would appear, left in places I'd never thought to look: behind rocks, beneath the old oak, or just outside my cabin, tucked between the roots of trees, as if they'd always been waiting for me.

Every time I opened one of those packages, I found exactly what I needed: a jar of honey, a bundle of medicinal herbs, a few tins of fish, some simple cloth, and sometimes, a small, carefully folded note in neat handwriting, *T.E.*

I never knew who it was, I never knew why she did it, but I trusted her. I had to, it was the only thing that kept me from slipping too far into the dark places of my grief.

"You were... always there when I needed you," I say, voice barely a whisper, the weight of the moment pressing against my chest. "I thought it was magic," I admit, almost laughing at the childishness of that belief. "I thought you were some kind of... forest witch or spirit, someone who could see my needs even before I knew them myself. I didn't know if you were real."

Thaleia waits, watching me in silence for a moment. She offers a soft smile, her eyes thoughtful and full of a kind of quiet understanding. I swallow hard, the lump in my throat refusing to budge. I look down at the pouch in my hands, running my thumb over the stitching.

"Thank you," I say, my voice thick. "For bringing these, for reminding me."

Her smile deepens, and she nods, understanding without needing more words. "It's my pleasure," she says quietly. "My garden gives me more than I know what to do with."

We sit and she pours tea from a travel kettle she's brought, cinnamon bark and violet leaf. The steam coils between us in gentle, fragrant ribbons. She talks easily, in that winding way she does, letting her thoughts meander like a brook cutting through meadow grass.

She tells me about her personal garden, tucked behind the old stables: how the marigolds have gone wild this year, how a crow stole her gardening shears and hasn't returned them.

She speaks of her old students in a tone halfway between fondness and frazzled. "They were sweet," she says, sipping her tea. "But one of them had a tendency to turn everything into a love story. I assigned them a treatise on spectral convergence and got back a thirty-page romance about a wraith and a priestess."

I laugh, surprising both of us. It feels good, light and unguarded.

Her voice quiets. "Your mother used to laugh like that."

I freeze, cup halfway to my lips.

Thaleia looks down, thumbs grazing the rim of her mug. "I knew them well and I miss them greatly."

My breath catches. "Lucien said that too. But he rarely talks about them."

Thaleia gives a small, understanding smile. "He doesn't grieve. But me, I keep it all, memories, stories, even the ache. Like seeds. Like stones in a pocket."

There's a gentle quietness between us, the only noise is the wind at the shutters.

She lifts her gaze to mine. "I taught them, you know, all three of them. Caliane, Auren, and Lucien. They were bright, bold and constantly challenging me. They were inseparable back then, the kind of friends who finished each other's arguments as often as sentences."

A faint smile touches her lips. "But even early on, I saw it, the way Caliane looked at Auren, and how he always found a reason to sit beside her. There was a softness between them, a kind of quiet gravity. Love, even then, just waiting for its moment. Your parents were always so full of love."

She leans back, thoughtful. "Things shifted over time. Caliane and Auren started staying after lessons, just the two of them. At first, it was debates and shared theories. Then laughter. Then looks. And Lucien..." Her voice trails off gently. "Lucien stayed close, but I think he knew before they did what was changing."

She clears her throat, voice warming. "Your mother once slapped an Educator across the face for claiming emotion had no place in theory. Said, 'how can we name the sacred if we don't feel it?' And she meant it. That woman lived every truth like fire: burning, illuminating, never hidden."

I blink back the sting in my eyes.

"Your father," Thaleia chuckles. "Once he started his guest lectures here, he used to sneak pastries from the kitchens and bring them to me. He always bribed me for more time in the hall. I always let him borrow mine when he wanted to teach."

"That sounds like him," I murmur.

"They were free, Sylvaine. Not careless. Not naïve. But full of something this place has forgotten how to carry."

I press the edge of my cup to my lips, though it's gone cold. The words fill the room like a second embrace.

I say it, before I can stop myself, "I'm not like them."

Thaleia looks at me, stills.

"I mean," I fumble. "They were blessed, chosen. My Mama carried Light like it belonged to her, and Pa cloaked himself in Shadow. I... I read well. I write fast. But there's no fire in my blood. No touch of the divine."

A pause, she doesn't interrupt.

"I keep thinking... maybe I was a mistake."

Thaleia leans forward slowly, her face open, weathered, utterly without pity. "Sylvaine. Not everyone who matters to the world is lit or cloaked from above."

She takes a breath, thoughtful. "The brightest torches burn out. The deepest roots never shine, but they hold everything up. You are not a mistake, you are a choice; a thread in the design that was never meant to glow, only to hold."

Something opens in me, gently; like a bud uncurling to morning air.

Thaleia reaches into her coat pocket and pulls something out, a worn slip of folded parchment, the edges weathered with age. She presses it into my hand.

"I wasn't going to give this to you yet," she says. "But maybe... it's time."

I open it slowly: a diagram, a sigil, notes in a familiar hand.

The ink pricks at something in my mind, like recognition trying to bloom.

"I don't understand," I whisper.

Thaleia smiles gently, rising to her feet. "You will. Not all blessings announce themselves with thunder."

She presses her palm lightly to my cheek, thumb brushing a stray hair aside.

"Keep growing, child. Even stone blooms, given time."

And just like that, she's gone, the door clicks softly shut behind her.

Outside, the mist begins to lift, revealing a morning painted in soft gold and for a moment, just one, I feel something shift inside me.

The next day drapes itself in silence. I spend the morning moving slowly through my cabin, cleaning more by instinct than necessity: rearranging shelves, folding blankets, brushing dust from window sills with a cloth already fraying at the corners. The kind of work that asks nothing of the mind but lets the thoughts wander.

I steep tea leaves in silence and let the scent of them unfurl through the room. I reread passages from texts I've half-memorized, not because I need to, but because the words feel different in the stillness of a free day: less instructive, more alive.

When the sun shifts past midday, I step outside barefoot, letting the light beams dapple across the porch planks, warm on the tops of my feet. That's when I see them: a small bouquet resting neatly against the doorframe.

Wildflowers, not the tidy, perfumed blooms sold in the shops. These are hand-picked: golden bells and moon-clover, a few asters like the ones I braid into my hair. Someone took time with this, not arranged for elegance, but for meaning.

There's no note, but I assume they're from Lucien.

He's not the kind to sign his name to softness. That makes it all the more tender.

I bend down, fingers brushing the stems. Something blooms in my chest; small, foolish and warm, a flutter that lifts me briefly out of myself.

It is a strange thing, to be seen, to be thought of when you are not in the room. Not as a symbol or a speaker or a vessel of Light-approved wisdom, but as a person, as Sylvaine.

I carry the bouquet inside, set it gently in water, and place it on the windowsill above my desk.

For a while, I let myself be still: I read without annotating, I sip tea without planning the week ahead, I watch the petals turn toward the sun.

It is good, no, *necessary*, to feel appreciated: even if only for a moment, even if only by *him*.

Unexpected Tension

BEFORE I KNOW IT, Veriday is upon me again.

The air tastes of old parchment and morning dew as I wind my way back to campus, the weight of the week settling over my shoulders like a ceremonial cloak, familiar and heavy.

I arrive at the lecture hall early. The space is quiet, still holding the stillness of dawn. Alone before class begins, I move through the room with purpose, fingers brushing the faint shimmer of the ward-ring etched into the stone. I trace each rune in turn; protection, clarity, containment, feeling the pulse of magic stir faintly beneath my touch, like breath beneath skin. The runes respond in kind, soft glimmers of light flaring for half a heartbeat before fading again.

When the students enter, I'm already writing; chalk in hand, focus narrowed. The board becomes a canvas for the day's provocations.

I hear the familiar scrape of chairs, the quiet rustle of cloaks, the shuffle of books, but I don't turn to greet them. Let them step into the lesson like it's a threshold, let them decide whether to cross.

"If knowledge is power," I say, turning to face them, "then who gets to decide what knowledge is allowed?"

The room shifts, bodies still.

Eyes flick toward one another, gauging the weight of the moment, the tilt of the air. There's a charged and waiting silence, like the inhale before a spell speaks itself aloud.

There's always a thrill in that silence: the edge of something, the moment before thought becomes sound, the precipice before someone dares to leap.

Mirielle jumps first. She always does.

"Those in control," she says, her voice steady, hands clasped in her lap like folded wings.

I nod. "Why?"

"Because if they can shape what we learn," she says, "they shape how we think."

"They shape what we believe," Aric adds, leaning forward, eyes sharp. "And what we're afraid of."

"Good."

I turn back to the board and write one word: *Censorship*.

My hand moves in long, deliberate strokes. As the chalk meets the slate, the enchantments woven into the frame hum faintly. One of the older bindings, truth-attuned, flickers in response, just enough to remind us that the room is listening too.

"Let's talk about that," I say. "What does censorship protect? And what does it destroy?"

Hands rise, voices follow, hesitant at first, then surer.

"They say it protects peace," Tomas offers. "But it really just protects the powerful."

"It protects a version of the truth," says Lenore, "a version that's easier to manage."

"It keeps people safe," one of the younger scholarship boys whispers, his fingers nervously plucking at the edge of his desk. "Safe from ideas that might get them killed. But... it also keeps them asleep."

I smile, this time it's real.

"You're all correct, and that's the danger. Censorship isn't always a knife, sometimes it's a lullaby."

The runes along the walls flicker; not much, just a shift in tone, a dimming, a response to the collective tension. Truth magic does that when you get too close to something raw.

I step forward, slow and steady, letting the quiet hold a beat longer before I break it.

"Now," I say, pacing a circle through the rows, "let's pair that with another idea: obedience. Who can tell me the difference between obedience and justice?"

The silence stretches: parchment rustles, someone clears their throat.

Then, unmistakably, there is the soft click of the door.

Lucien enters like mist: controlled, smooth, unreadable. He doesn't speak, just folds his hands behind his back and steps into the rear shadows of the room: a sentinel, a shape in the architecture.

The air shifts again, not colder, just heavier.

The students notice. I see it in their shoulders, in how they sit straighter, in how their breath stills.

Even the rune-lights seem to dim, as if tensing.

Lucien's voice answers, low and polished. "Obedience is the structure through which justice is made manifest."

He doesn't need volume, the enchantments embedded in the room carry his words like thunder wrapped in silk.

"Order only became possible after the kingdom shattered," he continues. "Before that, chaos ruled beneath a mask of unity. The Light does not simply illuminate. It disciplines. It governs."

I meet his gaze, remaining steady and level.

"Interesting theory," I say. "But what if structure becomes the thing we obey instead of justice itself?"

His head tilts, the motion slow, measured. "Then justice must be redefined."

I let the pause stretch, then ask, "and who defines it?"

He doesn't answer.

The silence that follows stretches like a drawn bow. I turn back to the students, keeping my stance loose and my voice warm.

"Justice and obedience often walk the same road," I say. "But one is a compass, the other is a leash."

I gesture to the board, the words glow faintly now under rune-burnished chalk:

Censorship. Obedience. Justice.

"Now," I say, "let's test those ideas. I want your next assignment to be based on the previous reading. Were the Furies just? Or simply vengeful?"

Their next assignment is not an argument, not an essay, but a reckoning.

The quiet that follows feels deeper; like something fragile has been set in the center of the room, and we're all afraid to breathe too hard.

Still, I push forward. We speak of divine wrath, of mercy, of gods who punish with flame and gods who forgive with open hands.

I ask who they'd follow, who they'd forgive, what they'd let burn.

"I'd forgive theft," Mirielle murmurs, "if it was for survival."

"I'd punish arrogance," Aric says. "People who think their power makes them holy."

"I'd worship only the truth," Lenore says.

And there it is again, that silence that listens back, a stillness with weight.

When the bell rings, it breaks like glass: chairs scrape, books close, the rune-lights brighten.

Lucien stays by the door. He speaks to a few students with soft, slow words. Compliments shaped like questions, never commands, but every phrase lands with the gravity of iron under velvet.

Mirielle is last to gather her things, her fingers shake slightly as she stacks her notebooks. Lucien spoke with her the longest, and she doesn't meet my eyes.

I want to call her back, to say something, but the words knot in my throat and then she's gone.

I remain in the silence left behind, a silence full of things we almost said.

I turn to the board one last time.

Censorship. Obedience. Justice.

Three words, each one waiting for someone brave enough to command them.

I stare too long, arms folded across my chest. There's a tightness under my ribs, not fear, just something too alive to ignore.

Maybe I've gone too far, maybe I mistook fire for Light.

I close my eyes, breathe.

What's done is done, the words are out, uncoiled, alive.

With one sweep, I erase the board and chalk dust falls like ash.

Then I gather my notes, adjust the cuffs of my sleeves, and turn toward the chamber of Enlightened Affairs, where the full weight of the Order waits for our first Illumination Meeting.

My footsteps echo down the stone corridor. The scent of lichen and wax drifts up from the flagstones, mingling with the bitter tang of old magic that always clings to these halls.

By the time I reach the Grand Hall, it's already half full. Robes rustle like dry parchment, candles hover midair, suspended in perfect stillness; no flicker, no wind, just that charged silence again, like static before a storm.

The long tables are arranged in two rows, separated by a central aisle that leads straight to three high-backed chairs at the front, the reserved seats of the Beacon of Light, the Hand of Light, and the Chancellor of Illumination.

I take my place near the end of the eastern table, beside Sealed Scribe Marrett, who greets me with a subtle incline of the head. Scribe Neve is already there, ink smudged along the edge of her sleeve, her eyes fixed on her notes as if they offer shelter.

Lucien stands farther ahead, near Elowen and Veyron, the Hand. Elowen's posture is as precise as ever, back straight, hands folded, gaze like a steel blade laid flat on velvet.

Then the bell chimes once, clear and cold.

"We begin," Veyron says, the words as ceremonial as breath.

Lucien steps forward.

"General curriculum evaluations," he begins, voice clipped and composed. "Several instructors have introduced interpretive frameworks this quarter. While a measured approach to theory is encouraged, we must ensure inquiry does not drift into dissent."

His gaze flicks to me, no more than a half-second, but it's deliberate.

"There's promise," he continues, "in challenging young minds. But untempered freedom leads to fragmentation, to chaos."

Elowen nods, expression unreadable. "Philosophy breeds unrest. And unrest, left unchecked, becomes refusal."

Alra, the alchemy Educator, leans in with a smirk. "One of my students quoted an ethics parable during combustion drills. He asked why we distill anything at all. I told him to distill himself out of my lab until he could follow a procedure."

A ripple of chuckles follows, dry and brief. I do not smile.

Lucien speaks again, softer now. "There are names we're watching. Curious ones, too curious." He names them: Mira, Lina, Laen. Names I know, voices I've encouraged: students who sit a little too long in silence, students who have stayed after class with one last question.

"Keep them close," Veyron says. "Flames burn brightest before they devour. We must learn which to contain, and which to extinguish."

Alra murmurs, not bothering to disguise it. "Snuff them out before they slip between the stones."

Something inside me stiffens, but I say nothing. The echo of the chalkboard still clings to my hands like ash.

The tone of the meeting shifts.

"We must discuss the festival," Veyron says. "The solstice approaches."

A scroll unfurls midair, its script glowing softly: gold ink, official, impeccable.

The Festival of Flame, held on the longest night.

For the next hour, we discuss logistics: sunrise chants, rotations of scripture readings, the public offering, flame-roasted and eaten in silence. Then comes the Forest Rite, performed in the altar grove, deep in the darkness beneath the stars.

Lucien's voice cuts through the quiet. "The Rite will proceed unchanged. The circle will be drawn. The path to the glade will be sealed. Only sanctioned initiates may enter."

"Students?" asks someone near the southern alcove.

"They may observe," Lucien answers, "but not approach."

"For reverence," Veyron adds. "And to remind them of order."

As if order is something visible, something that can be absorbed, like warmth from a flame. As if they won't feel the truth in their bones, that some fires burn without light.

A new voice chimes in, dry and weary. The main Archivist, Scribe Tellin, rarely one to speak.

"There are whispers," he says, eyes half-lidded, "in the libraries. Students citing restricted texts, debating the distinctions between truth and doctrine."

He doesn't say my name, he doesn't need to.

Neve stirs beside me, her hand stills on her parchment, but no one challenges the Sealed Scribes.

Lucien's gaze rests on me again, gentler now, almost amused. "What do you think, Educator Sylvaine?" he asks, too casual, too smooth. "Is there merit in letting them question their pillars?"

There's a pause, just long enough to notice. Heads tilt slightly toward me.

I keep my voice even.

"There's always merit in questioning," I say. "But it depends on what you want them to find."

Elowen makes a dismissive sound. "They don't know what they want. That's why we guide them."

"No," I say quietly. "That's why we teach them."

The silence that follows is sharper than anything else that's passed tonight.

Veyron doesn't address me directly. Instead, he turns back to the floating scroll, listing logistical adjustments for initiates and revised seating for the high chant.

The meeting drifts into the smaller matters: permissions, shifts in lecture schedule, recommendations for additional surveillance of students under the banner of "pastoral attention."

But I am not listening anymore. My mind is back in the lecture hall: with Mirielle, with Aric, with their unflinching questions, with the weight of three words written in chalk.

Censorship. Obedience. Justice.

Three doors and someone knocking on the other side.

A bell in the courtyard chimes, signaling the end of the meeting: chairs scrape, robes shift, the room begins to empty.

Elowen brushes past me, not quite stopping.

"You're still standing," she says, voice low, menacing.

"For now," I answer.

She nods.

But something lingers in her eyes, not a threat, not quite a warning; something colder, sadder, maybe, like someone watching a candle burn down and not stopping it, not because they can't, but because they've already accepted the dark.

It takes me only one lecture to notice.

My hall, once full with nearly forty students, now holds maybe twenty; a few more on some days, a few less on others.

It's not dramatic, not a walkout, just... a quiet loosening. A few empty chairs here and there, until whole rows, especially the ones near the back, usually claimed by the Light-born students, sit untouched.

I understand, they hadn't signed up for this.

They came expecting answers, not questions, certainty, not ambiguity; a neatly lit path laid out in scripture and sermon.

What they got instead were open-ended discussions, provocations, metaphors sharp enough to draw blood. They didn't want to interrogate the stories, they wanted to be reassured by them.

I won't give them that.

The students who remained had nowhere else to go, or maybe, in some quiet way, they didn't want to leave. They stayed through the discomfort, the silences, the strange turns our lectures took. They didn't always agree with me, but they were still here: still showing up, still trying.

I caught Aric watching the empty seats one morning as he flipped open his notes. He didn't say anything, just shook his head once, as if unsurprised.

I wasn't offended, not really. Teaching was never about being liked.

Still, as I stood before the room that had once been crowded and now felt only half full, I couldn't help the flicker of something small and sour settling under my skin.

They wanted me to speak of the Light like it was a balm, I offered it as a blade.

Some of them had walked away, and I let them, better that than pretend to be something I am not.

BLOSSOMING RELATIONS

L UCIEN STARTS SHOWING UP more often.

At first, it's occasional: passing glances in the corridor, the brush of a gaze across a crowded council room, a brief nod during Enlightened Affairs sessions that feels more like a warning than a greeting. We move in parallel, our interactions sparking like flint but never catching.

Soon it shifts, becomes habitual, intentional; a pattern I can't pretend not to see.

He begins appearing just outside my lectures, speaking quietly with the students who linger behind: always polite, always measured. His tone is always soft, but his questions are pointed. He praises their insight, then folds it inward, turning it into something colder, cleaner, safer; like sharpening a blade.

He appears at the library steps when I'm leaving late, one hand resting lightly on the railing, as if he's been waiting.

Other times, I find him in the garden cloisters, where the prayer-lilies bloom pale and silent in the evening shade. He never says much, but his silence follows me home.

He slips into my day like thread into cloth, one stitch at a time: not quite intrusive, not quite avoidable.

Then the runes begin to appear.

At first, I don't notice them, small inscriptions tucked into the grain of my office door frame, fine as embroidery. Then etched along the underside of my desk, folded between the lining of bookshelves, pressed faintly into the wood of my lectern.

Protective runes, anchoring glyphs. Some I recognize, symbols meant to ward off misdirection: to ground the mind, to shield memory from manipulation. Others are unfamiliar, older, more complex, like half-spoken prayers in a dialect no longer taught. I find one drawn inside the clay teacup I keep by the window, another curled like a spiral shell beneath the inkwell tray.

He never speaks of them, never asks permission, but the craftsmanship is unmistakable. Light-touched ink that glows faintly when the day is longest. They are woven with precision, held with care: too deliberate to be surveillance, too careful to be casual.

He is warding my space.

Why?

Sometimes, I tell myself it's curiosity: that he's observing, not interfering, that he wants to understand why my students still ask questions when others have learned to stay silent, that he's studying me the way a scholar studies a paradox, hoping that if he watches long enough, the contradictions will resolve themselves.

Is it protection?

Is it guilt?

Or is it something older than either of us, something he can't name any more than I can?

There are moments; when I find another rune tucked where no one should reach, when I feel the air shift like someone exhaling just out of sight, I can't help but think this is not about safety, but about control

And then I think, no.

No, this is about care: twisted through duty, etched in a language I was never meant to read.

I don't know which is worse.

I'm halfway through grading, red ink bleeding across the corners of a student's crumpled paper. The question was bold, too bold, and my notes trail off into silence, as if critique itself might close a door not yet meant to be shut. The lamplight is dim, and my eyes ache from squinting. Outside, rain murmurs against the panes, patient and persistent.

A knock, firm and deliberate, draws me from the margins.

I glance at the door, puzzled. My office is usually quiet at this hour, filled only with the scrape of quill on parchment and the slow sigh of time. The interruption feels out of place, like a breath held too long.

Lucien stands in the doorway, one shoulder resting against the frame. The last of the sun glints off his collar, catching in his eyes like polished wood. His expression is calm but familiar in the way water might be familiar before it floods the room.

"Sylvaine," he says, low, like he's offering the name instead of saying it.

I blink, surprised but careful not to show it. My fingers tighten around the paper. I settle on a neutral smile. "Beacon Corwell."

He steps in, brushing a lock of hair from his brow with that same easy grace that never quite feels casual. "Please, you know you can call me Lucien when it is just us. I thought you might appreciate some company."

I nod, slow and practiced. "I'm nearly finished, Lucien," I say, folding the paper with deliberate calm, tucking it beneath the others like a secret I'm not ready to name.

He doesn't sit; he moves instead to the tall, narrow window and eases it open just a fraction. A breeze slips through, cool, green and damp with garden rain. The scent of jasmine lingers in the air, soft as a lullaby. He closes his eyes for a breath and inhales like it's the first clean air he's had in days.

"I hear your students are fond of you," he says, turning back with a smile just wide enough to soften his edges. "That's rare, especially in your first year."

I tilt my head, searching the space behind the compliment. There's always space behind his words. "They're bright," I say carefully. "And curious."

"Curious," he echoes, like he's testing the shape of the word on his tongue. He steps forward again, and his fingers trail lightly along the edge of my desk, tracing the old scars in the dark wood, scratches left by other hands, other years.

"Curiosity can be dangerous." His voice drops, warm and quiet. But there's something beneath it... something coiled, sharp: not quite a threat, yet not entirely harmless.

I stiffen negligibly, but don't retreat. "So can silence."

A beat lingers before he laughs, just once. It's not unkind, but it doesn't reach his eyes.

"Perhaps," he says, almost indulgently. "But silence doesn't spread."

I glance at the stack of letters waiting for me, the ink still wet with questions: the kind that never quite fit into rubrics, the kind that flicker like sparks when read aloud.

"Is that what you're here to prevent?" I ask. "Spread?"

He watches me for a long moment: not answering, not denying.

Finally, he shrugs. "I'm here to make sure things stay... balanced."

I look at him then, at the man, not the Beacon: at the softness around his mouth when he isn't smiling, at the crease between his brows, just faint enough to suggest he's always measuring something. I wonder if he knows how much he gives away when he doesn't speak.

"Balance," I say, "isn't the same as stillness."

He doesn't respond to that either, but he holds my gaze for a moment longer than necessary, long enough to feel like a decision.

Finally, he straightens, brushing the front of his coat. "I'll let you finish," he says. "I just wanted to check in and thought you might want the window open."

He leaves with barely a sound and the door clicks shut behind him.

I sit still for a long time after, something warm lingers at the edges of the air, and I wonder, not for the first time, what it is he isn't saying.

Or what, exactly, he's trying not to feel.

Days later, I find a note slipped beneath my door. The parchment is thick, edges pressed with a faint, wax-less seal. The ink flows in elegant, deliberate script:

The garden path before curfew. I would like to walk with you. – L

No pretense, no explanation, just that.

I hold it longer than I need to, rereading the single line like it might reveal something new the third or fourth time, something hidden between the strokes of the pen.

I shouldn't go, I know that: not after the meeting, not after the students' names were spoken like smoke ready to vanish, and yet... I go.

The garden is a labyrinth of mist and perfume, branches heavy with night dew and the breath of unseen blooms. The moon is high, its glow a pale wash across the stone paths. Every petal shines distinctively silver, every leaf a deeper shade of green than it is by day. It's quiet here, beautiful in a way that feels deliberately constructed, as if the garden were designed not for walking, but for thinking dangerous thoughts.

Lucien waits by the rose arbor, hands folded behind his back, a single blossom held between two fingers. His face is unreadable in the moonlight, chiseled and still, as if caught between decisions. When he sees me, he doesn't smile, not fully, but his posture shifts; just slightly, the way someone might shift to welcome softness.

"Thank you for coming," he says.

"You didn't leave much room for refusal."

"There's always room, but fewer reasons."

His voice is gentler than usual, unguarded in the cool quiet of the garden. We begin to walk without speaking; the gravel crunches beneath our steps, rhythmic and steady. The scent of damp earth and rose clings to the air, softening the edge of the night. Somewhere in the distance, a night bird cries out, low and melodic. I tuck my hands into my sleeves.

A breeze slips through the hedges, cool and damp with the scent of rain-soaked stone. I try not to shiver, but the motion betrays me, small and involuntary.

Without a word, Lucien slows. I hear the soft rustle of fabric before I feel the weight of his cloak as he eases it over my shoulders. His hands linger for just a moment longer than they need to. The wool is warm, still shaped by his body, and the scent of him, pine, smoke, and something darker I can't name pulls close around me like a second breath.

His fingers brush the side of my neck as he adjusts the collar; just the barest touch, light as dusk, but it's enough to send a shiver down my spine.

He must feel it. I think he means to step away, to give me space, but instead, he pauses; not looking at me, exactly, just near me, as if proximity might say what words won't.

I glance up. He's not smiling, but there's something softened in his eyes now, less guarded. Like this, in the dark, beneath the moon and starlight, he's someone else, or perhaps more himself than he ever allows.

The silence isn't empty, it presses gently at the corners, full of things neither of us are quite ready to say.

Finally, he stops near a stone bench half-buried in ivy. He turns toward me, his expression touched by something quiet and distant. "There's much more to see here than most choose to notice."

I glance at him. "What do you see?"

He tilts his head, studying me, not coldly, not calculating, but like he's memorizing the way I look in moonlight. "The threads. The patterns beneath the surface. The choices people pretend they don't make. The truths they bury under duty or doubt. Most don't even realize what they've agreed to."

"And what have I agreed to?" I ask, softer now; not a challenge, almost a whisper.

He doesn't answer right away. Instead, he looks past me, toward the tree line beyond the garden. His voice is lower. "Something between silence and rebellion. I'm not sure which side you'll land on."

"I didn't realize I had to choose."

"You don't, not yet." A pause. "But the day's coming."

The words settle over us, heavier than the night air. I fold my arms, resisting the urge to pace. "You made me look weak in front of them: the other faculty, the Chancellor, the Hand."

His jaw shifts slightly. "I made you visible."

"And what am I now? A warning?"

"No," he says, stepping closer. "You're a question, and questions are more dangerous than answers."

The space between us tightens; not with threat, but something else, a heat, a pull, something neither of us name.

I should step away. I don't.

"You speak in riddles," I murmur.

"You answer in mirrors." His gaze moves over me, not possessively, but with a quiet reverence; like he's not sure how close he's allowed to be.

"I don't know what you want from me," I admit.

"That's the most honest thing anyone's said to me all week."

He reaches up, and for a breathless second, I think he might touch my cheek, but his hand only brushes a leaf from my shoulder.

Still, the gesture coils heat low in my chest. His touch is fleeting, but the awareness it leaves behind lingers like the echo of a forgotten song.

"You're dangerous," I whisper.

He doesn't flinch. "Only if you're afraid."

He says it almost like a question. I don't know what to say to that.

Part of me still aches from the meeting, from the way he named the students without hesitation. Yet, there's something in the way he says *we* without saying it, in the way he looks at me like I'm not just part of the Order, but something else entirely.

The silence returns, but it's full now, woven tight with what might be either confession or caution. I realize, too late, how close we are.

All too suddenly, I'm thinking of the kiss, soft and gentle, in his study after dinner; the way his hand trembled slightly before it found mine, the way the moment held its breath around us.

Finally, I take a step back. "It's late. I should go."

He nods, the smallest shift. "Of course."

As I turn to leave, his voice finds me again, quiet, almost casual, too careful to be unmeant.

"I want you to answer."

I pause. "Answer what?"

He doesn't look at me, doesn't move, just says, "What it is you're really afraid of."

The night holds its breath as a breeze stirs the petals at our feet. I wait, foolishly, for him to follow the question with something lighter: a smile, a parting word. He doesn't.

So I walk away before I can decide if I want to turn back, before I have to think of an answer.

A WAR UPDATE

Academy Bulletin: Morning Light Briefing

Glorious Victory in the Southern Hills:
The Light Battalion has cleansed another sector of
Shadow corruption near the southern border. Over
fifty Shadow insurgents were neutralized, and sacred
territory has been reclaimed for the Divine Path.
Citizens are urged to pray in gratitude and report
any suspicious behavior.
"With every battle, we reclaim not just land, but
purity." — The Hand of Light

Shadows Use Forbidden Magic on Children:
Recovered accounts confirm that the Shadow forces
have been using corrupted blood-rites to coerce
orphans into serving as spies and saboteurs. This
cowardice further proves that the enemy respects
neither innocence nor life. Stay vigilant. No whisper is harmless.

Thought for the Day:
"The Shadow promises freedom, but what is freedom
without Light? Only chaos, only pain."

```
Memoriam for the Fallen:
Five brave soldiers of the Night Watch ascended
into the Light this week while defending sacred
ley-lines. Their sacrifice fuels our salvation.
Classes will pause for a five-minute Radiance Re-
flection at noon.
Know the Signs of Shadow Corruption:
Unexplained dreams or visions, emotional volatility,
obsession with personal freedom or forbidden texts,
speaking in riddles or poetic metaphors, withdrawal
from structured group activities. If you or a class-
mate exhibit any of the above, report immediately
to a Luminary Guard.

Daily Affirmation:
Order is Peace. Peace is Light. Light is Eternal.
End of Briefing. May the Light Illuminate Your Path.
```

W E GET OUR FIRST war update in the form of the staff bulletin. One sheet: sanitized, clinical, euphoric.

We were promised updates from the front; regular, honest communication to keep us informed. A full moon cycle, and only now do we receive a carefully worded scrap of information.

It doesn't feel like the truth; it feels like control. Almost like they're afraid of what would happen if we *really* knew.

I lower the bulletin slowly, fingers tightening around the edge.

Unexplained dreams, emotional volatility, metaphors: the list of "signs of corruption" reads less like a warning and more like a mirror held to my own mind.

The silence in the room sharpens. My students sit frozen in the glow of the high windows, the filtered morning light casting long colored shadows across their desks. I can feel their eyes on me, twenty-two pairs: wide and waiting, curious and anxious.

I fold the page, carefully, deliberately, then clear my throat.

"Well," I begin, keeping my tone even, neutral, "we've finally received a war update."

A flicker runs through the room: a rustle of parchment, a few glances exchanged.

"Official channels only, of course," I continue. "It came folded inside the instructional bulletin. I'll read the summary aloud, then I'd like your thoughts." I let my gaze drift across the rows. "Particularly on the language. Don't worry, there are no wrong answers, not here."

That gets a few of them to sit up a little straighter. Aric shifts forward on his bench, pen already in hand. Calyra stops fidgeting with the strings on her sleeve, Laen, near the back, doesn't move, but I see the way his eyes narrow slightly, focused.

I unfold the page again, and begin to read.

My voice is calm, uninflected. I do not let the reverent tone of the passage seep into my delivery, though it clings to every sentence like incense smoke.

I glance up as I read, watching their expressions flicker.

Aric's brow furrows. Calyra bites the edge of her thumb. Even Mira, usually unreadable, tilts her head slightly, as if hearing something beneath the words.

I let the silence stretch after I finish. A bird cries out faintly somewhere beyond the courtyard walls. I fold the page again, slowly, and set it aside.

"Thoughts?" I ask quietly. "What stood out to you?"

A pause, long and silent.

Aric raises his hand. "They never say 'killed.' Just 'ascended.' Like it's not war. Like it's a... ritual."

Calyra doesn't raise her hand, she just speaks, voice low. "It sounds like a sermon, not a report. It's preaching."

Near the back, Laen shifts forward, his voice a little shaky but clear. "They said 'purity.' That the land had to be purified." He hesitates, eyes fixed on the edge of his desk. "That's not cleansing. That's... that's erasure."

I nod, slowly. "Why those words, do you think? What's language like this trying to accomplish?"

"To make it sound holy," Mira says immediately. "Not violent, not cruel, just... destined."

"Good," I say. "Yes. What else?"

Aric taps the edge of his quill against his knuckle. "The signs of corruption, they're not things you can measure. They're feelings, dreams, poems. How do you defend yourself against an accusation like that?"

A quiet voice from the second row, Lina. "You can't. That's the point."

Someone else, Rellington, mutters just loudly enough: "It feels like they're watching us through the words."

My pulse ticks faster. I school my expression, but inside, I feel that flare of something, fear, maybe, but also something electric. This is what teaching is supposed to feel like: vital, urgent, alive.

Dangerous.

Then the bell tolls.

They all rise as one, heads bowed, and for five long minutes we stand in stiff silence, bathed in the kaleidoscope of light from the stained glass windows. The colors shift slowly across their faces, blue over Aric's brow, red along Calyra's cheek.

When the final chime echoes and the reflection ends, the classroom exhales. The students begin packing away their papers. I remain still, my heart just beginning to settle, and that's when I see him.

Lucien stands in the doorway, framed in gold, dressed in tailored cream that catches the light like the edge of a polished pearl. A bouquet rests in his hand, flowers, delicate and rain-speckled.

He steps into the room with that same effortless composure, all smooth grace and studied charm.

"Beacon Corwell," I say, keeping my voice carefully neutral.

"Picked just outside the gardens," he says, holding out the bouquet. "They reminded me of your parents, wild, resilient."

The petals are cool with dew as I take them, the stems damp against my fingers.

"Flowers again?" I ask, shocked at the public display when the last gesture was so quiet.

He looks confused for a moment before regaining his composure. His hand lingers a beat too long against mine before he leans in, slow and deliberate, his breath brushing my cheek as he draws close to my ear.

"Lunch on Umbreday?" he murmurs, just for me.

I nod, too quickly, and hate the way it feels like surrender.

The rest of the day passes in a fog: I teach, I grade, I nod when spoken to. But one thought loops, quiet and constant: *the words are watching, and so is he.*

The rest of my day is a blur.

By the time the study session arrives, the corridors have thinned, and the building has begun to exhale. Lecture halls settle into silence, the last of the chalk dust drifting like tired snow. Outside, the late sun slants gold across the flagstones, catching on the edges of ivy and cracked statuary. The courtyard chimes ring; soft and uneven, like distant laughter, warm, or unreal, depending on how you're listening.

My office smells like dried ink and old paper, the scent of ideas that have sat too long in the dark. The windows catch the light in fractured panes, casting the room in the palette of an old painting: amber, smoke, and dusk.

Inside, my students gather: not the cautious ones, not the ones who color within the lines of doctrine.

These are my regulars; the spirited ones, the ones who argue, question, linger, the ones I worry about most because they still believe that truth is something worth chasing.

Calyra is the first through the door, moving like someone used to slipping through locked things. Sparks crackle faintly around her fingertips: harmless, showy.

Aric enters and she zaps his shoulder as he makes his way past her.

"Ow," he says flatly, without looking up. "Rude."

"You looked too smug," she says sweetly, and hops onto the edge of my bookshelf, legs swinging.

Aric, undeterred, shrugs off his coat and flings himself into the reading chair with dramatic precision. "I'm already tired of being enlightened," he sighs, summoning his journal into his lap with a flick of Light, small and shimmering like firefly wings.

Then Laen arrives, slower, quieter. He closes the door with a small pulse of magic and leans next to it, arms crossed.

They always come in like this: never quite on time, never quite asking what they're supposed to.

"Long day in the Light?" Calyra teases, examining a parchment on my desk. "You look like someone who's had to smile through a sermon."

"I teach four classes a day," I say, not looking up. "I always look like that."

"But especially today," Aric adds. "After that bulletin, 'In Radiance We Rise' or whatever they're calling it now. That was a lot of... glory."

"'Purity reclaimed,'" Calyra recites in a sing-song voice, her fingers idly tracing glowing sigils in the air. "I copied it down in blood-red ink. You're welcome."

"I saw," I reply dryly. "Your commitment to dramatic annotation remains unparalleled."

She grins. "Would you have preferred gold?"

There's a rustle at the door and two more appear: Tomas and Lenore. Tomas nods silently and sinks to the floor by the radiator. Lenore, with her usual quiet grace, wraps her hands around the kettle, and a soft glow blooms beneath her palms. Heat hums through the metal as if coaxed, not commanded.

"Tea's ready," she announces. "Red leaf from the archives lounge. Acquired via morally ambiguous methods."

"Stolen," Calyra translates.

"Liberated," Lenore counters, unbothered, as she begins pouring cups like a priestess performing a rite.

"Tea?" she offers.

"No sugar," I say, accepting mine, "I see you remembered."

"I always do."

Steam curls into the air, catching the sun like breath. For a moment, the room feels like a refuge.

Then Laen says, voice even, "is it true you're seeing him?"

I blink. "Seeing who?"

Calyra leans back theatrically. "Lucien," she croons. "The Beacon. The Warden. Campus saint. He of the white robes and over-polished boots."

Lenore giggles into her sleeve. Tomas just raises his brows and sips.

I should deflect, or lie, but I'm tired and they already think they know.

"He did bring flowers," I say. "Wild ones, from the outer gardens."

"Oooh," Aric hums, scribbling furiously. "'The Light courts in blossoms. Resistance blooms in root.' That's a line."

"Scandalous," Calyra murmurs. "He doesn't seem like your type."

"And what is my type, exactly?"

"Books," she replies immediately. "Obscure poetry. Moral ambiguity. Definitely not men who speak in capital letters."

Laughter ripples through the room like a current through a circuit. Even Laen smirks, briefly. Aric shoots a spark at the edge of Calyra's boot, she retaliates with a tiny bolt that ricochets harmlessly into the bookshelf.

"Hey!" I warn, though I'm half smiling. "Keep it up and I'll ban all magic use during office hours."

"Empty threat," Tomas murmurs. "We all know you like us too much."

For a moment, it feels safe, but the mood shifts again, quick, like static changing direction.

"Do you trust him?" Laen asks.

The question lands heavier than the others; not sharp, not soft, just solid, and inescapable.

I set down my tea. "I trust that he believes in what he's doing."

"Even if what he's doing isn't right?"

"That's not what you asked."

Tomas is watching me now too, his teacup forgotten.

"I think he believes in the Light," I say. "And I think belief, when it's that strong, can be both beautiful and dangerous."

Lenore, quiet until now, finally speaks. "Is that what you think about the Shadows as well?"

She isn't accusing, just asking.

"I think that anything with beauty can also hold danger," I say softly.

Aric scribbles something again. I glance over, he's written:

Conviction is gravity. It pulls even the reluctant into orbit.

"You used to talk more like us," Calyra says again, more gently this time. "Back when you told us stories instead of warnings."

It's not meant to hurt but it does.

"I still do," I say, though even I can hear how tired it sounds.

"You teach us how to question," Laen says. "But sometimes it feels like you've already settled your answers."

Tomas leans forward. "Do you think we're naïve?"

"No," I answer instantly. "I think you're brave."

"But also dangerous," Calyra adds, flashing a half grin. "You said so once."

"I said passion is dangerous," I reply. "You chose to wear it like armor."

Another pause, then Lenore mumbles very quietly, "do you think Shadow will lose?"

I take a long sip of tea before answering.

"I think losing looks different to different people. And I think survival isn't always the same as winning."

Outside, the bells chime again, another hour vanished into golden dust.

"Careful walking back," I say, as they begin to gather their things. "Especially you, Aric. Your metaphors are starting to get revolutionary."

He grins. "I hope so. That's how they'll know I'm real."

They trickle out slowly. Lenore last, after collecting the mugs and setting them precisely on my desk.

The door clicks shut behind them. The room exhales again, silence returning like a tide.

I gather my papers slowly and stack them with practiced care.

Outside, the sky fades to a bruised violet. The lamps along the stone paths flicker to life one by one, like lonely stars in the dark.

I make my way back through the winding paths, past the gardens and the silent sentries of stone. The chill in the air threads through my sleeves like a whisper.

The trees, tall and unmoving, loom like guardians with secrets of their own. The wind smells of turning leaves and distant firewood. Somewhere, a bell tolls faintly: too far to mark time, too close to ignore.

Dinner is quiet in my cabin; the kind of quiet that settles in the bones, not silence exactly, but something deeper: a presence shaped like absence.

I warm the last of the root stew over the small iron stove. The broth is too thick, over-salted from being reheated again and again, a little like doctrine: reused, reheated, increasingly hard to swallow. I eat standing up, my back to the room, staring through the small window above the sink as the sun fades completely beyond the treetops. The sky slips from indigo into pure darkness, and even the birds have stopped their song. It feels like the world is holding its breath.

I think about Lucien and the way he looked, standing in my lecture with those ridiculous flowers in his hand; earnest, soft around the edges, like someone trying not to look lonely. The golden boy of the Order, emissary of the Light, bathed always in purpose, glowing with belief.

Yet, at that moment, something about him felt... human: not the Light he carries, not the scripts he recites, just him.

Later, I curl into the corner of the couch, bowl empty on the side table, and pull a book into my lap.

The Star Thief.

The pages are thin with age, delicate with memory. In the margins there are hastily scrawled notes, years old now, wind between the lines: crooked stars, half-finished thoughts, question marks that look like hooks waiting for something to bite.

I trace one of the stars. The ink has bled, softened over time, like it always meant to fade. It was Lysander's copy once, given to me in a moment of unguarded belief. I never knew whether he was chasing shadows or fleeing them, before he disappeared into the night.

I try to read, I really do, but the words keep slipping from my eyes. The story unravels in my mind, threadbare; not gone, just... unwilling, like a spell that won't speak its name.

My thoughts drift. The students' voices still echo faintly, caught in the rafters of my memory: their questions, their laughter, their defiance wrapped in curiosity.

Laen's eyes, bright and watchful, narrowed with something dangerously close to hope.

Calyra's voice:

You used to talk more like us.

She wasn't wrong.

I set the book aside and let my head fall back against the couch. The fire has burned low, embers pulsing beneath a thin veil of ash. Outside, something rustles: wind, a fox, a memory, a shadow.

Light says it knows, that it sees, that it burns clean. But I have seen what it leaves behind: the burn marks, the silence, the sermons that sound like threats if you listen closely enough.

Shadow says it questions, that it protects the mystery of things. But I have seen what hides there too: the unspoken, the unchecked, the weight of secrets piled too deep.

I feel caught between the two.

Once, I thought I stood with Shadow, then, I thought I was above it. Now, I'm not sure where I stand at all.

Can I fall for Lucien without falling for what he represents?

Can I love the softness in his voice and still doubt the fire behind his words?

Can I kiss a man whose hands are wrapped in Light and not feel like I'm being branded?

Can I love again, when the last man I loved made a vow in the dark, but then left before dawn and took the stars with him?

My chest aches with the kind of uncertainty that doesn't feel like fear, just the hollow shape it leaves behind. I want to believe in something but I no longer know what.

Eventually, I rise. I move like I'm underwater: slow, muffled, half-dreaming. I turn out the lamps one by one, and each extinguished flame leaves a little more shadow behind.

My bed feels cold. The sheets are too crisp, but they do not welcome me; they tolerate me, as if they too have questions I can't answer.

Sleep does not come easily, it never does on nights like this. My thoughts gnaw at themselves, not strong enough to wound, just enough to fray. Something stirs beneath the surface of my mind: a shape, a memory, a door I locked years ago and pretended to forget.

Something is pressing against that door now, insistent, not knocking; no, not that polite, just... pressing: weight, presence, intention.

Whispers trail beneath it: faint, feral, familiar. I close my eyes and try to keep it shut, but even in sleep, I know...

Some doors do not stay closed forever, some lights are too bright to look at, some shadows remember your name.

A GATHERING OF MINDS

T HE SUN IS STILL low on the horizon. Its pale fingers creep across the sky, not yet casting shadows through the trees.

It's Sovinday. I should be savoring the rare quiet, but instead I'm awake earlier than I expect, wrapped in the stillness of the morning.

The cold air bites, and I pull my woolen shawl tighter around my shoulders, drawing warmth from its thick, worn fabric. The scent of dew and cedar lingers in the air, the forest outside whispering its secrets to me.

I've already gone through my usual morning routine: braided my hair with asters and starwort, tugged on boots that fit like old friends, and stirred the embers in the hearth. The fire crackles back to life, casting flickering movement along the walls and the warmth feels like a small rebellion against the chill creeping in from the windows.

The air feels thick today, like something's about to change. It's the calm before the storm, the brief lull in my life before the lectures start again.

I sip my tea, the steam rising in delicate curls; the scent of herbs mixes with the earthy fragrance of the morning.

A knock interrupts my quiet thoughts, a soft and unexpected sound that disrupts the silence.

I set my cup down carefully, the ceramic cool beneath my fingers, and rise to my feet. The knock comes again, still soft but more insistent this time. I hesitate for a moment, wondering who could be so bold to disturb me this early.

I cross the room quickly, reaching for the door, my thoughts already on the visitor I suspect is standing just beyond it.

I swing open the door and there she is, Thaleia.

Her radiant smile is the first thing I notice. Next is the way her eyes sparkle with mischief, though something serious lingers behind them. She's carrying a basket, the woven handle gripped tightly in one hand.

"Good morning, Sylvaine," she says, her voice soft and gentle like the morning sun, but there's an underlying warmth that's always present with her.

Before I can even respond, she steps inside without waiting for an invitation. I step back, blinking in surprise at her sudden appearance. The familiar scent of spices drifts from the basket, mingling with the cool morning air.

"You're up early," I say, arching an eyebrow, though I can't help but smile. Thaleia has a knack for breaking the quiet and I can't say I mind.

"Early mornings are good for the soul," she replies, her voice carrying that calming confidence that makes everyone around her feel just a little lighter. She shifts the basket to one arm before setting it down on the table before lifting the lid with a flourish.

"I brought breakfast," she says with a mischievous grin, her eyes gleaming. "I thought you might appreciate it."

I laugh though there's a touch of surprise in it. "You didn't have to…"

"I know," she interrupts, cutting me off with a playful glint. "But I thought you might like a bit of company this morning."

The way she emphasizes the word makes me tilt my head, curious. "Company?"

Before she has time to explain what she means, I hear the shuffle of feet beyond my door. Three figures step into the cabin, and my surprise deepens.

Educator Veyrien steps past Thaleia first, her presence commanding. Tall and angular, her silver hair gleams in the early light, and her eyes seem to glint like sharpened steel. Veyrien's shoulders are squared with a kind of defiance, like she's always prepared for battle, whether literal or intellectual.

"Morning, Sylvaine," she says, her tone cool and precise, as if she's already assessed the situation and determined there's no reason to waste words. Her eyes cut through me, sharp and calculating. "I brought eggs," she says flatly, setting a basket of neatly wrapped eggs onto the table with military precision.

Next, Educator Dael follows, his broad shoulders filling the doorway. He's not as tall as Veyrien, but his presence is just as imposing, if not more so. His rough hands are calloused from years of work as the academy's runic smith, and his voice carries the gravelly depth of someone who's never wasted a word.

"Hope you've got room for me," he says, grinning as he strides into the cabin, the door barely closing behind him. He carries flatbreads in his arms, some still warm, the scent of freshly baked dough hanging in the air. "Made these myself. Well, mostly," he adds with a shrug, as if it doesn't matter whether he baked them entirely on his own. The casual confidence is impossible to ignore.

Behind him, Educator Hallen slips inside, his lanky frame somehow making him seem like he's always on the verge of falling over. He's a bookish sort, glasses perpetually slipping down his nose, robes a little too loose. His hair looks like it hasn't been combed in a week, but there's a warmth about him, a quiet intelligence that draws you in despite his disheveled appearance.

"I swear, I'm always winded by the time I get across the campus," Hallen mutters, his voice carrying the exhaustion of someone who's been running too long. He runs a hand through his messy hair, pushing his glasses up. "Hallen, at your service," he adds with a sheepish grin.

"You're the last one to arrive, as always," Thaleia teases, though her voice is gentle. She picks up the jar of honey she'd brought and hands it to Hallen, her smile soft. "You can't blame the hills," she adds, her tone amused, though there's something more intimate in the way she says it.

I stand there, stunned and amused at the same time, my thoughts a blur. Thaleia had mentioned the idea of company, but I hadn't expected... this.

"This is a bit much," I say, gesturing at the now-crowded space. "I wasn't expecting..."

"Surprise," Thaleia says brightly, her voice upbeat and playful. "I thought you might enjoy some like-minded friends. I know it can be... lonely, out here on your own."

She looks at me then, her expression softening with something like sympathy, though it's carefully masked by her usual ease. She's right, of course, the solitude of my cabin, of the academy, weighs on me at times, though I rarely admit it aloud.

I take a deep breath and force a smile. "I'm not sure what I did to deserve this, but I suppose I'll make room."

The cabin fills with the sounds of unpacking food, the rustle of baskets and the clinking of glass jars. The warmth of the room grows as they settle in around the table, and I can't help but feel an odd sense of comfort in their presence, even if it's unexpected.

Veyrien takes charge of organizing the food; her eyes scanning the room, taking stock of what we have and what we still need. Dael sits down with a grunt, already tearing into the flatbread, while Hallen mutters something about the difficulty of fitting his long limbs under the table.

The conversation begins easily, a low hum that I fall into without thinking. They speak of the past month at the academy: students, lessons, the usual day-to-day matters.

"There's something in the air this year," Veyrien says, her tone heavier than before. "It's like the students are waiting for something."

"Waiting for what?" Dael asks, his voice gruff. "We're all waiting for something, aren't we?"

Thaleia's gaze flickers toward the window, her smile fading just a little. "The war," she says softly, the weight of the word hanging between us. "It's been brewing for a long time, and now..."

Hallen takes a bite of bread and then speaks, his voice quieter than the others. "We can only hold our breath for so long, can't we? Something is bound to change."

The mention of the war brings a chill to the conversation, and I watch them carefully, listening to the undercurrents of their words. There's tension here, an edge that even their laughter can't fully erase.

"We don't get real news anymore," Veyrien continues, her voice steady but edged with frustration. "Everything coming from the fronts is filtered, censored. Official reports are propaganda... nothing we can trust."

"Rumors spread faster than facts," Dael adds, shaking his head. "Half of what we hear sounds like stories from another world, or a nightmare."

Thaleia's fingers drum lightly on the table. "The students want to know the truth. They want to hear from those on the ground, not the Order's carefully crafted speeches."

Hallen leans forward. "But anyone who tries to send unfiltered news risks disappearing. It is far too dangerous, we all know that."

"Dangerous for whom?" Hallen asks, his voice thoughtful.

"Both," Dael replies bluntly. "If we're not careful, we'll all burn."

The mood lightens again, as Veyrien shifts the conversation toward some of the more interesting student projects, and Hallen starts talking about a new theory he's been working on in his spare time. I mostly listen, offering the occasional comment here and there, though I remain an observer.

I can see them becoming more than colleagues... maybe eventually mentors, guides. I find myself admiring them, though I wonder if they ever see me as anything more than a young Educator still finding her way.

When the conversation starts to wind down, Thalela stands first, placing her hands on the table as she pushes back from her seat.

"Well," she says, "we've overstayed our welcome, I think."

I stand, too, following her lead as the others gather their things.

"I'll see you around," she adds, her voice soft but her gaze deeper, as if reminding me of something unspoken. "Don't forget what we talked about."

"I won't," I reply with a small smile.

One by one, they leave, the door closing behind them with a soft click. The cool morning air rushes in as their footsteps fade into the distance, and I stand in the quiet aftermath, my thoughts spinning like the wind outside.

I watch the last of them go, and then I turn toward the desk, where papers and lesson plans wait for me.

There is still much to do, still more to teach, but for now, I allow myself to pause, reflecting: on the unexpected visit, on the weight of their words, on the lingering sense that change is in the air.

The truth they want, the truth they deserve... it's dangerous to find.

Later, I will return to the rhythm of the academy, but today, I hold onto the stillness, for just a moment longer.

An idea has begun to take shape in my mind; risky, reckless, but maybe it's the only way.

FLUTTERS AND SHADOWS

I WAKE EXHAUSTED. NOT from lack of sleep, though that, too, lingers like ash behind my eyes, but from something deeper; a tiredness that feels old, rooted, as if I've been carrying too many truths I no longer believe in.

Outside, the sky is a pale, unfocused grey, as if the morning forgot to arrive properly. Mist hangs low across the treetops, softening the shapes of things, blurring edges and making everything seem just out of reach.

There are no classes today: no summons, no ink to dry or words to weigh. There are just endless hours, wide and unwelcome, stretching in every direction. I don't know what to do with time like this, when it doesn't demand anything, when it just... waits.

I walk barefoot into the garden behind my cabin, and the cold earth presses up into the soles of my feet. Dew seeps between the flagstones. Everything is damp, alive, barely stirring. I've let the garden go a little wild, not out of neglect but because some part of me needed it that way: a place not ruled by structure, a place that grows without permission.

The rosemary is leggy and uneven, pushing out over the path like it's reaching for something. I brush my hand across it and the scent lifts into the air, sharp and grounding, I let it settle around me like a cloak.

Mama used to garden; every spare scrap of yard she could coax into bloom, she did: herbs along the kitchen steps, beans climbing trellises, petals pressed between book pages. I used to sit in the dirt beside her, watching every motion of her hands, gentle, patient, and sure. I never touched anything back then. I just watched, fascinated; like if I looked long enough, I'd understand how things grew, how she knew what needed cutting back, and what needed to be left alone.

I kneel by the valerian bed. Its roots run deep and quiet, anchoring the soft white flowers that rise above like little prayers. I've always loved that about valerian, the contrast; softness and strength, balanced in one body. I press my fingers into the soil beside it. It's cool, pliant and yields to me.

I don't know why that nearly breaks me.

I move slowly, without purpose; not harvesting, not tending, just... touching, feeling, being. I run my thumb over the furled edge of a fern where a spider has spun a delicate thread between two fronds. The web is full of mist, a silver net catching the weight of a morning that hasn't quite settled.

At the far end of the plot, beneath the mulberry tree, wild heather has crept in. It wasn't part of the original plan, but I never tore it out. It's messy, uneven, but it blooms anyway; a burst of small purples that refuse to apologize.

I find myself sitting in the dirt, arms wrapped loosely around my knees. The cold seeps in through my sleeves, through the seat of my trousers, through my spine, but I don't move. I just stare at the slow, living chaos around me and try to match my breath to its rhythm.

Somewhere deep in the trees, a bird calls. It is a soft, descending note that makes me feel like I've forgotten something important.

I close my eyes and the never ending questions return. They never truly leave, but here, in the stillness of green things and waking light, they feel louder.

What if I don't know what I believe anymore?

What if the Light isn't wrong, just too rigid?

What if Shadow isn't freedom, just another kind of blindness?

And Lucien?

Lucien with his impossible gentleness, his unwavering conviction, his eyes that see too much, too clearly.

Can I stand close to him and not be consumed by what he represents?

Can I want the sound of his laugh without wanting the source of his certainty?

I pull a handful of dirt into my palm, hold it there. It is just soil, just damp, dark matter, but it feels heavier than it should. I clench it, feel the grit scrape my skin, and let it fall.

I don't have answers, only soil under my nails and silence in my mouth.

Eventually, the grey sky begins to lighten; not bright, not gold, but enough to see by, enough to pretend it's morning.

I stand, brush off the dirt, and head back toward the cabin.

I have to get ready for lunch with Lucien and still, the questions follow.

Lunch on the terrace is beautiful, too beautiful.

Sunbeams spill across the white stone like warm silk, catching in the gold filigree of the railings and the delicate rim of china cups. Between the columns, ivy trails down toward the lower courtyard where students laugh and cluster in soft murmurs, their voices floating up in warm, harmless waves. From up here, the academy looks peaceful, deceptively so.

We sit in high-backed chairs carved from lacquered ash, our plates arranged with absurd precision: slices of citrus-glazed vegetables, violet-dusted rice, two delicate glass bowls of rosewater fruit.

Lucien gestures toward my plate with a small smile. "Eat," he says lightly. "You've barely touched anything."

I lift a fork and make a show of obligation, though the food turns slowly in my mouth. "I just have a lot on my mind these days."

He leans back, folding his hands loosely in his lap, with fingers steepled. "Then let me help you unload your mind. Tell me about your latest lectures."

I oblige again, offering the broad strokes: myth structure, comparative symbolism, early cultic rites. I speak with the practiced cadence of someone who's explained this a hundred times before: polished, safe, professional.

He listens, too intently.

His eyes don't wander, don't flick to the view or the sky or the steam rising gently from his tea. He watches me like someone studying a book unable to be translated. When I finish, he tilts his head, not in correction or challenge, but in curiosity.

"And where did all that come from?"

I blink, lowering my cup. "The lectures?"

He smiles, small. "No, the depth. Your grasp of cultural patterning, the way you deconstruct ancient narrative, it's not... standard. It's not rote. It's lived, sharpened." He lifts his own cup, watching me over the rim. "There's history behind it. You've carried something with you."

He's circling something. I can feel it, not with the words he's saying, but the ones he's leaving just outside the frame.

"You mentioned a boy," he adds after a moment, almost too casually. "From The Vale?"

I nod, slowly, hesitant to mention Lysander. "We read old academy texts together. Whatever we could get our hands on."

His expression doesn't change but something shifts behind his eyes. "That kind of hunger," he says quietly, "is rare. Most people wait to be fed. You," he stops, and I glance up at him. His gaze is steady and not unkind, "you burned for it," he finishes. "Didn't you?"

I look back down at my plate. "We studied what we could find. He was good at spotting patterns, and I liked to ask questions."

"What did you believe?" he presses. "Back then, when it was just the two of you. What did you think was true?"

My answer is careful. "We questioned things. Compared stories. Looked for contradictions."

"Surely he influenced you."

I meet his gaze. "Maybe, but it wasn't one-sided."

A breeze stirs the ivy, and a cluster of white blossoms drops from the overhead trellis, scattering across the flagstones.

He watches me a little too long, and the moment stretches between us like a string pulled gently taut. It doesn't feel like tension or discomfort, but something quieter, something attentive. Measured, but real.

Then, without quite thinking, he reaches across the table, and his fingers find mine. He doesn't take my hand; he just brushes his thumb slowly along my knuckles, a whisper of touch, like he's memorizing a detail he doesn't want to forget.

"Sometimes I forget," he says softly, "how young you are."

I start to pull back, not offended but unsure. He stills his hand.

"Not in mind," he adds quickly, "never in mind. That part of you... it's brilliant, sharp. Ancient, almost. There's a part of you that still remembers wonder."

His thumb lingers, just for a breath longer. I don't move. I don't speak. I let him touch my hand like it means something, and maybe it does.

The compliment settles between us, tender and unguarded.

"I don't say that lightly," he murmurs, drawing his hand back, slowly and carefully. "Wonder is rare. Most of us lose it, or trade it. We learn how the world works and forget how it ever made us feel."

For a moment, neither of us speaks. The air is warm and the breeze stirs a lock of hair against my cheek. I feel the place where his hand touched mine still tingling faintly, like the memory of sunlight.

He reaches for the teapot, graceful and unhurried. "More tea?" he asks, his voice a little lower now, a little gentler.

I nod, and he pours for me, the stream of liquid catching the light as it falls, fragrant and gold.

"Thank you," I say quietly, though I'm not sure whether I mean for the tea or the moment.

He meets my gaze as he sets the pot down. This time there's no distance in his expression, no guarded curiosity; just softness, and something close to affection.

I sip the tea. It's floral and warm and just a little too sweet... just like him.

The heat of the terrace still clings to my skin as I step away, heels clicking against sun-warmed stone. Lucien remains behind, sipping his tea with a look I can't quite name.

I don't look back.

The walk help me clear my mind. The breeze stirs the glass chimes nestled between ivy-covered arches, threading soft music through the courtyard trees.

I move without direction, letting the paths wind where they will. Students pass by in small knots, heads bent, books tucked under arms, laughter trailing behind them in muted ribbons. A few nod in greeting, most pretend not to see me.

Near the old statue garden, I spot Lina.

She sits cross-legged on the edge of the reflecting pool, ink-black braid swinging as she leans over a battered book. A second-year student whom I vaguely recognize sits beside her, scrawling doodles on his sleeve in charcoal. She looks up just as I approach and grins.

"Educator! You walk like a ghost," she says. "I didn't even hear you."

"Bad habit," I reply with a soft smile. "Good to see you, Lina. Studying outside today?"

"The library smells like mildew and politics," she mutters, wrinkling her nose. "And the view's better out here."

The boy nods, reverent and silent. I glance down at the book in her lap, its spine barely holding, the corners curled with age.

"Light reading?"

Lina smirks. "Old myths actually. I brought it from home."

"Ironic," I say, but there's no judgment in it, only the ghost of something like recognition.

She rises and falls into step beside me, the second-year trailing behind like a shadow. Lina talks as she always does, animated and unfiltered, her hands painting the air as she weaves through folktales and fragment-myths like they're half-remembered songs. I let her ramble, the rhythm is familiar... comforting, even.

As we pass beneath the cloisters, her voice softens. "There was one my mother used to tell me," she says, "as a bedtime story, actually."

I glance at her sidelong.

"The Myth of the Split Kings."

The words stop something in me, quietly and completely.

Lina continues without hesitation. "Before the gods turned on each other, before Light and Shadow were enemies."

Her voice changes as she speaks, taking on a cadence older than her years. She isn't reciting from the page, she's remembering, drawing something from bone-deep memory.

She speaks of the first king, mortal but chosen, of the twin gifts, of the covenant written in blood and rewritten by Earth. When she reaches the part about the twins, one with Light in his lungs, one with Shadow in his bones, she hesitates, just for a breath then continues.

"They ruled together," she says, "the crown and the hand. Two kings. One heart."

"But it didn't last," I say softly.

Lina nods. "When the gods fractured, so did the world. The people chose sides. And the twins... disappeared."

Her eyes lift to mine, earnest. "Do you think it's true?"

I pause, thinking of the only set of twins I knew: Lysander and Caelum, convenient that both of them have disappeared as well.

The reflecting pool behind us shimmers with ripples from the breeze. White petals drift from the canopy above, catching in the water like snowflakes too soft to melt.

"I think the myths we preserve are often less important than the ones we whisper," I say at last. "The ones someone risked remembering."

Lina's smile falters just for a second but returns, quieter.

"That's what my mother always said," she murmurs.

She looks toward the spires of the academy, whose stained glass catches the sunlight like a wound. Her voice, when it comes again, is smaller. "I like the idea of it, though. Two kings, equal, whole only when together. Balance, not conquest, maybe that's the real heresy."

The words fall between us like something sacred. She doesn't mean it as rebellion, she means it as hope.

We stop by a low wall overlooking the eastern orchard and she leans forward, resting her elbows on the stone.

"My mother said the old stories weren't just for dreaming," she adds. "She said they were left behind like seeds, meant to be planted when the world was ready again."

I study her face... young, but not naive. There's something ancient in her eyes, like memory passed through blood.

"You'd make a good Scribe," I say gently.

Lina smiles, but there's a strange heaviness in it. "Or a heretic."

"Sometimes," I murmur, "they're the same thing."

She laughs, the sound is bright, sudden and real.

The boy finally speaks, softly. I almost forgot he was with us. "It's a good story."

"It is," Lina agrees, "even if no one believes it anymore."

"They don't have to," I say, more to myself than to her. "It was never written for them."

They wave as I excuse myself, citing the usual stack of essays and the unspoken weight of what lingers, but even as I turn the corner and the cloisters hush behind me, her voice echoes through the stillness:

Two were born, one to rule, one to guard, both to bind what was broken.

I wonder, not for the first time, if the myths we whisper aren't memories after all, but warnings, or promises.

After spending nearly the entire weekend dallying, I know I can't afford to lose another hour. I spend Luminday cleansing and prepping so thoroughly, my Pa would have been impressed.

The next week's lectures won't prepare themselves, and the untouched stack of essays on my desk is beginning to feel like a personal failure. If I fall behind now, I'll be scrambling the rest of the term.

So I make my way to my office, letting the weight of routine settle over me like a cloak. The rhythm of responsibility is steadying and familiar.

But even before I unlock the door, I feel something is off: that subtle shift in air pressure, that faint, unmistakable wrongness that only comes from presence, from intrusion.

The room looks undisturbed, perfectly arranged, but I know it's been entered... handled.

A note waits on my desk, no seal, no crest; just a square of fine cream paper, folded with surgical precision. The ink is pressed into the grain like it belongs there.

Come see the stars tonight. —L

I stare at it longer than I mean to, pulse settling into something half-steady, half-curious. I set it aside without folding it, let it rest at the corner of my desk like an open possibility, and pull the stack of parchment forward: grading.

"If myth remembers, rather than invents, could it be that Light and Shadow were never meant to oppose, but to orbit? Not war, but gravity?"

My quill hovers, then scratches across the first page.

Strong premise. Push further, what does orbit require? What breaks it?

I move to the next.

"Light, as described in early hymns, seems less like salvation and more like hunger. A force that demands allegiance, not love. Might this explain the language of supplication?"

I pause longer this time. A thrill runs up my spine that I refuse to name. In the margin:

Excellent. Explore inversion, what is Light afraid of? Where does Shadow offer safety?

I set it aside, careful not to glance at the note again. The silence in the office is familiar, but too still, in a way that feels expectant, as if the room is holding its breath.

Lucien's voice echoes, unwanted and too close:

You don't just study these myths. You live them. Let them live through you.
That's why it matters.

Another essay, this one messier. The ink is smudged, margins filled with jagged annotations, as if the student couldn't write fast enough to keep up with the thought.

"My theory is that balance was too costly. Not just for the kingdom but for the gods themselves. The act of compromise stripped them of certainty. Of simplicity."

My hand stills above the page, balance was too costly. The words echo: not just academically.

I think of Lina's voice, weaving her mother's myth like thread pulled from a deeper garment: of the First King, of the twin sons, each born of a different breath, of a kingdom broken not by hatred, but by the impossibility of holding two truths at once.

I think of how her eyes had lifted to mine when she asked if I believed it, and how I hadn't lied but hadn't said everything, either.

And now:

Come see the stars tonight.

Lucien leaves no hour, no place, no reason... only certainty.

I don't have an answer, not yet.

I go, even though I am not sure I want to.

Because refusal might raise suspicion. Because part of me, small and stupid and still soft in places I thought long-hardened, wants to believe he means well. Because sometimes safety doesn't look like distance, sometimes it looks like wanting to be kissed.

The observatory door creaks open before I can knock.

Lucien stands beneath the great dome, silhouetted in the starlight, the ceiling rolled back to bare the heavens. Above us, the constellations stretch across the dark like ancient promises: beautiful, vast, and sharp-edged.

He looks at me like I'm one of them.

"Sylvaine," he says, his voice catching somewhere low in his throat. "You came."

"You asked." I smile, soft but unreadable, my armor.

He takes a step forward. "You outshine the stars."

I glance down. My robes are plain, but the way he looks at me, like I shimmer, like I belong in the sky, pulls warmth to my face before I can stop it. He offers me a glass of wine and our fingers brush.

I don't pull away. His touch lingers, and for once, I let it.

The wine is cool and fragrant, pear, yes, and something floral, wistful. He watches me as I drink, and I'm painfully aware of the shape of his attention. The way he doesn't look through me, but at me, like I'm something he's memorizing.

A table is set with quiet elegance: soft cheese, sliced figs, still-steaming bread wrapped in linen. The candlelight gleams in crystal, dancing on the silverware. Music hums from a corner, violin and cello; something old and mournful that somehow feels like it was composed just for this.

We sit. The space between us isn't wide, but it's measured.

Lucien tilts his head toward the sky. "I used to come here as a boy. My father said the stars were the only honest thing left in the world. Light, undiluted."

"Honest?" I echo. "Or indifferent?"

He glances at me, mouth lifting a limited degree. "Perhaps both."

Silence stretches, not cold... just heavy, deliberate.

Then he speaks: of legacy, of precision, of a world perfected through order and clarity, sculpted in unbroken Light.

"There's elegance in purity," he says, voice reverent. "When the Light is whole, it elevates everything it touches. No chaos. No Shadows."

"It burns, though," I murmur. "Doesn't it?"

He looks at me, really looks. "Only what refuses to shine."

I should flinch, I don't. I meet his gaze and hold it. He shifts closer, not threatening but intimate, earnest.

"You're not like them," he says. "You don't settle for echoes. You dig until truth bleeds. You could shape something better than this." His hand lifts, hesitates, then finds mine. "You already are."

My throat tightens. It's not with fear, but with the ache of being seen and not trusting the one who sees you.

"I don't want to see you wasted," he says, quieter now. "You're rare, Sylvaine. You deserve more than fading into someone else's shadow. Stay near the right hands, and you'll never have to fade."

I should pull away, but when he leans forward, I meet him halfway. The kiss is warm, slow, and not forgettable this time. It lingers, not because I need it, but because part of me doesn't want it to end.

I let myself want him: just a little, just enough to make it true.

Later, we walk the stone halls in silence, the kind that feels like a held breath. My hand brushes his once, twice. He doesn't try to hold it, but I feel the want there. I want to as well, and that's the dangerous part.

By the time we reach my cottage, the wind has picked up, tugging at my hair. He stops at the threshold and turns to me.

"I hope you saw more than the stars tonight," he says, and for a moment, he looks almost unsure, vulnerable.

I don't know what to say, so I don't say anything.

He leans in again, slower this time, lips brushing mine with the kind of softness that wants permission. I kiss him back, because I want to, because I shouldn't, because something in me is still uncertain, and that uncertainty is beginning to ache.

I notice a shift across the path, beyond his shoulder.

Shadows begin to move: slow, intentional, creeping. They slither along the path towards my cabin like smoke pulled by a breath I can't hear. Not toward him but toward me.

They ripple like silk in water, like thought, like memory. They shimmer, not like Light, but like truth, not cold, not cruel, just... calling.

Something inside me reaches back.

I pull away from Lucien, blinking as my breath catches.

"Sylvaine?" His voice is soft, uncertain now. "I'm sorry if that was... too much?"

"It wasn't that." My voice sounds far away. "I thought I saw something. Behind you."

He turns, of course he sees nothing.

"You're tired," he says, still watching me carefully. "It's been a long day. You should rest."

"I will." I try to smile but it doesn't quite reach my eyes. "Good night."

He hesitates, then nods, brushing a kiss to my cheek. "Good night."

He leaves and I close the door behind me, my hand still tingling from where he held it.

The feeling that follows, whispering behind my ribs, isn't about him. Rest doesn't find me, not tonight.

ASSIGNMENT OF LETTERS

THE NOTICE PINNED TO the door catches my eye, impossible to ignore even in this quiet space. The sharp sunburst shines back at me, a cruel, pristine reminder of the edict from the Order. The words are inked in cold gold, the text sharp and unwavering:

Ensure all coursework reflects the moral framework of the Light.

The phrasing feels oppressive, like a tightening of chains around my chest. I swallow against the bitter taste that rises in my throat, crumpling the notice into my coat pocket with a swift motion, as though I can hide its weight beneath the fabric of my clothing and hope it disappears.

I close the door to my office more quietly than I mean to, easing it shut with two fingers, as though I might go unnoticed by the empty room. The silence that greets me feels like an old, familiar weight, one that settles deeper every day. The wooden door clicks softly, and I pause, hand lingering on the handle, as if I might reconsider stepping into the world of lectures, students, and endless expectations.

The truth is, I can't shake the feeling that it's not just the edict weighing on me today. No, it's something else, something heavier that clings to the air in the hallways, something unspoken, but undeniably there.

I haven't even made it to my first class yet, but everywhere I go, I am followed by hushed conversations in corners, behind closed doors, in whispers that trail behind every passing student.

Lina is missing.

Nobody knows where she is, where she's gone. It's as if she's simply disappeared into thin air, as though she was never here to begin with: no explanation, no announcement, no one to tell us why.

There is just an unsettling silence where there was once her laughter, her sharp wit, and her gentle but steady presence.

I feel the weight of it all pressing on me as I move through the stone corridors; my steps are quick and sharp, but my mind is clouded. Faint murmurs of voices drifts down the hall, but it only deepens the silence within, making it feel more oppressive. My throat is raw, sore from too much talking, too little sleep.

I asked everyone I could about Lina and her disappearance when I heard the news.

No one has the answers, not yet, not that anyone is willing to share.

Shadows cling to the edges of the day like a warning I'm not ready to understand. The world outside the stone walls of the academy feels distant, unreachable, as if time moves differently here. The storm outside echoes my growing uncertainty.

When I reach the classroom door, I hesitate. My hand hovers over the handle, but before I can turn it a student catches my attention, Calyra. Her face is pale and drawn, her eyes wide with a mix of fear and uncertainty.

She whispers so softly I can barely hear her over the distant thunder. "Lina's still not back, she never returned last night, or this morning. No one knows where she is."

Her words settle on my chest like a heavy stone, making it hard to breathe. I nod, the weight of her statement almost suffocating. I want to offer comfort, but there are no words to make this better.

"I know," I manage, my voice tight. I force my hand to the door handle, pushing it open slowly. The creak of the door echoes through the room.

Inside, it is quieter than usual.

Lina's absence is both deafening and suffocating. Her seat is empty, the air around it colder for it. Her voice, once so familiar and bright, doesn't echo through the halls.

The students are sitting more rigidly, their backs stiff, their faces strained with anxiety. The low murmur of voices has quieted, their eyes flicking toward the door with each creak of the floorboards beneath my feet. The tension is palpable, thick in the air, an absence that haunts the room more than any lesson ever could.

I clear my throat and force a smile. "We'll begin," I say, though my voice feels like a lie.

I move toward the board, hoping that the familiar act of writing will ground me, steady me. I pick up a piece of chalk, gripping it too tightly, but as I draw the first line, it snaps between my fingers. It crumbles and falls to the floor in a soft, unforgiving break.

I stare down at the broken piece. My grip is too tight, my thoughts are too tangled.

Lina's absence hangs in the air like a question, unanswered and impossible to ignore.

How can I go on with this day, with the lesson, with the illusion of normalcy, when everything feels wrong?

The students are waiting for something from me, but I don't have the answer. I don't even have it for myself.

Slowly, I bend down to pick up the broken chalk, each movement feels deliberate, as if I'm trying to make time stop, to hold onto something familiar. The silence in the room grows heavier with each passing second. I stand, steadying both my hands and my breath, but the nagging feeling that something is coming...something terrible, remains.

I turn toward the board, forcing myself to focus, to fill the silence with words even if they feel hollow. I turn to the class, voice steady, though every breath feels like it's being measured.

"This week," I begin, "we finish our journey through *Orpheus*; the myth of love, loss, and the price of looking back."

The students stir; their eyes flicker to one another, then down to their desks. Even here, in this ancient story, they sense the parallels, or maybe they already know how close myth has come to truth.

I let the silence settle for just a moment, then I ask, "what do you think it was, love or control, or something else entirely that made Orpheus look back?"

The pause is longer than usual, then Aric speaks, his voice clear but tight. "Fear."

I nod, gently. "Fear of what?"

"That Eurydice wouldn't follow. That the gods' promises were lies. That he'd come all that way for nothing."

His words hang in the air like a dare, not just to me, but to something unseen. The ancient truth runes shimmering around the lecture hall flicker, as if they sense what is happening.

I walk slowly across the front of the room, letting the question bloom in the silence. "So... doubt? A failure of faith?"

"Or refusal to obey blindly," Mirielle whispers.

A few heads turn toward her. Her voice is quiet, but every syllable lands like a drop of ink in still water, her gaze stays fixed on the wooden grain of her desk, as if it might swallow her.

She has been more reserved since Lucien pulled her aside after class the other week. It seems that even now, his presence lingers.

I want to say it out loud: that questioning is not failure, that obedience without thought is death.

I bite back the words.

Instead, I turn to the board and I write in large, deliberate letters:

The Price of Disobedience

My hand trembles slightly, I hope they don't see it.

Calyra raises her hand, her voice is soft but sure when she speaks.

"Educator," she begins, "there's a story, from the time of the twin gods. Before the schism. When balance, not tyranny, held Vaeloria together. The gods ruled through respect, not fear. There was room for both Shadow and Light."

I glance at her. This is a branch of the same story Lina spoke to me in the gardens, the last story she told before she disappeared.

Her expression is calm, but her fingers are twisted in the hem of her sleeve. She knows the risk of saying such things aloud, they all do.

The class breathes in her words like they've been starving for them, like they didn't know they needed to hear it until now.

"Balance," I echo, my voice lower, almost reverent. "A word that's become dangerous."

Another silence, this one is not empty, but alert; like the pause before lightning.

The chalk trembles again between my fingers, but this time, I don't hide it. I steady myself, right as we hear the knock: loud and commanding. My heart clenches and I feel him before I even turn to look.

Lucien enters like a silk-clad blade, smooth, elegant, and impossibly sharp. The scent of clove and cold iron follows him, not his usual scent. He nods at me with the soft familiarity of someone who knows exactly what your limits are, and how to press them.

"Forgive the interruption," he says, but he doesn't wait for permission to continue. His eyes sweep over the students like a tide, all gentle surface and undertow beneath.

"I hope you're finding value in these lessons," he says. "The administration trusts that your understanding of the Divine Order and the consequences of disobedience deepens with every session."

He lets the last word linger.

His gaze finds mine and holds it, something cold and intimate passes between us.

"And remember," he says, voice lower now, so that the room seems to lean in, "myth is beautiful, but dangerous. It seduces with questions. It hides rebellion in metaphor. It dresses doubt as wisdom. But there is only one truth."

He smiles, it is not a kind smile.

"The Light asks not for understanding," he finishes, "but trust."

He pauses just long enough to see if anyone will speak, when nobody dares to, he turns slightly, glancing at the stack of papers on my desk: notes, essays, careful thoughts dressed as analysis.

"I admire how literature inspires creativity," he says, with that same smile. "But we must guard against the dangerous kind."

He steps closer, for a heartbeat, I think he's going to say something more damning. Instead, unexpectedly, his tone shifts into something almost tender.

"And Sylvaine," he says, using my name like a blade wrapped in silk, "you have a rare gift for guiding young minds, use it well."

Something flickers between us. I don't know if I'd call it affection, maybe recognition or perhaps a warning dressed as praise.

He turns, and with a final, deliberate nod, leaves.

The door clicks shut. The silence in the room doesn't just return, it thickens.

I stare at the chalk in my hand. I am left with the weight of his presence, the absence of Lina, and the tightening noose of the Light's gaze. Around me, the students sit frozen, unsure whether to breathe or speak, but their eyes are wide open now.

Mine are too.

Lina is back today, just as suddenly as she disappeared.

She hurried in, just a few moments late, slipping into a desk at the far edge of the room, her body tense and trembling like a leaf caught in a restless wind.

As my lecture progresses, I keep my eyes on her.

Every small noise, a cough, a shifting chair, the scrape of a foot, makes her flinch, eyes wide and darting nervously around the room. Her usual lively spark is gone, replaced by a raw, fragile fear that seems to grip her whole being.

She avoids my gaze completely, fingers twitching as they fidget with the edge of her desk, tapping and pulling at the wood like she's trying to steady herself. I want to reach across the rows and pull her into an embrace, but I stay frozen, caught between wanting to protect her and fearing I might break the fragile calm she's desperately holding onto.

My throat tightens. The ache from too much speaking and not enough rest gnaws at me like an invisible wound.

Is this what I've become?

A teacher trapped between roles: mentor, censor, conspirator.

The classroom feels smaller today, as if the walls are closing in like whispered warnings. The pale light filtering through the tall windows casts long shadows across worn wooden desks, their surfaces etched with countless names and secret symbols, remnants of students who dared to leave their mark. The air smells of chalk dust, ink, and something metallic... maybe rain seeping through the stone.

I stand at the front, my hands trembling ever so slightly as I smooth the folds of parchment before distributing them. The students' eyes flicker between me and the papers, uncertain, curious, and wary.

"I'd like for us to try something," I say, "something different. Not a book, not Light doctrine."

A murmur passes through the room.

"You've spent the term so far studying voices: gods, poets, rebels. Now I want to hear yours."

I move slowly between the rows of desks: the quiet shuffle of parchment, the faint scratch of quills, the breathless stillness of students watching, waiting. I hand each one a folded piece of parchment and a small stamped slip of paper; coded, unsigned, light enough to flutter like a secret smuggled through the cracks in the wall.

"This is a creative exercise," I say, voice low but clear. "A character study. You'll write anonymous letters to soldiers on the front, a blend of fiction and truth. Use the codenames provided, or make your own... but nothing traceable, nothing tied to your real name."

They know better than to ask why.

"This isn't sanctioned by the Order," I add quietly. "Officially, war reports are classified, sanitized. But this... this is a way to learn what's happening out there in real time. If the letters reach their marks, and some of them will, maybe they'll write back."

The silence thickens. Eyes dart from parchment to my face, even the walls seem to hold their breath.

"It's a creative exercise," I repeat, softer now. "But sometimes, fiction tells the truth better than doctrine."

Around me, the air tightens, not with fear but something sharper: curiosity, hope, hunger.

"Write what you would never say aloud." The words hang in the air like a blade suspended by a thread: a dare, a whisper, a door half-opened.

Quills begin to move, slowly at first... the careful scratch of rebellion.

Aric, ever the cynic, lets his usual smirk fade; his brow furrows in focus.

Mira exhales softly and begins.

Mirielle, still wary, hesitates. Her fingers curl tightly around the quill, eyes distant. I can almost feel the invisible leash around her neck tug tighter.

I walk back to the front of the room as the sounds of writing grow bolder, steadier. Beneath it all, something else hums, like a current running through the floor, coiled and electric.

They've been starved of the truth.

The Order's news scrolls say the front is stable, that peace is near, but the student letters passed between hands say otherwise: wounded cousins, entire towns vanished, soldiers rotated back with vacant eyes and mouths sewn shut by fear. These children know how to read between the lines, and more importantly, they know how to write in the space between them.

I pause near the window. Outside, the rain smears the sky in grey streaks, the towers of the academy loom like watchmen, like prison walls.

The classroom used to feel like a sanctuary, now it feels like a pressure point, tight with tension, one wrong word away from collapse.

But this? These letters? This is more than a lesson.

It's a message, a flare in the dark.

And I know, as they write, every word cloaked in metaphor, in myth, in carefully constructed fictions meant to pass unnoticed, that this is how it begins.

This is how truth finds its way past the walls, this is how they learn to speak, and maybe, one day, to fight.

I give myself a code name, too: Noctis.

It's not random. Noctis was the boy from *The Star Thief*, etched into my memory like the ghost of a flame only we ever saw. The boy who stole sky-fire from the gods and danced barefoot across battlefields, laughing as the world burned behind him. The first book Lysander and I ever truly shared, a battered cover passed between us in the quiet of forgotten corridors, dog-eared pages laced with the scent of dust and ink. A story, yes, but also a cipher, a tether, a secret.

The classroom is wrapped in brittle silence, I hear the faint scrape of quills like the tapping of moth wings. As I lower myself into my chair, my mind drifts.

Back to the boy I used to know, and the way he would read aloud softly when he thought I was asleep. Back to the books that carried more than stories: whispered promises, stolen hours, memories folded like pressed flowers between their pages.

Around me, my students continue to write, some cautiously, others with bold, angry strokes. The air in the room is thick with tension, electric, reverent, like standing beneath a sky before a lightning strike.

Anticipation, a sense that this, somehow, matters.

At the close of class, I gather their letters with slow, careful hands. Each folded sheet feels like a heartbeat, delicate and defiant. I promise to seal them, to send them by the village's goat post, the only system left that isn't fully watched. I don't tell them I'll read them first, they already know, and they trust I won't change a word.

I read not to censor, but to listen. I read to know them, to hear the truths they are too afraid to speak aloud; that is all I've ever wanted.

When the classroom empties and the door clicks shut, I sit alone, the stack of letters before me like a small bonfire waiting to be lit. Their weight presses down, not heavy in mass, but in meaning: my hands tremble, my pulse thrums high in my throat.

What have I done?

What if Lucien finds out?

The letters form a strange, silent chorus: one signs as Belladonna, another as Sunfall, one is a poem composed entirely of questions, another contains just a single, aching line:

"Do you dream of silence?"

That night, long after the halls fall quiet and the last lamp in the tower extinguishes, I sit at my desk, the candle guttering low. Wax spills into a tarnished dish like the slow drip of time. I unfold a piece of parchment, my fingers shake only slightly as I begin to write: not as Sylvaine, not as an Educator, but as Noctis.

Dear Soldier,
I wonder if you remember the silence before the storm, the stillness of a forest breathing beneath an endless sky.
Do you find moments like that on the front, or has the war swallowed even the quiet?
I don't write to offer comfort.
I write to ask... What keeps you moving forward when the world burns? Is it hope? Duty? Or something darker, something harder to name?
I have spent my life in books and shadowed libraries, trying to understand a

war I've never seen.

They tell us who is right and who must be cast into the dark.

But I wonder... are those lines real? Or are they drawn in ash, shaped by the ones who survive?

If you can hear me, through ink and distance, tell me:

What do you see when the sun falls?

– Noctis

No one sees the letters I slide into the post box at the day's end, each sealed in wax the color of blood.

The goat post is a closed-loop system, ancient carts pulled by aging, irritable goats, meant for student parcels and approved messages. No one is supposed to read them, it's guaranteed, but the goats have a reputation. They're mostly reliable, but like most things, they have opinions of their own.

The weight of those sealed letters presses against me, a silent threat, sharp as teeth beneath my ribs.

What if someone at the academy is reading them?

What if someone at the academy already knows?

The questions coil in my skull, tighter and tighter, until even silence feels loud.

I try to study, to lose myself in lesson plans and pages, but the words blur. My hand shakes. I realize I've been clutching the same quill for over half an hour without writing a single line.

Eventually, I stop pretending.

I need answers, or at the very least, I need a way to breathe again.

A DANGEROUS GAME

THE NEXT EVENING, RESTLESS and unsettled, I find myself drawn once more into the lower levels of the Umbraxis library; past the glowing lanterns that float like fireflies above orderly shelves, casting halos over polished marble and pristine rows of sanctioned knowledge. I slip downward, into the darkened veins of the library the administration prefers forgotten. Here, the lamps dim, the silence deepens, and the scent of paper gives way to something older, ancient, buried.

Dust hangs thick in the air, laced with the sharp bite of iron ink and something more elusive, memory, perhaps, or warning.

Every step into this unlit realm feels like crossing a threshold not just of knowledge, but of fate.

I move through the tight aisles, where the walls seem to breathe closer with every passing second. Shadows stretch and shiver in my peripheral vision. They don't recede, they watch.

My fingers trace the spines of long-ignored tomes, cracked leather and faded titles whispering of truths rewritten or erased. One calls to me, a heavy, dark-bound volume, brittle beneath my touch.

Chronicles of The Shattering;
The Shadow War.

The pages sigh open like dry leaves caught in a dying wind.

The opening is what I expect: dry, official, sterilized by the Light. It's an unyielding narrative of triumph over chaos, of the Light's supposed mercy, painted in blinding strokes of gold, but deeper within, something shifts.

Scrawled in the margins, as though written in haste and anger, are words not meant for public eyes.

The true spark was not on the battlefield but in the council chambers.
Peace demanded silence, not justice.
The Light doesn't save — it smothers what it cannot control.

I stare, transfixed, my pulse stutters.

These words burn, not with fire, but with forbidden clarity.

My hand trembles slightly as I tuck the book into my satchel. It settles against my side with a soft thump, but the weight is immense. I don't pause, I can't. I keep moving, deeper still.

Another spine catches my attention: thin, delicate, nearly dust. I cradle it with care, the paper threatening to disintegrate at the edges.

Of Light, Shadow, and Kings: The
Rule of Twin Flame.
It is said that long ago, the gods took
from themselves a drop of Light and
a drop of Shadow, and from these two
essences, the first king of Vaeloria was
born. Divine blood ran in his veins, not
of one god, but of both. A mortal child
with the strength of balance, and the

power to rival even the heavens.
But the gods feared what they had
made. One soul, touched by both Light
and Shadow, proved too great a force
for one body alone. So the line of kings
was split — each ruler henceforth born
as twins: one of Light, one of Shadow.
From that day forward, this was the
law of Vaeloria: every king would rise
with his twin beside him. The one chosen
to rule would carry the essence of either
Light or Shadow. The other, his brother,
would serve as the Hand of the King,
never to rule, but never far from pow-
er. Two halves of the same soul, forever
bound. One to reign. One to guide.
This is the way. This is balance.

I read, each word anchors something in me I hadn't known was adrift.

Twins, one Light, one Shadow. A divided soul made to govern in balance, one to reign, one to guide. A truth hidden in plain sight, now fading before the world could remember.

I press my palm flat against the brittle page and recognition pulses beneath my skin.

A faint noise breaks the silence, a soft echo of footsteps. My spine goes rigid and my heart gallops behind my ribs. I know that rhythm, that stride.

Lucien.

He steps into the end of the aisle, framed by the wavering lantern light like a painting come to life, a sentinel of marble and menace. His eyes lock with mine. I expect fire or frost, what I get is worse, softness; a terrible softness that twists the breath from my lungs.

"What are you doing down here?" he asks, his voice low and calm, velvet over stone.

I draw in a breath steadying the quake inside me. "I... lost track of time. I was searching for supplemental material. I must have wandered too deep."

His gaze sharpens like a knife turned slightly in hand.

"These sections are sealed for a reason, Sylvaine. You shouldn't be here."

"I know," I whisper. "But... I was curious."

A flicker passes over his face.

His steps bring him closer, soundless but deliberate. The shadows seem to follow him, bending toward his form. He stops just before me, his breath brushing my skin.

"Curiosity," he murmurs, voice almost gentle, "is dangerous when it leads people into places they're not meant to return from."

His hand lifts, slowly, deliberately. His fingers slide a stray strand of hair behind my ear and his knuckles graze my cheek. I don't flinch, I can't. His touch is warm, but there's something claiming in the gesture, something unmistakably his.

"You especially," he adds, thumb brushing the hollow of my throat. "You don't realize how much they watch you."

"Do you watch me?" I ask before I can stop myself. The words slip out raw, naked.

His gaze drops to my lips, then back to my eyes.

"More than I should," he says.

Then suddenly, he's closer. One hand is at my waist, the other against my back. I feel the heat of his palm through the thin fabric of my blouse, spreading like fire along my spine.

My body betrays me, I sway into him; not in surrender, but in confusion, drawn to something I can't name. My pulse flutters like wings beneath my skin.

His hand presses more firmly, fingers splaying across my hip, his grip both possessive and oddly gentle. I feel the strength beneath the surface, restrained only by sheer will. His lips brush the top of my head, not a kiss of comfort, a mark.

"You're valuable, Sylvaine," he says, voice a silken threat. "Don't make me choose between you and the order I serve."

"I never asked you to choose," I whisper, but the words feel hollow, foolish.

His hand slides higher along my ribs, lingering for a second too long, long enough to send heat coiling low in my belly. I don't understand this moment. I don't know if it's a warning or a tether. But gods help me, I lean into it.

Without another word, he steps back and cold floods in where his warmth once was.

He gestures, and I follow like a moth still dazed by the flame. He says nothing as we ascend, but his presence presses on me with every step, a shadow wrapped in longing and power.

Outside, the world feels sharp again, too real. The night air bites against my skin, cool and damp, as if trying to pull me out of the fever dream of the library's shadows. Each step toward my door feels stolen, weighted with the secrets I carry slung over my shoulder.

Lucien walks beside me in silence, his pace precise, every movement economical, controlled. I can feel the heat still radiating from him in waves, a furnace beneath iron. He doesn't look at me, but I sense the focus in him hasn't broken, not entirely.

We reach my door.

I fumble with the key, fingers clumsy, too aware of him standing so close. Then I feel his hand on my wrist, the grip firm, halting. It's not enough to hurt, just enough to take control.

Slowly, deliberately, his fingers glide up my arm, skimming my sleeve, tracing the inner line of my elbow before curving along my shoulder.

My breath catches as his knuckles brush the edge of my collarbone, then rise higher, along the side of my neck, to my jaw. His thumb presses lightly just beneath my chin, tilting my face up to meet his gaze.

Those eyes, dark and unreadable, search mine... not for answers, but for weakness, or maybe permission.

But he doesn't ask.

His mouth finds mine without warning, the kiss is hard, insistent, possessive. It claims, not in gentleness, but in certainty.

His hand slides into my hair, fisting just enough to tip my head back, deepening the kiss. His body crowds mine, pressing me back against the door. I feel the weight of him, all restrained strength and intention, and something deep inside me flares, both confused and hot.

I gasp softly against his lips, but he doesn't relent. If anything, he leans in further, his other hand braced against the door beside my head: caging me, surrounding me.

For a moment, I don't think. I just feel.

The warmth of him seeps into my bones, burns through the chill. My heart hammers, caught in that same rhythm it knew in the stacks. A rhythm born of danger, desire, and a growing, terrifying awareness that I may not be able to separate the two anymore.

Just as suddenly as it started, he breaks away.

His forehead rests against mine for a beat. His breath is shallow, ragged, like he's fighting something unseen.

"You play a dangerous game, Sylvaine," he whispers, voice hoarse at the edges. "And you don't even know the rules."

I want to speak, to say something clever, or safe, or defiant, but nothing comes. There is just the thunder of my heartbeat and the weight of his hand still wrapped around my wrist.

Instead, I nod once. The movement is small, controlled, like him.

If this moment and this kiss keeps his eyes off the secrets in my bag, if it keeps the door from slamming shut forever on the knowledge I've stolen, then yes... It's a game I'm willing to play, rules be damned.

Even if part of me, treacherous and trembling, wants him to kiss me again, even if part of me already wishes he hadn't stopped.

Two nights later, I return to the restricted stacks. My heart is a stone in my chest, every footstep echoes too loud in the hollow quiet.

When I reach the stairwell, I stop short.

The iron gate has been replaced; reinforced, heavy, rune-carved, and sealed with authority not even I can name.

My fingers press against the cold metal, helpless.

Behind it, the secrets still wait, but they wait in silence now.

I am alone.

THE LORE KEEPER

My STUDY SESSIONS HAVE become something I look forward to most, and tonight is no exception. Though tonight, we are not in an office and we most likely won't end up studying.

We are calling it a tea party, but really, it's a rebellion in miniature... a soft one, cloaked in warmth and laughter. The kind of defiance that comes with curling your feet under you and letting the world slip away for a while.

The idea, naturally, had been Aric's.

"We need a night off," he declared dramatically that morning, tossing a dog-eared copy of *Contested Cosmologies* onto my desk like it had personally betrayed him. "If I read one more paragraph about the ethics of divine embodiment, I'm going to throw myself into the river."

"You'd just float," Mira had muttered without even looking up. "You're too stubborn to sink."

He shot her a grin. "And too charming to drown."

"Debatable," she had said, though her smirk had given her away.

That evening, instead of being crammed into my tiny office like scholarly sardines, we ventured into the forgotten guts of the north wing, an area few even acknowledged, let alone visited. A broken archive blocked the hallway like a collapsed lung, and the only way through the door beyond was to lean into it like you were asking for its permission. The students had found the room, I didn't ask how. I'd learned long ago that mystery clung to them like a second skin.

The space itself felt like it had once meant something, but now it wears a thin veil of abandonment. Halos of dusk slant in the light. Shelves lean like tired old men, some still cradling curled scrolls or faded ledgers. A stone hearth yawns in the wall, dry but whole. The window has no glass, only a wooden lattice we've covered with scarves and old tapestries to soften the edges of the world.

Rellington is the first to sprawl across the floor; a thick tome perched on his stomach like a lazy cat. He keeps flicking it open and closed without reading a word.

Mira floats through the space, lighting lanterns low and carefully placing pots of honeyed tea beside mismatched mugs.

Aric uncorks a flask with exaggerated secrecy and pours a little into everything. Who am I to stop him?

Tomas, still moving like he fears breaking something, hovers near the edge of the circle until Aric tosses him a mug with the kind of aimless grace only he can manage.

"Sit down," Mira says, patting the cushion beside her. "You hover like guilt."

He sits instantly.

Even Lina made it. She has tucked herself into the hearth's corner, legs folded, arms wrapped around her knees, but her silence tonight isn't sharp or heavy. It feels... curious, resting.

I watch them all as the room settles, the flickering light reflects in their eyes like secrets just beneath the surface. These students, no, these companions, have seen too much to still be called young, yet there is youth in this, in the way they allow themselves softness.

The low crackle of magic hums softly beneath the conversation. Calyra, who had been quietly observing, suddenly flicks her fingers and sends a tiny bolt of lightning arcing across the circle, harmless, but enough to make Tomas yelp and jump.

"Hey! I swear I almost spilled my tea!" Tomas protests, laughing nervously.

"Careful, or I'll turn this whole room into a lightning storm," Calyra teases, her eyes sparkling.

I raise my eyebrows. "If that happens, I'm charging for the show."

Aric leans forward, journal open. "Speaking of sparks, does anyone have a handle on the new homework? That section on the mechanics of ethereal manipulation might as well be written in a dead language."

Mira nods. "Yeah, I keep mixing up the runes; my fire attempts ended up as a smoky mess."

"Here," I say, sliding over a sheet I'd prepared. "Try focusing your intent on the rune's core meaning. Let the energy flow around your will, not against it."

They lean in, murmuring questions. I guide their hands through simple incantations, watching as their magic flickers to life, a soft glow, a brief flash, a warming pulse.

The night stretches onward, punctuated by laughter, playful shocks, and quiet moments of shared discovery. Outside, the world may be heavy and uncertain, but here, in this hidden room with these bright sparks of rebellion, time feels like it bends just enough to hold hope.

I pour more tea with a mock-serious flourish. "So," I ask, "now that the assignments are out of the way, what shall we discuss tonight?"

"Dreams," says Mira without hesitation.

"Philosophy," Tomas offers, trying to sound casual and failing adorably.

"Whether gods bleed," mutters Rellington from the floor.

Aric raises his cup, eyes half-lidded. "To all of it."

We talk, we drift, time blurs at the edges.

Rellington recounts a dream in which the moon peeled open like a fruit and whispered secrets in a voice made of bird bones.

Mira offers a theory that gods are not entities but outcomes, unintended consequences of collective yearning.

Tomas shyly confesses he'd once believed the stars were tiny windows punched through the sky by long-dead kings trying to see home.

"You sound like my Pa," I murmur before I can stop myself; the words land like a pebble dropped into still water.

Everyone looks at me.

I swallow. "He used to tell me stories. Before the war. I... don't remember many. Only pieces, a garden, a song, a name I've forgotten but still dream of."

Lina's voice is barely a breath. "Is that why you came back to teach? To remember?"

"Maybe," I say. "Maybe that's why any of us are here."

A gust of wind moans against the scarf-covered window, almost downing out the sound of three knocks: soft, measured, intentional.

The air stills and we all freeze.

I rise. My breath feels heavy with dread, but when I open the door, Thaleia stands on the other side .

She looks like a memory wrapped in starlight: her silver hair is wild, bound in braids threaded with slivers of black thread like ink running through frost, her robes shimmer with constellations, literal constellations, glowing faintly as she moves, as if the fabric remembers the night sky better than the heavens themselves.

"May I join you?" she asks, like this is all perfectly normal.

No one moves, they look to me... am I their leader?

I only know they trust me.

I step aside.

She glides in, not walks, glides, like her feet were a suggestion the stone politely entertained. She sits beside the hearth, folding her limbs with a grace that makes time feel irrelevant.

"I was summoned," she says, smiling just enough to unnerve. "You spoke of memory, of kings and gods. That is my language."

Tomas, to his credit, only waits two seconds before blurting, "What are you?"

Her eyes gleam, deep and silver. "A witness," she says. "And a keeper of what should not be forgotten."

She places her palm against the hearthstone.

"You spoke of dreams," she says. "Let me give you one."

Her voice flows like smoke curling into silence.

"There were once two brothers," she begins, "born from Earth's first sigh."

"One was made of reaching, of radiance and impulse and need. He called himself Light. The other was made of waiting, of silence and rhythm and depth. He became Shadow.

They were not enemies. Not at first. They danced in tandem, spun the seasons between their fingers.

Light wove joy; Shadow, rest. Light made fire; Shadow, sleep. The world turned beneath their balance. But harmony is a delicate thing. And brothers are not immune to pride.

Over time, Light grew resentful of Shadow's quiet power. Why should stillness be praised? Why should people seek silence when he offered warmth and glory?

Shadow, for his part, pitied his brother's hunger, that endless need to be seen. He began to withdraw.

Earth, seeing her son's splinter, acted. She did not speak. She unmade. For a moment, just one eternal moment, she stripped the world of both Light and Shadow. No sun. No stars. Not even darkness. Just nothing. The absence. Time stopped counting. Days folded in on themselves like spoiled fruit. Without rhythm, crops failed. Animals wept or tore each other apart. Fire refused to catch. Children forgot their names. Madness bloomed. And then, when desperation had hollowed every corner, the brothers made peace. A brittle, blood-slick thing.

Earth allowed them to return. But not unchanged. Light came back dimmer. Shadow, deeper. And something had entered the world with the absence, something old, something true. A memory older than either brother.

Light began to whisper. That it had been Shadow's doing. That only Light had saved them. At first, it was only words. But words become laws and laws become kingdoms. Light crowned himself the savior and built Aureverra: all gleaming towers and blinding sermons. Where to question was to fall. Where clarity burned away doubt and souls.

Shadow retreated and built Velmourn in the hollows, where memory survived in whispers. There, truth did not arrive as dogma, but in dreams. Dangerous dreams. Wild ones. They called it the Shattering. Earth has never fully healed, and neither have they."

Her hand slips from the stone, the fire dims, her voice fades.

No one speaks.

Rellington stares at his hands. Aric looks like he's forgotten how to blink. Mira is still, eyes glassy. Tomas has gone pale, he isn't crying, but he looks close.

But Lina... Lina is crying; silent tears down still cheeks. She isn't looking at Thaleia, she isn't looking at anyone. Her eyes are fixed somewhere behind the moment, somewhere far.

I stand, alarm prickling behind my ribs. "Lina?"

She flinches, shakes her head. "I'm fine."

She isn't, because I know the story. Not all of it, but the bones of it, the rhythm. It parallels what she had told me once, in the garden, before she vanished and returned with scars shaped like runes and memories she refused to name.

Thaleia looks at her, just briefly: not with surprise but with recognition, with approval, like she had been waiting for Lina to remember.

The fire flickers, draws inward.

"Was it real?" Tomas whispers.

Thaleia tilts her head, touching the floor. "Is this?"

She stands, slowly, like drawing herself out of deep water.

"There are truths buried beneath this place," she says. "Some of you have already begun to remember. But remember this: truth is never safe, only necessary."

With that, she steps past the threshold. The door closes on its own, the fire sputters, the tea has gone cold.

Lina's shoulders shake, silent.

Aric finally speaks. "Well," he says, voice raw. "Shit."

No one laughs.

THE ONLY RESPONSE

THREE DAYS LATER, I find myself standing before the small, unremarkable mailbox assigned to me. It is tucked away in a quiet corner of the hallway, half-hidden behind a potted plant someone must have placed there to soften the space. It's my first real mailbox since I never had one in the forest I grew up in.

The academy rarely sends personal messages, and the letters I do receive are usually routine. Today, there's a subtle weight in the atmosphere, a tension that makes the simple act of checking the mail feel strangely significant.

I lift the metal flap, and my breath hitches. There's only one letter and it's not from the academy.

The envelope is thick, unusually so. The paper beneath my fingers is rough, textured, like it's been made by hand with care, not the kind of paper that you find in any typical mailroom. It feels significant somehow, like a thing that holds weight, almost like it has a history.

It is sealed in black wax, unmarked. There is no name, no insignia, no return address, only that rich, smooth black seal.

My heart beats a little faster.

I hesitate, my fingers tremble at the edges of the paper. Something about it feels alive, like it's waiting for me, anticipating my touch. It feels as if the letter itself is aware of me, aware of this moment. For a long while, I simply stare at it, feeling the pull between the words I haven't read yet and the knowledge that something about this envelope is beyond ordinary. A force I can't name presses against my chest, urging me forward, but also warning me.

I'm not sure what finally compels me, but I break the seal. The wax snaps away easily, as if it was meant to be done, not fought against, and I unfold the letter.

The handwriting inside is elegant, curved, flowing, with a flourish at the end of each letter that almost seems to dance across the page.

The pages are foreign, not like anything I've seen before; no ink, no script from the academy's archives or the old texts I'm familiar with. It feels like something far older, but the writing is familiar, poetic, as if the words themselves were meant to be spoken aloud, rather than just read silently.

The letter is short, but the words feel heavy, like they're carrying more than just their meaning. As I read, a sense of unease settles deep in my chest, but beneath that, a stirring of something else: curiosity, anticipation, fear. It's as if the letter itself is reaching out to me, beckoning me into something I wasn't prepared for.

I swallow, and my eyes return to the paper, feeling a strange mix of dread and fascination as I read.

To the one who calls herself Noctis,
Your words reached further than you meant them to. I am not the one you intended to write. I am the one you were told to fear.
But alas, your letter arrived like a breath caught beneath water, unexpected and unsettling.

The words drip with a certain eerie familiarity; as if they understand me, understand the silence that has followed me for so long, the very silence I try to push against. The writer continues, speaking of silence, but not in the way I know it. To them, silence is something altogether different.

The silence you speak of is a memory, a ghost.
Out here, the noise is unending: blasts, orders, the cries of the lost. The front is not a place for quiet reflection, but a forge that burns away innocence.
What keeps me going?
Fear, perhaps. Fear of forgetting who I was, or losing what remains of my soul.
Hope? Yes, Hope that this war will end, though the gods seem deaf to such prayers.
They call us Shadows, enemies of the Light.

My breath hitches. Shadow soldiers. The words hang in the air, heavier now, like the letter itself is weightier than just ink and paper.

We hold the shape of things that Light cannot reach: memory, pain, freedom.
Maybe that is why they fear us.
You ask what I see when the sun falls. I see the faces of those who have vanished into the Light, and I wonder if the Light ever truly saw them at all.
Keep writing, Noctis, if you can.
Your words are a rare flame.
Tell me...
What do you believe in, when the Light goes out?

I sit there, staring at the letter, as the weight of it sinks into me. The room feels too small, the silence too loud. The words seem to echo in my chest, pulling at something deep inside.

I had written a letter in passing, a quiet message to the void. Yet, this response, this invitation, feels like it's reached through the very fabric of my life and pulled me into something I wasn't prepared for.

What do I believe in when the Light goes out?

I don't know yet, but I can feel it now, deep within me just waiting to be discovered.

I fold the letter carefully, pressing the black wax seal against my palm as if it might help me hold myself together. My mind races, each thought spiraling like a whirlwind, and yet, beneath the chaos, a singular truth forms:

This is only the beginning.

The page in my hands carries a faint scent: ash, ink, and something distinct. It reminds me of moss, damp and green, the kind of smell that clings to the corners of a forgotten forest or the underside of ancient stones. It settles in the back of my throat, making the air feel heavier as I stare at the letter, unable to tear my eyes away.

I can feel my own shadow beneath me, stretching long across the floor, curling like it's alive, reacting to the words I've just read. It twitches, a sharp, sudden recoil, like a string plucked too hard.

Recognition.

The thought shudders through me, clear and visceral, like a jolt of cold water in the face.

I freeze, the letter still clutched before my chest, my heartbeat thundering in my ears.

I read it again, then again. Four times.

I force my eyes over the words, willing them to change, to become something else, something harmless. They don't.

Each reread only sharpens the unease coiling tighter inside me.

This could be a trap, I think? A test of loyalty, a trick planted in the dark to see who will flinch, who will fall.

I close my eyes, the darkness behind my eyelids offering no reprieve. I try to still the thudding of my heart, but it's no use. The letter feels heavier now, pressing down on me, smothering the air from my lungs. I shouldn't respond, I shouldn't even be reading this. I know that.

But something in the ink, in the shape of the words, calls to me in a way I can't ignore.

The shadow at my feet shifts again. It's subtle, barely a movement, just the briefest flicker, but it's there: quiet, attentive, watching, waiting.

I shiver, and it's not from the cold.

Against every instinct that screams at me to stop, to destroy the letter before it entangles me in whatever this is, I slip it into my coat pocket and move swiftly from the mailroom. My footsteps are soft against the cold stone floor, the sound swallowed by the shadows that seem to stretch and grow with each step I take. I don't look back.

In my office, panic tightens its grip around my chest, squeezing until I can barely breathe.

Where can I hide this?

My gaze darts around the room, scanning for any place safe enough to conceal the letter.

The desk drawers? They're too shallow.

Beneath the stack of unused parchment? Too obvious.

Inside the hollowed-out volume on obscure treaties? Too easy for someone to find.

Nothing feels secure.

I think of the letter, its presence in my pocket like a weight that drags me down. In a moment of desperation, I slide it under a book on my desk, pressing it flat just as my office door creaks open.

The sound sends a spike of adrenaline through my veins.

Lucien enters, as polished and composed as ever, his presence filling the room with that aura of controlled charm, the kind that always feels like a mask carefully put on for a performance. But today, there's something in the curve of his smile that doesn't quite reach his eyes; it's there, just beneath the surface, a flicker of something sharper, something dangerous.

"I hear your students wrote more letters," he says softly, his tone a blend of amusement and warning. His fingers trail across the surface of my desk, brushing lightly over papers, as if he's looking for something, anything, that might betray me. I watch his fingers, too aware of how they linger just a fraction too long on the edges of my things.

"They did," I answer, my voice steady, even though the muscles in my shoulders are taut, like a bowstring pulled too tight. "They've taken to using codenames."

Lucien raises a brow, his eyes gleaming with that typical, unreadable curiosity. "How inventive."

"It helps them process things," I reply, hoping my tone stays neutral. "The war and the weight of it."

His gaze lingers on me, too long, too searching. I feel the weight of his eyes like a pinprick on my skin, like he's trying to see right through me. I hold his stare, determined not to show anything.

"Inspiration is a beautiful thing," he murmurs, voice smooth like honey, but I catch the cold edge beneath the sweetness, the calculation that lies beneath every word. "But it is dangerous, in excess. Let's not confuse rebellion with therapy."

His fingers flick over the papers, restlessly straightening a stack of essays that didn't need straightening. He brushes against the edge of the book on my desk.

The book. The one where the letter is hidden.

I stop breathing, my pulse surges in my throat, and for a moment it feels as though the world has slowed to a crawl. He lifts the book just enough to glimpse beneath it and I freeze, but with a casual motion, he lets it fall back into place. The moment lingers in the air, stretching longer than it should.

With a soft exhale, Lucien straightens, his posture shifting from subtle predation to a kind of casual concern. He steps closer, his presence wrapping around me like silk: smooth, dangerous, too close.

"You're overextending yourself," he says, the words quiet, almost gentler than I expect. "I worry, you know. Not everyone at the academy understands your... passion for nuance."

"I can handle it," I say, keeping my voice firm, even as my heart begins to race again.

Lucien's smile softens just a touch, the edge of warmth creeping into his expression. It's almost tender, and I know it's deliberate, too deliberate.

"I know you believe that." His gaze sharpens though there is a flicker of something darker beneath the surface. "But belief isn't always enough, sweet Sylvie."

The way he says my name, the familiarity of the nickname, *the intimacy of it*, sends a shiver down my spine. It's not the first time he's used it like that, but today it feels different: a claim, a mark.

With a final, calculated smile, he turns and leaves, his footsteps soft against the stone. The door closes behind him with a soft click, but his presence remains: like perfume lingering in the air, like a warning, like silk wrapped around a knife.

I don't move, I sit there rooted to the spot, my eyes tracing the empty space where Lucien stood just moments before. The silence presses in on me, thick and oppressive, but I do not break it. I let the weight of his words linger, the coolness of his smile. I let the scent of him, the silk and the danger, hang in the air.

Time drips away, slow and deliberate.

Finally, I sit and the chair creaks beneath me. I pull out a blank sheet of parchment, the surface stark and white, a canvas that feels impossibly vast: it's too clean, too empty. For a moment, I just stare at it, the blankness mocking me, daring me to fill it with something.

My fingers twitch, but it's not fear that makes them tremble. No, it's defiance; something raw, something untamed that courses through my veins like wildfire. I don't want to move, I don't want to do this, but I will.

With a steadying breath, I place the quill to the page. The ink flows out in slow, deliberate strokes, tracing the words that have been circling my mind, waiting for a moment to break free. This is an act of reclamation, a return to something I had lost, or maybe something I never had but always knew was mine.

I feel the pulse of it, that sharp, unyielding energy that cuts through the fog Lucien left behind. Every word, every letter, is a choice; a choice to not let fear dictate my next move, a choice to not be controlled, not to bend under the weight of expectations or the smooth poison of threats veiled as concern.

The quill moves faster now, more sure of itself, as if the ink knows the truth I'm trying to claim. The words spill out of me: unfiltered, unrestrained, a silent roar against the walls that have always boxed me in. The letter, no, *the message*, is a thread, weaving its way through the darkness that Lucien's presence has left behind.

I will not be silenced. I will not be manipulated.

As I write, I can almost hear the echo of my own voice in my head, the defiance crystallizing in my mind:

I am not afraid of you.

I know there is no going back; what I write now will change everything.

With each word, the silence in the room grows thicker, more intense, until it's almost suffocating, but I breathe through it.

The letter is already in my hands, my voice already on the page, and when I lift the quill one final time, the words are clear. There is no fear, no hesitation. Only the truth, only the fire that has finally been lit in me, burning brightly, demanding to be seen.

I am done waiting.

Dear Stranger,

Perhaps it was fate, or the will of a stubborn goat, but you read something not meant for you, and yet, you responded. I find myself wondering why.

Your words haunt me. Not in the way most things do, but like a truth, uncomfortable and necessary.

They echo like the shadows of my childhood, when darkness felt like a friend, not a threat.

The world was wonder then. Now, stories are weapons, honed by fear and command.

You speak of fear.

I know it well. I live in it. But there is something else, too.

Not hope, perhaps, but the refusal to be consumed by what we've lost. The memory of something unbroken. Something worth holding onto.

I want to believe that freedom is more than just a word whispered in the dark, that it can be a light itself. Rebellion doesn't always shout; it waits, in the shadows, growing.

Write back, please.
— *Noctis*

⭐⭐⭐

It's been a fortnight since the students wrote their first letters to the soldiers, and the air in the classroom has shifted. Their restlessness is palpable; footsteps tapping, whispered conversations across rows, eyes drifting toward the windows only to snap back to me, silently asking questions they can't quite form.

Maybe it was a fumble on my part, or perhaps the blame lies solely with the goats. I'm not entirely sure what happened to all of the letters meant for the soldiers, but the delay is becoming hard to ignore. I've been dragging my feet, avoiding the conversation, pretending to sort through papers on my desk, letting the silence stretch long enough to become uncomfortable. Eventually, the silence breaks.

"They haven't written back, have they?" Elswyn asks.

I can hear the tentative hope in their voice, trying not to sound too hurt. They glance toward the others, and I see that same quiet ache mirrored in their eyes. Hope still lives there, stubborn and young, and it makes my chest tighten.

"No," I admit, my voice softer than I intend. "No replies yet."

The room grows quiet. Faces fall, lips press together, eyes turn inward. One student shifts uncomfortably in their seat, as though the weight of the silence is too much to bear.

"There's a strong chance they never received them," I add quickly, trying to repair the fragile thread I've just cut. "Goats wandering through a war zone aren't exactly the most reliable mail carriers, are they?"

A few students chuckle, half-hearted but thankful for the distraction. The tension in the room loosens by a thread.

Rellington leans back in his chair, hands behind his head. "Maybe the goats have finally had enough. Joined the rebels, found a cause."

"There's a coup in the pasture," someone murmurs. "Hooves and horns and righteous fury."

"They've been radicalized," Mira adds dryly. "All those late nights, chewing manifestos under the moon."

That earns a few more genuine laughs, soft but short-lived, like birds startled into flight.

Aric smirks. "Honestly, I'd trust a goat over half the Order right now."

Even Tomas, hunched over his notes with his usual tight grip on everything, manages a weak smile. "Don't give them ideas. If we start assigning familiars political leanings, I'm going to have to rethink mine."

I smile with them, letting the moment bloom, just briefly. The warmth doesn't reach my heart; it flutters at the edges and fades just before it can settle. Beneath the laughter, there's something brittle, not quite broken, but close. We're all pretending; pretending everything is normal, that the news isn't scarce, that our friends beyond the wards are fine, that the war is distant and theoretical, and not creeping closer every day.

Maybe we'll keep pretending for a little longer.

"I want you to keep writing," I say, my voice steady, even though my insides twist. "Use your codenames. Ask the hard questions. The ones you think no one wants to answer. We'll exchange letters in class, respond to each other, extend the ideas. Shape them into something bigger."

I hesitate before finishing softly, "I just... want to give you a space where your thoughts can breathe."

Some of them nod, a few look down at their desks, lost in thought. One or two already reach for their notebooks.

It eases my guilt, just a little, because I'm lying.

The truth is, I don't know if any of the soldiers ever received their letters, I don't know if they'll ever get a reply, and worse, I don't know if I even want them to.

Because, secretly, I've been getting letters. Not from the soldiers, but from him, the Shadow.

His letters come almost every night now, slipping through the cracks of stone, curling around my windowsill like shadows come to life.

I tell myself it's for the intellectual exchange, for the sake of the students' learning, for widening the scope of their world, and that's true, partly, but it's not the whole truth.

The whole truth is that his letters feel like breath after too long under-water. They're the only thing I look forward to anymore, especially with Lucien breathing down my neck: vague enough to haunt, firm enough to warn.

His words are raw, unfiltered, uncensored. They make me feel seen, and something about them feels so familiar, though not in the stories he shares. It's in the way he writes, in the rhythm of his thoughts, the careful pause between each word.

It reminds me almost of Lysander.

The boy who brought me worn paperbacks and stolen jam jars filled with summer pears. The one who whispered tragedies by candlelight, telling me we were too clever to stay silent forever. The one who made the world feel worth saving. The boy who vanished the day the war began, leaving me behind after promising me he'd return.

I braved the village to find him years later, asking everyone I could. They told me he enlisted, said it plainly, like it was something noble. I searched station after station, through enlistment logs, academy rosters. Nothing, no records, no postings, it was as if he had evaporated into smoke.

But now, a part of me wonders...

What if he didn't vanish?

What if he stepped into the shadows, became the Shadows?

Is he still watching, still whispering stories from the dark?

His recent letter ended with a single line. Just one sentence, but it cut through me like a blade turned inward:

Do you believe the Light has ever truly seen you, Noctis?

I didn't answer.

Back in my cabin, I take out his letters and read them, savoring his words. They feel heavy in my hands, the words lingering long after I've finished them. They settle in my chest, pressing against something I thought was already lost.

Once I feel as if the words themselves are burned into my soul, I fold them slowly, reverently, and slide the bundle beneath the ash bucket near my hearth, under a loose floorboard, like a secret I don't want to let go of. In this war-torn world, some things, some truths, are too dangerous to speak out loud.

Outside, shadows stir again, not to frighten, but to listen.

Dear Shadow,
The world beyond my window feels fractured, like a cracked mirror reflecting a sky I can no longer recognize.
Do the trees bleed when the earth is torn apart?
Do they remember the songs of Light and Shadow that once danced beneath their branches?
I cling to memories of silence and the quiet before the storm, before magic and fire reshaped everything.
It feels like holding onto smoke, something intangible, slipping away.
I want to believe in something beyond this destruction. Something that will

outlast the war and the ashes.

When the night is deep and still, do you hear the forest mourning too?

Does it remember those who stood and fought beneath its leaves?

Or will we all fade, ghosts swallowed by the ash?

I find myself longing for a sign that this world will be whole again.

If you can hear me, tell me what you see beyond the smoke?

— Noctis

Noctis,

I hear your words like wind through the branches; soft, aching, and too familiar.

The trees do bleed. Not red, but in the way they drop their leaves too early, or lean toward the ground as if burdened by what they've witnessed.

Some still sing, but the songs are different now, hoarse with ash and silence. Yet beneath it all, there is a pulse, faint and steady, like memory buried in root and stone.

Yes, the forest mourns. In the stillness between spells and sirens, I hear it. A low hum of grief that wraps around the bones of the world.

It remembers more than we do. The names. The Shadows. The Light. All of it.

Will it remember us? I don't know.

But I think the earth keeps record in its own way, not in stories or statues, but in scars and seedlings. Maybe that's enough.

And beyond the smoke? Some days, nothing. Just ruin.

Other days, I catch glimpses of green breaking through cracked stone, of a bird returning to a broken branch. Small things. But real.

Hold onto that. Hold onto anything that breathes, even if it trembles.

Eerily Calm Propaganda

Morning Dispatch From the Office of Enlightened
Affairs: To All Faculty and Students of Umbraxis
Academy

"Where Light dwells, peace follows. Where peace
dwells, all thrives."

Regional Stabilization Progressing Smoothly:
The eastern provinces continue to experience tranquil recalibration as Luminary Guards secure zones
previously disturbed by Shadow interference. Temporary interruptions to local flora and fauna are
expected and within control. Restoration rituals
have begun.

Emotional Dissonance Advisory:
Several students have reported vivid dreams, stray
memories, and irrational questions. This is a known
side effect of prolonged proximity to ancient texts
and will subside once order is reestablished within
the self. Those experiencing such symptoms may
receive quiet purification upon request.

```
Curriculum Reminder:
All syllabi must remain free of unapproved mate-
rials, including pre-Concordance poetry, mythos of
fractured gods, or writings that glorify individual
choice over divine unity. Exceptions are revoked
until further notice.
In Memoriam:
Three Luminary Guards of the Dawn Watch gave them-
selves in a tranquil last stand to prevent a Shadow
incursion near the Weeping Trees. They are at rest
now, their souls offered to the greater song. Please
observe a moment of gentle silence during your first
class period.

Observation:
Those who drift toward Shadow often speak of freedom.
But there is no freedom outside of Light, only
forgetting.
We See You. We Are With You. You Are Safe.
Stay lit. Stay obedient. Stay lit. Stay obedient.
```

THE CAMPUS IS QUIET this morning, too quiet; the kind of silence that tastes like control. As I climb the final steps to my office, I notice the stillness isn't peace, it's fear, vacuumed into every hallway.

Eyes lower as I pass, doors close quicker than usual, and then I see it. A single sheet of creamy parchment lies centered on every desk, every bench, every lectern. The academy seal gleams gold at the top.

My stomach knots.

Morning Dispatch from the Office of Enlightened Affairs: To All Faculty and Students of Umbraxis Academy

My fingers tremble as I snatch one from the department's notice board.

Regional Stabilization Progressing Smoothly. The eastern provinces continue to experience tranquil recalibration...

Tranquil recalibration? I bite down hard on the inside of my cheek, blood answers before tears do. I read on.

Temporary interruptions to local flora and fauna are expected and within control. Restoration rituals have begun.

Burning forests, scorched earth, screaming wildlife... all tucked neatly under the phrase "interruptions." I feel sick. My grip tightens as I scan the next section.

Several students have reported vivid dreams, stray memories, or irrational questions...Side effects of prolonged proximity to ancient texts. Quiet purification upon request.

Side effects, that's what they're calling it now. Gods forbid a student feels something, questions something, remembers something. By the time I reach the section titled *Curriculum Reminder*, I'm seeing red.

They're talking about me: my course, my students, my shelves. I scan the list again, mythos of fractured gods: that means *Orpheus,* that means *Hekate,* that means every story I've ever taught that breathes doubt.

The Office of Enlightened Affairs doesn't just issue guidelines; it manufactures obedience. It takes history, and binds it into hymns. They're erasing everything with a heartbeat.

The paper crinkles violently in my hand as I reach the final line:

Stay lit. Stay obedient.

Twice, like a hymn. No, like a curse.

My nails dig into my palm as I crush the dispatch into a hard, angry fist. I want to scream, I want to tear every copy from every desk and set them ablaze with the very Shadows they fear.

Instead, I breathe, slow and low, but it comes out a growl.

There is darkness curling at the edge of my soul that I can no longer ignore. Lucien's warning, subtle, but unmistakable, rings louder now.

And this?

This dispatch isn't a coincidence, it's a message. They're not just watching, they're warning me.

We See You. We Are With You. You Are Safe.

Lies, I have never felt less safe in my life.

They call it curriculum reform, but it feels like erasure; like what remained of Vaeloria's memory is being rewritten line by line, sealed in golden ink and silence.

All that's left is Aureverra, the realm of the Light. We don't even hear much about Velmourn, the realm that now holds the Shadows... never by name, at least; almost as if they're afraid that if by mentioning its existence it will invite doubt.

I stand before my students, hands clasped behind my back, eyes scanning the rows of quiet, wide-eyed faces. Each of them has a copy of the dispatch folded neatly atop their desks, like an accusation.

The silence is thick.

Some of them haven't even looked at me yet, as if to be seen paying attention might condemn them too.

I let the quiet stretch a moment longer, then speak. "I won't be summarizing the dispatch today."

A few students glance up, surprised.

"You've all read it," I continue. "Or at least you've seen it. You know what it says." I keep my voice steady, neutral. "So we won't waste time repeating its... contents."

There's a faint shifting of chairs. One student lowers their eyes, clutching the paper too tightly, another exhales, almost inaudibly, a breath they've been holding.

"Today," I say evenly, "we begin a new unit."

I hold up a thin, bland-looking volume issued by the Office of Enlightened Affairs. Its title is vague and sanitized:

The Doctrine of Sacred Order: Tales for Unified Minds.

The Light's idea of literature.

Around the room, there are barely-concealed looks of disappointment. One student sighs, another mutters something about missing *Orpheus and Eurydice.*

I smile, small and sharp.

"Though our official text has changed," I say slowly, "what we are studying has not. We are still exploring themes of obedience, agency, memory, and myth. These... assigned stories offer us new tools, different perspectives. We will read them together, closely."

Some of the students perk up: a boy up front lifts an eyebrow, a girl near the back starts to smile.

"Literature," I continue, "is not neutral. It never has been. What a culture chooses to preserve, and what it chooses to erase, tells us everything about its values. If you find something missing from these stories... ask yourself why."

No one moves but they're all breathing differently now. I walk slowly to the board and write:

Where Light dwells, peace follows.

Then underneath it:

Peace is not the absence of conflict, but the presence of justice.

I underline the second line. "That quote," I say softly, "is not in your assigned text. It's from a banned poet named Alea Ves. Consider that."

Someone gasps, another scribbles it down.

"I will teach what I must," I add, voice low but firm. "But I will never teach you to stop thinking. That part of the syllabus is not up for revision."

I turn to begin the lesson.

The lesson ends on a silence that hums, a quiet defiance passed hand to hand like flint. My students leave slowly, some with hesitant glances, some with determined steps, all clutching questions they're not quite ready to speak aloud.

As the door clicks shut behind the last of them, I let out a breath I didn't know I'd been holding.

I don't even have time to sit before the knock comes: measured, commanding, expected.

I smooth my skirts, gather the fragments of calm I have left, and open the door.

Lucien stands there, tall, elegant and radiant in his pale robes. Behind him, slightly to the left, is Elowen. Her robe is darker, academic bronze with golden cuffs, and her expression is already carved from disdain.

"Educator Sylvaine," Lucien says, with a nod just shy of warm. "Might we have a word?"

"Of course," I say, stepping aside.

They enter with the precision of a ritual, measured steps and unspoken intent. Lucien crosses the room, folding his hands loosely behind his back. Elowen remains standing by the desk. Her eyes scan the board, the desk, the discarded copy of *The Doctrine of Sacred Order*, her mouth tightening slightly.

"I trust," Elowen begins, "that the students received the morning dispatch with clarity." Her voice is silk spun over ice.

"They received it," I reply evenly. "Clarity is subjective."

Lucien cuts a quick glance at me. In his gaze I don't see warning or support, but something else, something complicated.

Elowen's lips curve, but the expression doesn't reach her eyes. "Subjectivity is precisely what we seek to minimize, Educator. You know that."

"I know what the dispatch said." I lift my chin. "And I followed the curriculum revision. We used the approved text."

Lucien steps forward, voice softer. "And yet... there were reports."

Ah, there it is.

I keep my tone calm. "Reports of what?"

Elowen's gaze is needle-sharp. "Of... editorializing. Deviations. Unrecorded remarks not found in the text."

I think, half-fearing at how swiftly whispers and reports have reached their ears. Class has only just ended, yet already the air is thick with knowing.

My thoughts drift, quiet as mist, to the wards etched in my classroom, to the runes that bloom unbidden, silent as snowfall, offering no reason.

Lucien glances toward her, as if to temper her tone, but he doesn't contradict her. He won't.

"Elowen," he says gently, "perhaps we might speak to intention first."

Her nostrils flare. "Intention is irrelevant when influence is involved. Sylvaine may believe herself clever, but subtlety is no shield from scrutiny."

I bristle, but Lucien speaks before I can.

"Let's not forget," he says with an edge of warning, "that Sylvaine has maintained top marks from her students. Their comprehension, engagement..."

"She charms them," Elowen interrupts, voice now laced with venom. "That's not the same as instructing them."

There it is, not just disdain but jealousy. Lucien hears it too; I see it in the faint tension in his jaw.

"Elowen," he says more firmly, "this is not a personal matter."

"But perhaps it should be," she snaps before turning to me, voice low and cutting. "You think you can cloak rebellion in poetry? That you're untouchable because *he* likes you?"

Lucien flinches, only slightly but he does.

I say nothing, I'm watching them both now, reading what isn't written.

"She deserves a formal review," Elowen fires towards Lucien. "An audit of her materials, her lectures, and a restriction on independent discussion until further notice."

Lucien looks at me and for the first time, I see the weight behind his usual softness. He's not just conflicted, he's cornered.

Elowen smiles, satisfied. "Enjoy your tenure while it lasts, Educator. The Light is patient, but it does not tolerate erosion."

She leaves without another word and the air feels scorched in her wake.

Lucien lingers.

"I can't stop the review," he says quietly. "Not after the dispatch. There are eyes on all of us now."

"But you don't agree with it."

He doesn't answer.

"I didn't report you," he says finally.

"I know," I answer.

"I can't protect you forever."

"I'm not asking you to."

A beat. The silence stretches long between us.

He looks at me. For a moment as a look back, I see something more than regret... it could almost be fear.

"She'll come for you again," he says.

"I'm counting on it," I reply.

He leaves and the door closes.

I let the quiet settle around me like a shroud. The review is coming, the fire is lit and I have already chosen my side.

After what feels like the longest day of my life, I finally reach my cabin.

The lantern above the door flickers low, as if it's just as tired as I am. I notice something resting on the doorstep, a small woven basket tied with twine. Inside there are sachets, five or six of them, each filled with herbs and dried petals: lavender, ginger root, passionflower, mint. There's a small tag tucked under the top bundle, handwritten in looping, precise ink: *T.E.*

Thaleia.

The scent hits me before I even open one: earthy, calming, a little bitter. My throat tightens, it smells like my mother's kitchen.

I carry the basket inside like it's something fragile and sacred, setting it beside my kettle. The shadows in the room stretch longer than usual, curling beneath the edges of my shelves and furniture, like they've been waiting.

I don't question them.

I brew a cup of tea, ginger and passionflower, and bring it to my writing bench. The steam curls into my face as I sit. I take a sip. It's not what I'm used to, less sweet, more grounding; a quiet kind of bitter, but it calms the noise in my chest.

Still, there's only one thing on my mind. I set the cup down beside me. The parchment waits and I begin to write.

Shadow,
What have they done to the truth?
This morning I found their lies printed and folded on every desk. I've at-

tached a copy so you can see it for yourself.

Do you know what this means, really?

They will strip out the soul. They'll call it Light, but it's just silence.

They're watching me. They know about the letters, or at least suspect.

I need to know what's really happening. Please... tell me what the Light is doing in the eastern provinces.

Tell me if the Weeping Trees are still standing. Tell me if the villages were spared.

They mention three fallen Luminary Guards. They mention nothing of who they were fighting.

Did anyone survive? Did you?

I want to believe this is still about knowledge, about understanding both sides.

But when I read your letters, when I read you, I feel something I don't know how to name anymore.

Like someone I lost is speaking through you.

Your words feel like memory, like home. The shadows around me are growing deeper, and this scares me.

If you are who I think you might be, let me know...

Write soon. Please. I don't want to be alone in this.

— Noctis

BLEACHED MEMORY

I'M SEVEN AGAIN.

The forest breathes around me, thick with green light, ancient and alive. Sunbeams filter through the canopy like spilled gold, dancing across the underbrush in rhythms older than language. My fingers are stained dark with blackberry juice, sticky with sweetness. My knees, scabbed from yesterday's tumble, throb faintly, but I don't mind. They are proof of motion, of freedom.

I am alone but not lonely.

Birdsong warbles somewhere above, a lazy kind of symphony, as if the whole forest is half-asleep and I'm the only thing awake enough to hear it. I hum to myself, and the forest hums back; the trees sway in time. The wind carries something that feels like a memory; not mine, exactly, but known to me anyway, something deep, old, and true.

The moss beneath my feet is soft as breath; with every step I take, it seems to lift to meet me, as though the earth knows my name and means to cradle me in it.

Then I hear a rustle: sharp, startled. It's not the forest but something else, someone else.

I turn and he is there.

The boy from The Vale, the closest village to my family's land, older by maybe a year, but somehow already ancient in the eyes. His hair is a mess of wild curls, and his silver eyes glitter with mischief and melancholy. In one hand, he clutches a weather-worn book, too large for his frame, in the other, a half-eaten jar of jam; stolen, by the look of it.

He grins at me, gap-toothed and wicked. "You looked like you needed a story."

I almost cry.

Instead, I sit. He lights a stub of candle from his satchel, melted to the nub but still brave enough to glow. He reads, low and careful, tragedies, mostly: gods punished, lovers lost, empires buried. Not the kind of tales you tell children.

I drink in every word, every fall, every silence between the lines.

His voice curls around me like smoke, warm and secret. In that moment, the whole world becomes candlelight and quiet wonder.

Then the candle flickers: once, twice. The flame stretches. The glow elongates, thins into a spear of too-bright light and then breaks.

The dream shifts, snaps, curves into something colder.

The trees begin to straighten, rigid as soldiers at attention; their trunks narrow and grow tall, unnaturally so. Branches twist skyward, now jagged like spears. The soft moss chars beneath my bare feet, blackening with a hiss.

The green light, *my light*, drains, bleaches... becomes sterile, white, humming with voltage.

The forest is no longer mine.

I whirl to him, to Lysander, but his face is wrong now: flickering, fractured. A golden seal blooms across his lips, glowing with Lightscript.

Divine gag.

His eyes widen. He tries to speak. Nothing comes.

Figures emerge from the tree-line, smooth as sliding blades. They move in perfect synchrony, their white robes whispering across the deadened earth, laced in gold thread and sanctified cruelty. I know them by name, by nightmare:

Verse-Keepers.

Clerics of the Sacred Flame, keepers of the Light, censors of the soul.

They have no faces, only mirrors polished to blindness. They speak as one, their voices chime like hollow bells dipped in venom.

Where Light dwells, peace follows.
Where peace dwells, all thrives.

I try to step back, to run, but the moss is gone and my feet are stone.

They surround me, closer, closer.

One of them raises my book, the one filled with marginal drawings, notes and half-thoughts, the one I read until it fell apart. They burn it. Page by page. Not with flame, but with touch.

Their fingers sear with holy light. Pages curl into ash without smoke, the words vanish screaming.

I scream too, but my voice is swallowed before it can rise, devoured.

Lysander tries to reach me. I see it in his face, behind the seal, his hand lifts, trembling. Golden chains erupt from the ground, wrapping around his wrist like serpents, yanking him backward.

He disappears into the Light. His outline flickers... gone.

The Verse-Keepers close in.

Curiosity leads to fracture.
Choice leads to forgetting.
You are not safe.

The trees are gone, the forest is gone, he is gone. Only the Light remains and it burns everything.

I am screaming but no sound escapes.

I wake with a start, lungs dragging in air too fast, too shallow.

My sheets cling to me, soaked in sweat. The dream still grips my chest like a claw, the images already smudging at the edges. The feeling remains: searing, hollow, a warning still echoing through my bones.

For a long moment, I just sit there, heart hammering in the dark.

A tap at the window startles me, it's not loud, not urgent, but precise, rhythmic; like knuckles on glass, like a question.

I turn, pulse skittering. Part of me braces for Light to come blazing through the panes, to rip away the dark like it did in my dream, but there's no blaze, only moonlight, silver and solemn, casting soft reflections across the stone floor.

Slowly, I rise.

At first I see nothing beyond the glass, only the black outlines of the trees, unmoving. But then I spot it, a raven, perched just beyond the ledge: not pecking, not fluttering, waiting.

Its eyes find mine, steady and black, ancient.

Normally, I'd be annoyed, maybe even unnerved, but tonight... I'm grateful. The silence in my room feels too loud, too watched. I cross the floor, barefoot and breath held. The window creaks open with a reluctant sigh of old wood.

The bird doesn't enter but something else does.

At first, I think it's a trick of the candle stub still burning on my desk, the flicker of flame against glass, but then it moves.

A Shadow: thin as smoke, fluid as breath.

It slithers over the sill with unnatural grace, not cast by anything, not attached to any form; just Shadow, a sliver of living dusk.

It ripples toward the floor, coils like a serpent, then it reaches toward me; not with malice, not with violence, but intent. As if offering, as if obeying some command older than language.

I freeze.

The raven watches in silence, unmoving.

The Shadow stretches upward, the tip of it forming into something like a hand; five wisps of darkness, each one barely tethered to reality. Within its palm, something begins to form; a piece of parchment, thin as breath, inked in silver that glows faintly against the black.

The Shadow sets it gently on my desk and with the grace of a bow, it dissolves, as if it had never existed.

I stand, stunned, heart thudding like a drum in a sealed box.

The raven croaks once: low, rough, almost sympathetic. Then it lifts off the ledge and disappears into the night.

I stare at the letter, still faintly glowing where the Shadow touched it. I haven't even broken the seal, but I already know who it's from.

The parchment is tied neatly with dark twine, my fingers tremble as I undo it. I read:

My Noctis,
You ask what the Light has done.

The Weeping Trees still stand, though their roots run crimson. The soil drinks what it must.

The children of the ridge were hidden before the first torch touched bark. The villagers... not all were so lucky. But some live. I saw to it myself.

Three Luminary Guards fell, yes... but not in "tranquil last stands." They died screaming, beneath arrows fletched with memory.

One begged for his mother. Another for absolution. None for the Light.

You ask if I survived. I did.

Not because the Light failed to kill me, but because I refused to be unmade by their version of salvation.

As for who I am... I cannot say. It is not safe, but I can say this:

You make me believe that even in a world divided, some souls would never forget the forest.

I know that the Light would fear you if they ever truly saw you. Maybe they do now.

Shadows are gathering. They know you. You do not command them yet. But they wait.

They respond not to force, but to memory. To longing. If you speak, not with your mouth, but with your marrow, they will listen.

Try it. In the quietest moment of your doubt, call not with words but want. You may be surprised what stirs in response.

You are right to question. But be careful. A curious mind is a dangerous thing to those who rule by certainty.

I will write again soon. Leave your letters in the hollow beneath the twisted hawthorn near the edge of the wood, it is safer than the post, and birds can be intercepted.

I sit there long after the ink has dried on my fingertips, the letter open on the desk like a wound I can't close. Outside, the world is held in the breathless stillness before dawn, but inside me, something has already begun to stir.

The Light wants obedience, it wants silence, but I am remembering now, what it felt like to believe in something wild, something tender and defiant.

The shadows at my doorstep no longer frighten me. I now know they are Shadows, magic from the gods, not just dark shapes produced by something coming between rays of light and a surface. If they are waiting for my voice, then perhaps it's time I stop whispering. Perhaps it's time I answer.

I rise from the chair, the wooden floor cold beneath my bare feet. The room feels unfamiliar suddenly, like a skin I've outgrown. Books on the shelves that once offered comfort now hum with something electric beneath their spines. The air itself is thick with possibility.

The Shadows shift along the floor: not menacing, not sinister, but alert, curious.

I cross to the window. The night is pale with half-light, the moon slung low, hanging like a question. The edges of the garden paths are blurring, the darkness curling around the hedges like smoke that's begun to remember it once had a body.

I close my eyes.

Not with your mouth, but with your marrow.

My chest rises, trembles. I do not speak aloud, I do not need to. I let the longing speak for me, the ache for truth, for story, for resistance that doesn't wear armor but wears softness like a shield. The want that lives in the places I've kept hidden: beneath duty, beneath discipline, beneath the curated masks of civility.

The Shadows answer. They do not speak, but they tilt, as if listening, as if leaning closer.

A breeze stirs inside the room though the window is shut, and the candle flickers sideways. On the hearth, the ashes of the dispatch scatter upward in a slow spiral, drawn toward something unseen.

I take a step back from the window. My heart beats like it remembers another rhythm, older than hymns. I think of the twisted hawthorn: of the boy with silver eyes, of verses that end in rupture, not reunion.

This is not just defiance, it's remembering, and remembering, I realize, is the first form of rebellion.

I gather the letter carefully, wrap it in cloth, and tuck it into the loose floorboard, where I keep my most dangerous things: truths, mostly. Then I reach for a fresh page, my hand no longer trembles: not a report, not a lesson plan, not an apology, a reply.

Let the Light preach silence.

Tonight, I choose to speak.

A SILKEN LIE

THE KNOCK ON MY door is firm and deliberate.

I'm curled in a loose knot on my chair, the remnants of last night's reading scattered across my desk; half-burned notes, marginalia that veer dangerously close to banned doctrine. I straighten quickly, smoothing my dress with more care than I feel.

Opening the door, I see Lucien, though he is wearing the face of The Beacon of Light today.

His posture is usually marble-solid, but today there's a crack in the stone. His shoulders are drawn tighter, eyes wary, like he's trying to calculate the temperature of the room before stepping fully in.

The familiar scent of pine and incense drapes off him like always, but there's something underneath it now: hesitation, guilt... or something more self-serving.

"Sylvaine," he begins, voice low, "about the dispatch..."

He pauses, then shrugs, half-smiling, a gesture he must think makes him seem disarming. "I'm sorry if it upset you. I was only doing my duty. Orders are orders. No hard feelings, I hope."

I study his face.

It's a practiced apology, the kind that's less about making amends and more about smoothing the edges of consequence. He expects me to nod, to thank him for his restraint. He expects me to forgive him for twisting my words, for dragging my name into his doctrine-spun pageantry, for using me as a cautionary tale.

And yet... beneath his polished performance, I can see it, not shame, just justification; because to him, what he did isn't betrayal, it's obedience, it's survival.

That's what frightens me most.

"The Chancellor's been busy," I say lightly, but there's iron beneath it.

Lucien's gaze flickers, just barely.

"Elowen's new mandates reached my door at dawn," I continue, voice even. "Lecture audits. Curriculum transparency declarations. Faculty interviews without notice. She's not just targeting contraband texts now, she's targeting tone, implication, ambiguity."

I don't add: *she's targeting me.*

Elowen has hated me since I stepped on the academy grounds: my teaching, my defiance, my name. But lately, it's changed; her disdain has sharpened into something more personal, not just ideological, territorial.

"She believes a little fear is good for the soul," I say. "Her words. Not mine."

Lucien exhales slowly, but doesn't argue: doesn't defend her, doesn't offer the usual script about how Chancellor Elowen is simply 'protecting the purity of learning.' That silence is more telling than anything he could have said.

"She's always been... rigorous," he offers finally, but even he hears the hollowness of the word.

"Rigorous," I repeat, dryly. "Is that what we're calling forced reassignments and sealed libraries now?"

A pause stretches between us, taut and bristling. The truth coils there, unsaid but suffocating.

I want to spit it at him, that the dispatch turned my voice into a weapon, turned curiosity into heresy. That the Chancellor's tightening leash is not about enlightenment, it's about control. I want to tell him I see through his sacred mask.

But rage won't get me what I need, not now, not yet; so I swallow it down like poison and smile with practiced grace.

"It's... understood," I say carefully. "You have your duties as the Beacon of the Light, and Light Warden, and I have mine as an Educator."

Lucien's eyes soften for a breath. The apology almost returns to his lips but he says nothing.

I step back, just enough to allow him entry.

He hesitates, one foot still in the corridor, his fingers curling slightly at his side. The threshold between us is not just physical; it's a ritual, symbolic, and I can see it in his posture...

He knows crossing this line means more than stepping into a room, it means stepping into whatever this is, into me. Maybe he doesn't want to; or maybe he wants to too much, maybe it will cost him.

The Shadows in the corners of the room seem to breathe, as if recognizing the shift, as if waiting to see who he'll be, once inside. I turn away before I can watch him choose.

He enters.

His footsteps are careful across the floor, as if he's walking through something fragile, sacred, or forbidden.

"Good," he says finally, voice softer now, lower, more uncertain. "Now... about us."

I stiffen slightly... that phrase, *about us*, is both an invitation and a warning.

He moves closer, just enough to let the distance hum between us like a live wire.

"I feel as though I've been... neglectful," he continues, gaze resting somewhere just over my shoulder. "I realize I haven't been the most clear with my feelings."

I glance at him from the side, one brow arched, but say nothing. Let him speak, let him unravel.

"I haven't planned our time together," he says, but the words sound rehearsed, carefully chosen, precisely placed, like stones on a chessboard. "And for that, I apologize."

His tone is warm, almost tender, but it's the kind of warmth a fire gives just before it burns out; because this isn't about affection, it's about control, reassertion, damage control in velvet gloves.

"I thought distance might keep you safer," he adds, quieter now. "But perhaps... I misjudged."

I finally turn to face him, the candlelight catches the edge of his jaw reflecting off the gold thread at his collar. His face is still composed, still curated, but there's something frayed in the corners of his eyes... something that looks almost real.

"You didn't misjudge," I say. "You calculated and decided the risk was mine to carry."

He flinches, just barely, but he doesn't deny it.

We stand there in the solitude of my quarters, between what we are and what we pretend to be.

He takes a breath, the kind that precedes either confession or manipulation.

"I do care for you, Sylvaine. I know I haven't always shown it in ways you might recognize. But I am... trying. Things are shifting. Elowen, she watches everything now. Every alliance. Every whisper. If she suspects I've let someone close, she won't come for me. She'll come for you."

There it is, the admission: wrapped in affection, wrapped again in threat. He's not wrong, but that doesn't make it kindness.

I look at him, really look; at the man caught between conviction and self-preservation, between the Light's doctrine and whatever flickers in him when he looks at me.

"I'm not asking for protection," I say. "Just honesty."

He doesn't respond right away but when he does, his voice is quiet.

"Then I'll try to be honest. Starting now."

But even then, he doesn't say what he's really thinking, because neither of us trusts the walls anymore.

The Shadows, still waiting in the corners, remain very, very still.

His performance is convincing, but I've been around too many wolves dressed as prophets. Still, a new thought roots itself in me, one that chills and thrills all at once.

If I keep him close... maybe I can see more, learn more, eavesdrop on the holy secrets he spills when he thinks no one's listening. If I listen carefully enough, I might find a way to starve the Light from the inside.

I meet his gaze, steady and bright, "I appreciate that," I say, my voice a silken lie. "It's been a long semester. I think we could both use a break."

His smile is victorious... if only he knew.

Solara, the capital city, beyond the academy walls, feels alien, alive with rough edges and restless energy. It's been years since I walked these streets, and tonight, every clang of a horseshoe, every bark from a vendor, every stray note from a distant string instrument feels alive. The city is a contrast:

raw and unfiltered. It strips me of the academy's polished silence and makes everything feel too loud.

We duck into a tucked-away tavern, dim and musky with sweat, roasted meat, and stale ale. Orange light swings from old lanterns, casting Lucien in shifting shadows, a predator trying to look like a companion.

We sit at a sticky table near the back and I glance at the menu, brow furrowing. The dishes sound like random animals culled from the wild, tossed into the cauldron with reckless abandon. My stomach twists in protest.

Lucien watches me, not with affection but with calculation.

I decide to play along. I order a glass of red wine and let the burn spread through me, loosening the tightness in my chest. When he orders, I watch his expression carefully, noting the slight twitch of impatience behind the polite smile.

I drink again, and again: to calm my nerves, to give myself courage, to play the part he wants, the part I need him to believe. The wine is sharp and sweet, loosening my limbs and my tongue.

Soon, I'm leaning closer, laughing too easily. My fingers brush his arm... accidentally, or maybe not. My voice dips into velvet, teasing and inviting.

The performance begins.

He responds just as I expect, eyes darkening, voice low and warm. He laughs at things that aren't funny.

We're performers in a masquerade of intimacy.

For a moment, just a flicker, I almost forget why I'm here. For a flicker, his goodwill feels real. The weight of war, the forbidden letters, the Shadows that press at the edges of my life, it all disappears for just a moment. His attention is like a balm, or a trap, and I'm teetering between forgetting and remembering.

Reality returns: sharp and cold, like a blade pressed to my spine. I swallow it down with another sip.

Eventually we leave the tavern, both of us unsteady, the night air brushing cool against our flushed skin. The streets of Solara are quiet this late, just the occasional torch flickering against ivy-covered stone and the echo of our footsteps against the walkway.

He's looser now, almost reflective. "You know," he murmurs as we walk, "you're not like the others. Most of them... they're all theory and obedience. But you..." He glances over, eyes glassy. "You still have teeth."

"I try to be interesting," I reply lightly.

He smiles at that, and the silence that follows is oddly fragile, like something he wants to break open but can't.

The academy looms ahead, its towers rising like fingers clawing at the moonlight but instead of veering toward my cabin at the edge of campus, he guides me gently but insistently up the winding stairwell of the tallest spire, his private quarters. It sits at the crown of the campus like a throne, and he walks as if he belongs to it, as if it was built just for him.

Inside, his chambers are warm, saturated with the scent of cedarwood, candle smoke, and aged books. No fire crackles in the hearth and the darkness seems intentional, calculated. I hover near the shelves, unsure where to stand, how to place myself in this performance's final act.

He wastes no time and I let him, this is what I came for.

The kiss is all heat and entitlement. No tenderness, just possession.

His hands find my shoulders, then my waist. I don't resist, this is the moment I planned for, the cost I accepted.

He kisses me like he already owns the answer. His breath is hot with beer, and the taste makes me want to gag. Still, I let him.

My body doesn't fight, even as my mind curls inward, away from this.

His fingers are rough, impatient. The delicate pretense of civility vanishes as he tugs at my clothes with little care, almost ripping the fabric in his eagerness. He stumbles as he undresses, muttering something slurred and half-laughing, as if this is still part of a game.

I let him kiss me, let him undress me; because I chose this, and I will own the cost.

He takes what he wants like it's owed, like my silence is consent, like this is closeness.

The bed behind me is too large, the sheets too cold.

He doesn't pause, doesn't ask. No preparation, no protection; it's a good thing I have all the herbs I need to make a contraceptive draught.

He thrusts into me like a soldier breaching a gate, forceful and unrelenting. He's not particularly large, but it doesn't make it any easier. Pain bites sharp at first. I tense, but I don't make a sound. I stare past him, to the ceiling, to the flickering Shadows on stone.

The intimacy, if you could call it that, is hollow, practiced, like a ritual he's performed countless times. His hands only touch the places he wants, his eyes stay closed the entire time.

He never asks what I want, never once considers if I need anything at all.

When he finishes, it's with a satisfied grunt and a sigh that sounds like pride. He glances at me briefly, breath still heavy, and asks, "That was great, wasn't it?"

I summon a smile, dreamy and delicate. Or at least I try, it probably looks more like a grimace. Hopefully he's drunk enough not to notice. He doesn't wait for an answer, sleep takes him quickly, sinking into the mattress like a man who's earned something. I lie beside him, unmoving. My heart beats too fast, my mouth is dry.

The ceiling above is still, but I feel it watching me... this whole room watching me, the Shadows are watching me. Secrets press in from every corner.

The air feels heavier now, cloaked in a silence that screams.

Careful not to wake him, I slip from the bed, every step slow, calculated. I dress in silence, my hands shaky but practiced. Each movement is deliberate, rehearsed a hundred times in my head. I reach the door, freedom just a breath away, but pause. My eyes flick to the desk in the corner of the room, a monolith of polished oak, burdened with disorganized papers and half-burned candles.

I hover there, breath catching in my throat... *don't, just leave*, but something tugs at me, a gnawing pull I can't ignore. I tell myself it's for the sake of knowledge: for truth, for the students I swore to protect.

There's something else too, the selfish, trembling part of me that needs to know if I'm right: if he's who I think he is, if the mask he wears is hiding something darker than rumor.

I hesitate, the weight of the choice thrums at the base of my spine. Then, slowly, I cross the room.

His desk is cluttered, but not locked, not guarded: a hubris I can exploit. My fingertips graze the edge of the topmost letter, hesitant. I know I shouldn't read it, I know the moment my eyes track the ink, I'll lose something I can never get back, but curiosity is a curse that has never let me go.

I unfold the pages. They're clinical, almost elegant in their detachment: dozens of names, ages, allegiances, outcomes. Each line feels like a blade. *Subject 218B: refusal to renounce Shadow-aligned rhetoric. Continued noncompliance after three weeks. Initiated second phase. Results pending.*
Subject 443A: Educator reported excessive questioning in lecture. Relocated for assessment. Silence protocol activated.

I can't breathe.

As I continue reading, I notice there are students on this list, my students: the ones who dared to ask about dual interpretations, the ones who lingered after class, whispering curiosity into the bones of dead philosophers. Their names are written in the same sterile ink as the rebels, no distinction, no hesitation.

They are being labeled, processed, and *purified*.

Underneath the stack, I find something else, a folded letter. The paper is softer, worn with time, not the same institutional fiber as the others, the ink flows in loops, delicate and unmistakably familiar, Mama. My fingers tremble as I unfold it and begin to read:

Thaleia,

You must forgive the secrecy. I have little time and fewer allies.

I fear by the time you read this, it may already be too late. You of all people know this.

Please, if we do not survive this, I beg you, watch over Sylvaine.

Keep her safe. Teach her to question, to feel, to see.

She must know the truth, not the truth Lucien will offer her, polished and sharpened like a blade, but the truth that lives in the quiet and the Shadows.

Lucien was different from the beginning. Too bright, too certain.

Light, when held too tightly, burns. You saw it, I know you did. The gleam in his eye was not illumination, but hunger.

He speaks of purity. Of order. Of one truth.

But truth has many voices, Thaleia. It always has. You taught me that.

If he has begun to rise, if the Order has started to turn inward, then the corruption of Light is no longer a whisper.

It is a reckoning. And Lucien stands at its heart.

You were always the one I trusted. You, not him.
— Caliane

My breath catches and my hands curl into fists, crumpling the edges of the letter.

This is the letter, the one they must have written before everything fell apart. It wasn't meant for Lucien, it was never meant for him. They hadn't trusted him to guide me; they'd warned against him.

And somehow... he had it, he kept it, he hid it.

Thaleia never got the letter. All these years, I believed Lucien was my protector, my mentor.

He was a thief, a liar. No, he *is* a thief, a liar.

Whatever warmth once flickered in my chest now ignites into fire, into fury.

I fold the letter back with surgical precision and return it to the stack. My hands do not shake. I have learned the stillness of the hunted. I leave everything exactly as I found it. There is no sound as I move, just the ache of a breath held too long, the cold settling into my joints like winter beneath skin.

The smile I wore for Lucien has long since peeled off, what's left is sharper, quieter. The candlelight no longer seems warm. I slip out through the door without a word, and the world resumes its slow turning.

The corridor outside Lucien's quarters is suffocatingly quiet. The heavy door clicks shut behind me, and for a long moment, I just stand there, staring at the candlelit stone archways ahead. My footsteps echo like warnings down the empty hall as I begin the walk back to my cabin. My mind is buzzing, unraveling, calculating.

The night air hits me in waves as I leave the main building, cool and scented with burning wood and the metallic tang of coming rain. I keep my hood up, head bowed. Even in the dark, the academy watches.

I tread the path I know by heart, the one leading from the inner courts to the wooded edge where my small cabin waits. Tonight I take it slower, letting the silence speak. The path to my cabin is the same as it always is, but I am not.

Lucien thinks he has me. He believes I've bent under the weight of his gaze, that the fear has finally seeped through my marrow and made me docile, and he's right... in part. I am afraid, but fear sharpens, it slices clean the illusions I've clung to.

I bite the inside of my cheek until I taste blood. I walk faster.

I need to keep pretending, to teach the required texts the way they want them taught: coldly, cleanly, with no inflection.

The Light will get my lectures, polished and pure, but my students will get something else: in whispers, in hidden corners, in locked rooms beneath stone.

A club, a sanctuary, a place where we can speak in full sentences: where questions aren't betrayal, where books are not burned, but devoured. I will teach them what the Light has buried and I will build something under the surface.

The wind stirs the trees like breath, somewhere in the distance a bird calls once, sharp and sudden, then vanishes into silence. I resume my walk, slower now, each step a deliberate decision. I will teach their truths in the daylight, but at night, we will remember, we will reclaim what was taken.

Let Lucien believe he owns me, let the Light keep watching.

They won't see what's coming.

Obedience is Clarity

I STAND BEFORE MY class like a statue.

Today's assigned reading is *On the Divine Path* by Solarius Vire, a Light-approved relic of rhetoric, wrapped in the gilded language of piety and obedience. The text is hollow, bloated with proclamations.

"Order is clarity. Clarity is sanctity. Submission is the highest form of freedom."

I read aloud, voice measured and flat. There is no invitation in my tone. No inflection, no provocation; just words, words the Light wants, words I must say.

The students sit in stiff rows, eyes down, quills scratching dutifully at their parchments. Not one of them looks up, not even the bold ones; because today, we are not alone.

Lucien is at the back of the hall, his posture is relaxed but it's a performance. He watches with surgical attention, eyes narrowed like a man who's already made a judgment and is now waiting for confirmation.

Next to him stands Elowen, her presence curdles the air. Her hands are clasped before her, still and smooth. Her expression is unreadable, not because she hides it, but because she has perfected it, a mirror polished by power. Still, her gaze settles on me like frost.

The room has changed since she entered. My classroom, once my sanctuary, now hums with the cold geometry of surveillance. I can feel the added wards layered into the corners, the shimmer of cloaked listening glyphs stitched into the crown molding and etched beneath the lectern. Their presence is subtle, but I know them.

They do not just record, they *interpret*.

If I speak too freely, if I suggest that obedience is not the only path, if I ask a question I am not sanctioned to ask, they will trigger. They will not raise alarms, they will *muffle;* a thrum will slip into the air, a distortion of sound. My voice will vanish, swallowed by sanctioned silence. The students will not even know what they missed, that's the beauty of these wards.

The Light doesn't censor you, it erases you mid-thought. So I recite Vire's lines like scripture, tone flat as marble:

"To bend the will is to align with purpose. To align with purpose is to be made whole."

I pause. The silence after the sentence stretches long. I let it linger, heavy and uncomfortable.

No commentary, no context, no questioning. I have been instructed not to provoke interpretation today, I am to "guide through reverence, not speculation."

A page turns somewhere in the back, slow and deliberate.

Lucien's smile prickles like a splinter down my spine, I don't have to look to know it's there: half-affection, half-warning.

Good little Educator, it says: compliant, reformed, safe.

He thinks I've surrendered.

And Elowen... Elowen does not smile, she does not need to. Where Lucien performs, Elowen observes.

She watches the way a hawk does just before it descends; still, but utterly lethal. Her eyes scan the classroom with clinical precision, noting posture, eye movement, tone, syllable cadence. She notes silence, most of all. She's not looking for wrong answers, she's looking for thought.

This is no longer a lecture. It is a performance, and I must give the Light a show worth believing.

So I finish the final passage of *On the Divine Path* with flawless cadence:

"To resist divine order is not to defy control, but to flee from healing. Light does not punish, it corrects."

I close the text with reverent quiet.

What they don't know, what Elowen and Lucien, in all their robes and rank and sanctified certainty, cannot see, is that every assigned copy of the book has already been tampered with; just enough to leave no trace, just enough to let hope in.

Inside the spines, pressed gently between pages sixty-two and sixty-three, where the chapter on "Submission as Liberation" begins, I've tucked thin slips of parchment.

They're impossible to detect unless you know where to look; to the untrained eye, they are merely aging fibers in the fold of a page, but to those who question:

> *Burn this after reading. We will gather soon.*
> *No Light. No rules. No lies. Stay cautious. Be patient. Truth lives.*
> *Location: TBD.*

I watch them now, my students, filing out one by one, their expressions calm, compliant, but their eyes... linger on mine, just long enough.

The silence between us is not passive, it holds breath; like something sacred... or scared.

I offer no smile, just a nod. I dismiss them quietly.

When the last one vanishes through the arched door, I begin stacking scrolls, gathering lecture notes with deliberate care, ritual motions that buy me a moment of peace.

But I'm not alone, Lucien is leaning in the doorway again. Sunlight cut across his cheek like a scar. He waits until the last footstep fades before moving closer, that practiced smile already on his lips.

"You're very... composed today," he says softly, walking toward me like a man confident of his welcome. "A clean lesson. Clear message. The Order will be pleased."

His tone is almost affectionate but underneath it hums with both possession and expectation.

I incline my head, subtle and perfectly measured. "That is my goal, isn't it?"

Lucien steps closer and lays a hand lightly on my wrist. "I missed you Vaelday morning," he says, his fingers brushing warm across my pulse. "You vanished after our dinner. No note. No goodbye."

Before I can reply, he leans down and presses a kiss against my cheek, just a whisper from the corner of my mouth: a performance, a mark, a warning.

"I had to prepare my lectures," I answer, the picture of apology. "The new mandated texts aren't as self-explanatory as one might hope."

Lucien studies me for a beat too long. The softness drops a degree. His eyes search mine, not for truth but for deviation; he's always watching for the edge of the mask.

"You're always working," he murmurs, voice tilting toward pout, though it doesn't quite reach sincerity. "Let me make you dinner tomorrow. Something simple. Wine. Candles. You deserve softness, Sylvaine."

My smile is gentle, breathless, masked. "Tomorrow's no good," I say lightly. "I'm behind on annotations. The next inspection is due, and... well." I shrug, sheepish. "You know how it is."

Lucien's smile tightens at the edges, a flicker, not quite anger.

"Soon, then."

"Soon," I echo, and it tastes like ash.

He watches me gather my things, watches my fingers slip too-neatly around a stack of Light-sealed scrolls, and I know he's counting every motion. I let him.

When I finally walk past him into the hall, the corridor swallows me like the end of a prayer.

My shoulders drop half an inch: still composed, still controlled, still performing.

But not for them, not anymore.

My thoughts race ahead, faster than my steps, pulling me toward the woods, toward the hidden edges of truth, of memory, of him.

The walk is brisk, the cold air biting but welcome. The air around me is thick with the kind of silence that hums in the bones, a listening silence. The trees don't rustle, the wind doesn't call, even the birds seem to hold their breath.

When I reach the edge of the clearing, I stop and scan the darkness.

I pause long enough to feel the difference between presence and threat, a habit now.

I slip into my cabin and lock the door behind me, three swift clicks of old iron and wood. The creak of the hinges sings softly, familiar and imperfect, the way real sanctuaries are. It is the only place that still feels mine.

I kneel beside the hearth, where last evening's fire is nothing more than a grey echo, the bucket of ash sits heavy, harmless. I move it aside and press my fingers against the warped floorboard beneath.

The wood shifts with a low groan, and there, beneath it, waits my hidden stack of letters.

I ease it out slowly, reverently. The letters are curled from time and the heat of so many secret nights. Their edges are singed in places, the way a truth pressed too close to the world will begin to burn.

The scent rises up to meet me: charred paper, ink, smoke, something darker... longing.

I pull the newest one free, careful not to disturb the rest; I collected it just last night but hid it before I had a chance to read his words. I sit cross-legged by the hearthstone. A candle flickers already, casting shadows that dance over the cabin walls like ghosts with stories to tell.

The seal breaks like a sigh and inside is the voice I've been waiting for:

Star stealer,
The quiet is growing louder. Even the birds avoid the northern outposts now.
They say rebels are being "recalibrated" in sanctuaries of Light, but none return.
Tell me what you see, what they whisper behind golden doors, what they burn.
I often dream of peaceful forests, though I haven't seen one in years.
Do you dream?
Do you remember what it felt like to be unafraid?

I exhale but the breath catches on something fragile inside me; not grief, but the thing that precedes it, the ache of recognition.

I clutch the parchment tighter, knuckles pale.

His words carry a stillness I know well, a knowing of what silence can become when turned into doctrine: the forests, the rebels, the ones who do not return, they weigh heavy. But it's the last question that undoes me.

Do you remember what it felt like to be unafraid?

I stare at the letter for a long time, then reach for the fresh parchment waiting beside me, the one I always keep prepared, just in case. Ink touches the page before I know exactly what I'll say, but it knows.

Shadow,
They call it purification.
I've seen the names, students, children, anyone who dares to ask why.
They're breaking them without touching them. The silence is a weapon now.
I wish you could see them, my students. The way they stare at me, wondering if they are next, wondering if I can save them.
I am trying.
I used to dream of someone. A boy who taught me how to trust, love and listen to the earth.
Now I only dream of fire and bindings, of voices screaming behind walls of gold, and books turned to ash.
But sometimes... sometimes I still dream of him. He had eyes like moonlight. And he made me laugh before the world went silent.

I stop there, my hand hovering, unsure whether to write more, but I know it's enough. It always is.

I don't sign my name. I don't need to. He knows the shape of me in ink, just as I know his in ash.

When the words have dried, I wrap the letter in its usual cloth, black, soft, damp-resistant, and bind it tightly. My fingers work fast, practiced, the ritual of rebellion. I rise and slip back out into the dark, following the barely-beaten trail to the twisted hawthorn at the edge of the wood. The hollow beneath its roots is small and careful, I press the letter inside like an offering.

He always finds them, or perhaps... his Shadows do. Either way, the truth is moving again and I am not alone.

The moon is absent tonight. Begrudgingly, I make my way to the Temple Hall for the Solis Rite.

Attendance is not optional and absence is its own kind of confession. The procession is quieter this time, not solemn but subdued, weighted.

Something has shifted in the days leading up to this Rite. This is the fourth Rite held this year, and each has been more exacting than the last; the first still clung to tradition, the second tightened its grip, and by the third, the messaging was nearly scripted. Now, it's all choreography and control, serenity sharpened into spectacle.

Something has shifted for sure. There are whispers of rebellion, a sudden disappearance here and there. Elowen herself has issued three edicts in as many days. Edicts cloaked in serenity, but cut sharp with control; new restrictions on student gatherings, curfews for outer-tier academies, the appointment of "Clarity Overseers" in select halls: thought-censors in polished robes, wardens disguised as mentors.

The Light is afraid and fear breeds precision.

We descend the alabaster corridor like pale blood through stone veins, the scent of sun-leaf and root-glow denser than before. It clings, not purifying but smothering, like incense used to mask rot.

I move with the tide, draped again in ritual white, but the fabric scratches this time. The golden threads at the hem seem tighter, pulling the shape of me smaller, narrower. I used to feel invisible in these robes, now I feel exposed.

When we pass beneath the arch into the hall, the hush arrives again, but it doesn't fall like snow this time, it lands like a command.

The chamber is unchanged: perfect, sacred, lifeless.

The mural glows overhead, Light splitting the sky, the sun bursting through a painted heaven. The same sunburst pattern glimmers on the floor, veins of gold radiating from the altar like a spider web spun from law but tonight, the space feels colder, like the warmth has been leeched in preparation.

The Verse-Keeper is already in place, his mask a blank sun. Beside him, not Lucien, but Elowen, Chancellor of Illumination: voice of law, mirror of flame.

She stands cloaked in ivory, though hers is stitched not with sunrise thread, but woven strands of opal-light, a living shimmer that shifts with her breath. Her face is bare, no mask. Elowen does not require one. Her expression is colder than any iron façade. She is still, still like a blade sheathed too long.

When the hymn begins, she does not join, she only watches.

The choir rises around her, voices trained and trembling:

> *We rise in Light, from ash and flame...*
> *We speak one name, we hold one*
> *claim...*

The words feel hollower this time, even as they echo off the domed glass. I mouth them again, as I must, but my voice does not follow; it crouches in my throat like a hunted thing.

There is a rustle in the pews, movement. Elowen raises her hand, interrupting the choir mid-praise.

The music halts instantly, the sudden silence slices cleaner than any blade.

She speaks. "The Light has given us warning."

Her voice is low, beautiful and terrible. It does not echo, it doesn't need to.

"Obedience is no longer assumed. Clarity must be proven."

A ripple moves through the congregation. Fear, maybe, or just memory of fear.

"There are false stars rising," she continues. "Whispers in lecture halls. In margins of approved texts. In minds softened by indulgence and pride. The Light will find them. And when it does, it will burn away what does not belong."

She looks directly at me.

I cannot move, I barely breathe.

Behind her, the Verse-Keeper lifts the Scroll of First Flame. He begins the recitation but it sounds different tonight: sharper, less like faith, more like decree.

Let all who bear doubt cast it aside.
Let Shadow be revealed. Let heresy be
cleansed.

A second voice joins him.

Lucien, late, but shining. He emerges from the side arch in full ceremonial regalia, his eyes bright with borrowed righteousness. He bows before taking his place beside the Verse-Keeper, completing the trinity of Light.

Candles are passed again, but slower this time. Each bearer pauses longer between hands, like inspecting for tremors, searching for guilt.

I hold mine steady, I must.

As the flame reaches my row, I hear the Benediction begin, not from a choir now, but from Lucien himself.

> *Light without limit. Flame without fear...*

His eyes catch mine. He holds them, long enough to twist the meaning of every word.

> *Let your shadow fall behind you.*

I bow with the others.

When I open my eyes, I find Thaleia again, only this time, she is not in the pews. She stands at the very back, unmoving. Her robes hang the same, soft with memory but tonight, her eyes burn with something new. Not memory, not kindness, resolve.

She nods once, almost imperceptibly, then disappears into the shadow between the braziers.

My chest seizes, I almost forget the rest of the rite. The candlelight wavers around me, smoke coils in the vaulted air.

> *Obedience is clarity. Clarity is peace.*

Something inside me is no longer clear, something inside me is choosing, and it is not the Light.

MEMORY IS REBELLION

THE HYMN STILL ECHOES in my bones as I climb the north steps alone, boots biting the stone. The halls here are nearly empty now. This wing was abandoned after the Shadows fled in the early stages of the war; the northern wing became a place no one spoke of. It's too cold, too quiet, too far from the Light's daily reach.

Perfect for uninterrupted meetings.

I knock once.

Thaleia opens the door immediately and pulls me in with more force than warmth. Her office is small and cluttered with stacks of banned texts masked under coded bindings. The air is dry, laced with dust and chalk.

Inside, Educators Hallen, Dael, and Veyrien are already seated around a low stone basin etched with shallow glyphs. Candles flicker at the edges of the room, their flames unnaturally still.

Thaleia wastes no time. "Did they notice you?"

"No," I say, breathless.

She nods once then gestures to Veyrien.

"I'll ward," she says.

She crouches near the door, trailing a pale ash mixture in a careful circle around it. She murmurs as she draws her hand across the glyphs, her voice low, laced with something older than the current dialect. The air folds again. I've come to recognize the sensation as the feeling of a proper silence, not quiet, but sealed.

I sit and then I speak. "I've been writing to someone," I confess. "A soldier. Shadow-marked. I don't know his name."

The silence is immediate and sharp. Dael's brows draw together, Hallen leans forward, Veyrien stops tracing the ash for a moment.

"After our last meeting," I continue, "when we discussed wanting unfiltered news from the war, I had my students write letters to soldiers. Just... harmless prompts. I wrote one too. We only got one response, and it wasn't from a Light soldier."

"Wait," Dael says, his voice even. "You had your students reach out to active soldiers?"

"The prompts were generic, filtered, nothing traceable. Questions about food, dreams, memories. Just... connection."

"That's a dangerous thing to assign," Hallen says. "Even for Educators, let alone students."

"I know." I don't flinch. "But we're already risking our minds by staying silent."

Veyrien raises a brow. "And this Shadow soldier answered you?"

"Yes, quiet, small things. Fragments of what it's like on his side, things that don't match the Light's version of the story."

"You kept writing," Thaleia says, softly.

"I did, and the more I wrote, the more I realized how much we aren't allowed to know." I meet each of their eyes in turn.

There's a pause, long and weighted, then Dael leans forward, voice quiet but pointed. "And what about *Lucien*?"

The name hits the air like a blade.

Thaleia narrows her eyes slightly, but it's Hallen who speaks next. "We've seen you with him, more than once. He's not just watching you. He likes you, and you're letting him get close."

Veyrien adds, abruptly. "He's Light-marked and of the highest rank. You think they won't notice if you get too close?"

I exhale slowly. "I know what I'm doing."

"Do you?" Dael asks. "Because from out there, it looks like you're leaning too close to the leash you're trying to escape."

I meet their eyes, each in turn. "At first... I was blinded by him. By the way he spoke, the ease, the charm. He made the Light seem gentler than it is. I almost believed him."

Silence. I note a flicker of disappointment or worry, on Thaleia's face.

"But not anymore," I say. "I let him get close because he wanted to, and now? Now I keep him close because it's safer that way. He talks when he thinks I'm soft. He lets things slip."

"You're using him," Hallen says carefully.

"Yes."

Dael nods once, slowly. "Good."

Veyrien smirks faintly. "You may not have magic, Sylvaine, but you're far from powerless."

"I want to do more. I want to form a group, something quiet and student-led. Not protest but a preparation; a place to read the banned works, to ask the forbidden questions, to think without the Light listening."

Hallen shifts, considering. "And if they're caught?"

"They won't be. Not if I'm careful, not if we all are."

Veyrien folds her arms. "You'd trust students with this?"

"I'd trust the right ones, only those already asking. You know the type, they're already drifting, already suspicious. This would give them direction."

Thaleia watches me closely, then asks, "Where would this group meet?"

"I'm working on that," I say. "I'll find somewhere abandoned, hopefully low-traffic. We can ward it, disguise it."

"They can invite others," I add, looking to each of them. "You as well, if you know students who are questioning things. But only with care, trust is earned."

"You're talking about subversion," Hallen says.

"No," I say. "I'm talking about survival, and real clarity."

Thaleia leans back, finally satisfied. "Then let's make sure this doesn't fail."

She opens a drawer and pulls out three smooth, palm-sized stones etched with glyphs.

"For your rooms," she says. "They won't block the Light's surveillance completely, but they'll muddy it; smudge the transcripts, cause interference. Use them only when necessary"

Each of the Educators takes one; Veyrien studies hers carefully.

"I'll start making a list," Thaleia adds. "Students, Educators, those with eyes still capable of seeing."

"I'll send word once I've found a place," I promise.

"We'll be watching," Dael says, his voice no longer skeptical. "Not to stop you, just to help you stay standing."

The candle flames flutter, the ash circle dims. Something else glows now, a wick lit in darkness; not a blaze, but enough to warm the cold.

Three days pass before the next letter arrives. The ink is smudged, hurried, the parchment warped as if dampened by sweat... or blood.

The trees here don't move anymore. Even the wind avoids us.

We lost another group. Captured, not killed. That's worse. You know that now.

There are stories... whispers of new facilities. Light-branded compounds where even time bends beneath their hands.

They call it "holy reclamation." They say they are burning the madness out. But you and I both know what they burn first: memory, will.

You're in danger. You walk among them, but you're not invisible. Not anymore.

I miss the world before the hymns. I miss you.

—

The star is inked: small, sharp, nestled against the fold of the page.

I freeze, not because it's strange but because it's familiar.

A memory slices through me like lightning over still water: our old books, smuggled and passed between hands. The margins were cluttered with riddles, maps, half-translated glyphs... and stars, always the same five-pointed star, drawn with the slightest curve on the bottom tip, like it was leaning forward, eager.

Only one person ever drew it that way, Lysander.

My heart goes still. The air around me folds in, dense and distorted, like the moment a ward seals shut, like I've slipped behind a veil.

For a moment, I'm in the forest again.... seventeen, breathless, heart caught in the space between love and fear. Lysander had mud on his boots and fire in his voice. *"The Light isn't pure,"* he whispered. *"It's sick. Corrupt."*

He kissed me like a vow, then vanished into the trees.

He promised to come back, he never did.

I thought he was dead.

He's alive, he's fighting, he's been writing to me, all this time: through letters hidden in ash and code, through warnings wrapped in metaphor and restraint.

It's been him, it's always been him.

The letter trembles in my hands as I clutch it to my chest, and something inside me shifts.

It is not grief, not hope, but fury.

The candle burns low, a stub of trembling flame, wax pools along the base like a melted hourglass.

I sit in the silence long after the letter falls to my lap. I don't remember lying down, only the feel of sleep swallowing me: heavy, endless, already burning.

I carry one thought with me into the dark:

Let the Light come, let them try to reclaim us.

I remember now and I will not let them take anything else.

I'm a child again.

The woods are soft and green, steeped in golden dusk: everything glows, everything hums. The air smells of pine sap and wild thyme, and the light falls in slanted beams that turn dust to gold.

Lysander is ahead of me, climbing the twisted trunk of the old weeping tree with effortless grace. He laughs, full and bright, like the forest itself is laughing with him.

"Too slow, Sylvaine!" he calls, grinning down at me.

I scoop up a pinecone and throw it at him, it misses. Another laugh, and I hurl two more in protest, pretending to be angry.

"Get down!" I shout.

"Make me!"

We're children again, pure in a way only memory allows. We laugh until the wind begins to steal our voices and the trees start to shift: bark unraveling into scripture, branches curling like glyphs. The golden haze dims, and the leaves fade to ash, the woods begin to rot.

Then night falls, sudden, final, like a blade.

The dream fractures, the forest dissolves and I am somewhere else entirely: the Temple Hall, the sanctum at the heart of the academy.

It yawns around me: a great marble rotunda crowned by a ceiling of gold and stained glass, a thousand sunlit stories etched in holy fire.

It should be beautiful, it isn't.

The Verse-Keepers stand in a perfect circle, twelve of them, draped in robes that shimmer like still water. Their faces are voids, nothing but pools of molten light, where their eyes should be, halos: burning, endless.

Lysander is on his knees in the center of it all, gagged with radiant silk, Lightscript flickers across the band like shifting commandments. His wrists are bound in front of him, and they bleed not red, but Light, bright and unnatural. Light that sears the skin where it touches him.

I scream, try to run, but my feet won't move. The floor beneath me is slick with ink and ash, thick as spilled truth.

They begin to chant.

> *Order is peace.*
> *Obedience is salvation.*
> *Emotion breeds madness.*
> *Memory is rebellion.*

Each word hammers through the chamber, a spell written in rhythm. Each phrase strikes something inside me, like it's meant to undo me.

One of them steps forward, torch in hand. They approach a raised brazier carved with scripture. One by one, they begin tossing books into it.

My books: journals, field notes, essays, poems I wrote in the dark, pages I tore from forgotten volumes.

They curl into glowing cinders.

"No," I try to say. "No, stop..."

But my arms are suddenly bound, my mouth sewn shut with threads of Light, like gold, but alive, worming, burning.

I can't scream.

Lysander turns his head, his eyes find mine; they are filled with sorrow, rage, and love. He tries to speak, but the fire roars louder than our childhood.

Then he's gone, everything's gone.

I wake gasping.

Sweat slicks my skin, the sheets a knot around my limbs. The candle has gone out and Shadows pool at the edges of the room: thick, watching, still.

They do not speak, they do not leave.

The dream comes again, and again, and again.

And every time, I burn a little less with fear and a little more with fury.

My star,

Your letters arrive like a soft breath in a room full of shadows.

You were right: memory is the first thing they burn. But some of us are smoke-stained and still breathing. Some of us carry ash like armor.

I saw your mark. I knew it instantly. Strange how a single shape, small and familiar, can realign an entire world. Like a compass, or a promise.

I can't say more yet, but hopefully soon. Until then, hold the line where you are. I'll do the same.

I hope this letter finds you well, wherever you are.

Noctis,

Your words reached me. Even through the smoke, I knew them.

We used to talk about constellations that don't show up on any map, shapes we invented between the stars. I think I see a new one now.

It bends toward the horizon, looks a little like hope, if you squint.

You remembered the mark. That means something held, they haven't taken everything, not from you.

We're scattered out here, but we're still watching. Still listening. Even silence carries meaning, if you know where to look.

If you're planting seeds, plant deep. The Light scorches the surface, but it rarely digs.

If you find others who still dream, remind them: not all ghosts are dead, some are just waiting to be named again.

Be careful with your fire but don't let it go out. Until the sky clears.

LIVING NIGHTMARE

I THINK THE STRESS is starting to get to me. I've stretched myself too thin; worn the mask too long, let the seams fray.

I've been teaching the Light's doctrine with a steady voice I no longer recognize. I've been enduring the Order's constant surveillance. I've been sidestepping Lucien's warmth like it's not laced with warning. I've been avoiding Elowen's gaze, lest she see too much. I've been stealing time for hushed meetings with Thaleia and the others. I've been writing letters to Lysander that are half code and half confession...

I am beginning to crack, not loudly, not visibly, but quietly, internally; hairline fractures beneath the surface.

I no longer feel rooted in my own life, as if I've become unmoored from linear time, drifting sideways through moments that repeat, distort, and split apart mid-breath. My waking hours feel like echoes: warped, stretched thin over the bones of reality.

The fraying starts small...

A flickering lantern in the corridor, pulsing in a rhythm that matches my heartbeat. A chalkboard that split down the middle without being touched: clean, surgical, like it had simply had enough.

Yesterday, the ink in my quill turned to smoke the instant it touched the page: no warning, no smell, just ink one second, smoke the next. My words were erased before they could exist.

Today, it was the Shadows, my students' shadows move *before* they did: not delayed, but anticipatory, gesturing before hands rose, tilting heads before thoughts were formed, mouthing answers to questions I hadn't asked yet. They twitched at the edges of my vision, always just shy of direct confrontation, like they knew they shouldn't be seen.

I excused myself mid-lecture, my voice cracking on a syllable I don't remember, my heart pounding like war drums in my chest. It was deafening in the hollow silence that followed. I didn't wait for their reactions, I didn't offer an explanation, I ran.

My shoes struck the stone too hard, too fast, the echo of each step sharp as a snapped twig in a silent forest. I kept my eyes forward, afraid that if I looked behind me, Shadows would follow.

Am I unraveling?

Am I coming loose from the thread of what is real, what is safe, what is mine?

Fraying. Wild at the seams. Uncontainable.

If Lucien sees this, it's over. One misplaced word, one tremor too strong, one breath held too long, and the Light will descend; not as justice, but as a cleansing, and I will not survive it.

Control yourself, Sylvaine.

That's what I tell myself, over and over.

But how do you control what you don't understand?

How do you bind something that no longer obeys the laws of the world?

Who can I even ask for help in a place where questions are sedition?

In a place where curiosity is called corruption?

The cold finds me quickly once I'm outside, needling through my dress and cloak, wrapping itself around my limbs like a second skin. The garden path is rimmed in frost, light illuminating the cracks in the stone.

I walk past shuttered windows, dead fountains, statues of saints I no longer name; hoping the cold will wake me, hoping the stillness will offer clarity. The silence outside only amplifies the chaos within: every step feels both too loud and not loud enough, every breath is a strange and foreign thing.

I stand beneath the withered arbor of night-blooming ivy and press a hand to my ribs. My breath stutters then steadies.

Breathe, in, out, in again: until the panic dulls to a low throb, until the Shadows stop swaying, until I remember who I'm pretending to be.

Focus. You have to look calm, always calm... they only hunt what panics.

Underneath the surface, beneath the mask, the discipline, the stillness... the Shadows still move, not violently, not wrongly, just... *present.*

They pulse with my breath, stretch with my thoughts. They feel familiar, like something I used to know, something I once belonged to; no, something that once belonged to *me.*

I press a trembling palm to my stomach, to the deep center of myself where the Light dares not reach.

I can't stay here.

I find my way into the main corridor again. Back in the academy halls, everything feels half-abandoned: the lanterns have burned low, the corridors are veiled in a hush of soot and candle-smoke, silvered by moonlight and threaded with shadow. I move softly, cloaked and alone, fingers trailing along cold walls.

The air in Umbraxis holds its age like a scent, *magic,* long asleep but not quite dead. It breathes around me, slow and patient, like something remembering itself.

I knock along walls, gently, carefully, searching for hollows, listening for what others have forgotten.

The old ballroom comes first. Its chandeliers are shattered, frozen mid-fall like crystal raindrops never reaching the floor. The parquet is cracked, warped by time, but the golden inlays still glint in the dark like veins. It's too exposed, too open to watching eyes, too many stories caught in the walls.

The conference hall is worse. Once the stage of debate, now a tomb of silence: broken benches, long-dead arguments. The windows gape like wounds, baring the room to the wind. The cold there doesn't feel natural, it clings, it waits.

I keep walking, deeper. As the corridors narrow, the air thins.

At the library, I try the lower stacks, but the iron gate is still sealed, runes pulsing ephemerally: warding, watching. It is almost as if the books themselves have teeth, and know not to trust me, and still...something watches me back; not cruel, just curious, like the walls are listening.

I pause before one of the lesser-used wings, an annex once meant for foreign diplomats, long since closed. The door is warped, the handle rusted, but it yields when I press. The hinges groan like something roused from sleep. The room beyond is shrouded in dust and dimness, but it's dry, walled in thick stone, with no windows and only one entrance.

This could work, if I don't find something more secure. I mark it mentally and I will return.

On the way back, I feel a shift again.

The sensation is faint, like the air rippling just behind me: a breath that isn't mine, a whisper without words. The kind of presence you'd miss if you didn't already know what it felt like to be haunted, or chosen.

Am I losing my mind?

Or remembering something I was never meant to forget?

Days blur into nights: I teach, I smile, I survive.

But beneath the rhythm of lectures and doctrine, beneath the dull chant of Light-approved truths, something else pulses; something dark, and deep, and not unkind. It is not evil but free.

The Shadows no longer wait behind me, they walk beside me now and I think, no, *I know*, they have been waiting for me to wake up.

At faculty galas, I sip wine with shaking hands and let the laughter of others carry mine. My smile is faultless, polished like glass. When Lucien offers his arm, I take it with a practiced grace, weaving through the room like a woman who belongs.

"You've adapted well," he says one evening, handing me a glass of something dry and expensive. His fingers brush mine for a second too long. "Better than most."

I meet his gaze for half a second, cool, unreadable, then glance away as though I'm simply shy, not cautious. "It's easier when you don't ask questions."

He hums, low and amused. "That's the spirit."

I can't tell if he's mocking me or admiring the lie. His expression never changes, but his eyes always seem to know more than they say. I nod politely and say nothing, I never say too much.

It's a dance now, isn't it? One we both know the steps to.

I pretend not to notice how tightly he watches, he pretends it's admiration, or trust, or perhaps something else entirely.

In the classroom, it's worse.

His eyes follow me like shackles, invisible but unyielding. I feel him in the back row, silent, motionless, watching me more than the students. Watching not just what I say, but what I don't, measuring the space between my words.

I teach the mandated texts, brittle things, all surface and silence; sterile histories scrubbed clean of blood and rebellion. My voice flattens as I speak them: no inflection, no nuance, no questions.

Never any questions.

Every time I quiet a student's spark, every time I pretend that myth is truth and truth is myth, something inside me fractures. It's a slow erosion, a soul worn thin by compliance.

Today, after class, one of the braver girls lingers. She's clever, I've seen it in the way she hesitates before speaking, the way her eyes follow more than just the words on the page.

"Educator?" she asks, clutching her journal like a shield. "Was there... was there meant to be more to the story? It feels like something's missing."

I freeze, just for a moment. The air in the room thickens. The wrong answer could ruin us both.

I glance over her shoulder, Lucien is just outside the door, speaking with another Educator. His posture is relaxed, but his head tilts slightly, listening.

I want to tell her everything. I want to unseal the vault of truth and let it flood these quiet halls. I want to rip the lies from the walls and let the truth bleed through like ink through silk. Instead, I lower my voice.

"There's always more," I say softly, almost too soft to hear. "But not all stories are safe to speak aloud."

She stares at me, eyes wide. She's young but not naive, she hears what I'm really saying. The silence between us hums with shared understanding.

She nods, almost imperceptibly, and hugs her journal tighter.

In that moment, something small and flickering passes between us, not rebellion but the beginning of something that could be.

She leaves without another word.

I sit at my desk for a long time afterward, staring at the hollow text I've just taught, wondering how long I can keep pretending, wondering how many more sparks I'll be asked to smother before I forget how to burn.

After class, after Lucien, after the daily theater of compliance and careful silence...

I slip free from the polished corridors and gilded gazes. I let the mask fall from my face the moment no one is looking. I become only breath and bone again: quiet, unseen.

I search, again.

The ballroom, the conference hall, the locked lower stacks of the old library, they're no longer enough. They echo but they don't speak and the strange pressure in my chest, that quiet gravity pulling me inward, downward, refuses to relent... so I follow it.

By moonlight, I trace the forgotten tilework beneath worn rugs, finger-tips brushing ancient carvings barely visible beneath layers of plaster and neglect. I let my steps be guided more by instinct than logic, led not by knowledge, but by memory I shouldn't have.

One night, I find it.

Deep within the south wing, beyond the lecture halls and cabinets filled with obsolete scrolls and dust-laden ledgers, I come upon a breach in the wall: a collapsed alcove concealed behind a moth-eaten tapestry, where vines curl through shattered stone. At first glance, it appears to be nothing more than rubble and decay.

Yet as I step closer, the ivy gives way. The stone groans. A narrow tunnel, shrouded in shadow, slowly opens before me.

My breath catches.

I squeeze through sideways, shoulders scraping cold rock, the darkness swallowing the lantern light behind me. The air changes into something damper, older. It smells of deep earth and leaf-litter. The corridor narrows, then abruptly expands into a clearing, a forgotten garden, long surrendered to time.

The walls fall away.

Trees rise, not towering, but dense and ancient, their branches braided into arches. Moss chokes the crumbling stone benches, ferns spill over marble paths cracked by root and frost. Here, moonlight filters through a tangle of branches like fractured silver.

The silence is so complete it hums. The air feels untouched, sacred, and still wild.

I step inside like I'm crossing a threshold into a memory I've never lived: each footfall lands with reverence, each rustle of leaf and snap of twig sounds too loud in the quiet.

This is the place.

I stand in the center, heart pounding like a signal drum, head bowed like I've arrived at a chapel. My hand curls to my chest. The pull that brought me here settles, quieter now, as if it has reached home.

I pace the garden's edge, cautious but purposeful. My breath plumes like fog. The trees lean in, listening, the Shadows do not shrink from me, they shift, soft, like animals settling near a fire.

Back in my cabin, I light only a single candle, the wax drips slow as rain while I write, hands trembling.

Meet me past the south tunnel. Do not speak of this.
No questions are forbidden. No voices silenced. Burn this after you read it.

The ink runs slightly where my tears fall, I don't wipe them away.

By morning, I've written more. Each message folded with care, the handwriting clean and sure even as my pulse stutters.

In class, I slip them into textbooks and satchels when no one is watching: one in a poetry anthology, another between the pages of a copied sermon. Each placement is deliberate, careful, a risk calculated and taken anyway.

At dismissal, I say nothing, I only watch.

Some students glance down, surprised to find folded parchment, some don't notice at all. I don't blame them, fear is a kind of blindness... it's taught that way, bred into us like obedience.

I walk back to my chambers alone, the weight of what I've done presses against my ribs like a second heartbeat.

I don't know if anyone will come. Maybe none of them will and still, I wait.

I believe: despite the silence, despite the danger, despite the weight that is always Lucien's gaze... I believe my students will come, and when they do, they will come to more than a garden.

MAGIC SURGE

I T IS THE NIGHT before our first meeting, the night before everything changes. My heart is a frantic drum, caught somewhere between hope and terror. Excitement prickles my skin, but so does the cold bite of doubt.

Do we need a name?

Something sharp, like a blade?

Something unforgettable, like a legend whispered by ghosts in half-forgotten tongues?

A name that will echo across time, long after we are dust and memory?

I lie in the dark, eyes tracing the silver filaments of moonlight through my shutters. Gods, listen to me... what does it matter what we're called if we're caught before we even begin?

I breathe deep, slow, steady. I cannot let myself spiral. Everything will work out, it has to.

Despite the trembling beneath my skin, sleep finds me. It's not like before; this dream is different.

There is a darkness that breathes; whispers that taste like honey and ash.

A hush falls over the dark. A breeze, scented with wildflowers and dusk, curls around me. The air softens.

Suddenly, I feel seen, desired, known.

Lysander is here, or maybe not. Maybe I conjured him from the ache that lives just behind my ribs. In this place, he feels realer than reality.

He walks through the darkness like it's water, like it bends around him. His smile is a secret just for me. His eyes are lit from within, silver, gleaming, infinite. He reaches out and when his fingers touch mine, the dream blooms.

We're in a meadow that doesn't exist in the waking world...

We are surrounded by moonlit grass, petals that float like stardust, and a sky that breathes in hues I don't have names for.

Time forgets to move.

We are in Velmourn's forgotten soul, a place lost to the waking realm, buried in memory. It looks a lot like the forest I grew up in; a sacred glade, untouched by war, untouched by fire.

Some say the god of Shadow still walks the dream-veil, whispering to those who remember the world before it burned.

Sylvaine, Lysander whispers, and my name sounds like a promise.

He kisses me like he's never been allowed to before, like we've been waiting lifetimes for this moment. His hands are slow, reverent, aching with need.

Each touch is a vow, each sigh is a confession. We sink into the meadow, the earth soft beneath us, damp with memory, humming with recognition. His mouth trails down my throat like a benediction, poetic and reverent.

My back arches into him. His fingers skim my skin, and the world pulses with our desire.

All around us there are flowers blooming, stars falling, roots curling around us like an embrace.

The ground drinks our heat. The sky sighs. The air feels like a witness.

His hands memorize me. His mouth worships me.

I offer myself freely, utterly, without shame or fear.

It's dreamy, drenched in lust, but more than that, it's holy.

There is nothing gentle about the way our bodies meet.

It's not fragile. It's desperate, consuming, something ancient in its hunger. It is like the first fire, like the last breath; a communion, a claiming, a ritual older than speech.

When I cry out, it's not a name but a surrender, a release of everything I've ever been. Just before I shatter completely, he looks into me and says:

You asked me to count the stars to show you my love, so I did. One for every breath you took, every silence we didn't get to share, and still, the sky is endless. So here I am, still counting.

I hover somewhere between sleep and waking, my skin warm, limbs heavy.

I think I hear my name again: soft, reverent, wrapped in longing. Something touches me, not a hand but a feeling.

I open my eyes, fully awake now, and something is still touching me, not just in the dream.

Shadows.

I start to panic, but calm as they slide over me like silk drawn taut, tracing every curve, every hollow, every trembling inch. They know my body better than I do. They curl behind my knees, under my spine, across my breasts.

When the Shadows find my nipples, tweaking, rolling, teasing, I gasp, and heat floods through me. I feel myself grow slick, aching. The sensations are too good, too much.

This can't be happening. This has to still be a dream.

As if sensing my thoughts, mocking them, the Shadows twine around my neck, holding me still, restricting my breath; not quite painful, but deliberate, dominant.

They slither lower with wicked patience, taunting, making sure I know just how real this is.

They reach between my thighs and part them indulgently and soak up my wetness as they begin to circle my clit, lazy and cruel.

My back arches. My lips part in a soundless cry. Pleasure shudders through me like a living thing.

I never feel this with Lucien; never like this and never this much.

As if offended by the comparison, the Shadows slap my clit, sharp and punishing. I choke on a gasp.

Okay, they definitely know my thoughts.

They return to their rhythm, more relentless now; stroking, circling, filling me with thick tendrils that stretch and press and claim. My walls clench around them, needy and desperate.

The pressure builds. The pleasure blinds.

I gasp, but no air comes.

There is no breath here, only sensation.

Pleasure surges through me: violent, exquisite, unrelenting. My body feels like lightning, born of memory and hunger. My back bows.

It isn't gentle, it isn't soft, it's all-consuming. Brutal in its beauty.

Do these Shadows belong to me?

Do they belong to someone else?

Can Shadows even work that way?

They feel like Lysander; heavier than a memory, hungrier than a ghost.

My hands tremble. My thighs ache. Magic thrums just beneath my skin, ravenous. The candle beside my bed has melted down to a puddle of wax.

I can still feel it, him, them?

For a moment, I don't move.

I simply lie there, staring at the ceiling, waiting for my heartbeat to settle, but it doesn't.

There's a pressure in the air, a hum beneath the silence. The shadows in the corners no longer resemble the soft silhouettes of furniture shaped by flickering flame. They feel sentient now: watchful, patient, waiting.

My fingers twitch.

I sit up slowly.

My nightdress clings to me, soaked through, nearly translucent at the chest and hips. My thighs are slick with the evidence of what happened.

I bring my fingers to my neck where I feel a faint tenderness, a ghost of pressure. There are no bruises but my body remembers, and worse: it *aches* for more.

I swing my legs over the side of the bed and inhale deep, sharp, trying to pull myself together. Something catches in my breath, a hitch, like magic still clinging to the back of my throat.

I look down at my hands.

They're trembling faintly, and not just from the cold, They're trembling from something deeper, something resonant. My fingertips tingle, like they've been dipped in starlight. The skin across my palms is flushed, glowing faintly; not gold like the Light doctrine teaches, like the sanctioned glyphs and runes etched into the academy's altar stones.

It is something else, warmer, wilder; a shimmer that shifts like oil in water, hues I don't have names for, fleeting, almost imperceptible.

Then it's gone, not burned away but drawn inward, absorbed.

I flex my fingers. They feel different, denser, like power has settled inside my bones and hasn't decided yet if it wants to stay.

I rise on unsteady legs and cross to the mirror. My reflection meets me, wide-eyed and flushed, lips parted, neck flushed pink. I don't recognize the woman looking back at me, or maybe, for the first time, I do.

My hair's a mess. My body's still pulsing from the memory of him and yet I feel... whole, seen, claimed, and that terrifies me more than anything.

I whisper his name, barely audible: "Lysander." It is the first time I've spoken it aloud in years.

The mirror darkens slightly, just for a heartbeat; like something heard me, like something answered.

I stumble back.

The candle beside my bed is entirely gone now, not burned down, but melted. Even the holder is warped, scorched in a strange spiral. Magic residue crackles faintly in the air, like static just beneath the surface of thought.

I grip the bedpost.

What the hell happened to me?

I sit again carefully, as if the floor beneath me might vanish. Outside, the sky begins to lighten; morning presses faintly against the horizon.

The day of the first meeting has come.

I should be preparing. I should be focused.

Instead, I sit in the quiet, waiting for my hands to stop shaking, waiting for my heart to remember its rhythm, wondering how much of me still belongs to me at all.

THE FIRST MEETING

THE *FLARES* ARE GETTING worse: bigger, bolder, less interested in hiding.

At first, I think I am imagining it. A shimmer in the far corner of the lecture hall. A ripple across the stone like heat on glass. A torchlight twitches, but there's no breeze. A curl of Shadow where none should be, pressed flat against the marble, wrong in its angle, its texture, watching.

I blink and it's gone, or pretending to be.

I press on.

Midway through my morning lecture, I feel it again, a low buzz at the base of my spine; not fear, not pain, just... awareness, something there. The shadows from the ivy above the blackboard rustles faintly, like breath caught between words. I glance up and it stills.

My throat tightens and I grip the chalk harder.

I continue speaking in flat and practiced tones This is *The Radiant Order,* a text so sanitized it practically hums with sanctimony.

"Obedience is the truest shape of love," I recite. "And the purest love is silent."

My voice is too calm, too measured. I don't believe a word of it.

The students are quiet, they always are. The Light does not reward curiosity.

I turn to scrawl a passage on the board when something flickers at the edge of my vision. My stomach drops as I look down.

The Shadows at my feet are moving, not twitching, not shifting with the light, but *moving*.

They stretch slowly across the floor, then slither up the side of the podium, dark and gleaming, fluid, like ink in water: reaching, curious, sentient.

The front row sees it. I hear a gasp. A girl's quill clatters to the floor. I snap the chalk in half in my hand without realizing it.

There is a beat of silence that is both thick and electric.

I force my voice out, too loud, too sharp. "Order cannot exist," I say, eyes fixed forward, "without something to contain it."

The room holds its breath as the Shadows still.

I continue, softer now. "Light defends itself against the dark."

There's a ripple of tension across the students, a few nod, cautious, thoughtful, others shift uncomfortably in their seats. They all feel it: something's off, something's here.

But no one speaks, they never do: not here, not in front of me, not where every question feels like a trap.

I hold until the last student files out, until the last set of footsteps fades down the corridor, then I move fast.

I slam the textbook shut and stack my notes with shaking hands. My fingers are clammy and the chalk dust clings to my skin like ash. My breath is short, shallow. My heart races in time with the Shadows still curling near the corners of the room.

I try to make it look routine, just another day, just another lecture, but I'm unraveling inside. Under the fear, sharper, hungrier, is hope.

It's reckless, it's dangerous, and I can't stop it from blooming.

The moment I step into the corridor, Lucien appears.

Of course he does.

"Sylvaine," he says, voice smooth as silk, polished and practiced. He offers a polite nod, all courteous charm. "Another compelling lecture. You're making quite the impression."

I force a smile but it feels brittle on my face. "The rune transcriptions must be reaching you faster these days."

He chuckles softly, just enough to be disarming. "Efficiency is everything."

His gaze lingers; not just on my face, but through me, like he's peeling back layers. He always watches. I feel it like heat on the back of my neck, like shackles tightening.

Then, too casually, he brushes a stray lock of hair from my cheek. His fingers are cool, possessive, measured.

He kisses my forehead, a gesture that should be intimate but it leaves my skin feeling cold. Then he walks away as if nothing ever happened, as if he doesn't know what he just took.

My robes swish against the stone tiles as I turn the next corner. The air in the corridor has shifted, quieter than usual, tense; like the moment before thunder breaks.

I barely make it to my quarters before the panic overtakes me.

I drop my satchel and my books spill across the floor. I don't care.

I strip off my teaching robes and throw on my cloak, fingers fumbling the clasp. I don't eat. I don't light a candle. I don't sit. I just move.

Later, I leave my cabin; no one sees me slip out. I don't light a lantern.

The wind cuts sharp as a blade, frost needling through the seams in my boots. My breath curls in the air, pale and fleeting. I pull my cloak tighter, hood low, and begin the slow walk east, then south.

The path is uneven. No paved stone or curated trail, just frostbitten grass, bramble, and the crunch of frozen earth beneath my feet. I move quickly, heart pounding. Every window I pass feels like an eye, every branch is like a reaching hand.

The southern entrance looms ahead, half-swallowed in ivy and dusk. The wind shifts and carries something with it, wildflowers and smoke, or maybe memory.

I don't hesitate, I press forward.

The tunnel mouth looms ahead, hidden beneath the thick veil of ivy.

The ivy doesn't resist me but yields to me; it parts beneath my hand like breath, like a curtain pulled back on something sacred. I slip inside, heart pounding.

The earth here is cold, old and alive. My boots press into soil that remembers. The wind nips at my cheeks, stings my eyes.

One by one, my students arrive as shapes moving through the darkness, cautious but steady, steps muffled, hoods drawn low. I count them first by motion, then by breath. The frost crunches lightly beneath their feet, but otherwise, the night holds.

My chest tightens as each figure enters the clearing.

Lina is first, sharp eyes catching every flicker of movement, every tremor of the trees. Her mouth is a thin line, her jaw set like stone. She used to make me laugh during study sessions, used to argue for the sheer joy of it. Now she's quieter, hardened since the week she disappeared, since she came back different.

Mira comes next, always trailing behind, but never lost. She is quiet, strategic. The kind who watches first, speaks later, and only when it matters. She doesn't make a sound now, but her gaze scans the glade, already assessing.

Laen follows; heart far too soft for this world, even softer for this school. His magic used to pulse like music, bright and uncontrolled. Now it shivers inside him, barely visible. I feel it under his skin when he passes near: stifled, caged.

Then Aric, with that same unimpressed slouch he wears in lectures. He scoffs at everything, especially the sacred texts, especially himself. But he's here and that means something.

Tomas, of course, holding a leather-bound book too tightly, fingers smudged with ink. The poor boy memorizes ancient languages the way others memorize songs. He looks terrified but determined.

Mirielle; tender, upright, eyes clear. Her presence steadies me.

Calyra, her flame barely disguised, always simmering beneath the surface. She never speaks unless she wants to burn something down. Her smile tonight is small, dangerous.

Elswyn, golden child of the Light, the one who should not have come, and yet here they are. They once turned in a paper so dazzlingly faithful to Light rhetoric it was published, but I know what they really believe. I see it in their eyes now.

Rellington, all quiet muscle and brutal grace. He barely speaks in class, but when he does, it slices clean. He nods to me as he enters, a silent affirmation.

And Lenore, a blade in girl's clothing. Her essays made me weep once. Her eyes meet mine now with something between warning and worship.

Nine.

Then Thaleia steps into the clearing, her cloak tugged tight. Gods. My breath catches. Sweet, sweet Thaleia, too perceptive, too knowing. She doesn't speak, but her gaze locks with mine like a whispered challenge, but it's not just her.

Three figures follow behind.

Educator Veyrien, tall and sharp as a winter blade.

Educator Dael, older, with eyes like cracked glass.

And Educator Hallen, quiet but heavy with power.

Behind them, more students, nine, maybe ten, their faces unfamiliar but lit with the same cautious defiance. Called not by me, but by whisper, by rumor, by hope.

My voice catches in my throat as I step forward.

There is no podium, no chalkboard, just the earth beneath our feet and the wild canopy above.

"You came," I say softly.

Some nod, some don't, but none turn away.

"It's not safe," I continue. "You know that. You knew before you ever set foot in this place and you still came."

They wait, breaths held, Shadows listening.

I pace the edge of the fireless circle. "The Light's grip is tightening. You feel it. I know you do. The lectures are thinner, censorship is thicker. My hours with you aren't mine anymore and I miss you."

A few heads lift at that. One of the new students chokes softly on a sound that might be a laugh.

"I miss your questions. I miss hearing your minds open. I miss not being afraid to wonder with you."

A flicker, not from a torch, but from the Shadows in the trees, curling and shifting like they're inching closer to hear.

"We were taught that knowledge is illumination," I say. "But the light we're given? It's too bright. It blinds. It bleaches out the edges, the colors, the contradiction."

"Control," Lenore mutters. "Wrapped in devotion."

"Exactly." I nod. "*The Radiant Order*? It teaches obedience as a form of divinity. But obedience to whom? For what?"

A low murmur moves through the group.

Mira steps forward. "They scraped out the bones of the old myths. Left us the shell."

Tomas unrolls a scroll, hands shaking. "I cross-referenced three copies of the same sermon, five years apart. The original says nothing about divine submission. That was added."

"I've seen it too," says Veyrien. "Pre-schism texts called the dark sacred. Not sinful. Sacred."

"Until they decided only Light was allowed to speak," Dael adds, voice bitter.

One of the unfamiliar students, the youngest, shifts uncomfortably. "If it's all lies, why are they so afraid of us finding out?"

I step closer. The Shadows around me pulse faintly, reacting to the tension, to the truth. The moss beneath our feet glows for half a second, like breath, like heartbeat, then stills.

"Because stories are power," I say. "And the truth is a story they didn't write."

A thick silence follows. Then Elswyn drops to their knees, draws a circle in the dirt with one finger. Their head is bowed, but not in prayer, in defiance.

"We should name it," someone murmurs. "This place. This gathering. It matters now."

"Nox's Hollow," Mira suggests.

"Nightroot," Calyra counters.

Mirielle tilts her head. "No, naming binds it too early. Let it stay fluid."

They look to me and I pause, heart pounding.

Magic coils in the clearing: uneasy, electric, expectant. It does not blaze or burn, it waits, like a question no one dares to speak aloud.

In the branches above, something rustles: not wind, not animal, *attention.*

The trees seem to lean in. The Shadows hold their shape, as if watching, listening. For a moment, we are not students, not teachers, not rebels or traitors. We are witnesses, we are rememberers.

Something has begun that cannot be unmade.

Then, quiet as dusk, Thaleia moves.

She steps forward, soft-footed, lowering herself to the earth with a grace that doesn't disturb even the frost. She doesn't look at me, doesn't look at anyone, only at the dirt beneath her knees, the raw and waiting soil.

Without a word, she begins to draw with her finger in the soft soil.

A shape takes form, not a symbol from the academy's scrolls, nor from the Verse-Keepers' canon. This is older than all of it.

A circle, open at one edge, a spiral nested within, a line that cuts through, but does not break. The shape is strange, gentle, and complete. It is half root, half moon, wrapped in thorns. I know it, of course I know it.

She gave it to me weeks ago, in silence, in trust. She gave it to me as a child, in strength, in memory.

Finished now, it seems to hum in the soil, vibrating at a pitch I can't hear but feel: low, deep, true.

When Thaleia finally speaks, her voice is a hush that still somehow carries.

"It's not a rune of Light, or Shadow, or even magic," she says. "It came before those. Before language. It is called the First Rune. Earth's rune."

A ripple moves through the group, uncertain, awed.

"It means balance," Thaleia says. "Among other things. It means cycles. Breath. Root. Return. It means all things in harmony, even the ones we're told should not be."

The clearing responds.

The ground beneath the rune vibrates, faint but real, as if recognizing itself. A murmur rises from the soil, like a memory stirring. Some step back instinctively, others lean in, hungry.

I step toward her, knees bending to meet her at the edge of the mark.

She whispers, only so I can hear. "I offered it to you before, but that was like sowing a seed before the soil was ready."

"And now?"

Her eyes lift to mine. "Now it's ready. You are ready."

I place my palm over the rune. The vibration warms against my skin, no Light flares, no Shadow coils, just *life*.

Balance.

Around us, the circle draws a little tighter, not by command but by gravity.

We don't speak. We don't need to.

The earth remembers and now, so do we.

A Tightening Leash

THERE ARE GUARDS IN the back now, lined along the walls of my classroom like statues: eyes forward, hands within easy reach of their hilts. Their uniforms gleam, stitched with the white-gold sigils of the Luminary Guard, immaculate even beneath the dust of old chalk and older ideas.

Lucien says they're there for "safety," that "recent unrest" has made vigilance necessary. His tone is always smooth, his concern just warm enough to sound genuine.

But we both know the truth.

They're not here to guard me, they're here to watch me, contain me, remind me.

Someone from the Order sits in on every lecture now. Most days, it's Elowen; severe, silent, her hair always scraped back like it's ashamed of softness. But more often, lately, it's Lucien.

He never sits in the front, always the back row, arms folded, legs crossed with casual elegance. His half-lidded eyes always look bored if you don't know what to look for, if you don't understand that his stillness is a kind of violence.

He watches everything: the cadence of my voice, the inflection when I quote doctrine, how I pause between ideas, who among the students dares to nod.

He watches me, and he watches them.

Sometimes he intercepts me in the corridor between lectures, always when the halls are empty, always with that practiced ease that makes intrusion feel like flirtation.

He leans just close enough to make stepping back look like weakness.

"Glowing review from the Order," he murmurs. "They adore how you make doctrine feel like poetry."

His hand brushes the small of my back; just a touch, a pressure that says *obedience*, that says *mine*.

"There is something waiting for you in your cabin," he adds.

He never raises his voice, he never threatens, he doesn't have to. Lucien is fluent in implication, in the seduction of power and proximity. He wears charm like a blade dressed in silk.

I stand still, spine straight; a puppet carved from poise. Around us, conversation flows like wine, sweet, cloying, and just as intoxicating. No one sees the strings, not here, not among them.

The chandelier above us glitters with captured starlight, or some arcane imitation of it: too perfect, too bright. Everything about the hall is like that; marble polished to a mirror, golden banners embroidered with the sigil of the Light, columns etched with scripture no one here truly follows.

Lucien's hand rests lightly at the small of my back, guiding me through the crowd like I'm a thing he owns but hasn't quite unwrapped yet.

"Smile," he murmurs, lips barely brushing my ear. "They're looking."

I do, just enough. My lips curve with the precision of a blade, but my eyes do not gleam.

I can't remember the last time they did.

The gown I wear tonight is champagne silk: sleeveless, backless, and perilously tight. It was waiting for me in my quarters.

It fits so tightly I can't take a full breath, but the intent is clear: stillness, silence, submission dressed as elegance.

Heels bite into my arches as I walk, each step a reminder that even movement can be curated, restrained.

Around us, the banquet hums with laughter and clinking glasses. Politicians in robes spun with threads of Light discuss tariffs on "heretical provinces." Verse-Keepers toast to "moral purges." A general chuckles about "how quickly fire makes believers of the stubborn."

I nod. I sip. I don't choke.

My smile says *how enlightening,* my heart says *run*.

Lucien steers me toward a crescent of Light-born nobility gathered near the golden fountain at the hall's center. Its waters shimmer with spell light, charmed to mirror the constellations wheeling overhead. The surface ripples as we approach, catching the light in a way that feels too deliberate, too choreographed.

Heads turn, robes shift, deference stirs the cluster like wind through tall grass.

"Ah, Educator Sylvaine," coos a High Luminary in gold-threaded vestments. His eyes glint, calculating. "Still outshining half the faculty, I hear."

"She's more than that," Lucien replies, smiling with effortless warmth. "She's a revelation. Her lectures illuminate doctrine in ways even the old priests struggle to emulate."

There is a beat of polite laughter. One bishop bows his head, a general offers a slow, approving nod. Someone murmurs my name as if tasting it.

Lucien's hand hovers at the base of my spine, a touch light enough to pass as fondness, but firm enough to steer, to display.

"I hope you've had the chance to speak with her," he says, gesturing me forward. "Her work with the Order has already produced remarkable shifts in engagement. You should see the archives, her lesson copies circulate like relics."

I see a flicker of genuine interest in a few faces. A Verse-Keeper leans in slightly.

"She teaches the Light not as dogma," Lucien continues, "but as devotion. As a story. Flame woven into language. You'd think she was born beneath the sun itself."

More smiles, more toasts. The compliments swirl like incense, rich and suffocating.

"She brings clarity," he finishes. "A rare thing in these times."

I offer the expected smile, soft as moonlight. I incline my head. I let them believe I am all the things he says.

What I do not say is that some of the students cry after class. That some of them don't recite doctrine, they rewrite it. I don't say that I keep a stack of burned parchment and secret questions, whispered in rooms with no windows.

Lucien lifts a glass, voice rising just enough to catch the attention of those nearby. "To Sylvaine," he says, "who reminds us all that the Light is not only law, but language. Not only discipline, but beauty."

There's a ripple of clinking flutes, a toast, a murmur of approval. I sip the champagne and let it burn.

"She's a force," someone says.

"She's the future," Lucien adds, his eyes never leaving mine.

The chandelier above us scatters starlight like shattered glass. Every face turned to me glows with reflective gold, but none of it feels warm.

I raise my glass again. I smile again.

I nod. I perform.

But beneath the silk and ceremony, something coils tighter with every word spoken about me rather than to me, every compliment that doubles as a cage.

Lucien's hand hasn't left my back. When a lesser guard stumbles too close, eyes bleary with drink and curiosity, his fingers press a little deeper, a subtle tilt of possession.

This one is claimed.

I see her then, Elowen, drifting toward us with her usual elegance, lips painted like blood-roses, posture precise. She's surrounded by two Luminary Guards and a pale-haired Scribe, but her eyes are locked on Lucien.

And on me.

She smiles, but the sharpness of it cuts. "Educator Sylvaine," she purrs, her voice sweet with false civility, "how radiant you look this evening. The gown suits you. Someone chose very well."

Lucien chuckles. "I have excellent taste."

The corners of Elowen's mouth twitch, a twitch too brief to be called a smile. "Oh, I've never doubted that."

Her gaze drags down the length of me, neckline to hem, and back again. Noting the skin, the closeness, the way Lucien's hand rests comfortably against the curve of my waist.

"Such poise," she continues. "It's almost easy to forget how recently you were appointed. Not everyone ascends so quickly." The implication glistens beneath her words like a knife beneath satin.

Lucien's grip tenses almost imperceptibly. "Merit rises fast in times of need," he replies smoothly, eyes still on me. "And Sylvaine has proven indispensable."

"Mm," Elowen hums, tilting her glass but not drinking. "Indispensable. Of course."

The silence that follows is brief, brittle. Another guard leans in with a joke about doctrine and diplomacy, and the group's attention shifts.

Elowen lingers a heartbeat longer, gaze flicking between us. Her smile fades, and what's left behind is raw and unmasked; want, not of me, but of what I represent, of *him*.

She walks away without another word, gown whispering over the polished stone like a departing curse.

Lucien leans in again, lips brushing too near my ear. "Don't mind Elowen," he murmurs. "She lacks your... elegance."

I manage a sound, soft, somewhere between a laugh and a breath. "She's not the only one watching."

He smiles. "Let them."

We make another circle. He introduces me again, each title more gilded than the last.

"A rising scholar of the Radiant Doctrine."

"A voice of renewal."

"A living hymn to the Light's grace."

He never says "mine." He doesn't need to but everyone understands, and I... smile. I toast. I play my part, even as something wild and restless stirs beneath my skin, begging to be unbound.

I finally excuse myself, murmuring something about the air, the heat. His grip lingers just a heartbeat too long, enough to remind me that even my exits are permissioned.

Outside, the night air slices through silk and illusion. My lungs expand, raw and grateful. The wind smells of stone and star-fire.

Above, the sky pulses beyond the Light ringing the academy.

I wonder what the stars see.

I wonder what they remember.

I wonder how much longer I can keep being her, Sylvaine: scholar, symbol, silent consort.

The Shadows inside me?

They're not whispering anymore, they're watching, and they are hungry.

We make it to my cabin after the banquet. Lucien is already stumbling, half-dressed, laughing too loudly, as if he stops, the night might collapse under its own weight. His mouth finds my throat as I push the door shut, and I let him. The laugh still echoes in his chest when he starts pulling at buttons and sleeves, guiding the momentum. Jacket, gloves and gown fall in a trail like offerings I don't remember choosing.

There's nothing left between us but heat and hands and the hollow ache of performance. I keep my face turned toward him, but my thoughts are elsewhere. I'm too tired to name the feeling crawling under my skin, and maybe I don't want to.

I just need to keep the façade intact.

Later, the fire's burned low. My slip clings to my thigh where the silk is stuck with sweat, and his shirt is still crumpled on the floor. The cabin smells like smoke, sex, and the ghosts of too many things we won't say out loud.

Lucien sits beside me on the edge of the settee, close enough that our knees touch. His hair mussed in that deliberate way of his. He looks relaxed but Lucien never truly relaxes, not even after this.

"You seem different," Lucien murmurs, his voice as low as the firelight in my cabin. His fingers trail the bare skin of my arm, feather-light: just enough to pass as affection, just enough to feel like a test.

"Restless," he adds. "Distracted."

I shift slightly, turning toward the hearth to hide the way my breath snags. My face catches the glow, soft gold on skin gone too pale.

"I'm exhausted," I say.

True, but not honest.

Lucien doesn't nod, doesn't smile. He studies me like a puzzle he half-remembers solving once. His head tilts, gaze sharpening. I can feel him trying to decide whether I'm cracking or merely tired, whether there's a fissure wide enough to press through.

"Strange," he says softly, eyes still on me. "You missed the last Rite."

My blood turns to ice.

The Solis Rite.

I'd completely forgotten. It was three nights ago.

The Shadows had been crawling up the walls of my bedroom like ivy. My hands wouldn't stop vibrating. I couldn't even hold a pen without the ink flaring blacker than it should have been. The Shadows humming in my veins had been loud, feral. I'd stayed locked in, curled on the floor, trying not to feel it rise.

"I..." I force a laugh. I try to keep it light, keep it careless. "I wasn't well. Fever, I think. It passed quickly."

He watches me, too long.

"I would've sent someone," he says at last. "The Order asked after you."

"I didn't want to cause alarm," I answer smoothly. "I know the Rite is mandatory, I just... I wasn't in any state to stand before the Light."

His smile doesn't quite reach his eyes. "No," he agrees. "But for someone in your position, it is expected."

I nod, duck my head slightly, let my lashes cast shadows. "Of course. It won't happen again."

He reaches out, tucks a curl behind my ear. His fingers linger at my jaw, trailing down the side of my neck. "I've been thinking," he says.

That's never a good sign.

"You and I... this thing between us," he begins, like it's something delicate and sacred, not calculated and dangerous. "It could be more... official."

I still. "You mean..." a breath, "marriage?"

He smiles, a slow, gleaming thing. The kind of smile a predator gives just before it closes its jaws. "You'd be protected. Elevated. Respected."

Owned.

The word pulses beneath my ribs, I feel it like a bruise forming under the skin.

I swallow it, swallow everything and answer with slow, practiced grace, "Let me think about it."

He kisses my cheek, just above the bone, before rising.

"I'll give you time," he says, and with a final glance at the fire, at me, he slips out the door.

I don't move until I hear the latch catch.

Then, only then, do I collapse.

The slip loosens around me in halves. I sink to the floor, trembling, breath shallow and fractured. My hands curl in my lap like claws. I feel the seams of myself straining, stretching, about to tear.

Teacher, lover, traitor, and something else entirely.

Magic seeps through the cracks in my body like oil through paper; it smells like ash and rain. At night, I dream of hands wrapped in Shadow pulling me down, down, *home.* I wake with sparks behind my teeth and darkness curled under my tongue.

My control is slipping.

I sit on the floor of my cabin, barefoot and bare-armed; the moonlight pouring through the window. The hearth is cold, my candles unlit. Still, something burns.

Inside me, the Shadows hum: low, patient, hungry.

They've been louder lately, closer. They no longer wait at the edges. They curl around my ribs like smoke, seep through my veins like a second bloodstream. Sometimes I catch myself whispering in a language I've never learned. Sometimes I wake with ash on my tongue.

What are you? I ask in silence.

What am I becoming?

They don't answer in words, they answer in rhythm, in thrum, in pull. They are not separate from me anymore, they are me.

I press my palm to the floor and the stone warms beneath my skin. The ivy on the windowsill rustles as though stirred by breath. Something vast, something old, stretches its limbs deep in my bones.

Stillness is no longer safety; it is communion.

I don't fight it tonight, I breathe instead. But fear still curls at the edges of my mind, not fear of the dark, but fear of what it means if I'm made of it. So I rise, and I write.

To my star,
I don't know where else to turn.
All my life I have held nothing but the faintest flicker.
But now, it is undeniable. The Shadows, they move without will, they respond
before I even think to command.
It's not casting. It's... something else.
I am becoming something I don't understand.
I'm terrified, and I need you.
What if this power ruins everything I've built?

How can I teach and blend in when Shadow writhes beneath my skin?
You always seemed to understand things I couldn't even name.
I need you now more than ever.
I am not afraid of the dark. I'm afraid of what it might make me lose.
— Noctis

My Star Stealer,
Never doubt that you have a place to turn.
I remember those early days, how frustrating it was for you, watching others wield with ease while you struggled to grasp even the smallest spark. And now?
What you feel is not a curse but a transformation. The Shadows are not separate from you, they are part of your truth, a force that has waited patiently beneath the surface for you to claim it.
Fear is natural. Control takes time.
You will falter, you will stumble, but you will learn.
You must trust that within you lies the strength to bend this darkness without breaking yourself, or the world you've built.
Do not fear what this power might make you lose; fear instead the possibility of denying it and losing yourself altogether.
I am proud beyond words of the woman you are becoming.
Keep your heart steady, and remember: the night is darkest just before dawn.
—

THE LONGEST NIGHT

T HEY CALL IT SOL Infinita, the long night. A night wrapped in fire and shadow, sacred and unforgiving. A holy day etched into the marrow of our order. A night of ancient pageantry, parable, and ritual flame.

The Festival of Light marks the winter solstice, the darkest night of the year, when Shadows press closest and the Light demands its due. We feed it well, with flesh and spirit, with fear and devotion.

Before the first breath of dawn, the city stirs with whispered anticipation. From every courtyard, balcony, and tower window, a buzz rises; low and swelling, like the tentative flutter of wings.

As the sun creeps above the horizon, that buzz blooms into a chorus, voices layering over one another in a raw, trembling crescendo. It is the Sunrise Chants, a ritual older than any living soul.

The words are ancient, scraped from tongues long dead, languages cracked and faded like brittle parchment. They have been hollowed out, emptied of all but their sacred core, and sanctified anew by clergy who pierce their skin with golden needles, weaving blessings into the flesh of their words. Each syllable falls sharp and clear, slicing through the frost-bitten air like a blade. Each note is a shard of light cast into the lingering darkness.

Next to me, my students kneel in rows, a sea of bowed heads and clasped hands. Their faces are glazed, eyes distant and unfocused, as if caught in the sway of something far beyond themselves. Their lips move in flawless, automatic rhythm, repeating prayers we no longer believe in, echoing truths we can no longer hold.

I mouth the words alongside them, the shape of prayer on my lips, a mask I wear for their sake, lips tracing ancient shapes that feel foreign against my tongue.

> *O Infinite Flame, we are thy fuel, we are*
> *thy gift.*

The prayer spills out, a chant layered with sacrifice and submission.

The cold bites deep, the air crackling as frost sparkles on every stone and leaf. My breath billows before me in misty clouds, each exhale a fragile ghost that vanishes in the rising light. The sun, a pale, bleeding orb, floods the colonnade with soft gold, turning stone to amber, shadows to liquid fire.

Everything glows, and yet, everything feels hollow.

By midday, the feast begins. The garden squares swell with life and ritual. Fire pits roaring like ancient beasts beneath spits turn slowly, roasting whole animals; venison, boar, pheasant, filling the air with deep, smoky aromas. The scent of caramelizing fat and crackling skin twists through the frosty air, drawing a silent crowd around each blaze.

The scent makes my stomach curdle.

The offerings are laid out meticulously and with solemn reverence. Loaves of bread shaped into radiant sigils and runes of protection rest beside bowls of seared fruits whose edges curl black with flame. Root vegetables harvested from sacred soils lie dusted with ash and coarse salt, their earthiness softened by ritual fire.

The air is thick with the sacred silence of restraint; no voices rise, no laughter breaks the spell. Only the crackle and snap of flame eating the gifts, a fierce hunger answered by reverent whispers of thanks that flutter like smoke among the gathering.

I sit at the long stone tables with most of the other members of the Order, hands folded in my lap, spine straight and unyielding as a priestess's vow. Lucien sits beside me, his laughter low and easy at some whispered jest shared with a passing noble, his goblet raised like a chalice, lifted with a ceremony all its own. His robe shimmers with intricate white-gold embroidery, a sun bound in golden chains, marking him unmistakably as chosen by the divine.

"This year's tone feels devout," he murmurs, eyes dark and sharp, tracking the slow, silent procession of servers as they carry offerings to the flames. A faint, almost predatory smile quirks his lips.

"More guards, too," I murmur back, voice steady but low enough to keep between us.

"Security is devotion, darling," he replies, a glint of amusement or something sharper shines in his eyes.

His fingers brush against my wrist beneath the table, light, deliberate, claiming.

I do not pull away.

My smile is perfect, carved and practiced like a mask. But beneath it, every breath tastes like smoke choking the back of my throat, and the warmth of the fire feels colder than the winter air outside.

As dusk bleeds into night, the rites deepen and twist, drawing shadows long and sharp. The Forest Rite begins just as the final strands of light dissolve into a violet-black sky.

Hundreds of us fall into solemn procession, the crunch of frost-hardened earth beneath our feet the only sound besides the occasional creak of ancient branches swaying overhead. We move toward the altar grove beyond the southern gates, a place where the trees rise like colossal cathedral pillars, towering sentinels of bark and bone, black silhouettes against the star-flecked heavens. The cold gnaws mercilessly at any skin left bare, stealing warmth even through layers of ceremonial robes.

At the heart of the grove stands the altar stone, massive and worn smooth by generations. Crowned above it burns the Offering Flame, an otherworldly fire without fuel: no wick, no oil, no wood. It is a flame born of faith, sustained by blood and silence. It flickers with an unnatural light, humming softly like a living thing. The air around it shivers with a power both sacred and terrible, drawing a hush that presses deep into the chest.

Here, the Narrative Keepers take their place. Their voices rise in measured parables, each word polished and sharpened to perfection. The stories they weave glorify Light-born martyrs whose sacrifices shine eternal. The stories condemn heretics reduced to ash and forgotten. The stories celebrate the "sweet grace of submission" to the eternal order. The cadence of their speech is hypnotic, a ritual weaving that threads like silver through the crowd.

Children, their faces solemn beneath hooded cloaks, carry carved lanterns, fragile vessels of flickering light, their glow as tentative as hope itself. Around us, Verse-Keepers chant in spirals, melodies coiling and uncoiling like smoke, threading through the gathered throng. We kneel in frostbitten silence, breath rising in pale clouds, drifting like smoke into the dense canopy of leaves far above.

I kneel with them but I do not pray.

The Ritual begins at midnight. I do not run. Instead, I stand rooted in the biting cold, the moonless sky pressing down like a dark promise.

Lina finds me first, her eyes fierce beneath her lowered hood. Then Calyra, Aric, Laen, Elswyn, Mira. Others drift in like whispered threads, weaving around me in a circle of quiet solidarity. No words pass between us, there is no need.

Our presence speaks volumes: steady, unbroken, a silent vow. We are still here.

Our hoods drawn low, breaths misting in the frosty air, fragile clouds swallowed by night.

Around us, torches flare to life, arranged in concentric rings that ripple outward from the altar grove. The flames leap and dance, casting flickering gold that makes the embroidery on every robe gleam like armor forged in fire. The clergy form rings within rings, their chants rising as one, voices melding in perfect harmony, unyielding and sharp. At the center, the High Luminary stands, palms lifted high to the empty, starless sky.

Let Light endure. Let the dark dissolve.
Let the Order bind us all.

Each word strikes like a command, each command a blade slicing through the frozen air. The crowd sways with the rhythm, some weep quietly, others press trembling hands to their hearts, faces drawn and pale with fervor. My circle remains still, unyielding as stone. Even Mira does not blink, her gaze sharp.

There's a terrible beauty in the ceremony, the way truth hides beneath layers of gold and fire and music, how conviction drowns the senses like a rising tide. It's unbearable, a poison wrapped in light.

Suddenly, the chanting ceases.

The night exhales into a heavy hush. Even the wind seems to hold its breath.

From the far edge of the grove, twelve guards emerge, their armor gleaming blindingly white, faces swallowed beneath cold, faceless helmets. Between them stumbles a man, an Educator I recognize only vaguely. He once taught metaphysics in the minor wings, Educator Ilven. From the little I've heard of him, I know he is gentle, kind, with a smile that no longer reaches his eyes.

Lucien steps forward, voice smooth as honey, each word weighed with cold, deliberate precision.

"We honor the Light not only with praise but with vigilance."

They drag the Educator toward the altar, his bare feet trembling on the cold stone. He kneels, searching desperately for mercy, but finds none.

A Luminary in pristine white robes steps forward, voice rising in grim grandeur.

"Let this be a lesson. To teach is a sacred act. To twist the truth is treason. Tonight, we return one of our own to the Light."

I shift just enough to see clearly.

The Educator pleads, words swallowed by Lightscript, divine gag. A sharp strike from a guard follows before his wrists are bound, cold Light biting into flesh. Then comes the lashes, twelve brutal strokes, one for every lesson that dared stray from Light's doctrine. He makes no sound, not until the final moment when the flame touches his skin.

His body ignites, a living silhouette burning away, crumbling into ash. The Light devours him utterly, merciless and absolute.

Around me, the crowd looks away, voices rising in a familiar, sacred chant:

Order is peace.
Obedience is salvation.
Emotion bleeds madness.
Memory is rebellion.
O Infinite Flame, burn us clean.

We do not avert our eyes, we do not join the chant, not my circle.

Rellington's grip tightens on Calyra's hand. Aric's jaw clenches so hard, his knuckles whiten. Elswyn's face pales, as if the flames might leap from the altar to consume their own heart.

I hold my gaze steady, even when Lucien steps back to the stage and intones with chilling finality,

"Let this be a lesson in truth. He is now forgiven, marked by Light."

Something inside me tears; not a wound, but a rupture, a silence breaking free from years of quiet endurance.

Tonight, the Light revealed its terrible truth, and we are done pretending not to see.

A Circle of Silence

AFTER THE DISASTER OF the Light Festival, we need an emergency meeting. There is no time to send messages, signals. We rely on instinct, and the way grief calls us back to each other.

We meet in the clearing, just past the old southern entrance of the academy where the path fractures into roots and memory. The stone arch looms half-swallowed by ivy and dusk, a relic more skeleton than gate. The wind shifts as I pass through, it brings with it the scent of wildflowers and smoke, or maybe that's just the ghost of a warmer season, something my body remembers even if the world doesn't.

The earth here is cold, old, and alive. My boots press into soil that remembers.

Fog curls low around us, ghostlike, coiling through frostbitten grass and bare branches. Even the stars seem to have turned their faces from us. The trees breathe around us in silence, ancient and indifferent.

They arrive one by one.

Mira is first, her hood drawn low, her hands balled into fists. Her voice cuts through the stillness like a blade. "That wasn't justice," she says, flat, final.

Lina paces the outer ring of the clearing, boots chewing frozen earth, arms crossed like she's holding herself together by force. Her silence is louder than a scream.

Aric's hands are shoved deep into his coat pockets, but I see the tremble in them.

Elswyn's lips are bloodless, drawn taut with something fragile and fraying.

Calyra stares into the trees like she's expecting them to open and swallow us whole.

Mirielle's voice snaps through the cold. "Say it."

She whirls on us, hair loose beneath her hood. Her face is raw with fury. "Say what we're all thinking."

Mira lifts her head. "That wasn't a lesson," she says. "That was a performance."

"A sacrifice," Elswyn mutters. "They silenced him."

"No," I say quietly. "They burned him."

Aric laughs, sharp, bitter. "Is there even a difference anymore?"

The silence that follows is ugly, tense; grief coiled too tight beside rage, beside guilt, beside fear. The clearing has been a sanctuary but tonight it feels like a wound, open and raw, echoing with things we don't want to admit.

Mirielle kicks a half-buried root, hard enough to crack bone if she missed. "We stood there. We watched. We didn't stop it."

"We couldn't," Mira snaps. "What would you have done, Mirielle? Thrown yourself between him and the flame? You'd be ash by now."

"Then maybe that would've meant something!" Mirielle hisses. "Because standing there in silence, that meant nothing. That meant *we* are nothing."

"You think silence is nothing?" Calyra's voice slices in, sharp and unexpected. She's trembling, not from the cold. "I memorized every word of that parable, every lie they wrapped in poetry. I will not forget the way they looked away or the look on his face when no one stopped it. Silence is not nothing. Silence sees."

Elswyn sinks to the ground, legs folding beneath them like paper.

"We're all going to burn," they say, soft, sure. "Maybe not today, but soon. They know. They always know."

"They don't know everything." My voice is steadier than I expect.

"They will," Aric mutters. "Lucien watched us. He saw who didn't chant, who didn't look away."

"Then let him see," Mirielle spits. "Let him *see us*. I'm done hiding in the cracks. I'm done folding paper birds while they burn people alive."

Mira kneels beside Elswyn, murmuring something low. Calyra begins to pace now, mirroring Mirielle's restlessness. Aric stays still, but he's shaking, his breath fogging in sharp bursts.

There is a sudden breath of warmth in the cold and the fog parts.

Thaleia steps into the clearing.

She doesn't speak at first. She just walks to each of us, arms open, her cloak trailing behind her like smoke and silk. Her eyes are soft but steady, rimmed red with weeping that didn't steal her strength.

She hugs Mira first, long and tight, fingers pressed between her shoulder blades. Mira stiffens, but only for a moment, then sinks into it like someone who forgot they were drowning.

She moves to Elswyn, brushing their hair back, kissing their brow.

To Calyra, who flinches at the touch but doesn't pull away.

To Aric, who leans in like he doesn't know how not to.

To Lina, to Mirielle, and finally to me.

Her arms go around me like they've always known how. She smells of sage and river moss; home, in the way nothing else is anymore.

She offers no words, just presence, just knowing.

From her satchel she draws small bundles of dried herbs wrapped in thin leather, bound with green thread. She presses one into each of our hands. The scent is earthy, sharp, grounding: valerian, juniper, maybe crushed firethorn. I don't ask what's in them, I trust her.

She circles back, and this time she doesn't hug; this time, her fingers lift.

She stands before Mira and touches two fingers to her forehead. Her fingertips glow faintly in the dim light, barely visible, a shimmer of blue-white like moonlit ink. She draws a symbol, slow, deliberate; a rune for strength, for stillness in the storm.

She makes her way to Elswyn, then Calyra, Lina, Mirielle, Aric, me.

Each mark feels different: not cold, not warm, just right, like being recognized by something older than language.

The runes vanish almost instantly, absorbed into skin like breath into frost.

No one interrupts her, we just let her work.

When she's done, she steps back into the shadows. She doesn't speak, just nods, once, a silent promise.

I step into the center of the clearing.

"This ends one of two ways," I say. "We fracture. We run. We try to outpace their fire and pray it doesn't catch. Or... we stop being a circle of silence. We start being something else."

They look at me, one by one. Their faces are clouded and full of storm.

I take a breath.

"There's something I haven't told you."

The clearing tightens and the fog seems to draw closer.

"I've been exchanging letters with someone I knew before the war. A friend I grew up with, he's with the Hollow Guard."

Aric stiffens, his breath catching. "You are not serious!?"

I nod. "You know I am."

"That's..." He falters. "That's a death sentence!"

"No," I say, "it's a risk, but it's a risk I've already taken."

The clearing stills around us.

The Hollow Guard, the name alone hangs like a curse.

Everyone knows the stories, Shadow-born warriors who defected when the first cities fell: saboteurs, assassins, ghosts of the old. For decades, they've waged their own war in the dark, against the Order, against the Light, against the rot they couldn't purge from within. They're not myth, they're a scar the Light can't quite cauterize.

Elswyn shakes their head slowly. "They say the Hollow Guard lost half their number in the Sunfall raids. That they've gone underground, feral, broken."

"They're not broken," I say. "They're regrouping and he found me. He remembered who I was before I started pretending."

"Why now?" Aric asks. "Why reach out after all this time?"

"Because the Light is cracking. He says the fractures are growing beneath the surface, where no one's looking. There's movement. Something is coming and they're watching us."

"Us?" Mira's eyes narrow.

"They've heard whispers, about me, about *us*. There is something else you should know," I say quickly, before fear can stop me. My voice cuts through the fog like a frayed thread. "I've been learning, slowly. I think I am Shadow-wielding, or at the very least I am starting to."

The words hang there, heavy and dangerous.

Mirielle swears under her breath, low and sharp, like she's been struck. Calyra recoils a step, as if the admission itself is something volatile.

"But I thought you weren't blessed?" Calyra hisses. "Do you know what would happen if anyone here found out you wielded Shadow?"

"I'm not blessed," I say, steady. "Not in the traditional sense. I wasn't chosen, and did not show any signs of magic until just recently. I think these Shadows are... just, me? My blood, my will, my *choice*."

"That's not how it works," Calyra snaps. "Magic without the blessing has never been heard of."

Elswyn's voice is barely above a whisper. "You could be executed for just discussing Shadow magic, much less wielding it."

"I will be executed," I say. "Maybe not today, maybe not tomorrow. But one day, the wrong eyes will see too much, and they'll call it heresy. They always do. That's why I stopped waiting for permission to survive."

Aric shakes his head slowly, like trying to clear fog from a mirror. "Why are you telling us this now?"

"Because I don't want to hide anymore," I say, fiercely. "Not from you. You deserve to know who stands beside you. I won't lie to your faces while we pretend we're not already living on borrowed breath."

"You think we deserve to know," Mirielle murmurs. "Or you're testing if we'll betray you."

I meet her gaze. "Maybe both."

A long silence stretches out again, no longer brittle, but humming with something older, something breaking and reforming all at once.

Mirielle lets out a shaky breath, rubbing her hands over her face. "What does this mean, Sylvaine?"

"I think it might be time we stop surviving their way, and start living our own."

"So what?" Aric says. "You're asking us to risk everything"

"No," I say. "I'm telling you we *already are,* every time we choose silence instead of praise, every time we refused to kneel when no one was watching. That wasn't survival, that was resistance."

They stare at me, silent.

"I'm not asking for loyalty," I say. "Just readiness. I think that when the time comes, the Hollow Guard will light the fuse. And we need to be ready to strike."

Mira steps forward. "And when that day comes?"

I meet her gaze without flinching. "Then we stop surviving. We start *fighting.*"

Mirielle's breath shakes. "And until then?"

"We pretend," I say. "We play the part. Perfect little pupils, chant your prayers, bow your heads. Let them think they still own your bones."

"And when?" Lina whispers. "When do we stop pretending?"

"When the cracks are deep enough to split the stone."

The fog coils tighter, the wind shifts again: cold, urgent, ancient.

"We stay quiet. We stay close. We watch. We listen. When the moment comes, we strike."

Mira rises slowly. Calyra nods once. Aric's jaw sets.

They believe me, or at the very least, they want to.

For now, it's enough.

The night wraps around us like a pact; no more silence, no more looking away, let them watch us, let them mark us.

They won't see the blade until it's already buried in their chest.

Unhinged Propaganda

FROM THE HAND OF LIGHT FOR IMMEDIATE CONSUMPTION

GLORY UPDATE: THE SHADOW BLEEDS AND CRAWLS BACK

Traitors of the Vale extinguished:
Their screams fed the sky. Their ash feeds our
crops. DO NOT MOURN THEM. They chose darkness over
discipline. The war moves ever onward toward Holy
Purification.

MIRACLES ON THE FRONT:
LIGHT-SCORCHED EARTH: The Blessed Day Watch set
fire to an entire Shadow grove using Divine Verse,
witnesses say the air itself turned gold. Some claim
to have seen angels. This is what loyalty earns.

BLOOD-LETTERS ON CAMPUS?
Have YOU seen parchment that moves on its own? Heard
whispers in your sleep? Do your classmates mutter
about "truth" or "freedom" in corners?
REPORT. THEM. IMMEDIATELY. The Shadows are infiltrating.

KNOW THEIR LIES. MEMORIZE THESE TRUTHS:
The Shadow is rot disguised as poetry. "Feeling" is
not a right, it is a temptation. Those who say "both
sides have merit" are already corrupted. The Light
sees everything!

MESSAGE TO THE SHADOWS: You will not hide in roots.
You will not whisper in halls. The Light is not
coming. The Light is ALREADY HERE.

T HEY PAPER THE WALLS with it before sunrise; thick, bleached sheets
nailed into every door frame, every hallway column, even the gates
of the academy garden. Red ink, gold seal, and a headline that shrieks like
it was written with blood:

*The Traitors of the Vale extinguished. Their screams fed the sky. Their
ash feeds our crops. DO NOT MOURN THEM. They chose darkness over
discipline. The war moves ever onward toward Holy Purification.*

I stand frozen in the entry arch of the west courtyard, barely breathing.
The parchment crackles in the breeze and something inside me twists.

The words sear themselves into my skull like a brand, each phrase more
violent, more triumphant in its cruelty. My stomach lurches. I clutch the
stone wall behind me to steady myself, but the cold doesn't ground me; it
burns. I taste bile. My hands shake and I can't swallow.

The world tilts by a whisper, like a floor has shifted beneath me but I
didn't realize I was standing on. My pulse is a drum in my ears.

Students walk past the posters wide-eyed, pretending not to see it. A few
read. One retches into the hedge.

Another dares to whisper, "Is this real?" and is instantly shushed.

It continues:

*The Blessed Day Watch set fire to an entire Shadow grove using Divine
Verse, witnesses say the air itself turned gold. Some claim to have seen angels.
This is what loyalty earns.*

That grove was once part of Vaeloria's sacred lands, blessed by both gods, Light and Shadow, before the Shattering, before the lies.

"Angels," I murmur aloud, too bitter to stop myself. "Or the echo of a god too bright to see without going blind. The Shadow god never demanded worship through fire, only presence, only memory."

No one dares to meet my eyes.

By the time I reach my classroom, the full sheet is plastered beside the door like some kind of holy edict.

Do your classmates mutter about 'truth' or 'freedom' in corners? REPORT. THEM. IMMEDIATELY. The Shadows are infiltrating.

The two guards have become eight, but they are thankfully posted outside of the room today, silent and unblinking.

My blood runs cold and another wave of nausea coils low in my belly. I swallow hard, steadying myself on the doorframe before pushing it open.

They know something, or they're grasping in the dark and hoping fear will do the rest.

Inside, the classroom is quieter than ever. There is no chatter, no laughter, just twenty sets of eyes watching me, more like surveillance than curiosity.

"Morning," I say, though the word feels brittle in my mouth, like glass about to crack. My voice doesn't sound like mine; it drags too low, too distant, like it's echoing from somewhere deeper than my own throat.

I slip the rune-carved stone from Thaleia out of my pocket and set it gently on the edge of my desk, making sure to keep it visible.

The moment it touches the wood, the air seems to tighten, just slightly. The runes etched into its surface glint faintly with a shimmer not visible to untrained eyes, only those who know the old languages would see it: the warding, the silence, the scramble. It is a cloak over truth.

I've been careful these past weeks, every word in class weighed, every lesson sanitized. The runes, those etched into the room's corners, into the chairs, into the floor beneath the lectern, they watch, they listen, they report. I have bent myself into something narrow enough to avoid their notice, but not today.

I exhale through my nose and rest my hands atop the lesson plans. They shake slightly but I still them.

My eyes flick to the windows, closed, curtains drawn. The glyphs carved into the stone beyond them flicker like faint brands, Light-bound, still active, still listening. But Thaleia's rune thrums quietly, like a small shield raised against a storm.

I whisper a silent prayer to please let it hold.

Silence stretches across the classroom like a wire strung too tight. My students wait, uncertain, eyes darting. I try to smile, try to meet them where I always have, with calmness, with certainty.

But the smile slips: it feels wrong, it feels false.

They know what's happening, even if they pretend not to. Some of them look at me the way you'd look at something that might catch fire.

I know they've seen it, the sheet, the warnings, maybe some of them even believe it: that Shadows creep in on whispers and paper, that a question or a letter could kill them.

I feel one of my letters burning in my satchel, one I haven't yet sent. The Shadow's last words replay in my mind:

Keep your heart steady and remember; the night is darkest just before dawn.

He's hundreds of miles away, buried in a war of ash and bone, and still, he feels it; still he sees what's coming.

Here I am, standing not in a classroom, but on a fuse just waiting to spark.

I clear my throat. "Let's begin."

No one moves, not at first, then there is a rustle of parchment, the creak of a chair. A few reluctant hands reach for quills. The silence doesn't break, it stretches thinner.

"I know what you've read," I say at last, softly. "I know what they've told you."

A sharp inhale. Someone drops their quill, the sound is loud in the tense quiet.

"They want you to believe that questions are dangerous," I continue. "That ideas spread like sickness. That Shadows live in paper, waiting to pounce. But let me ask you something."

I step away from the desk. My voice is quiet, but clear.

"If Light is so righteous, so pure, why is it so afraid of words?"

There is a beat of silence before Calyra speaks.

She's seated at the far left, near the wall. Today, she looks different. Her posture is tense, her hands balled into fists in her lap, her voice, when it comes, is flat and low. "Because Light needs silence to survive."

Every head turns toward her, I see a flash of alarm in a few eyes. Elswyn looks like they might physically recoil. Everyone next to them shifts slightly away, subtly, as if distance might save them.

Calyra stares straight ahead.

"It needs obedience: unquestioning, unflinching. When that falters, it lashes out: like it did with Educator Ilven at Sol Infinata, like it will do to any of us who speak wrong."

"You shouldn't say that," Lina whispers. "Someone could hear."

"They're *always* listening," Calyra snaps, eyes sharp with a dangerous gleam. "That's the point."

I step in before the panic blooms.

"Calyra," I say carefully. "I hear your anger."

She meets my gaze. There's no fear in her, just fire.

"I'm not afraid of them anymore," she says. "Let them come."

"Don't invite them," Mirielle hisses, voice nearly cracking. "You think they'll stop at you?"

"Maybe they should be afraid of us for once," she growls.

The room holds its breath.

I step back toward the desk and let the quiet settle again, heavier now, a dense and living thing. Still, I feel Thaleia's rune pulsing faintly, the only shield I have.

"We are not here to call down fire," I say softly. "We are here to think, and right now, that may be the most dangerous, and necessary, thing any of us can do."

They stare at me, but something shifts.

A few nod, just barely. Others look down, but not in shame, in fear. Fear, I understand... it's the price of clarity.

I glance at the rune. It hasn't cracked, not yet.

"For the rest of class today, I want you to write," I say at last. "Not what they've told you to, not what you think I want, just the truth. Yours, even if it's ugly, even if it burns."

Slowly, one by one, they begin to write.

Calyra is gone by afternoon; no warning, no summons, just gone.

Her bunk is stripped bare, the trunk at the foot of her bed emptied, the thin mattress rolled and tied like it was never used. Her name has been scrubbed from the dormitory roster of the eastern hall. Not crossed out, not redacted, but erased; like she was never here at all.

It doesn't feel real.

A few students linger outside her room at first, pretending they're passing through. I see them slow, glance at the bare doorframe like it might offer answers. No one touches the handle, no one knocks. We all know better.

The silence that follows has an impact, ringing and raw.

The silence has weight now, shape, texture; the kind that coats the tongue like ash.

Her seat in class is as clean as the day she first sat in it: no personal marks, no carved initials, nothing to prove she'd ever claimed that space. And yet everyone keeps looking; as if something might grow there, as if teeth might bloom from the fabric, or fire.

The administration posts a single note:

> *Student Calyra has been removed from campus for advanced Shadow corruption. Cleansing deemed necessary.*

That's all it says. No one asks how, not out loud; we can all imagine it, and that's the point.

I can't help but think that this is my fault. That the rune I used cracked, that Thaleia's gift faltered. That someone reported what Calyra said.

But maybe it was something else?

What if she said worse, *more*, somewhere else?

Or what if she'd been writing or hiding letters?

I don't know what's true. I only know she's gone, and I can still feel the echo of her voice like flint behind my ribs.

Something in me wants to scream, but no one screams here; that, too, has been scrubbed clean.

We are all quieter now; not because we understand, not because we agree, but because we saw what happened to the girl who didn't look away.

Lucien finds me in the library, of course.

He always does. Whether it's the guards, or the wretched ivy outside my window that's suddenly begun curling toward the sill like it's listening, he knows. The persona he wears today is not Lucien, not the man who once quoted poetry in low candlelight. Today, he is the Beacon of Light. The divine's golden Light.

His robes catch the lantern glow like flame on glass. His steps make no sound.

"Sylvaine," he says, voice honeyed, smile like frost, "did you see the bulletin?"

"I did."

"A necessary clarity, don't you think?"

"I think fear rarely produces clarity."

"Ah," he muses, tilting his head, "but it produces obedience and that's far more useful."

My throat tightens, but I keep my face still. Stillness is the only armor I have left.

He walks closer, fingers brushing the back of a nearby chair, pausing beside the reading table where I've laid out three old texts I'm not truly reading. He glances at them briefly, then back at me.

"You've been quiet," he says. "Withdrawn. Is something... troubling you?"

Everything.

"I've been reflecting," I answer smoothly, "on the sanctity of our mission and your proposal. I think I'm close to an answer, I just need a little more time."

He watches me for a moment longer than is comfortable, the air between us tightening like thread drawn over a blade. Then, slowly, he smiles.

"Good girl."

He lets the silence stretch just long enough for it to settle beneath my skin, then he adds, almost as an afterthought, casual, conversational:

"A tragedy, really, about Calyra. I know you were fond of her."

I say nothing. I don't blink.

"She showed promise, once," he continues, idly tracing a fingertip along the gold filigree of a nearby volume. "But passion without purpose? Dangerous. Like a candle left too close to parchment. Such a shame, when potential turns inward and burns."

He looks at me again, sharp, assessing.

I do not flinch. I do not speak.

He leans in, voice almost tender.

"Don't squander your light, Sylvaine. I would hate to see it wasted."

And with that, he's gone, his robes brushing the marble as he disappears down the aisle, silent as ash.

That night, I light no candles. I leave the hearth dark, the drapes undrawn. There is no warmth, no softness; just the cold wood and the whispering dark outside my windows. Even the ivy is still.

I hold Lysander's letter from the other week. It is creased, smudged, and slightly torn at the edge from how often I've touched it. His words burn hotter than the fire I refuse to light.

Keep your heart steady and remember; the night is darkest just before dawn.

I hold it until my fingers go numb, knuckles white with grief. I think of Calyra's seat in the lecture hall, emptied like a pulled tooth. Scrubbed clean, erased, and then passed over as if she had never mattered, as if she hadn't stood up and *spoken*.

I want to cry. I want to scream. I want to run barefoot into the forest and disappear beneath its roots, let the moss seal over my name and be forgotten.

But I don't.

Instead, I kneel on the cold wooden floor of my chambers, the same way we do in the rites but this time, there are no clergy watching: no doctrine, no Light.

Just me.

I press my palms to the stone and I *breathe*. Once, twice; slow, centered. Shadows come at once.

They don't crash, they don't claw, they slip in, quiet and certain, like water filling a vessel. They rise through the floor, through the cracks in the stone, through the hollow ache inside my chest. They curl around my spine like vines seeking light, but there is no light here, only will.

They brush against my throat, not to choke, but to *anchor*.

They slip through the lattice of my ribs, not to hollow me, but to *steady*.

They rise behind my eyes, not to blind, but to *clarify*.

They *remember,* and this time, I do not flinch.

This time, I open myself. This time, I *choose* them.

My voice is low, but firm. There is no trembling.

"Teach me."

Shadows hum in response; not words, not commands, but presence, memory, invitation.

The air shifts. The cold deepens.

And somewhere far beneath the stones of this sacred place, something ancient begins to stir.

THE CITY BENEATH

THE MEETING IN THE clearing lingers in my mind long after the fog has settled and the chill of the night has thawed. The weight of the silence, the unspoken promises, and the new paths I've set us on, press down on me. Every step feels heavier, and yet, there's no turning back. I know what I've started, what I've asked of them, what I've asked of myself.

But what if it's not enough?

What if our rebellion is nothing but a spark, a fleeting flame, bound to be snuffed out before it can catch fire?

We need more. We need knowledge. We need power.

I find myself in the Library again. The musty scent of old parchment and dust clings to me as I step into the familiar maze of shelves, the stone walls closing in like the echo of my own thoughts. I can almost feel the weight of their gazes: my friends, my students.

I can't afford to fail them.

I begin with the indexes, though I know they're all but useless. The war archives, those carefully constructed histories of the Light's rise, its purity, its salvation, are sealed away behind layers of red tape and lies. They're framed as untouchable truths, narratives that fit neatly into the world they want us to believe in. But I know better; there's always something hidden, some scrap of truth left behind, some detail buried beneath the layers of polished rhetoric.

I know how to find it. I will find it.

By the second week, I've mapped every inch of the accessible wings in my head, each turn, each section of shelves that holds its secrets just out of reach.

The war histories stand pristine, untouched. They speak of the Rise of Divine Order, the Cleansing of the Vale, and the Shadow Epoch as though they're gospel. But they're nothing more than a lie dressed up in fine words, neat bindings, and gold-leaf titles.

I skim through them, page by page, and what I find only sickens me more: dates that don't align, villages that never existed until the Luminary Guards forces marched through, names that disappear only to reappear in unexpected places, as if the Scribes themselves are trying to rewrite the past.

I write down fragments. I collect names; names of rebels, names of scholars, names of those who simply vanished one night: students, healers, poets, children. My stomach churns with each passing page. Truth is never lost; it's buried, and I will unearth it.

But I need more; I need to go deeper.

I push past the boundaries of the official archives, sneaking into the forgotten rooms, back hallways, unlit corners, and unindexed shelves where the real secrets lie, gathering dust. I search for something that might give me control, something that might allow me to wield the power inside me without being consumed by it.

One night, in the quiet shadows of the third-level wing, I find something. It is a single entry, hidden in the margins of a translation manual, so faint I almost miss it:

> *Testimony restricted: see Lore-binders*
> *(Order 317.4) and Echo-Scribes of the*
> *Hollow Archive.*

There's no direct record, no corresponding volumes. Just this cryptic, almost imperceptible note, buried like a forgotten whisper, and for some reason, that's enough to pull me in.

Lore-binders, Echo-Scribes; titles I've never heard of, but they're strange enough to draw my curiosity. These aren't just names, they're rebellion. They're history's ghosts, memory-keepers who didn't bow to the Order's will.

I scour through the indexes, tearing through cross-references, each dead end more frustrating than the last. But then, just once, I find a mention, buried in a footnote of *The Compendium of Faithful Legacies*:

> *Let the false tongues of the Lore-binders*
> *be silenced. Let no trace of the Hollow*
> *Archive remain. Their oaths were not to*
> *Order, but to memory.*

The Hollow Archive.

The name pulses with something ancient, like the beat of a heart beneath the floorboards. I press my fingers to the page, feeling the faintest thrum, the distant echo of something that has been hidden away for far too long.

I need more. I need answers. I need control, before whatever is rising inside me devours everything I've fought for.

It's been just over two weeks since I sent the letter detailing everything that happens after the Sol Infinita: my confession, the dangerous path I've set us on, the way I've brought my students into this.

In the letter, I had told Lysander about the meeting in the clearing, about the fragile resolve I'd seen in their eyes, about the silent promises that seemed to weigh more than any words could. I explained my plans, my search for knowledge, for anything that might give us a fighting chance, and for answers that could guide us out of the darkness. I trusted him with the truth. I had no choice.

At the time, I was certain that when he received it, I would hear from him soon.

Lysander was always so deliberate with his responses, so careful in his words. I imagined him reading my letter, processing everything in that quiet way of his, before sending a reply filled with wisdom, reassurance, or a plan of action that might help us. It has been almost a full moon cycle since I've received my last letter and as the days dragged on, still I had received nothing.

At first, I told myself he was just busy, caught up in something urgent. There was always something urgent with the Hollow Guard: missions, reports, decisions that weighed heavy on him. It was possible, I thought, that he was tangled in some mess too dangerous to explain, some task so vital that it kept him from writing.

I was willing to believe that. I told myself I'd hear from him soon.

He always came back when he was ready.

But as the days passed, the silence settled in like dust, quiet, suffocating, and persistent. It clung to my thoughts, no matter how many times I tried to sweep it away.

I try not to let the worry turn sharp, try not to imagine worst-case endings blooming in the dark.

What if something's gone wrong?

What if he's caught in a trap?

What if… what if he's no longer able to write at all?

The thoughts spiral, but I push them away. I have enough to do: students to teach, secrets to uncover, power to control. But the silence from Lysander is like a gathering storm, swelling darker with each passing day. It haunts me, though I refuse to admit it aloud.

Then, at dawn, it comes.

It doesn't arrive with fanfare. No knock at the door, no Shadows carrying urgent news or a warning. Just a slip of parchment, pushed beneath my door, like a secret pressed into the quiet morning air. At first, I think I imagine it, no more than a shimmer in the corner of my eye. But there it is, unmistakable and real.

A scrap of paper; no seal, no crest, no signature, only Lysander's handwriting, although shakier and clearly rushed.

The paper feels damp, the edges curling as if it has been hastily folded and shoved into place. My fingers tremble slightly as I unfold it, as if the message itself is too heavy, too fragile to hold. My breath catches in my throat as I read:

Beneath root and ruin, there's a path. Just past your cabin. The earth remembers. Follow the hum.

A cold knot forms in my stomach. My heart stutters, unsure whether it's relief or fear that seizes me.

It could be a trap, a ruse. Maybe someone has intercepted his letter, or worse, it's a message from the Light, something designed to pull me into a snare.

My thoughts spin, fingers tightening around the parchment, crumpling the edge as if that could somehow anchor me to reality.

The rational part of me hesitates. I could turn back, I could ignore it, I could stay in the safety of the known, keep myself hidden.

But then, there's that pull. That feeling, deep in my chest; like a hum beneath the earth itself, like the very ground is calling to me, urging me forward.

I feel it even then, the way it resonates through me, as though I've been waiting for this moment. It's a thread: thin, delicate, undeniable. It tugs at me, promising something old, something forgotten, something waiting beneath the roots and the ruin.

I can't ignore it. I can't let it go. So, that night, with my heart pounding like the drumbeat of war, I leave.

I move swiftly, a knife hidden beneath my coat, my footsteps muffled, knowing that this path, whether it leads to Lysander or to something else entirely, is the only choice left.

I don't know what I'll find, but I've already crossed a threshold. Whatever comes next, there will be no turning back.

The forest welcomes me like it's missed me. The trees lean closer than I remember, as though eager to brush against my skin, to claim me again. The air is thick with the scent of moss and damp earth, and the path beneath my feet is barely recognizable now, overgrown, tangled with vines and brambles that seem to whisper secrets I've forgotten. The way is hidden, but not from me.

I find it. Past my cabin, there's an opening, a forgotten space hunched beneath a curve of ancient ash trees, half-swallowed by ivy and the creeping tendrils of the wild. The air here feels heavier, older. The trees groan with age, and the earth beneath me thrums like a heartbeat, steady and unyielding.

I pause only a moment before pushing past the curtain of ivy that hangs like a veil, hiding the path from view. He said beneath it, beneath the roots, beneath the ruin.

I move forward, and that's when I first feel it, the undeniable hum.

It starts soft, a pulse deep in the earth, just barely perceptible, like a distant whisper calling my name, a vibration that resonates through my bones. It grows louder as I follow the overgrown path, pulling me forward with an almost magnetic force. A hum I have never heard but somehow know, a sound as old as the world itself.

The tunnel appears before me, veiled in thick vines, so well hidden that I don't see it until I'm almost upon it. My fingers tremble as I part the curtain of green, stepping into Shadows that seem to shift and writhe with their own life. I step into the dark, feeling the weight of the world drop behind me. The air is cooler now, damp and full of something ancient. Something that knows me.

The tunnel is narrow, suffocating, but not in a way that makes me panic. It's intimate, as though the earth itself is breathing around me, watching, waiting. It doesn't feel wrong, it feels... inevitable. The walls are slick with moisture, the stones smooth, too smooth to be natural, too well-formed to have been made by time alone. It's not carved, it's shaped, like the earth itself moved aside for someone it recognized.

I walk, each step deliberate, until the air chills and the scent of stone and memory fills my senses, overpowers everything else. The hum is louder now, vibrating through me, echoing against the walls, seeping into my bones.

And then I see it, the door.

It's made of ironwood, dark and unyielding, with sigils etched deep into its surface, markings older than any doctrine, older than any power I've known. The symbols sing a low, quiet song, their meaning lost to most, lost even to me. When I touch the door, the world seems to disappear, and Shadow engulfs me. It's thick, disorienting, pulling me in every direction at once. It presses against me, surrounds me, until I can't tell where my body ends and the darkness begins.

I can't breathe but I don't panic. I don't fight it. I feel as if I am both drowning and have too much oxygen all at once.

Old magic coils around me, unseen, unspoken, watching with hidden eyes. It presses against my chest, my ribs, squeezing and stretching until I think it will break me. It stops abruptly.

The weight lifts and the pressure dissipates. I'm now standing in front of another door, almost identical to the one before, but different. Everything around me feels different.

I reach for the handle; it assesses me, almost thinks, and it opens at my touch.

I step into what I instantly know is the Hollow Archive.

It is not merely a room; it's a cathedral of knowledge, of forgotten memories.

Stone shelves stretch in spirals, infinite and awe-inspiring, filled with scrolls, ledgers, maps, and journals, each one older than the last, each one whispered about in legends, hidden from the world. Lanterns float above me, dim but warm, casting long, dancing shadows against the cold stone walls. The ceiling is painted in silver, symbols etched into the rock in a language I don't know but understand deeply, as though I've seen them in a dream long ago.

This is Shadow work: ancient, preserved, and somehow... waiting for me.

I move slowly, reverently, feeling a deep, undeniable connection to every item around me. My fingers graze the edges of forbidden pages, and I feel the pulse of something lost, something forgotten. The air here is thick with secrets, with knowledge lost to time, and as I read, I can't help but feel that these are the very memories of the world, buried and forgotten by those who feared them.

One scroll catches my eye: notes, written in a hurried, almost frantic hand, coded names, intercepted orders, and a map with a jagged line drawn through the Vale. The names are familiar; I recognize them from whispers, from the stories that still trickle through the cracks of this broken world.

Another list; this time it is student names, side by side with chilling phrases:

Uncleansed.
Re-education failed.
Purified.

Calyra's name is there. So are twenty-three others. Gone without ceremony, without a trace.

I bite down a scream. The parchment shakes in my hands, my heart thundering in my chest. My vision blurs, but I refuse to look away. I have to keep reading. I have to know the truth.

And then, I find Lysander's name, scrawled in the margin of a war report, hastily scribbled like a curse:

Lysander Draven Ardent of the Hollow Vale.
Butcher. Shadow-wrought.

The words hit me like a physical blow. The body count listed in the report is staggering. Ambushes, fires, precision strikes; everything he had done, everything they had accused him of. They call him a monster. They call him a butcher.

But I see the truth.

He's not killing for power. He's holding back a flood. He's the dam, the only thing keeping the Light's machine from swallowing everything. He's the last line of defense between them and utter annihilation.

But that's not what makes my breath catch. No, what stops my heart is the last name, Lysander Ardent.

His last name, the name of the late king: the ruler of our land, the monarch who stood above all. I may have been an orphaned forest girl, but even I knew the name of King Ardent. He told me he was Lysander Draven. He never mentioned the rest of it, and now I think I understand why. He was one of two set to inherit the throne. The boy-kings, Shadow and Light born, the ones they erased from history, the missing twins.

My legs buckle beneath me. I sink to the floor, the parchment shaking in my hands, my breath coming in short, ragged gasps.

Lysander. *My Lysander.*

Memories flood back: his laughter, his defiance, the fire in his eyes even as children. I always knew he was noble, with the way he carried himself, the way he dressed, even so young. I knew it in the way he vanished after the Vale fell, after everything was torn apart. It always made sense, but this?

How could I not have known?

He's war-forged now, sharpened into something necessary.

A weapon, but somehow... I don't fear him for it. I respect him more than I ever did.

Grief wells in my throat; not for what he's done, but for what it's cost him, for what it's made of him. He was once a boy who sang to trees, now they call him a butcher, and yet, I understand why.

As I sit there, crushed beneath the weight of the truth, I feel a pull. It tugs at me, drawing me to the far end of the chamber. There, beneath a hollow arch, stands a lone pedestal, untouched, waiting.

A single book rests atop it: leather-bound, blackened by time, unmarked by any hand save the one that wrote it.

I reach for it and it glows; not violently, not brightly; just a soft, pulsing thrum, as if it recognizes me, as if it's been waiting for me.

The instant I open it, words blossom across the page. They don't appear in ink, but unfold themselves, as if the very pages are alive, fluid, breathing.

The words are written in a language I shouldn't know, but somehow do.

> *When the Mother chooses its vessel, the vessel remembers; not all at once, not gently, but truly.*

My hands go numb.

The book knows me. It was waiting for me.

Tears sting my eyes, blurring my vision as the truth crashes over me, a quiet devastation.

I don't sleep that night. I don't eat. I read until my eyes burn, until my magic trembles in my bones. I scour through prophecies, warnings, visions of what's to come if the Light consumes the last wild parts of the world. The final entry catches my breath, its words haunting in their finality:

We do not burn the world because we hate it. We burn it because they salted the roots. Something new must grow.

I close the book, and I know exactly what I have to do next.

THE THREAT

BY THE TIME I return from the forest, the pale light of dawn has overtaken the sky, washing everything in a bruised silver. The trees rise around me like sentinels, their limbs skeletal in the early mist, reaching skyward as if in warning. The silence is uncanny; too complete, too knowing, but it doesn't frighten me anymore.

It *recognizes* me.

My body aches from what I am assuming is a portal; I don't know how to describe the old magic at the door any other way. It does not help my aches that the satchel at my hip feels twice its weight.

The book inside it thrums steadily, as if aware of what's coming. Its presence presses against my ribs, warm and watchful, like a second heartbeat. I can still feel the shape of the words it gave me etched behind my eyes.

I'm almost to my cabin when my breath catches; something twists in my gut, a cold, low pulse of wrongness.

The door is ajar.

I freeze mid-step. The wind stops moving, no birdsong, no rustling; just stillness, heavy and anticipatory, like the world is holding its breath.

My feet crunch softly on the path as I inch forward. The porch groans beneath my weight.

I reach for the door with a shaking hand, my pulse pounding in my ears. The wood creaks beneath my touch.

There sits Lucien, in my chair like he's always belonged there; like this cabin is merely another part of his domain. Legs crossed, fingers laced, entirely at ease, his silhouette is framed by the weak dawn light streaming in through the window. A steaming cup of tea rests beside him: my cup, my tea.

He doesn't look up immediately.

"I was beginning to think you weren't coming back," he says at last, voice mild, almost amused.

I don't move. The satchel strap bites into my shoulder. One of my hands still grips the doorknob, the other is clenched at my side. My throat dries.

"What are you doing here?" My voice is quieter than I mean it to be.

He lifts his gaze. His eyes are too bright and too calm.

"I needed to speak with you," he says. "Privately."

"You broke in."

He chuckles, as though it's all a misunderstanding. "Don't be dramatic. You left the door unlocked."

I didn't. I know I didn't. .

He gestures to the chair across from him, casual. "Sit. Please."

"I'll stand," I say tightly. "Say what you came to say."

His smile thins and I notice a flicker of irritation behind his eyes. The mask is cracking already.

"You've been wandering, Sylvaine," he says, tapping one finger against the wood of the desk, a slow, measured rhythm. "Into the woods. Avoiding your duties. Skipping Rites. Ignoring direct summons. And then there are the letters."

My eyes flick to the corner of the room. The ash bucket is out of place, one floorboard is not sitting quite flush... my hiding spot.

My pulse spikes.

"I've been preparing lessons," I lie, too fast. "Fieldwork. The woods help me..."

"Don't insult me by playing dumb."

His voice cuts like a whip. He stands abruptly and the chair scrapes back with a screech. The quiet cabin constricts around me like a breath being held too long.

"You're undermining the Light," he says, voice rising. "I brought you here. I protected you. Raised you up from the dirt. And you repay me with *this*? Defiance? Secrets?"

His fury comes fast, laced with something more dangerous than rage, disappointment.

He strides across the room, closing the distance in two strides. I back up, but not fast enough. He grabs my arm and his grip is like iron.

"You think I can't feel it?" he snarls, nose inches from mine. "The change in you? The *pull* in the air around you? What have you touched?"

I try to wrench away, but his fingers only tighten. Pain blooms under my skin.

"You don't know what you're doing," he growls. "You've been infected. But it's not too late. I can help you. I *will* help you."

"I don't need help," I grit out. "I need you to let me go."

But he's not listening.

A flicker of something shifts behind his eyes, conflict, or maybe grief. His jaw clenches. Then he speaks, low and almost to himself.

"Elowen warned me. She said you were never one of us. That you were pretending. That you were leading my students into the dark. I told her she was wrong. I told her she was jealous. *Faithless.*"

His gaze snaps back to mine, wide and glittering.

"I didn't believe her. I *refused* to believe her." His voice cracks on the last word, and something inside him begins to unravel.

"I love you, Sylvaine," he breathes. "I always have. Your mother... I thought she was the one. But she was just the start. She gave me *you*."

The room tilts. His hand brushes my hair back, mock-tender. I go still, cold creeping over my limbs.

"You were never meant to be small," he whispers. "You were made for more. To stand beside me. To *rule* beside me. You've just been fed lies. Taught to fear your own Light. But I see you. I've *always* seen you. You were crafted to be flawless. The Prophecy predicted it. So tell me... where did the cracks begin?"

My heart pounds so hard it hurts.

"The cracks?" I breathe. "They appeared the moment you demanded perfection. The moment you named Light as the only truth. You burned it into my skin, carved it into my bones, and called it armor. But perfection isn't purpose. And Light? Light is the lie. It's a cruel kind of magic." I lift my chin. "You say I was made flawless, but I was born to be real: to fall, to bleed, to rise, to break. I was born to break and still go on. The flaw isn't in me, it's in your obsession with flawlessness. It's in your blindness to anything that isn't shining."

"You can still be mine," he says. "Just one cleansing. One moment of pain. Then you'll be pure. And we can finally begin."

Something inside me shatters; it does not break, it unleashes.

Shadows rise.

They peel from the corners of the walls, long and serpentine, moving like water with purpose: the room darkens, the air changes.

Let. Go.

The words are not mine. They are *everywhere*. The walls pulse. The windows tremble in their frames.

Lucien stares at the darkness blooming behind me, eyes wide, breath stuttering in his throat. He doesn't understand.

"What... what is that?" he chokes, stumbling backward but his grip on my arm doesn't loosen. He's still dragging me with him, not realizing the truth, not *wanting* to.

That the Shadows aren't following me, they're *coming from me*.

The air splits with a low, resonant hum, like the groan of the earth before it breaks. The darkness coils and spills across the walls, alive and pulsing, responding not to threat, but to *need, to rage*. It wreathes the corners of the room, dripping like ink, climbing like ivy.

He blinks at it in disbelief; like if he just stares long enough, it'll make sense, like if he refuses to name it, it won't be real.

The Shadows know the truth and they are *done* hiding.

They rise, slow and deliberate, like the tide before a storm. They answer him, not with words, but with presence; a vast, inhuman stillness that presses in from every direction, ancient and intimate.

Lucien flinches and in that heartbeat, I finally see *him:* afraid, weak.

They surge forward in a wave: living, breathing, furious. They wrap around my limbs, my shoulders, my face, not to bind, but to *shield*.

"I said..." I lift my hand, fingers splayed, every nerve alight, "Let. Me. Go."

The explosion is silent, but total.

The darkness surges from me, not creeping but roaring, a tidal wave of ice and lightless fire. It howls through the air, sharp and radiant, as if the void itself had learned to scream.

Lucien's eyes widen in that last instant, not with fear, but recognition.

Too late.

The blast hits him square in the chest. His body lifts like a puppet cut from its strings, limbs splayed. Behind him, the shelves burst apart in a spray of ancient wood and yellowed parchment, scrolls spinning like dead leaves.

He hits the floor with a sound I feel more than hear, a brutal, final thud that shudders up through the soles of my feet.

Ash floats like snow in the air, catching the fractured moonlight filtering through the shattered windows. The cabin groans softly, wood settling into its broken bones. Wind whistles low and mournful through a crack in the far wall. I can taste iron on my tongue, sharp and real, grounding.

My breath comes in ragged gasps, each one scraping the back of my throat. Shadows curl tighter around me, thick as smoke, alive. They rise and fall in time with my heartbeat, pulsing like wings; guarding, loving, protecting what I've become.

Lucien is alive. I know it before I see him move; some small, imperceptible tether between us humming faintly in the wake of ruin.

He stirs, barely.

One hand twitches at his side, blood trickling between his fingers. His chest rises, shallow and slow. There is no accusation in his gaze now, only pain, and something else too dim to name.

I step toward him. The Shadows follow, loyal as breath.

For the first time in a long time, I examine him as a whole.

I see him; not just the man who helped raise me, not just the scholar, the mentor, the man who brewed tea when my hands shook, I see what I *missed*.

The signs were always there, subtle, creeping: the dull sheen in his eyes where once there had been fire, the way his posture bent inward, not with age, but with slow surrender, the lines etched into his face, not from time, but from strain, holding back doubts, biting down on truth. He's been unraveling piece by piece, trading himself away for the Light's promises; too slowly to notice at first, too carefully to question.

He's not the man I grew up knowing.

The Light took him gently, methodically: whisper by whisper, choice by choice.

The Light took from him until nothing was left but this twisted version: corrupt, hollow, gleaming.

He is a man who believes that love is control, that purity is obedience, that salvation can be *forced* into someone, if he just pushes hard enough.

My throat tightens. For a moment, pity flickers beneath my fury.

But pity won't save him, or me.

I straighten. The Shadows curl closer, drawn by my stillness.

Lucien blinks up at me, glassy-eyed and lost. He reaches for me like a child reaching for a ghost, but I am not his.

I turn away. I do not wait.

I grab my satchel and run: into the trees, into the dark, into something older than night.

The wind slices against my skin. Branches whip past my face, catching in my hair, tearing at my sleeves.

I don't care. I just run.

My feet barely seem to touch the ground. My body is moving, but it feels distant, puppet-like: a thing on strings.

The satchel bangs against my hip, rhythmically, like a war drum. The book inside is burning hot now, *alive*, almost, pulsing through the canvas, through my coat, through my bones. It sears against me like it knows where I'm going, like it's eager.

The forest blurs, all teeth and darkness. Trees smear past in streaks of grey and black. The air is thick with the scent of moss, sap, and something deeper, something metallic and ancient.

My breath roars in my ears, ragged and panicked, too loud, too close, like it doesn't belong to me.

I don't remember choosing the path. My feet find it on their own, familiar, inevitable. The ground twists beneath me like it's leading me somewhere I was always meant to go: toward the outcrop, toward the mouth in the stone.

By the time I reach it, my legs betray me. They buckle, and I stumble to my knees, catching myself on the jagged edge of the stone walls with trembling fingers. Blood wells up in my palm, unnoticed. My vision doubles. I crawl the last few feet, scraping through dirt and wet leaves, into the tunnel's yawning throat.

It welcomes me like it's been waiting.

The air changes instantly: colder, heavier. My breath turns to fog. The walls are damp and lined with roots, pulsing faintly like veins under skin.

I fall into the old magic: slowly, clumsily.

The Shadows deepen around me, until it feels like I'm moving through water, thick and soundless.

My knees buckle again as I reach the threshold of the hidden archive. I stagger across it like a drunkard, gasping.

Books line the walls in impossible volumes, their spines whisper as I pass. The room is lit only by the strange, soft glow of phosphorescent moss and the light from the flickering orange lanterns. The Shadows are alive here, breathing, curling at the corners of my vision like ink in water, never quite still.

I press a hand to the nearest shelf to steady myself. The wood hums beneath my palm, like it recognizes me.

I can't think. My thoughts slosh like wine left too long in the heat. My skin feels too tight, my bones too far away. Everything is too bright, or too dark. I can't tell anymore.

The adrenaline starts to drain, slow and punishing. That's when the shaking sets in.

First my hands, then my legs, then everything. My body becomes a shiver.

"Get it together," I whisper, gritting my teeth. I clutch the shelf harder, as if it can anchor me. "You're safe now. You're safe. You're..."

But then I hear it, a voice. No, *voices*.

Soft, layered, not spoken, not exactly. More *felt*, like wind through leaves, like memories falling into water too deep to reach the bottom.

> *Stone will whisper, soil will cry, and*
> *bones long lost will rise and fly...*

My breath freezes in my lungs. I spin around, wild-eyed.

Nothing is here with me, just the shelves, the dark, the quiet hum of old magic.

> *The ground will speak in breaking*
> *groans, she walks alone. She is the*
> *key. The hidden flame. Unmarked by*
> *blood, unclaimed by name...*

"No..." I backpedal, stumbling into a stack of books that topple with a crash. "No, stop. This isn't real. This is just... I hit my head. I'm halluci-nating."

> *Raised by silence. Cloaked in night. Her*
> *heart the blade, her truth the Light.*

The room contracts; breathless, as though something has just noticed me.

The voice rises, not in volume but in gravity. It *presses* on me now, vibrating in my chest, my ribs, my spine.

> *She bears the wound. She is the thread.*
> *The door, the fire, the book unread. Let*
> *sky be shattered on her spine, let Earth*
> *split wide along the line...*

My mouth is dry. My heartbeat stutters.

> *The orphaned child must choose it all, to*
> *rise in flame, or let all fall. And in the*
> *wreck of gods grown cruel, she will bleed.*
> *She is the rule.*

"No," I croak, backing into the stone wall. "Please, stop..."

I see movement at the far end of the archive, through the veil of Shadow, through the ink.

Something shifts. Not something, but *someone*.

A figure steps forward, slow and soundless: tall, unhurried, draped in night like a second skin. The Shadows don't just surround him, they cling, *obey*. They move for him, curl around him like smoke returning to fire.

His hair is dark and wind-tossed. His frame is lean, carved in sharp lines and subtle grace. And his eyes...

Gods, those eyes: silver, burning, *familiar*.

My breath catches in my throat.

He looks like Lysander: wild, whole, undiluted by fear.

297

"Who?" I gasp, stumbling a step back.

He stops at the edge of the light. The Shadows swirl around his boots like they're reluctant to release him. His eyes widen as they settle on me, see me. Recognition crashes into his expression: soft, disbelieving, reverent.

"Sylvaine?" he whispers, so softly I barely hear him.

My name, spoken like a question, like a prayer's final word, like he's been waiting an eternity just to say it.

My knees give way. The ground vanishes beneath me. The world tilts sideways.

Just before the dark claims me, something wraps around my waist, gently, surely; Shadows, warm as breath and soft as memory.

They catch me, not like a stranger but like something that has always known me.

Roots of
The Past
Flashbacks

The Star Thief by The Bleeding Quill

Once, when the world was still young and the stars hung low enough to kiss, there lived a boy named Noctis who dreamed of fire.

Not the kind of fire that burned bread crusts or warmed weary toes; he dreamed of sky-fire, the kind that lives in stars, the kind the gods kept hidden in their pockets.

Noctis was a strange boy: he never wore shoes, he never told lies, and he never looked away from sorrow.

"Why do you stare at things that hurt?" the wind once asked him. And Noctis said, "Because I want to remember where they fell."

One night, while the gods were asleep in their golden sky-palace, Noctis climbed a ladder woven of spider silk and silence. Step by step, heartbeat by heartbeat, he rose past the moons, past the clouds, past the songs of the birds, until he reached the vault of stars... until he found it, hidden behind a curtain of Light, sky-fire.

The gods had hoarded it, locked it in crystal jars, but Noctis saw what the gods had forgotten. Fire isn't meant to be caged; it's meant to be danced with.

So he stole it: one jar, then two, then all of them. And the stars began to fall.

The gods awoke in fury. They cast down their thunder. They screamed of sin and sacrifice. They built new walls and brighter prisons. They swore they'd scrub the world clean of his name.

But Noctis was faster than shame. He ran through the skies, barefoot and laughing, scattering flames like dandelion seeds.

Down below, the world was at war. Men marched in lines, women wept in fields, children forgot how to dream. But as sky-fire rained across the broken earth, something ancient stirred. Flowers bloomed in ruins, ghosts whispered to trees, and the forgotten began to remember.

They say Noctis still dances, barefoot over battlefields, a flame in his chest and shadows in his wake. He never stays long; just enough to plant a spark in the hollow of someone's heart. And when children cry out in the dark, when their dreams are taken, their questions silenced, their stories burned, a little star might flicker in their hands.

They'll know: The Star Thief lives, and memory can never be truly stolen.

THE PUPPET SHOW

AGE 5

MAMA'S HAIR SMELLS LIKE honey and pine when she picks me up. I bury my face in her shoulder and pretend I'm small enough to stay there forever. Her arms are strong but soft, like tree branches wrapped in the warmth of the sun. She smells like home, like the forest after rain, like everything that feels safe.

"Did the mushrooms talk today?" she asks, her voice light, teasing, but there's a warmth in it that wraps around me like a blanket.

I nod, feeling the tiniest flicker of excitement dance in my chest. "They wiggled," I whisper, as if saying it too loudly might disturb something fragile, something secret.

Mama's eyes widen and she gasps, her face lighting up with delight. "Did they?" she says, voice lilting in awe. "Then it's time to leave them an offering."

I nod again, a smile tugging at the corners of my mouth, knowing exactly what she means. The mushrooms, our mushrooms, are special, and when they speak, it means the forest is calling us to listen.

As we walk into the cabin, I feel the warmth of the fire wrap around me like a familiar hug. Pa's at the stove, the fire crackling under the heavy iron pot, sending ribbons of smoke curling into the air. The smell of wild garlic and roasted roots fills the room, earthy and comforting, making my stomach rumble with hunger and anticipation.

Pa's humming a low, deep tune, one I don't know the words to yet, but it's familiar: it feels like safety, it feels like bedtime, it feels like *him*.

Our cabin is always warm. Even in the dead of winter, when the forest crunches beneath our boots and our breath turns to clouds, the inside is golden; not the flicker of candlelight, but something truer, something woven into the very fabric of our home. It's like warmth has been stitched into every corner, every log, every thread of the blanket draped over the chair. It's the kind of warmth you can feel in your bones, the kind that doesn't just keep you from the cold, but keeps your heart full too.

The walls are made of logs stacked like puzzle pieces, their edges softened by time. Moss grows thick in the cracks, keeping the cold out like a secret, like something only the forest knows how to protect. The ceiling is high, and sometimes, when the sun dips below the horizon and the light dims, I see the bats up there; tiny, sleeping blankets hanging from the rafters. I wave at them, though I know they'll never wave back. I like to think they do, in their own way. They're my silent friends.

The window above Mama's herb shelf is my favorite. It's round, big and full of light, like the moon; I love to press my forehead against the cool glass.

Tonight, it's raining. Each drop taps against the window like a gentle knock from a shy ghost asking to come inside. I close my eyes and listen, letting the sound of the rain fill the quiet spaces of my mind. It feels like a secret, shared just between me and the night.

"Set the table, little fox," Pa calls from the stove, his voice as steady as the rhythm of the fire. "Three bowls, three spoons."

I jump down from Mama's arms, my feet light against the wood floor. I run to the low drawer where we keep the good spoons. Not the shiny, metal ones that gleam like strangers, but the wooden ones; the ones that are carved with love and care. I pull out mine, the one with a fox etched into it, its tail curling toward the tip like it's about to pounce.

Fox and Nox. I think we would be friends if we ever met. I smile to myself at the thought.

I set everything carefully, even the napkins, folding them just like Mama taught me. They're a little lumpy, but Mama always says that it's the care we put into the folds that matters, not the perfection. I like the idea that something doesn't need to be flawless to be special.

We eat with the crackle of the fire beside us, the logs popping in rhythm with Pa's deep voice as he tells his story. It's the one about the time he met a bear who loved poetry and only spoke in rhymes. His voice dances with the words, and I feel the warmth of his laughter in my chest.

Mama rolls her eyes in mock exasperation. "It was a raccoon, and it was sick."

Pa waves his hand, dismissing her. "It had elegance," he insists, his voice thick with affection.

After dinner, I ask for a story; a real one, the kind that makes the world outside the cabin feel far away.

Mama moves softly around the room, turning off the lights, starting with the little oil lamp near the hearth. It's like she's shutting out the world so we can be alone, wrapped in the safety of our home. She pulls me into her lap, cradling me like I'm still the small girl I once was, still the one who needs her comfort, her light.

Pa sits beside us, cross-legged, close enough that I can feel the steady beat of his heart in the air around us. I snuggle between them, resting my head against Mama's chest. For a moment, it feels like the middle of a book, when everything is perfect and the story is just beginning.

"Which one tonight?" Mama asks, her voice warm and gentle.

"Tell the one about the girl who speaks to trees," I say, my voice a soft whisper.

"The sapling?" Pa winks, a mischievous glint in his eyes. "She roots for herself."

Mama swats his arm lightly, a playful sound escaping her lips. "Stop," she says, but her smile is soft. I know she loves this story too, even if she's heard it a thousand times.

I giggle, a sound that seems to melt into the warmth of the room.

Mama lifts her hands, summoning her magic. A small orb blossoms in her palm, lit from within like morning mist caught in glass, casting a glow that dances along the walls. It is soft and steady, like she's caught a star and coaxed it to rest there. She raises both hands, and the Light stretches outward, casting long, reaching shadows across the small room.

Mama begins the tale, her voice low and sweet, like the sound of rain tapping against the window.

"There once was a girl born beneath the canopy," her voice rich with the weight of the world. "So deep in the woods, the sun had to ask the leaves for permission before it reached her..."

Pa's fingers flick through the air, weaving Shadows into the shapes that match Mama's words. The darkness dances and bends, twisting into a cradle beneath a great tree, then shaping into a tiny girl, curled up and sleeping inside. The figures come to life, flickering and shifting, as though they have their own thoughts, their own stories to tell.

I know this story by heart. I know what will happen. The girl will find a wolf cub, the wolf will grow strong and loyal, and together, they'll save the forest by listening when no one else would. Although I have it memorized,

I listen. Because when Mama tells it, it feels new, like it's happening for the first time, just for me, like even the trees outside are leaning in to hear.

As the story unfolds, I close my eyes, and I'm with her: the girl, the wolf, the trees. I feel the warmth of Mama's Light in my chest, and I know she's right there with me, just as Pa's Shadows are right beside us, guiding us through the tale.

Before sleep claims me completely, Mama bends close, her breath soft against my ear. "You are special, little sapling," she whispers, and her words make the world slow down, the way the last light of day stretches long into twilight. "You are balance, and that is sacred."

I don't understand what it means, but I believe her. I believe her with everything I am.

LESSONS OF THE FOREST

AGE 6

THE SUN SLICES THROUGH the canopy like rich, warm honey, spilling golden light over everything it touches. It lands on the back of my neck, soft and steady, as I crouch beside the stream.

Around me, the air is alive with the cool scent of wet moss and crushed fern. The creek sings a bright, burbling song, and my fingers hover just above its surface, still, expectant.

A silverfish darts by, quick as the flash of a falling star. I strike, too slow. My hand breaks the surface with a sharp splash, sending the fish scattering in all directions, no more than glimmers vanishing into the current.

"Almost," Pa says from beside me. His voice is calm, patient; never sharp, never scolding, just steady, solid, like the roots of the trees around us. "Wait for the ripple behind the eyes. That's the moment it lets go of its fear."

I nod, teeth clenched, trying to swallow my frustration. The rocks beneath my knees are slick and cold, pressing through my pants. My hands ache from staying so still, every knuckle stiff with effort.

But I stay there because I want this. Because he's already caught three, and I haven't caught any. Because I want to be good at this, not just good, but capable and worthy, like him.

"There!" My breath catches. A flick of silver, a pause... then, just behind the small black eye, a ripple comes, a hesitation.

I lunge.

This time, my hand closes around something solid and alive, slippery and wriggling, squirming between my fingers. My grip tightens.

"I got it!" I cry, jumping up, triumphant. Cold water pours down my arms like ribbons of glass, sparkling in the sunlight.

Pa laughs, and the sound makes something warm bloom in my chest. He claps me on the back, the weight of his palm a kind of benediction. "Well done, little fox. That's our breakfast."

His smile is quiet, tucked into the corners of his mouth like a secret, but it's real. There's pride in it, beneath the gentleness, beneath the careful hush he always carries like a second skin.

Around us, the forest sings, birds calling high above, wings flitting through the branches like bright leaves come to life. Deeper in the green, I hear the soft crunch of underbrush, elk, moving through the trees, their steps rhythmic and ancient.

The forest is alive in ways that don't need words. It breathes, and I feel like I belong to it.

We walk back together, the fish strung between us on a line that glints like captured sunlight. I hold one end, Pa the other, and between us swings our quiet victory. My other hand curls into his, small inside the rough, warm grip of his palm. The path home winds uphill, tangled with ferns and old roots, flanked by towering pines that murmur as the wind moves through them like an old memory, something half-forgotten and half-holy.

Mama's already at the firepit when we return. Her dark curls are tucked into a faded scarf, sleeves rolled to her elbows. Her hands move with quick familiarity as she stirs the smoking pan. Wild onions sizzle, filling the air with their sharp sweetness, softened by the scent of herbs I helped her gather yesterday, chamomile, pine tips, and something minty I still don't know the name of.

When she looks up at us, her face instantly brightens.

"How many this time?" she calls, grinning.

"Four," I say proudly. "Three his. One mine."

"That's one more than last time," she says, winking. "You'll out-hunt your Pa by next season."

"Don't encourage her," Pa mutters, though he's grinning, too. He hands her the fish with a reverence usually reserved for gifts or offerings. "She's already impossible."

We eat outside, perched on logs worn smooth by years of fires, stories, and sunrises. The plates are warm in our hands. The fish is crisp, the skin crackling, the herbs bright and green against the smoke. The air is sharp in our lungs, clean, with the kind of cold that feels alive.

Mama tells stories while we eat, her voice low and rich, curling through the air like the smoke above the fire. She tells of star-wolves that howl in constellations we've forgotten how to name, of root-spirits who sleep beneath ancient trees, of twin gods who once walked barefoot through these woods and left their footprints in the stones.

Her voice catches on certain names: names older than history, names that still matter. She says that some names are spells, and to speak them is to remember what the world has tried to forget.

Halfway through a bite, the question tumbles out of me before I've even had time to shape it. "Why don't you take me into the village more?"

The quiet that follows is instant, weighed.

They glance at each other. It's quick, barely there, but I catch it.

Mama's smile softens at the edges. Her voice lowers. "It's safer here, Sylvie. Things are changing in the world, and not all change is a good thing."

"But you always say we can't control the way things change," I say, frowning. "Like the seasons. We just have to let them."

"That's right," she says gently, tucking a curl behind her ear. "But the changing of seasons is *natural*. It's the rhythm of the world. It brings balance. It makes space."

Pa stirs the fire with a stick, brushing ash from his pants. His eyes stay on the flame when he speaks. "The changes happening in the village aren't like the seasons. They're made by people, and when people force change, especially with power they don't understand, they leave things broken behind them. Even if they think they're building something better."

I chew slowly. I don't fully understand but I *feel* something.

They've been different lately, quieter, tense when they come back from the village. Mama, with her fingers deep in the soil longer than usual. Pa, slower to joke, faster to silence. They speak in hushed voices when they think I'm asleep: about the Order, about Lucien, about the Light.

They say that name like it used to be a prayer, but now it sounds like a warning.

"Is Lucien still our friend?" I ask, because I need to know, because part of me already does.

Another pause, another glance.

Mama's lips press into a line. "We hope so," she says. "He's... searching. And sometimes, when people go looking too hard for answers, they don't realize how many bridges they're burning behind them."

Pa leans forward, elbows on his knees. His voice is low, like something old. "The Light isn't evil. Your Ma proves that in her very being. But Light, true Light, isn't what they think it is. It's not just fire, not just vision. When it's wielded without balance, it consumes. It devours. It blinds."

I look toward the trees, where the sun gathers in the hollows and hangs beneath the boughs like breath. "But aren't Shadows part of the world too?"

"They are," Mama says, and her voice is soft now, barely more than a breath. "And that's what people forget. We need both. One cannot live without the other."

I don't understand it all yet, but I am beginning to feel the weight of it.

I see it in the way Pa's shoulders tense when he hears footsteps too close to our land, in the way Mama's hands tremble just slightly when she seals her letters for the academy, in the way the path down to the village looks longer than it used to.

I don't know what's coming, but I know we are standing in the space between things: between Light and Shadow, between story and truth, between what was and what's waiting. And I know my parents are trying to shield me from something they can't name out loud.

THE VILLAGE KID

AGE 7

THE VERY NEXT MORNING, they leave together: Mama with her woven basket looped over one arm, Pa with a scroll case slung across his back.

"Be good, sweet Sylvie," Mama says, kissing the top of my head. Her curls smell like rosemary and smoke. "We'll be back before dusk."

"Don't burn the forest down," Pa adds, with a wink.

"I make no promises," I grin.

They vanish down the path, the forest swallowing them like it always does, soft, green, and endless. I watch until they're gone, then turn back to the trees.

By midday, the quiet feels louder. The birds are chatty. The creek laughs at its own jokes. I pack a satchel with a half-loaf of bread, my bone-handled knife, and a twist of dried apple. Then I wander, probably farther than I should.

The moss I find near the hollow tree grows in thick braids over the bones of an old stump. I crouch beside it, fingers trailing through the green. It's soft. Softer than anything, like hair. I start to untangle a strand.

Maybe I'll weave it into a crown. A crown of forest things, one the wind won't dare knock loose.

"Hey."

The voice hits me like a thrown stone. I jerk and nearly fall backwards. A boy stands at the edge of the clearing, arms crossed, glaring like I've insulted his Ma.

"You're not supposed to be here," he says.

"You're not either," I shoot back.

"This is my forest."

"No, it's mine."

We glare. He's taller, probably older by a year or two. His curly hair is trimmed and tidy, too tidy for the woods. His shirt is spotless, his boots polished. No burrs or dirt anywhere. Village kid, probably noble.

He tilts his head. "What are you doing out here?"

"Making myself a crown." I gesture at the moss. "See that strand? Perfect for weaving. A crown, because this forest is mine."

He chuckles, finally. "A crown. So you're royalty?"

"Obviously."

He steps in, hands on his hips. "You live out here?"

I nod. "With my parents. Who are very good at setting traps, I'll have you know."

"I wasn't going to hurt you," he says quickly.

"Good," I answer, straightening. "Because you'd lose against the traps."

Something shifts then. His mouth twitches, it is not a smirk but something softer, a half-smile.

"I'm Lysander. Lysander... uh, Draven."

I nod back, regal as I can manage. "Sylvaine Nox."

He glances around, then walks a bit closer. I don't move.

"You really live out here? All the time?"

"Yes."

"You don't go to school?"

I wrinkle my nose. "No. My Mama teaches me."

His brows rise. "What, like reading and numbers?"

"Yes. And also how to track elk by broken twigs, how to call owls in three tones, how to bind herbs so they don't rot."

"Sounds... intense."

"It's called *education,* village boy."

He snorts. "I go to the academy in the eastern region. I am top of my class."

I eye his perfect boots. "Of course you are."

He looks vaguely proud, but then glances toward the trees. "I grew up near the edge of The Vale, not far from here. We have an orchard behind our home, apples, mostly, and a few stubborn plums. I used to race my twin brother through it. We'd get in trouble for knocking down the fruit too early."

"You have a twin? My Mama tells stories about twins!"

"Yeah, his name is Caelum." His smile fades a little, just for a second. "But we aren't close anymore; he never wants to play."

I stare at him, offering no response. I don't have any siblings, so I am used to playing alone.

"He is the loud one," Lysander continues. "Gets in a lot of fights. Broke his arm falling off the academy roof once. I was the quiet one, still am, I guess."

I nod slowly. "My Pa says quiet people carry louder truths."

He gives me a strange look, like he's not sure if that's wisdom or non-sense, then he sits down beside the stump.

"So... this moss crown. Are you actually going to wear it?"

"Obviously. I'm the forest's queen."

"Then I should help. I was top of my class in..." he pauses, smirking, "...botanical weaving."

"Liar."

"Only a little."

We sit there for a long time, weaving together in half-silence. He hums something, a song I don't know. I hum back. Mine's older, the kind of tune the trees remember.

I tell him about the ridge where the wolves live. I tell him about the time I tracked a stag for two days and Mama made me promise not to do it alone again. I tell him about the grove where the mushrooms glow blue with phosphorescence, but only if you don't blink.

He listens, really listens, eyes wide.

"My Mama says the forest remembers what we forget," I say. "That it holds old things, sacred things, things no one should try to change."

He swallows. "My father says the forest is full of superstition. Says it's time we move on, past myths."

"Then your father is an idiot."

He laughs, I wasn't being funny.

Later that night, when my parents return, the wind has shifted. Mama's curls are damp with rain, and Pa's fingers are smudged with ink and charcoal.

The hearth is lit. A stew bubbles low. I stir it with a carved spoon and try to sound casual. "I met someone today."

Mama lifts an eyebrow. "Did you?"

"A boy."

Pa sets down his scroll slowly. "A boy?"

"He said his name was Lysander Draven. He was polite. Mostly. He had the craziest eyes I have ever seen, they glowed like the mushrooms do, but they were silver! I didn't say anything though, I am sure that is the first thing people say when they meet him. Do you know his Ma and Pa? "

They both freeze, just for a second. Then Mama moves again, peeling off her shawl and hanging it by the fire. She grabs the herb knife. Her hands move quickly, too precisely.

"Lysander," Pa repeats, voice unreadable.

"He said the forest was his," I continue, watching them closely, "but don't worry. I let him know it was mine. I even made him help weave me a crown from the moss by the hollow tree."

There's a long pause, the kind that makes silence feel heavy. They exchange a glance, one of their looks, filled with something I'm not supposed to see; knowing, worried, but they don't say anything.

GROWING TOGETHER

AGE 8

F ROM THEN ON, HE returns nearly every day. At first, he pretends it's by accident; just passing through, gathering firewood, hunting alone because no one else can be trusted with a bow anymore. The excuses change, but the intent doesn't. By the third or fourth time, I stop asking and he stops pretending.

He never brings much: a half-eaten lunch in a satchel, a scroll tucked under his arm, a belt knife he's clearly not supposed to have. His shirts get less clean. His boots scuff and wear. His hair grows longer than any boy from the village is allowed to keep it. And his smile... his smile becomes easier, looser; it starts to reach his eyes.

One evening, as he kicks pinecones off a log with studied frustration, he says, "I don't like being home. The walls feel too close, like a palace with no windows."

I don't understand what he means but I nod anyway. Here, in the woods, he's just a boy. So that's all I let him be, a boy, and a friend.

We meet wherever the forest feels most like ours: the moss-covered stump, the stream where silverfish dart between roots, the hollowed out tree covered in moss, guarded by owls. Sometimes, he brings books he pretends he doesn't understand, scrolls with looping glyphs, diagrams of bones and joints, star-charts peppered with mistakes.

"Help me," he groans, flopping into the grass beside me. "This makes no sense."

The parchment crackles between us, edges softened from the oils of his fingers. The inked symbols curve and tangle, more like vines than letters, more art than alphabet.

"You didn't even read the question," I murmur, frowning at the script.

"I did. It's in something ancient, said to be the language of the gods. I'm only fluent in being confused."

I smirk, brushing a strand of hair behind my ear.

"That's not a language."

"Tell that to Educator Drell. He speaks it fluently."

I take the scroll, eyes scanning the glyphs. My finger traces the arc of a particular rune.

"This one, *laerith*, it doesn't just mean 'to burn.' It means *to transform through flame*. It's more poetic. There's a difference."

He blinks at me. "How do you know that?"

"My Mama taught me." I glance up. "She says language is like soil. What you plant in it grows differently depending on what you feed it."

He sits up straighter, brow furrowing with something that looks a lot like reverence.

"That's... weirdly beautiful." A pause. "Do you think she'd teach me too?"

"Maybe. If you stop talking like a city prince."

He laughs, *really* laughs: head thrown back, teeth bared. It echoes through the trees.

"That's fair."

And just like that, something shifts, quietly, like a door opening somewhere deep in the woods.

We grow together like roots twisting beneath the same soil.

One day, he brings a book in a battered canvas satchel. When he pulls it out, it's wrapped in cloth like a relic, and he holds it with both hands like it might shatter if he's not careful.

"*The Star Thief,*" he says, reverent and a little sheepish. "My mother used to read it to me before bed when I was younger. My Pa said it was too soft for boys, so I read it twice as hard."

He presses it into my hands.

The cover is frayed, the title nearly worn away. I can still make out a boy with a comet-blade and a cloak stitched from nebulae. He looks angry or maybe lost.

We take it to the hollowed tree near the ridge, where the moss is soft and warm from the sun. He stretches out beside me, arms behind his head, eyes half-lidded like he's trying not to care how much this matters.

"You *love* this book," I tease, flipping to a page already covered in scribbles and underlines.

He snatches it back, grumbling. "I was little."

We spend hours like that. He reads a page in his stiff, careful cadence, every word deliberate like he's marching through them and we scribble our theories into the margins until the book looks like it's arguing with itself.

At one point he says, "It's not about the plot, it's about the *feeling*. The ache."

I stare at him. "That's... actually kind of beautiful."

He immediately throws a twig at me.

Later, the sun dips low, and the shadows stretch. We're lying shoulder to shoulder now, the book open across our knees. There's dirt on the pages, smudges where our fingers left traces of ash or ink. The Star Thief faces the end, alone on the sky-bridge, sword at his side.

"Do you think he exists?" I ask.

We don't say anything for a while. The only sound is the wind in the leaves and a bird calling in the distance.

He's quiet for a moment, "I think a little bit of him exists in all of us."

The book closes with a sigh.

Later, when the night comes and we're running again, barefoot, breathless, half-mad with stars, I glance back and call: "Come on, Star-boy!"

And he laughs, loud and bright and fearless.

"I'm coming, Noctis! Just, just don't forget me if the sky changes again!"

He teaches me village slang and the stiff cadence of military drills. I teach him the three ways to identify poisonous mushrooms by scent alone, and how the sky lies... how the new constellations don't match the old ones because the stars, like memory, forget themselves over time.

We climb cliffs just to see what's behind them. We sneak into ruined temples with rotting altars and shattered mosaics, laughing too loudly, daring the ghosts to find us. We find a bird skull etched with strange carvings and carry it around all day like a holy artifact.

And at night, we run barefoot through the dark, breathless and wild. The moon spills silver across the canopy, and the shadows slither and stretch like they're alive.

"Come on, Star-boy," I shout over my shoulder. "You're slow."

"I'm being *cautious*, Noctis!" he yells back. "You don't know what's out here!"

"I do. Everything."

He catches up just as I leap the old creek bed. We tumble down together into wet moss, limbs tangling, laughter breaking from us in gasps. Lysander rolls onto his back, chest heaving.

"I think I love this place."

"You didn't say that when the squirrel attacked you."

"That was a violent squirrel! You *saw* it."

I turn my head. He looks different here, untucked and untamed. Dirt on his cheek, twigs in his curls, and none of the stiffness he wears like armor back home.

"What's it like, your home?" I ask, voice low.

He's quiet at first, staring at the page like it has accused him of something. Then, slowly, "It's... polished, clean. Too clean, like it's pretending to be something it's not. My father's never wrong. My mother's never loud. And my brother..." He trails off, lips pressed thin.

"Your twin?" I ask, softly.

He nods, and when he speaks again, his voice is thinner, like thread pulled taut.

"Born minutes apart. But you'd never know it. Caelum is... Light. Literally. Saffron hair, amber eyes that always catch the sun. He never stops talking. Always *there*, filling every space. People love him for it: Educators, commanders, strangers. He makes the world look easy."

He doesn't say *and I don't*, but it's in the pause that follows.

"We used to be close. Real close. I thought we had the same blood, the same thoughts. Then one day it was like he started speaking a language I'd never heard before." A bitter little laugh. "Now I don't know who he is anymore. Maybe I never did."

I don't press. I just reach out, slow and quiet, and let my fingers brush his. He doesn't pull away and neither of us say anything for a long time.

He listens when I ramble about dreams I can't explain. He always asks, *"What do you think it means?"* Like nonsense can still have meaning.

He challenges me, pushes back. Laughs when I'm too serious and grows quiet when I ask the wrong questions.

He tells me stories of the village: the watching eyes, the suffocating expectations.

His father demands perfection. His mother rarely speaks. His brother is isolating himself, and no one says his name.

"Do you miss him?" I ask, one afternoon, while braiding cedar bark into a bracelet.

He's silent for a long time.

"Yes," he says finally. "But not in the way I think I'm supposed to."

I don't ask what he means. I just keep weaving, letting the silence hold space.

We lie side by side on our backs in the clearing, a torn star map spread across our chests. It's old, half-destroyed, rescued from some forgotten academy archive.

"See that one?" I say, pointing. "That's Dhalon's Cross. It's used when the moon is hidden."

"It looks like a kite."

"You look like a kite."

"That makes no sense."

"Exactly."

He elbows me and I giggle. Then he turns his head, eyes catching the starlight.

"Do you ever wish for more?"

"More what?"

"I don't know. Just... more. A bigger world, one where we don't have to pretend."

"I don't pretend," I lie, but I know what he means.

"I wish I could fly," he says. "Not with wings. Just... go. Be wind. Be free."

I close my eyes, "I wish I could remember the names of the stars before people renamed them. What they really meant."

He smiles, "That's such a *you* wish."

We press our pinkies together; a promise with no words but full of meaning.

We have bad days, too.

Days when he doesn't show and I wait too long. Days when he's distant and throws punches at trees until his knuckles split. Days when I speak and he flinches, like truth has claws.

It's been three days since he last visited.

By the fourth, I'm pacing like a trapped fox, half-mad with waiting. When he finally returns, rain plastering his curls to his skin, eyes red-rimmed and wary, I'm already there.

"You left," I say, sharp.

He doesn't speak.

"Did I do something?"

"I wasn't allowed to leave," he snaps. "My father found out I've been skipping my private lessons to come here. He's been watching. He thinks..." A breath. "He thinks you're dangerous."

The silence between us is instant and deep.

"I am dangerous," I say. "Just not in the way he thinks."

He stares at me, unsure whether to laugh or break. "I didn't want to stay away."

"But you did."

A pause, "I'm here now."

Rain hisses through the leaves like static.

"Then stay."

And he does.

Life is fuller now, brighter. Like spring stretching into the corners of a winter that had forgotten how to thaw.

Learning becomes play with him. Books turn into puzzles we solve together.

We argue over the phrasing of proverbs, over the structure of vanished spells. We laugh too hard and too long and forget to be careful.

Every question he asks makes me want to know more. Every answer I give feels like passing a sacred thing between cupped hands.

And I think, no, I *know:* I would've gone on like that forever if the world had let me.

POWERS AND LETDOWNS

AGE 9

LYSANDER BURSTS THROUGH THE underbrush like a storm, limbs flailing, breathless and loud. His shirt is half-untucked, twigs caught in his curls, and his whole body seems to hum with something just out of sight, like he's been touched by twilight turned inside out; not the shadow of night, but the moment before, when the world holds its breath.

"Sylvaine!" he pants, wide-eyed. "I *did it!*"

I don't look up right away. My fingers are busy with the moss, carefully etching a looping sigil into its soft green with a sharpened bone shard. The lines have to be delicate, perfect, otherwise they fade before they're finished. The act of making them grounds me.

"Did what?" I ask, not unkindly.

He flings his arms out like a magician mid-spell. For a heartbeat, there's nothing but the sound of wind through leaves and the charged stillness of the trees leaning in, as if even they are waiting.

Then there is the faintest flicker.

From his outstretched fingers, a curl of something rises; not smoke, not quite. It's darker than smoke, softer too, and yet somehow sharp at the edges, like a shadow that doesn't belong to anything, reaching blindly toward the light. It wavers in the air for half a second, shivers, and then vanishes.

I blink. "That's it?"

His grin widens, radiant. "That's *everything.*"

His whole face glows with the kind of joy that only comes when the world finally says *yes* to something you thought it never would.

I can see it, that deeper thing beneath the excitement. This isn't just pride: it's belonging, it's proof, it's the quiet fear in him finally letting go.

I try to smile; I do, but it feels tight around the edges, like something forced into shape.

"I thought it would be bigger," I say, voice soft.

"I thought I didn't have it at all," he replies, breathless with laughter. "But then last night, under the moon, I felt it. Like something behind my ribs cracked open. Like I stepped sideways inside myself, and there it was, waiting."

He drops to the moss beside me, knees knocking into mine, and starts scribbling wild spirals into the dirt with a stick, his whole body vibrating like a string pulled taut.

"I want to try something. Give me your hand."

I hesitate for just a second, then offer it to him. His palm is warm, calloused from climbing trees. His fingers close around mine with the easy familiarity of years. He closes his eyes, breathes.

A tendril of Shadow rises again, slower this time, like smoke in reverse. It reaches toward my skin, brushes it.

The moment it makes contact, it flinches back, retreats.

My hand feels colder after; not numb but *emptied.*

"Now you," Lysander says, gently. "Focus. Call the dark to you."

I nod. I try.

I close my eyes and call to the things I've known: caves where the air tasted like stone and water, moonless nights curled beneath pine boughs, bruises I never explained, words that stung more because they were never shouted, only whispered like truth, every time I bit my tongue until it bled instead of answering back.

I reach for all of it and nothing answers.

I try again, and again.

Still nothing.

Lysander doesn't say anything when he lets go of my hand, but I feel the way his joy folds in on itself; shrinking down to something polite, something quiet, like a song he's afraid to sing too loud in case I break.

"It's okay," I say quickly, before the silence can thicken. "I don't think I am blessed by the gods."

He opens his mouth, hesitates, then frowns and starts digging through his pack. He pulls out a small book, bound in pale leather, edges worn smooth. A sunburst is stamped on the cover, gleaming gold.

My stomach knots.

"I thought you might say that," he mutters, not looking at me. "So I... I stole this from Caelum's room. It's about channeling Light. I thought, maybe you're not like me. Maybe you're like him, like your Mama."

The idea makes my chest go tight. I stare at the book like it might bite.

"I don't think so," I say, my voice comes out flat.

"But you could try," he says, pushing it into my hands.

It's warm from his pack. The sigil on the cover glints like it knows something, like it *wants* something.

I flip it open. The pages are filled with precise, curling script" lines of invocation, sun-chants, hymns to clarity and flame. I try reading one. My tongue stumbles over the syllables, some of them sharp like broken glass, others smooth like river stones.

I raise my hands to the light as I imagine fire, embers, the gold-glow of dawn through mist.

Nothing. Nothing but the sound of my own breathing and the whisper of wind through the branches.

"I don't feel anything," I mumble.

Lysander watches me, face unreadable. Then he shifts closer. He doesn't touch me, but I feel the nearness of him anyway; the apology he doesn't know how to say.

"It's not fair," I mutter.

"No," he says softly. "It's not."

I close the book. The sun catches the gold on the cover, and for a moment it gleams so bright it hurts to look at, like it's laughing at me.

We sit like that for a long while.

The Shadows grow longer, curling around our feet like cats. His come when he calls, but mine don't even know my name.

LESSONS OF LIGHT

AGE 9

THERE IS A KNOCK at the door, hurried, but hesitant.

I hear the soft creak of the old hinges, the whisper of wind trying to slip inside, and a voice I don't recognize at first.

Mama answers. From my bed, I catch the gentle exchange drifting down the hallway like smoke.

"I'm sorry to bother you, ma'am, but I've been waiting every day by the stream for Sylvaine, and she hasn't shown up," Lysander's voice is low, edged with a worry he's trying to hold back. "I was wondering if she was alright."

"You've been waiting for her?" Mama asks, her voice warm and knowing, the kind that understands more than it says out loud.

He shifts on his feet, I can almost hear it. He hugs a bundle of books to his chest like a shield. "I didn't want to knock too hard. I thought... maybe she was mad at me."

"She's been sick," Mama interrupts gently. She turns, and from the doorway, she gives me a subtle wink. I blink at her from beneath the heavy quilts, the scent of cedar thick in my lungs, and my heart stumbles between relief and something sharper.

Mama opens the door just enough to let him in. Relief breaks across his face like morning.

He steps over the threshold carefully, reverently, like he's stepping into something sacred. His boots scrape softly against the stone floor, worn smooth by time and generations.

The cabin hums with quiet life: dried herbs above the hearth, beeswax candles flickering golden light, the faint smell of pine smoke and something bitter beneath it, medicine, or maybe magic.

Lysander's bundle is smaller than usual. The books are new, leather spines stiff and pale, still bound in coarse twine. He crouches beside my bed, settling into the space without disrupting it, and opens the top book.

"It's been a while," he says, voice uncertain, eyes flicking to the hollows beneath mine. "You scared me."

"I'm glad you came," I whisper, my throat raw. "I haven't been able to read much."

"Then we'll read together," he says, and offers a smile like the sun through storm clouds.

He opens the first book. Its pages gleam, un-creased and untested. His voice is steady as he begins, but the words land strange, too sharp at the edges.

"The Light illuminates the path of the faithful, burning away the darkness of ignorance and sin. It is pure, unwavering, the source of all that is good and just."

The pages are full of sermons, delicate script and angular diagrams of radiant beings, sunbursts and glyphs, each etched with painful precision. The ink is dark and final. The tone is not a song, but a command.

I listen and frown.

"That's not how I see it," I say softly. "The Light can't be everything. It needs Shadow to exist."

His eyes flash, surprise, then something like hope. "I think so too," he says quickly, then hesitates. "But the sermons say the Light is pure and good. Shadows only hide lies, fear."

A weak laugh rattles in my chest. "You sound like those village brats again. Light without Shadow is blindness, Lysander."

His jaw tightens. He looks down, fingers clutching the book too tightly. "Tell that to the instructors at the academy, or to my brother."

He doesn't usually bring him up so I wait.

"They praise Caelum for everything he does," Lysander says finally, his voice low and bitter-soft. "They say he's a blessing. That the Light sings through him. The Verse-Keepers call him chosen, proof that our family was touched by the divine."

He pauses, watching the fire like it might offer an answer. The flames crackle and spit, casting long shadows that dance along the floor.

"They don't say I'm cursed," he adds. "Not aloud, but they say I'm... *unclear*. 'Contrary to the natural order.' One of the Light-masters said I was 'tainted by old forces.'"

My breath catches in my throat.

"I showed them my Shadows because I thought it would mean something," he says, fingers tightening around the edge of the book in his lap. "I thought if I could prove the Shadow answered me, if they saw it was steady and quiet and real, they'd recognize it as divine, not dangerous."

He gives a dry, brittle laugh. "But they didn't panic. They didn't argue. They just smiled that tight little smile and told me not to worry about it. Said it was probably just residual energy, or a phase. That it would pass once I found my 'true alignment.'"

My stomach twists.

"They told me to stop practicing," he says softly, like he's ashamed of even admitting it. "Not because it was wrong, but because it was *irrelevant*. Said the gods make their intentions clear, and Caelum's Light is all the clarity we need."

I reach for his hand. It's trembling, cool with frustration, warm with pain, and I hold on tight.

"My father made me swear never to call to it again," he says, quieter now. "Especially not around Caelum."

"Your own brother?"

He nods once. "He's not cruel. He just... believes them. He thinks I've been led astray. That I'm something to be fixed." Lysander swallows. "But I know what I feel. The Shadow don't demand anything from me. It *welcomes* me. It doesn't burn. It listens."

His voice thins, almost breaking. "They say only one of us can rule and I guess I already know who it will be."

I squeeze his hand. "But you were chosen too."

His eyes lift to mine, wide and wounded.

"Exactly," he whispers. "But they only have room for one kind of miracle."

Footsteps sound outside the door: slow, deliberate, familiar. Pa's boots, and Mama's softer tread behind. They pause just beyond the threshold. Their voices are low, but not so low that I can't hear them.

"Would you two mind," Mama says gently, "if we old folks join you for a bit? Seems like there's a conversation worth having."

Pa enters first, settling into his worn armchair like he's folding himself into the forest. The firelight casts deep shadows across his lined face, but his eyes are steady. "Light without Shadow," he says, the words calm as rain, "is like a blade without a hilt. Beautiful, deadly and impossible to wield."

Mama kneels beside my bed, brushing a strand of hair from my cheek. "Balance is everything. The forest thrives because sun and shade take turns. One without the other would wither the roots."

Lysander is silent, staring down at the book like it's something rotten he's only just smelled.

"I didn't realize..." Lysander says, voice soft, breaking.

Pa nods. "That's the danger of dogma, son. Makes you think questions are curses. But Shadow isn't evil. It's shelter, it's rest, it's truth too deep for the sun to burn."

Mama's eyes meet mine. "It's in the space between light and dark that most real things grow."

Lysander looks to me, uncertain. I reach out and take his hand again. It's still trembling, but it's warmer now, steadier.

"We have to remember that," I say. "Even when they try to make us forget."

Pa leans forward, elbows on his knees, voice low but firm. "If you want, I can teach you more. The old ways. What was passed down in quiet. The kind of knowing that doesn't need a pulpit to stand."

Lysander blinks, startled. "You'd do that?"

"I want to," Pa says. "You have a gift. It deserves tending, not burying."

For a long moment, Lysander doesn't speak. Then he nods once, and it's the kind of nod that means everything.

The cabin holds us close, firelight dancing on the walls, shadows curling into corners like stories waiting to be told. Outside, the wind moves through the trees, carrying the night deeper into the bones of the world.

And somewhere, unseen but near, Shadow waits.

Not as a threat, but as a promise.

CRUMBLING

AGE 10

MY WORLD CRUMBLES.

Mama and Pa left early that afternoon, their packs heavy with books and maps. They said they'd be back by dinner, just a quick trip to the academy to meet with an old friend. I watched them go, the sky already bruised with gathering clouds, the air thick with the scent of the coming rain.

Mama turned at the edge of the clearing and lifted a hand in farewell. Pa looked back only once, his brow furrowed like he'd forgotten something but couldn't name what.

Now it's raining, the cold, relentless kind that taps against the cabin roof like a warning written in code only the old trees can read. I curl up by the hearth, trying to hold on to the last flickers of comfort. The logs burn low, pulsing embers giving off a faint, red breath. I feed the fire, one log at a time, but the shadows stretch longer with each heartbeat, reaching for me like fingers through water.

Outside, the forest is alive in the way things are just before they die, but it is too still. The trees sway but don't whisper. The leaves tremble but don't fall. Even the wind feels like it's waiting for something. I press my hand to the cool wood of the window frame, watching the droplets run down the glass like they're trying to escape.

Inside, the silence grows too loud. Every crackle of the fire is a shout, every ticking second is a scream. My body feels separate from me, like I'm watching myself wait from somewhere else, somewhere deeper and darker.

Hours pass. The sky blackens as day slips into night like a thief. Still, they don't return.

By dusk, the forest feels wrong, like a mouth clamped shut mid-prayer. It is then that I see it, a white light pulsing from the ridge beyond the trees: unnatural and cold, too perfect to be fire.

It doesn't flicker. It is blinding and silent, like the stars themselves have fallen and decided not to forgive us.

I run.

The ground slips beneath my feet, all mud and rot. Branches slap my face. My lungs burn. My heart pounds an uneven rhythm, screaming not just to run, but to *run faster*.

I crest the ridge and find nothing but ruin: ash, shattered pines, the earth burned down to bone. There are no bodies but I know. I know in the hollow way a scream lives behind your ribs long before it ever leaves your mouth.

When I return to the cabin, the fire has gone out.

The next day, Lucien comes; his coat is pressed, his boots clean, his hair dry and neat as always. No ash clings to him.

"Sylvaine," he says, too smooth, too easy. "I am so sorry. It was the Shadows, rebels. We tried to stop them with the Light, but we were too late."

He doesn't flinch when he tells me this, doesn't blink.

"I can take you back with me," he says. "You shouldn't be alone."

I try to follow but my feet won't move. The forest *won't let me go*.

Something old, something wild and root-deep, presses against my spine. It doesn't speak, it remembers, and I feel it coil around me like ivy on a trellis, quiet and firm.

Stay.

Lucien frowns when I refuse to leave. He says something about grief, about stubbornness, but I don't care what he thinks.

Days pass. I don't count them.

One night, around dusk, Lysander finds me curled in the hollow of the tree where we first met. The bark is rough against my skin, but grounding. The scent of pine is thick and green, bitter with sap and old wind.

"They're gone," I whisper. My voice cracks like ice. "They never came home. There was a light, unnatural. I ran as quickly as I could but I didn't find any bodies. I couldn't find them."

He doesn't speak. He just kneels and wraps himself around me, not to fix it, not to explain it, but to hold it with me. His arms are shaking. His breath comes in short, sharp bursts.

When my sobs finally break open, they come from some place deeper than language. I cry until my ribs ache and my throat is raw. When the storm in me quiets, he leans close, his lips near my temple, and says, barely audible, "Caelum is also gone but I don't think he is dead; I think I would feel it."

The weight of his words is like a stone dropped into the dark, rippling outward; loss braided into grief, grief becoming something shared.

The forest around us doesn't interrupt. It bears witness.

Somewhere above, a raven croaks once. The sound echoes: low, hoarse, final. Beneath us, the earth holds still.

Lysander's arms feel both strong and breakable, as if he's clinging to me to keep from falling apart.

His curls are soaked, tangled with twigs and rain. His face is pale, lips cracked. His eyes, once filled with mischief and flame, are dim, haunted.

"It's not just them," he murmurs, voice rough like stone against stone. "It's everything. The Light's taking more than it's giving. I see it. I *feel* it. And the more it tries to burn the Shadow out of the world, the more I think... maybe it's afraid."

I look up at him. There's something old in his face now, something that wasn't there before. Not entirely wisdom, but the beginning of it.

I nod, my hand finding his. "We can't let it win."

"We won't," he says. "We'll find the balance, like your parents taught. Even if we have to build it from ruins."

The forest exhales around us. The wind shifts, gentle through the leaves, brushing over our shoulders like a benediction.

We rise together, mud clinging to our boots, the last threads of twilight spilling through the branches above. The trees stand tall. The sky opens. The stars begin to speak in light again, but not loudly, just enough to remind us the dark is never empty.

Deep within the woods, beneath root and shadow and silence, something ancient stirs, Not to punish, not to destroy, but to remember and to rise.

Unopened Doors

Age 10

Lucien starts to show up more often.

At first, it's just once; a soft knock, a call of my name that I don't answer. Then he shows up again the next week, and the next. He returns like the rain: patient, persistent, unwelcome.

It is always the same.

His footsteps are muffled by the wet earth followed by the soft rustle of his satchel brushing the tall grass. He never lingers long, never speaks through the door anymore. He leaves small offerings at the edge of the porch: a loaf of bread wrapped in muslin, a jar of honey glinting like captured sunlight, bundles of herbs tied with crimson string. Sometimes dried lavender, sometimes rosemary, never mixed.

His presence is a storm cloud on the edge of my world. I never let him in.

Through the dusty window, I watch him; his coat too neat, his face too calm, as if grief is something he's practiced in a mirror and pressed into polite shape. He places notes with careful hands, folding each one twice, weighing it down with a stone like a prayer nobody asked for.

It's dangerous to live like this, one reads. *You need the Light.*

The Order can protect you, says another. *But you must return. We can't guard you out here.*

He starts leaving books, smooth, pale volumes bound in cream-colored leather, Light doctrine, always a new edition. Their pages are crisp, their spines stiff. They smell like cold ink and rules. The symbols pressed into the covers shimmer faintly when the firelight hits them. They remind me of frost.

Still, I do not open the door.

Eventually, I begin to find packages, and those I do open. The first one came two weeks after Mama and Pa disappeared. I knew they weren't coming back, but still I refused to go with Lucien.

I was trying my best.

I boiled pine needles into tea. I soaked lentils overnight and hoped that meant they wouldn't make me sick. I burned one side of the bread the first time I tried to bake without Mama's hands guiding mine, but I still ate it.

That morning, I found a small brown box tucked beneath the edge of the woodpile. It hadn't been there the night before.

No knock, no footsteps in the mud, no note under a stone.

There were two letters, smudged in black ink along the side: *T.E.*

I stared at it for a long time before touching it. Something about it felt different, not just because Lucien would have knocked, or left a note, or called out first, but because there was no Light symbol, no clean edges, no wax seal. It didn't *want* to be seen.

Inside were dried mushrooms, a sealed pouch of barley, a small jar of pine sap salve, and a flat disc of hard cheese wrapped in waxed paper.

I tested everything carefully and waited. Nothing burned, or twisted, or left me sick. The food was clean. The medicine worked.

I ate for the first time in weeks without trembling.

More came, always without warning, weekly, then sometimes every few days.

A tin of sweetened tea, a bundle of soft cloth for mending, small vials of tinctures that steadied my breath when fear curled in my chest, coins, sometimes; it was never much, but it was always enough.

The handwriting was always the same; rushed and uneven, like someone who knew how to write, but hadn't been taught to slow down. It was always just *T.E.*

One parcel included a folded paper with a strange sigil drawn in charcoal: half-moon, half-root, wrapped in thorns. I didn't understand it, but it didn't feel threatening. It felt... familiar. I pressed it between the pages of *The Forest Almanac* and shelved it beside Pa's maps.

The string on every bundle was the same, too, mossy green, tied in a knot I couldn't quite replicate. Nothing about the parcels felt like Lucien. They weren't crisp or perfect. They weren't offerings or bribes.

They were survival, and so I trusted them.

Inside, the house smells of cedar and smoke. The fire burns low but steady, its glow a quiet heart in the dark. Dried herbs hang from the rafters, their scent mingling with the musty warmth of old paper, the faint sweetness of jam, and the sharp tang of salt.

I've turned the hearth into something sacred. Part memory, part promise: a photograph, a candle stub in a dish Mama once used for ink, a carved stone owl, its wings spread wide, the one that always watched from Pa's desk.

This is my sanctuary now.

I am almost eleven, living alone in the forest on the edge of the world. I am doing my best and holding on.

Lysander still comes.

Unlike Lucien, he does not announce himself. He never knocks. He moves like rain through leaves; quiet, inevitable, like the forest knows him, and lets him pass.

Sometimes he's soaked to the bone, hair clinging to his forehead in tangled curls, his cloak dripping puddles onto the threshold he never crosses without invitation. Other times he's barefoot, dry despite the mud and mist, his presence so soft it barely seems real, more dream than boy, like the forest shaped him out of longing and moss.

But always, he brings books: never clean, never new... not anymore.

Their spines are cracked, their covers peeling. The pages are yellowed and dog-eared, filled with margin-notes in his crooked hand, ink that curls and loops like vines reaching for light. They're books no one else would keep, stories that feel like secrets: folktales, field guides, forgotten things.

When my hands are too heavy with grief to turn the pages, he reads them aloud. His voice is quiet, uneven sometimes, but steady in the way rivers are, soft but certain. It carries the rhythm of the woods: moss and damp roots, rustling leaves and birdsong far away. His breath hitches when the words are too close to wounds we share, but he keeps going. He always keeps going.

Sometimes he brings jam, wild berry, dark and rich, stolen from somewhere he won't name. The lids are scratched, the jars don't match, the labels are half-torn or faded to nothing, but the sweetness is real. We eat it by the spoonful, sticky-fingered and silent, daring the world to take one more thing from us.

Once, we ate a whole jar without speaking. Just sat on the floor by the hearth, trading the spoon back and forth like it was the last honest thing left in the world.

When he sits beside me, the cabin feels warmer. Not because he burns the Shadows away, but because he knows how to *share* them. He never flinches from the silence, never tries to chase it out. He fills it in gentle ways: with a story, with a presence that doesn't press or prod, with a look that says *I know and I'm here.*

There's a kind of magic in that.

He carries comfort in his eyes, and compassion in his hands. They are rough sometimes, dirt under the nails, scratches from brambles, but when he brushes my shoulder or hands me a cup of tea, he's always careful, like he's learned how to be soft without being afraid of breaking.

He never asks me to speak, never asks me to remember, or explain, or move on. He just comes, and stays, and listens to the fire crackle while the wind presses against the windows.

From then on, we are different; two ghosts, drifting through the wreckage of our childhoods, tethered not by what we've lost, but by what we've learned to survive.

He becomes my anchor, the steady pulse I cling to when grief threatens to pull me under, the breath I match when my own feels too ragged. I become his tether, the rooted stillness he needs when the Light inside him flares too bright, too cruel, too sharp.

He tells me once, quietly, so the trees won't hear, that Light can blind just as fast as it can guide. That his brother didn't see the edge until it was too late. I squeeze his hand, and he doesn't say more. He doesn't need to.

In the hush of the woods, we hold hands.

We are ten and twelve, bruised but breathing, raw but not ruined. Children who grew too fast and too sideways, shaped by fire and absence, by promises broken and paths refused.

But we are still here.

When he can stay, or doesn't want to go home, we sleep on woven mats near the fire, our backs to the woodpile. We watch the flames and whisper stories to them, half-truths, maybe-truths, things we wish were true. We count the stars we can see through the gaps in the canopy of trees. We dare ourselves to hope, just a little.

We are learning to live in the between, in a place that is not quite Light, not quite Shadow.

The trees stand watch, dripping with the last of the storm. The sky bruises toward dusk, all purple and silver and a whisper of fire at the edge. Somewhere deep in the forest, a fox cries, high and sharp, like the echo of something half-forgotten, the kind of sound you only hear once and always remember.

And behind it all, something waits: old as root, soft as ash. Not Light, not Shadow, but the thing that grows in-between.

TETHERED BY GHOSTS

AGE 11-17

THE YEARS BLUR LIKE watercolors in the rain, bleeding into one another, soft at the edges, indistinct. Time loses its grip, slipping between my fingers like mist. Even through the haze of the years, there are moments that carve themselves into the hollows of my ribs, into the fragile corners of my heart. They are the moments that hold the weight of everything, without ever speaking it aloud.

We learned how to exist in silence; not the strained, aching kind of silence, but the kind that grows between people who have been through too much together. The kind of quiet where every glance says everything, where every gesture is filled with the unspoken things we've lived. We stopped needing to speak every hurt aloud, stopped needing to explain why the spaces between us grew wide sometimes, or why the air felt too heavy to breathe. Instead, we moved through the days like two ghosts stitched together by shared grief, by breath, by pulse.

At eleven, I learn how to grieve without crying. I learn to carry loss like a second skin, something I wear beneath my clothes. It's not something that shows on the surface, but I feel it every day. The loss is there, like a dull ache in my chest, a whisper in the corners of my mind. It weighs differently every day, sometimes like iron, sometimes like fog. Some mornings, I wake up with it pressed so hard against my ribs that I can't breathe. Other times, it's a quiet thing, a weight that lingers just beneath the surface.

Lysander doesn't try to fix it. He doesn't tell me I should feel better, or that I should move on. He doesn't try to heal the wound. He just walks beside me, his presence a steady beat in the rhythm of my life. That, somehow, is the only thing that helps. The quiet company of someone who doesn't ask me to explain, someone who knows grief in his own way. We don't speak of it, not often, but there are times when the silence between us is full, thick with understanding.

We spend our days in the fractured places left behind by the world: crumbling stone gardens overtaken by moss, old paths overgrown with wildflowers, the forgotten corners of the village where no one else bothers to go. In a world that has turned away from us, we turn toward each other. We find solace in these broken places, these remnants of something that once was. In the silence, there's a kind of healing, not from the pain, but with it.

Sometimes, we go to the riverbank where the reeds buzz with insects and the water forgets where it's going. The current moves slowly, as though it, too, is trying to forget something. We lie back in the tall grass, listening to the soft, rhythmic flap of dragonfly wings, the low murmur of the river's secrets. He reads aloud from the scrolls we've salvaged, books that no one else cares about, filled with forgotten knowledge and stories that are as strange as the silence between us. His voice steadies me, low and sure, a thread I follow back to the present. In his words, I find something solid, something I can hold onto when everything else is slipping through my fingers.

While we sit near the bank, he finds long blades of grass, and his fingers work them with quiet concentration.

One day, he weaves a loop from a single strand and places it atop my head, the delicate grass weaving through my hair like a crown of forgotten things.

"You're a queen now," he says, his eyes serious, as though the weight of the title means something.

"Of what?" I ask, the words soft, half-smiling at the absurdity of it.

He thinks for a moment, brow furrowing, before he answers, his voice quiet but certain, "ghosts and broken things."

I wear it until it falls apart and then we don't speak of it again. The memory of it lingers in me, more real than anything else, more lasting than the fragile crown of grass.

There was a time I knew how to gut a fish in thirty seconds flat, how to silence a hare with a single stone. My parents taught me that. Mama's hands were always quick and precise, showing me the ways of the forest. Pa always laughed when I smeared blood on my cheek by accident, his fingers brushed it away with gentle care.

They taught me reverence, how we took only what we needed, never more. It was a practice born of respect, an understanding of life and death that was as natural as the air we breathed.

But now? Now, I can't bear it.

I haven't hunted in months. I haven't fished since the river froze the winter after they died. I try, sometimes. I'll go out with traps or a hook in hand, trying to reconnect with what was once so familiar. But the moment I see eyes, real, living eyes, not the cold, glassy eyes of something dead, something inside me twists. My fingers shake. My breath becomes too shallow. I can't do it. I won't.

Lysander never says anything about it. He never tells me it's okay to stop. He just leaves extra berries on my side of the cloth when we share food, his quiet way of saying he understands. Sometimes, he slips me the softest part of the root stew, the tender bits that he knows I'll eat. He pretends not to watch when I push aside the dried meat, when I can't bring myself to swallow the things that taste too much like loss.

I carry that, too, like I carry everything else, quietly, close to the skin, and always held within me, like an unspoken truth.

There are days when the silence between us is heavier than others, when the weight of all that's unsaid presses down on me, but Lysander doesn't push. He doesn't ask for more than I can give. In that quiet, I find something I never thought I would again. A kind of peace, not the absence of grief, but the quiet acceptance that grief and love can exist side by side. In the end, we don't need to fix each other; we just need to be.

This is enough.

By twelve, we've built a world between us.

It's stitched from Shadow and thistles, from the scent of stolen bread and the weight of the silence we've made ours.

We've learned how to weave grief into the space between us. We've learned how to navigate the gaps without ever asking for anything more. The world we've built is ours alone, fragile yet strong in ways we can't explain. It feels safer than the real one, the one that keeps turning its back on us, the one that feels like a dream we're too afraid to wake from.

One night, we make a fire just off the road, its flames licking at the night sky. Smoke curls upward, twisting like a question we're afraid to ask. The forest around us is still, save for the occasional rustle of leaves and the soft murmur of the wind through the trees. It's the kind of night where the air feels thick, heavy with things left unsaid.

I sit cross-legged, knees pulled to my chest, watching the fire with a kind of quiet intensity. The flames are alive, flickering and dancing, and for a moment, I feel like I could reach out and catch the fire in my hands, if only I dared.

"You're too quiet," Lysander says, his voice low, barely cutting through the crackling of the fire. He pokes at the embers with a stick, sending a few sparks spiraling into the night.

"I'm thinking," I reply, my voice softer than I mean it to be. I feel the weight of the words even as they leave my mouth, as though they carry more than just the truth of the moment.

"About what?" He doesn't look at me but I can hear the curiosity in his voice, the way it lingers between us, asking without pressing.

I hesitate, the words feeling strange on my tongue. I've been turning this thought over in my mind for days, ever since I saw the birds circle above the cabin, the ones that always appeared in the quietest moments, the ones I used to believe brought messages from the past.

It's a question I've never asked aloud, not even to him, but tonight, with the fire flickering and the world stretched out beyond us, it seems like the right time to ask.

"I was wondering if people disappear for good when they die," I start, my voice a little shaky, "or if they leave pieces behind."

I don't meet his eyes. Instead, I focus on the flames, watching them twist and curl like they're trying to tell me something, like they hold an answer I can't find.

Lysander doesn't speak at first. He just watches the fire, his face bathed in the warm, flickering glow. His eyes, dark in the night, seem distant, lost in thought, but his silence doesn't feel uncomfortable. It feels like he's listening to something I can't hear, something deeper than the crackling wood.

"I think the pieces stay," he says at last, his voice steady, sure in a way that makes the night feel less heavy. "In other people. In places. In the air."

His words hang between us, suspended like the smoke rising from the fire. I take a slow breath, letting them settle into me, trying to understand them, trying to hold onto them. There's something in his words that feels true, a kind of quiet certainty that resonates in a place inside me I don't often reach.

I nod, though I'm not sure if it's for him or for myself. The fire continues to burn, and with each flicker I feel a sense of connection, a sense of something stretching across time and space.

And then, just like that, I swear I can smell my Mama's perfume. It is the faintest, sweetest hint of it, like the memory of something tucked away in a drawer I can't quite open. It's so subtle that I almost think it's just my mind playing tricks. But I know it's real, a trace of her that lingers, a piece of her left behind, just as Lysander said.

We fall into silence again, but it's not the kind of silence that feels like an absence. It's the kind of silence that fills the space between us with understanding. We sit in the dark, the fire crackling in front of us, its warmth wrapping around us like a blanket.

Later, when the fire is nothing more than a few glowing embers, we curl up on opposite sides of it. The night is cooler now, the air sharp with the promise of dawn. I pull my knees closer to my chest, the fabric of my cloak soft against my skin.

The world around us fades into the quiet of the forest. I let myself drift into sleep, the rhythm of the night, of the fire, of the wind, of Lysander's quiet breathing, lulling me into dreams.

When I wake, the fire has long since died down, leaving behind only the faintest glow. The stars above are fading as dawn begins to creep over the horizon. I blink, disoriented for a moment, and then I feel it: his hand, close to mine, almost touching. The warmth of it is enough to send a jolt through me, a quiet surge of something I don't know how to name.

For a long moment, neither of us moves, neither of us speaks. It's the kind of stillness that feels like something shared, something unspoken. And for a heartbeat, I wonder if I'll ever have the courage to close that gap between us, to let the touch linger a little longer, to see what might happen if I do.

I don't. I let the distance stay, because in that moment, it feels just right. It feels like the only thing I can trust in a world that's never been quite so certain.

So I stay still, breathing in the air of the forest, the lingering scent of the fire, and the soft warmth of his presence beside me, and I close my eyes again, letting the quiet carry me back to sleep.

In the space between us, everything seems possible.

By thirteen, we've gotten good at stealing.

The hunger we carry between us is always there, a quiet pressure that never lets us forget how fragile survival is. For him, it's just another game, a thrill that sparks in the moment and fades just as quickly. For me, it's something else entirely. It's sharp-edged, cutting through the weight of everything we've lost. Hunger strips everything down to its core, makes each decision simple, clean. Guilt is a luxury for people who have enough to eat.

There's a day when we snatch fruit from a merchant's cart, figs and plums, their skins are soft and ripe. Our hands are quick, practiced. The plums practically tumble into our grasp, and in the frenzy of it, our fingers brush against each other, a fleeting touch, but it feels like something more, like a spark that goes unnoticed at first.

We run, breathless and wild, our feet pounding against the cobblestones, dodging under low-hanging laundry lines and through crooked alleyways, laughing like we've just pulled off some grand heist.

The world is a blur of motion and sound, our shoes hitting the ground, the call of birds overhead, the hum of the city that we've learned to navigate like ghosts. Our laughter rings out, raw and free, like it belongs to a time we can't quite hold onto.

When we're finally safe, hidden away in the hollow of our tree, the one place that feels truly ours, untouchable, we collapse into the mossy nook. The air smells green and damp, filled with the quiet hum of the forest, and the earth beneath us is cool against our backs. I'm still laughing, breathless, as I sit up and peel the skin from a plum, feeling the soft fruit give beneath my fingers.

I dip it into some honey before I bite into it, the juice running down my chin and wrist, sticky and sweet. Something in his gaze makes the moment feel heavier, more real than it should be.

"What?" I ask, still laughing, licking the honey from my fingers, my mouth full of fruit. The sweetness tastes like freedom, like escape.

He doesn't answer immediately. Instead, he just watches me. I feel a strange pull, something deeper in the way he's looking at me, something I can't quite place. His brow furrows slightly, like he's trying to figure out a puzzle he's been staring at for too long. Then, with a small movement, he leans forward, his hand reaching toward me, slow and deliberate.

"You've got honey here," he says quietly, his voice softer than I expected. He touches the corner of my mouth, his thumb brushing lightly against my skin.

I freeze for a moment, caught in the feel of his hand there, the simple pressure of his touch, but I don't pull away. Instead, I look up at him, and there's something in his eyes that makes my heart skip a beat; a flicker of something I haven't seen before, something sharp and tender, like the knife-edge of a storm.

Instead of wiping the honey away like I expected, he does something different, something I've never imagined, never expected.

He kisses me.

It's slow. Not clumsy, like I always imagined a first kiss would be, but like he's been waiting for this moment, waiting for years, and now that it's finally here, he wants to make sure he doesn't forget a single part of it. His lips are warm, familiar, and they fit against mine with a quiet intensity. Like a secret we've been keeping but didn't know we were hiding. Like a promise we haven't made yet, but somehow both of us know it's there.

My heart stutters in my chest, and for a heartbeat, time stops. There's no rushing, no urgency, just the feeling of him close, of his hand still resting lightly on my face, of the world falling away until all that's left is the press of his lips against mine and the soft, rhythmic thud of my pulse.

When we pull apart, the silence between us feels different. It's heavier, charged with something unspoken, something that hangs in the air like the smell of rain just before it falls.

I don't know what to say, or if I should say anything at all. So, we just sit there, in the cool shade of the tree, surrounded by the sounds of the forest, the rustle of the leaves, and the steady beat of our breathing.

The plums and figs lie forgotten between us, the honeyed sweetness slipping away as we both try to catch our breath, both of us unsure of what this means, or what it's supposed to mean. My mind races, trying to piece together everything I'm feeling, but for once, I don't have the words. I don't need them.

I look at him, and he looks back. His cheeks are a little pink. His eyes wide like he's not quite sure what just happened. His expression is a mix of surprise and something else I can't place. I can feel my own face heating up, my stomach doing a funny little flip.

I open my mouth like I'm going to say something, but the words don't come. Instead, we both just sit there giggling nervously, unsure whether to look at each other or away. The silence between us is different now, more awkward than anything. I can't stop blushing, and neither can he.

After a few moments, he clears his throat and shifts a little, brushing his hair out of his eyes, and I do the same, pretending I'm not as embarrassed as I feel.

I finally glance up at the sky, watching the sunlight fade behind the trees, and for a long time, neither of us says a word. We just sit there, still and quiet, the laughter slowly dying away as the evening settles around us.

Every so often, we sneak little glances at each other. When our eyes meet, we burst into giggles again. It's a strange, fluttery feeling, and neither of us knows quite what to do with it.

When I finally reach for a plum, its sweetness no longer tastes like hunger, it tastes like the beginning of something I don't yet understand.

At fourteen, everything shifts; not suddenly, but like a tide creeping in.

It's a subtle change at first, so small that I almost don't notice it. His shoulder brushes mine more often when we're walking side by side. His eyes linger when I'm not looking. When I catch him watching, he quickly looks away, but there's something in the way he does it, like he's not really embarrassed, just... unsure. I start to miss him like a limb when we're apart, like something I didn't know I needed until it was gone.

We spend hours beneath our favorite tree, the one with bark that peels like old paper, curled and soft in my hands. He carves little symbols into the wood, runes that mean nothing and everything all at once. Sometimes, he traces them with his thumb, like he's trying to make sense of them too. He makes up stories about them, about things we'll never understand. I trace them with my finger like they mean something, and maybe they do.

In those moments, I don't need to understand anything. The world feels just right, like we're part of something larger, something that's been waiting for us.

In the quiet of those afternoons, I begin to notice the changes in us. My body feels different. Not just in the way it moves, but in the way it's starting to take shape. Things I'm not sure how to deal with. His voice, too, deepens, cracking sometimes like ice in thaw. He laughs when it happens, a little self-conscious, but it's not as awkward as it used to be. His laughter is warmer now, softer, as if it's finding a new place to settle.

One afternoon, we sit side by side on the mossy ground, the scent of pine thick in the air, reading our mismatched books in comfortable silence. The sun filters through the trees, casting dappled shadows on the pages. At once, I realize that I haven't thought about Mama all day. The thought hits me like a wave, unexpected and heavy. Guilt rises in my chest, sharp and uncomfortable, like I've forgotten something important. For a moment, the world around me feels too big, and I can't quite catch my breath.

I close my eyes, trying to push it away, but when I do, I feel his hand slip into mine. It's a quiet, simple gesture, but it steadies me in a way I don't know how to explain. I don't tell him what I'm thinking, because I don't have to.

He already knows. He always knows.

Fifteen feels like the edge of something; not a cliff, not yet, but a precipice I can't quite see over.

We lie in the tall grass, our bodies stretched out beneath the vast sky, staring up at the stars. They blink in and out like they're tired of being watched, flickering like old bulbs that know they won't be around much longer.

The air is still, thick with the hum of summer. Everything feels too quiet and too loud at once. There's a weight to the silence, a question that hangs between us, unspoken but understood.

"Do you think we'll always be like this?" I ask, the words slipping out before I can stop them.

It's a small question, but it feels enormous in the dark, like it might swallow us whole. My heart beats a little faster, like I'm waiting for an answer that will change everything.

His hand is close enough to feel the warmth radiating off him, but not touching, just an inch of space that seems impossibly wide. I feel it.

He takes a long time to answer, like he's measuring his words, making sure they won't fall apart when he says them. "I don't know. The world doesn't like things that don't fit."

I chew on his words, trying to make sense of them, but I can't.

"But we fit," I say softly, the certainty in my voice surprising even me, because it's true, we fit. Somehow, we always have. I think we always will.

He turns to look at me then, his profile outlined in the moonlight. His face is a study of contrasts, the silver light turning the sharp lines of his jaw and the curve of his cheek into something dreamlike, something impossible. He looks at me for a long time, as if I'm a question he can't answer. His eyes are so full of things neither of us know how to say.

"I know," he whispers, and there's something in his voice, something raw and heavy. "That's what scares me."

My chest tightens, a knot forming where my heart used to be. The words sting more than I expected, and I don't know how to respond. The weight of them presses down on me, heavier than the silence that has been settling between us for weeks now.

Before I can say anything, I reach out and thread my fingers through his. His hand is cold, the kind of cold that seeps into your bones, but maybe it's mine. It's hard to tell anymore, whose warmth is whose, whose coldness belongs where.

I give his hand a small squeeze, as if I can hold onto the moment, as if that will make it stay.

He doesn't move, doesn't speak. He shifts, lying his head on my shoulder. The shift of his body is slow, like he's been carrying something heavy and finally gets the chance to rest.

I stay awake, counting the stars that haven't yet disappeared. There aren't many left, but I try to remember them: the ones that hang on, the ones that refuse to fade into the dark.

No matter how hard I try, I can't forget the weight of his words, or the way they feel like they're carving something new into the space between us.

In the quiet of the night, I wonder if we can fit forever, or if, one day, the world will take the one thing that makes us feel like we belong.

By sixteen, the world starts to press in, harder, crueler.

It creeps up around the edges, slipping through the cracks of the world we've made, squeezing into the corners of our lives until there's no space left to breathe. People begin to notice us, to wonder, to whisper.

At first, it's just a few sideways glances, a murmur here and there, but soon, it's more than that: more eyes, more questions, more people who think they know who or what we are.

We're nearly caught one day sneaking out of a shuttered bakery, our cloaks heavy with old loaves of bread that still smell of yeast and flour, warm in the early morning light. We've done it a hundred times, and for a second, I almost believe it's safe. But this time, there's a flash of movement: a guard, turning the corner just as we're about to slip into the alley. My heart stutters. We run, fast and silent, barely out of reach, our breath ragged in our throats.

Another time, we return to find our hollow tree gutted by fire. The stump stands blackened and charred, smoke still curling lazily from the ashes. Our scrolls, the only things we've ever really owned, are gone. The tiny symbols Lysander carved into the bark, the stories we wrote in the margins, the things we kept secret have turned to nothing. I stand there, frozen, the familiar weight of the world sinking deep into my chest.

Lysander doesn't say anything at first. He just stares at it, at the remains of the one place that has always been ours. His fists curl, his knuckles going white. Before I can stop him, he punches the tree beside us, his hands pound against the rough bark until blood spills from his knuckles. He doesn't make a sound, not at first, but I can see the rage in him, feel the heat of it in the air between us. His shoulders shake with it. His body trembles as if it might split open from the force of it all.

I can't breathe and then tears come; not because of the fire, not just because of the tree, but because of everything that's happening. Because of what we're losing. Because of the world creeping closer, like the tide, always rising, always taking.

I sit in the dirt, pressing my hands into the earth, grounding myself in the only thing that hasn't been destroyed. For the first time in months, I cry. The tears are heavy, and they come slowly, as if my body's been holding onto them for so long it doesn't know how to let go.

"Everything good disappears," I say through the tears, my voice thick and raw, like it's been buried with everything else.

Lysander doesn't answer right away, he doesn't need to. His arms are around me, pulling me close. His voice is soft, steady, like the calm after a storm. "No," he says, his lips close to my ear, "it just hides; it changes shape."

I let the words sink in, even though they don't make it all better. They don't stop the ache in my chest, the emptiness that stretches across everything we've ever known, but they're something. They are a kind of truth I can hold onto for now.

We sit there for a while, our breaths slow, the quiet around us heavy with the weight of the day. Then, as the sun begins to set, we gather what's left of the world we used to have.

We find a small box, old and weathered, and we fill it with what we can: charcoal pieces, fragments of things that used to mean something, a melted coin, bent and worn from years of use, a ribbon I used to wear in my hair, now faded and frayed. We bury it deep in the roots of the tree, beneath the blackened wood, a funeral for the version of ourselves who thought the world might leave us alone. The version of ourselves who believed we could carve out a space, a small one, just for us, and that it might stay that way forever.

The world doesn't let things stay. It doesn't let things be.

As we cover the box with dirt, I feel something shift between us, something that settles in the space where the hollow tree used to be. There's no turning back now, no way to go back to the way things were before. But maybe, just maybe, the world has more shapes to offer us: more spaces to claim, more things to hold.

Even though I don't believe in forever anymore, I believe in us. That's enough for now.

Seventeen tastes like smoke and wine, like the kind of night that slips through your fingers before you realize it's already slipping away.

There's something sweet and sorrowful about it, a quiet urgency that lingers in the air, a promise that smells too much like goodbye, even if neither of us wants to name it yet.

The heat between us doesn't burn anymore; it blazes, low and steady, like coals that never die. It's a fire that smolders deep inside, something we carry without needing to tend it.

The summer swarms with life. The forest alight with fireflies. We are shrouded in the scent of pine and earth, the heavy weight of warm air wraps around us like a blanket. The world feels alive in a way that's both comforting and suffocating, as though it's holding its breath with us, waiting for something that neither of us can name.

One evening, we wander deeper into the woods than we've ever gone before, to the glade where the ferns grow high, and the sky can't quite reach us. It's a place that feels carved from the heart of the forest, untouched by time or hands. The ground is warm beneath our feet, soft and damp with the last remnants of the day's heat. The shadows stretch long and languid, and the only sound is the rustle of the leaves in the breeze.

It feels like we're the only two people left in the world, and in that moment, we might as well be. The weight of everything falls away, everything but the two of us.

We kiss like it's the only thing keeping us whole.

The world feels different now. It's deeper, slower. Every touch carries the weight of everything we've never said, everything we've never had to say. There's no rush, no urgency. It's not just desire, but something older, something deeper, a connection that we've been building for years without even knowing it.

Our bodies are not just bodies, they are history.

They are the memories of all the days we've spent in this forest, tangled in the spaces between Light and Shadow, between laughter and tears.

We undress with shaking hands. Not out of lust, but reverence. We don't need to explain it, and we don't try. We move slowly, as though each piece of clothing we shed is an offering, an act of trust and devotion.

There's a tenderness in the way we touch, a sacredness in the way we come together, as though the very earth beneath us is holding its breath, too. Our love is a ritual now, older than both of us, as old as the roots that twist through the ground, as timeless as the sky above.

After, he holds me close, and I feel the steady thrum of his heart beneath my cheek. His arms are strong, a promise of safety, a promise of forever that neither of us dares to say aloud. I rest my head on his chest, listening to the rhythm of his heartbeat, counting each pulse like it's the only thing that matters in the world.

One, two... a thousand.

The sun begins to rise, spilling soft and golden through the trees like forgiveness, like a gentle kiss on the forehead after a long and difficult night. I feel the warmth of it on my skin, and in the quiet, I can hear the world waking up around us, slow and steady.

"I love you," he whispers into my hair, his voice low and filled with something I can't quite name.

"I know," I whisper back, the words tasting like truth, like the one thing I've always known without knowing it. "I think I loved you before I even knew what it meant."

It feels like a promise, the kind of promise that doesn't need to be spoken aloud, the kind that doesn't need to be broken.

We don't say goodbye. We never have to. Not while the forest still keeps our secrets. Not while the trees continue to stand watch over us. Not while his hand still finds mine in the dark. Not while the memory of starlight and honey and the hollow of each other's names still burns beneath our tongues.

We are two souls caught in the quiet wreckage of the world, stitched together by something stronger than words, something that doesn't need to be explained.

Goodbyes and Promises

Age 17

T HE SMOKE COMES FIRST. It rises like a bruise across the sky. Thin, grey tendrils bleed upward into the blue; too faint to smell yet, but enough to make the birds fall silent, enough to make the breath catch at the back of my throat.

I stand on the cliff where the wildflowers once bloomed, Our cliff, the place we named stars and traded secrets like treasure. It should be green below me, topaz with the late summer light, alive, vibrant, just as it's always been.

But today, everything feels wrong. The air is brittle, stretched too thin, as if the world itself is holding its breath. There's a quietness in the way the wind lingers, as though it's waiting for something to break, something to shift.

I don't hear him arrive, but I feel him. I always do.

Lysander comes fast, his horse lathered and wide-eyed, his cloak torn at the edge. There's dirt on his cheeks, sweat on his brow, and something in his eyes, worse than fear; grief, tangled with urgency, a look I've never seen before.

When he sees me, his shoulders drop, but only just. The relief is brief, tired, haunted. The kind of relief you get when you're running from something too big to outrun.

"I knew I'd find you here," he says, breathless, his voice raw.

"You always do," I reply, but there's no smile in it this time, not like there usually is.

He dismounts quickly, stepping forward with that familiar determination. He takes two steps before stopping, as if unsure whether to reach for me or run in the other direction. His hands tremble, the way leaves tremble in the first gust of wind before a storm. He pulls off his gloves, staring at me as though I'm the only thing left tethering him to this place.

"Something's happening," I say quietly, before he can speak.

His jaw tightens. "The villages... they're being purged."

I blink, trying to comprehend what he's saying. "What?"

"The Order is calling it a rebellion," he says, his eyes fixed somewhere behind me, as though looking at me too closely might break something inside him. "But it's not that. It never was. They're targeting anyone with even a trace of Shadow in their bloodlines: Educators, families, children."

The ground beneath me seems to shift, just a little, as if the earth itself flinched at his words.

I swallow, my chest tightening. "But that's not possible," I whisper. "There is no Light without Shadow. Everyone knows that."

But even as the words leave my lips, I feel the crack in them. The doubt that I've pushed away for so long comes rushing back. I remember Lucien's words after my parents died, his hollow tone as he explained everything so simply.

It was the Shadows, rebels. We tried to stop them with the Light, but we were too late.

I didn't believe him then. I wanted to, but somewhere deep inside me, something always questioned it.

Lysander's voice is low, a rasp in the silence. "That's what we were taught but the truth doesn't matter anymore, not to them."

I cross my arms, trying to hold myself together. The air feels colder now, like the world is watching us, waiting for something to crack.

"Even those of us who can't channel anything, we carry both inside us. That's balance. That's the point," I say. "I tried for years to draw from both Shadow and Light. I never could. I thought it meant I was broken, not... dangerous."

He nods, slow and heavy, as though the weight of it all presses down on him, too. "The new doctrine calls it impurity. They don't care what you are. If you don't shine, you burn."

His words hit me like a physical blow. I feel my legs tremble beneath me, but I stand tall, even as the world tilts on its axis.

"I didn't want to believe it either," Lysander continues softly. "But I've seen it. People disappearing after random flashes of Light. Families gone overnight. Entire towns silenced."

My mind races, darting through every corner of my memory, searching for something that might make sense of it. I think of the vanished books, the names no one speaks of anymore, the whispers that grew louder as the years passed.

"But Light is supposed to guide," I whisper, the words tasting like ash in my mouth.

He looks at me then and I see the boy I once knew buried beneath someone hardened by too much truth, too much loss. The soft curve of his features has been replaced by something more set, more determined. There is a hardness in his eyes that I didn't want to see.

"It can," he says. "But too much Light?" He shakes his head. "It blinds."

The silence stretches between us, heavy. The smoke climbs higher in the sky, thickening the air. Finally, Lysander takes a step closer, his gaze intense, locked onto mine. "There's a caravan," he says. "Families, sympathizers, the ones with nowhere else to go. They're heading west tonight. I know the way through the forest. If we leave before nightfall..."

"Leave?" I echo, the word unfamiliar, foreign on my tongue. "Just like that?"

"It's not safe here anymore, not for people like us." He looks at me, and I see the weight of his words hanging between us, the unspoken truth settling into the cracks that are beginning to form in my chest.

I shake my head, my heart a weight in my throat. "But the forest... it's always protected us."

"It's slowing time," he says softly, his voice strained. "Buying us days, maybe hours, but it can't stop what's coming."

I know he's right. I feel it too: the stillness in the trees, the silence in the river that runs just a little quieter now. The forest is bracing for something. Something we can't outrun.

Still, I hesitate, because this is the only home I've ever known. Part of me still believes that if we wait just a little longer, maybe things will go back to how they were. But that version of the world, the one where wildflowers bloom, where we steal fruit and lie in the grass and believe in stars, that world is already gone.

Lysander watches me with that same patient ache in his eyes. He looks at me the same way he looked at me when I first let him into the hollow tree. He looks at me the same way he held when he held me under the canopy of leaves, with cicadas singing like a hymn in the background.

He steps closer, his hands tremble as he cradles my face in both palms. His thumbs trace the lines of my cheekbones like he's memorizing me, like he knows this might be the last time.

"I love you," he breathes, his voice raw. "More than anything."

"Then stay. Prove it," I say, the words shattering the fragile space between us. It feels like a fracture, a break I don't know how to heal.

His breath catches. "If I stay, I'll die. Or worse..." He presses his forehead to mine, and for a moment, the world feels quiet again. "I'll become something I don't recognize, something that serves their Light."

I understand, but it doesn't do anything to dispel the hurt blooming in my core.

"You want me to prove my love for you? I can't, not in any way that would do it justice. You could ask me to count every star in the sky, and still, there wouldn't be enough. The sky may be endless, but my love for you runs even deeper. You don't have to decide now," he whispers, his voice breaking. "But if you change your mind, follow the birch trail past the ridge. There's a marked stone. Wait there before sundown."

He presses something into my palm, *The Star Thief*.

It is his copy. The one we passed back and forth for years. It's full of scribbles, underlined words, and secrets that only we understood. The spine is fraying. The pages smell like moss and river water, like all the things we've left behind.

I feel the weight of it. It's a promise or maybe a goodbye.

"I'll come back for you," he says, his voice a whisper in the growing wind. "I swear it."

I open my mouth to answer, but he's already turning, mounting his horse. He rides away, the sound of hooves echoing in the distance like a heartbeat too far from my own.

I don't stop him. I watch him disappear into the trees, and then I wait. I wait until the smoke thickens. I wait until the sun dips below the ridge. I wait until I can no longer see the wildflowers. I wait until I can't hear the river anymore. I wait and I try not to follow him, but I want to.

Eventually I go to the ridge. I find the birch trail, pale and thin as thread beneath my feet. My heart is lodged in my throat, each step a prayer I don't know the words for. The air grows colder, the trees more watchful, as though the forest itself is holding its breath.

I pass the crooked root where the ground dips like a secret. I move through the grove that only opens under moonlight, its silver leaves trembling, watching me. The air feels full of old names whispered in the dark. I find the marked stone, half-buried, moss curling around its edges, chipped and worn from time.

I press my hand to it, as though it might bring him back, as though stone could hold memories better than we can, and I wait.

I wait there, trembling, every heartbeat loud as thunder in my chest. I count the breaths between rustlings in the trees. I listen for hooves, for footsteps, for the crack of a branch, anything that might mean he's near.

But nothing comes: only wind, only the distant sighing of the trees.

The light fades. The shadows grow long.

Finally, I turn back.

I return to the cabin, walking slower than before, as if time might change its mind. The trees feel taller now, more silent; less like guardians, more like watchers, witnesses.

Inside, I sit by the fire. I stare into the flames, but they don't speak. Night falls. The stars come out, cold and scattered, blinking like they don't know what I've lost.

I wait until the fire burns low, until the shadows crawl across the floor like they, too, are searching for something. I wait until the silence becomes something deeper than quiet, something hollow, vast, echoing. I wait until I start to wonder if I dreamed the whole thing. If he was ever really here at all. I wait until the silence swells, and the forest forgets him.

He doesn't come back.

I begged the earth to open, but he didn't come.
The forest did not weep, but I did.

THE YEARS THAT FOLLOW

AGE 17-20

T HE FOREST IS THE only thing that stays.

Seasons come and go like visitors with no faces, never staying long enough to leave a mark, never staying long enough for me to learn their names. Rain softens into frost, frost gives way to green. Sap rises, petals unfurl, mushrooms bloom from rot and vanish just as quickly. The trees sway and bend, their branches groaning under weight I'll never know, whispering secrets among themselves that I will never hear.

I do not change, not really; not after Lysander disappears like a breath lost in winter.

At first, I try to live like the forest does: by cycles, by rhythms. I wake with the sun and sleep when it sets, trying to trick myself into believing I can be like the land: endlessly turning, endlessly renewing.

But grief is not a season, it does not come gently or pass when its time is done. It does not make its peace with time, and time does not make peace with it. It devours, then leaves you hollow and echoing, like the wind in a forgotten hollow, long after the storm is over. It presses on you until the space around you feels too small. It presses on you until every breath is a labor.

I wait, I grieve, I rage, then I stop feeling much of anything at all.

The first year, I count the days on the cabin wall in charcoal slashes. Every dawn, a tally; every dusk, a wound. Each line marks the passing of time as if time itself could be contained by such a simple act. It becomes a ritual, a way to carve order into the chaos that is my mind.

By the second year, I lose track of the months. I forget my own birthday. The dates on the wall blur together. They don't mean anything anymore. Time becomes a river I refuse to step into. I stay still so it can pass around me, unscathed. Let the world drift on without me; let the years pull away like the currents of a stream, too swift to hold.

I live alone in the old cabin, the one the forest built around me, plank by plank when the world burned. I tend the hearth like it still means something, like the flames will remember the warmth he gave when he stood beside me, when we sat by the fire and listened to the wind carrying stories. I whisper to the shadows, though they never answer back. The cabin echoes back my voice, soft and distant, as though it, too, is unsure of the weight it carries.

I plant seeds in shallow furrows, tend them gently, and watch nothing grow. The soil is stubborn, clinging to its grief like I cling to mine. The land doesn't want to let go, and neither do I.

I make dream catchers from willow branches, weaving them by hand with memories of laughter and late-night talks. I hang them from the rafters, hoping to keep the old dreams at bay. Hoping that maybe, just maybe, I can tie the fragments of my heart to them, and the dreams will carry them away. Some of the catchers catch nothing but dust. Others, perhaps, hold fragments of forgotten hope.

I don't know. I don't really care.

Every week, I visit the marked stone on the birch trail, even when it snows. I lay offerings there: pinecones, tiny carved birds, poems I never finish. Some get taken by squirrels, others vanish in the wind, carried away to some place I cannot follow.

I don't know why I keep going. Maybe I think that if I leave something behind, it will make the waiting easier. Maybe I think I can somehow speak to him again, that the stones will have a message for me, or the moss will whisper his name, but they never do.

Once, and only once, I go into town.

I wear my cloak low, pulling the hood over my face to hide the tired lines beneath my eyes, the hollows that have grown too deep to ignore. I keep my head down, moving through the village like a ghost. It's smaller than I remember, or maybe I'm just seeing it differently now. It's quieter, the people moving slower, as if the world here has felt the weight of time in ways I can't understand. I move through it like a ghost, like something that used to belong but doesn't anymore.

I ask carefully, cautiously. My voice is a whisper in a town full of dull murmurs.

"Lysander," I ask to the baker, the stable-boy, the tired woman outside the chapel with ash on her boots.

None of them know him.

Some say he must've gone to war. "Plenty of boys did," one man shrugs, stuffing his pipe into the crook of his mouth. "Didn't come back, most of 'em. But what can you do?"

I search the old postings on the chapel wall, my fingers brushing over each name, each familiar face that I've forgotten and tried to remember in equal measure. I sift through parchment at the archive station, searching for something, anything. But there is nothing: no records, no names, not even a whisper. It's like he never existed at all.

I come home that night, the quiet of the cabin swallowing me whole, and I cry for the first time in nearly a year. Deep, ugly sobs twist my chest and soak the wooden floor.

The fire burns low in the hearth, its flicker nothing more than a reflection of my despair. The forest watches, but it does not move. It never moves. It is as still as I am, and that thought only makes the ache in my chest grow deeper.

I try to tell myself it's just another phase, just another way that grief wears its face, but in that moment, I know it isn't.

This is different.

The forest doesn't cry for me, and neither do I... not anymore.

All that remains is an ache, an empty space where something should have been.

I think of Lysander, of the last time I saw him, the promise he made me to return. I wonder if he's somewhere out there, just out of reach, waiting to be found. Or maybe he's already gone, like everything else. Maybe the forest is all that's left because it's the only thing that knows how to endure, how to keep standing even when there's nothing left to hold on to.

The wind sighs through the trees outside, and I lie on the floor, feeling the cold seep into my skin, into my bones. My heart beats in time with the slow rise and fall of the wind. It is the only rhythm left.

For the first time, I wonder if I'll ever truly be able to leave this place behind.

COST OF SURVIVAL

AGE 21-25

LIKE FROST THAT KILLS the last tomatoes, he comes again.

Lucien. It is the first time I have seen him in years.

He arrives without warning, without letter or reason, just the sound of hooves crunching dead leaves underfoot and the weight of memory dragging behind him like a cloak too heavy to carry. It is a cloak I used to know well, when our paths were tangled and the future seemed like a simple thing, one we could shape with our hands. That was before the sun set on everything.

I step outside, knife tucked in my belt, heart lodged in my throat. He doesn't come with soldiers or fanfare. He comes alone, just him and that familiar, hollow silence that always seems to follow him.

Lucien looks almost the same, but sharper. Finer robes now, gold-trimmed and pressed, too clean for these woods. His mouth is thinner, jaw set like stone. He has carved himself into something harder, something colder. His hair, once wild and loose, is now short. It's disciplined, tamed. But his eyes... they carry something old, something brittle, cracked beneath the surface: a sadness lacquered over with a thick coat of faith.

"I thought you might want this," he says, holding out a leather-bound book, the Light's sigil gleaming on the cover like a beacon for something long lost.

I say nothing.

"It's not scripture," he adds quickly, as if to explain the reason for its existence, but I'm not listening to his words anymore, not really. "It's theory. Philosophy, on balance. The nature of the Divine Order. We were close once, Sylvaine. I thought..." He stops. His voice falters, like a thread pulled too tight. He swallows hard, eyes dropping to the ground. There's something he doesn't say: a name, a memory, a regret, a guilt that presses down on him in ways that he can't hide, no matter how hard he tries.

"You don't have to stay out here forever," he says, voice soft but insistent.

"I do," I reply, even as I feel the lie twist in my throat. I do because I can't go back: not to the world he wants, not to the world that devours itself in the name of faith.

"You were meant for more than this." His words ring in the silence, as though he expects me to believe them, as though I've forgotten what I was meant for.

"I was meant for peace," I reply, turning away. His words are hollow, and so are the promises wrapped up in them. I've learned enough to know that.

He leaves the book on my doorstep, but I never open it. The rain swells the leather, and moss grows along the spine. The forest swallows it whole, hiding it from my sight, from my mind. Eventually, I bury it under the old oak: deep enough to forget, deep enough to make it a secret between me and the roots of the earth.

When he returns, I don't open the door. I see him from the window, tall and patient, standing in the clearing with a bundle in his arms, a new cloak lined with pale gold thread catching the light. He doesn't knock. He simply waits, but I wait longer: as if the time itself can slow down, as if it might turn back if I stand still long enough.

Eventually, he places the bundle by the door and walks away. His footsteps are steady, like this is something he's done before, like this is something he planned, something he's come to accept. I don't touch what he brought for two days. I let it sit there, untouched: a reminder, a burden.

Under the excuse of needing salt, I untie the bundle: salt, ink, a half-loaf of travel bread that is still soft, a small book titled *Harmony Through Light: A Layman's Guide to Balanced Faith*.

A sickening, hollow weight settles in my chest at the sight of it, the light from the window flickering on its cover. I don't think twice before tossing the book into the fire, watching the pages curl and blacken. The rest I keep: the salt, the bread, the ink. These are not promises, not false hopes. These are practical things, things I can hold, things that don't burn when you touch them.

The next time he comes, I hear him before I see him: the crunch of his horse's hooves over frozen ground, the soft click of metal against leather, the knock on my door, slow and deliberate, the way you knock when you know no one will answer.

I stay seated, a pinecone half-carved in my hands, the sharp smell of resin filling the air. The world outside is quiet, still, waiting. I wait until he leaves. He does. He always does. He leaves behind a heavier parcel. No book this time, but it is more practical: a bundle of new socks, oiled leather boots, dried ginger root, a coil of twine, and a sealed jar of honey. The honey jar sits there, untouched, gathering dust like the things I can't quite let go of.

By the third visit, I scowl at him from the porch, arms crossed over my chest, the wind biting at my skin.

"You're persistent," I say, voice flat, betraying none of the turmoil I feel inside. His persistence is a sharp, steady thorn in my side. He knows nothing of what it costs me to stand here and listen to him.

Lucien gives a lopsided smile, his eyes flickering with something too familiar, something I refuse to acknowledge. "I've always been good at waiting," he replies, his tone even, like he knows how this game goes. Like he knows I might try to push him away, but I can't.

"You weren't invited," I say, trying to keep the hurt out of my voice, trying to keep it buried where it can't get out.

"I know." But he doesn't leave. Instead, he sits down on a stump near the edge of the clearing, loosening his cloak. His robes are still too fine, but the edges are muddy now, fraying in places, like he's been walking through the world I tried to escape.

"I brought dried peaches," he says.

I don't thank him, but I take them.

We stand there in the quiet, him watching me with eyes that are too full of things I don't want to see. And me, trying to remember a time when I didn't feel the weight of every choice I've ever made. A time when I didn't have to carry the memory of who I used to be. A time when it was easier to pretend I was still the same person, still together, still whole.

But the peaches are sweet, and for a moment as I chew, I let myself remember.

It's deep winter when I let him inside for the first time, almost a year after his first visit.

The cold is sharp, the kind that makes the floorboards snap at night, like old bones cracking under pressure. The wind howls through the pines, a sound like something wounded, a thing that once had voice but now can only scream in its own hollow ache. It seems to pierce the thick walls of the cabin, making the fire flicker as if it might be extinguished, as if it's as fragile as everything else. I don't expect him to come today, not in this weather, not when the forest is holding its breath, waiting for the spring that never seemed to arrive.

He knocks but I don't answer. I know it's him, even before the sound reaches my ears; the cadence of the knock is too familiar, too deliberate, but I don't bar the door. Maybe, on some level, I've been waiting for this, for him, for the moment when the silence between us could finally be broken. I stand motionless for a moment, my hands still clutching the rough wood of the table, but I don't move to open the door.

It creaks open slowly, like a prayer whispered in the dark. He steps in with snow still clinging to his boots, trailing in the cold from the outside world. The door shuts behind him with a soft thud but the chill lingers, wrapping itself around my spine like an old friend.

"You can sit," I tell him, nodding toward the stool near the hearth. The fire crackles softly throwing its light across his face, but I make no move to add more wood. The flames are warm but they don't reach my hands, and I'm not sure I want them to. "If you speak Light at me, I'll throw you out."

He holds up both hands, a gesture of surrender, one that feels old between us. He's learned the language of silence well. "Fair," he says, and there's a quiet acceptance in his voice, the kind that knows the weight of every word left unsaid.

He hands me a satchel of apples, firm and red and impossibly fresh, as if they've been plucked from some distant orchard, far from this barren stretch of earth. The scent of them is bright and sharp, a reminder of warmer days. "From the lowlands," he says, rubbing his hands together, trying to coax some warmth back into his fingers. "Bartered for them on the road."

I take the apples without a word, setting them on the counter beside me. The quiet between us is thick, as it always is, but there's a gentleness in the way he moves now, like he's forgotten how to rush, or maybe he's learned that there's no need for it anymore. I stew the apples with a little honey, the sweetness filling the cabin. We don't speak while I cook. The fire snapping between us is the only sound. The apples soften and we share the small meal in silence.

When I glance at him, I see a new hollow under his eyes, something worn into the skin beneath them, but I also see something softer in the lines of his mouth, as if the world has weathered him in ways that neither of us ever expected. He's still Lucien, but he's also become something else, something broken and reformed.

Eventually, during his visits, we talk, only a little. He doesn't tell me where he's been or what he's seen, and I don't ask.

I wait. I am always waiting for something he hasn't said.

He tells me how the Order is rebuilding the Temple spires. How sermons now speak of "the cleansing fire" and "illumination." He says it with a guarded tone, like a man tasting something bitter but familiar; something he's swallowed before, and will again, because he believes it's good for him, even if it burns going down. The words turn sour in my mouth, and I wonder how he still believes.

"You sound tired of it," I murmur, my voice quieter than I mean it to be, as I watch him over the rim of my mug. His eyes flicker briefly, like they're chasing something just out of reach.

"I sound honest," he replies. His voice is steady, certain; the voice of someone who's made peace with a truth he still holds, even if it costs him. "Don't mistake that for rebellion."

I don't respond right away. Instead, I pick up the book he's brought with him; a slim volume, bound in pale leather, its pages filled with elegant script, all the markings of a work that's been approved, passed through the right hands, the kind of work that feels sterilized before it even touches the world. The margins are redacted, whole sections blacked out. He lays it out like an offering, like it's something precious, something he's risked to bring me.

"I thought you might want to understand how they think," he says. "You always liked puzzles."

"I like truth," I reply, flipping through the volume on ley-line theory, where the entire section on Shadow-casting is missing. It's easy to see through the veil, easy to pick apart the layers. "This is polite propaganda."

"Even propaganda holds pieces of truth," he says, his tone soft, but there's a hardness behind it, a resignation.

"Which pieces?" I ask, my voice steady, though I can feel the old fire rising again, the anger that has burned in me for so long. "The ones that serve, or the ones that survive?"

Lucien sighs, and for a moment, I see the weight of it in his shoulders, in the way his chest rises and falls. "Do you want to debate me, or do you want answers?"

I look him in the eye for the first time in a long time, really look at him. It's harder than I expect, harder than it should be. There's a crack in his expression, a tension I recognize. He's been holding something in, something he hasn't told me.

"Both," I reply, the word a promise and a challenge.

We begin to speak in longer strands. We talk of doctrine, of balance, of the shifting tides of the world. By candlelight, he explains how the new doctrine is shaping the Order; how the Light is now redefined as a divine will, not just an elemental force. He explains that power is no longer about balance but purity. Purity, it's a word that chills me, makes the fire seem colder.

"Balance is hard to control," he says one night, fingers wrapped around a chipped mug, his eyes faraway, haunted. "But purity? That you can measure. That you can punish."

"And that's better?" I ask, voice thick with disbelief. "To boil the world down into clean and unclean?"

He doesn't answer, his gaze fixed on the fire. Eventually, I begin to ask harder questions.

"I thought you were here to teach me," I press, leaning forward, my heart racing against my ribs.

"I'm here to keep you safe," he replies, voice low, but there's an edge to it now, a sharpness that makes the air between us grow thinner.

"That's not the same thing."

He leans forward, eyes locking onto mine. His hands curl into fists on the table, but I don't flinch, not this time. "Some truths don't serve you, Sylvaine."

"Then they're not truths," I say, voice steady now. "They're secrets."

The silence that falls between us is heavy, like the weight of the world itself settling into the space. I know what he's hiding, what he's afraid to say.

His hands curl tighter, but his voice doesn't rise. "You don't understand how fragile things are. The Order is watching everything. Even me."

"You chose this." My words are quiet but sharp, a simple reminder that the path he walks now is one he took willingly.

"I chose survival," he replies, his voice quieter now, like the weight of his choices is crushing him, pressing him down until he can't breathe.

We don't speak for the rest of the night. The fire dies down, the night grows deeper, but neither of us moves. We're both holding on to something, something that can't be put into words.

He keeps coming, always alone, always with something in his hands: soup, books, winter blankets. I stop pretending I don't wait for him, stop pretending that it doesn't mean something to me, even if I won't say it out loud.

Sometimes we eat in silence. Sometimes we debate, our words tangled in the warmth of the fire. He teaches me what he can, and I keep pressing for what he won't.

One night, as I'm cleaning the kettle, I ask the question that's been burning in my chest, the one I haven't dared to ask before.

"Do you believe it?"

He looks up from his mug, his brow furrowing as if the question is foreign, like he hasn't thought about it in a long time. "What?"

"The Light. The way they teach it now." My voice cracks just a little, but I don't look away.

He hesitates. His voice is quiet, the weight of the world in it.

"I believe in power. Control. Justice and truth."

For the first time in years, I feel something sharp and small break loose in my chest. Hope, maybe, or grief dressed in gentler clothes. It's too much to bear, too much to hold in.

"If you still believe in truth, then what are you doing, Lucien?" I ask, my voice thick with the weight of it.

He doesn't answer, but he stays, and maybe that is an answer, too.

We never speak of Lysander or my parents.

It's as though their names have been buried, and we've agreed to let them stay there, beneath the weight of the years and the silence that thickens with every passing season. In the quiet of the cabin, I can almost imagine the memory of them dissolving, melting away like frost under the heat of the fire. But then, just as quickly, the ache surges again, sharp and jagged. I push it back, lock it behind the walls I've built inside, and go on with my days.

The years pass and I forget the names of flowers, their colors fading like old paintings left out in the sun. I memorize the sound of every owl in the valley. I know which trees groan before they fall, their warning carried on the breeze like a whisper just before the storm. I mark the passage of time by the thaw of the river, the slow march of elk migrating across the mountains. I find solace the nights the auroras tear across the sky like a great seam being ripped open, the colors swirling overhead in shades I could never name.

I sing less now. I used to hum, the melodies slipping out of me like the wind through the branches, but that's stopped. Now, I sleep more. The nights feel long, sometimes endless, and I lose myself in the quiet hum of the fire, its crackling the only sound that keeps me tethered to the world. Some nights, I fall asleep with a book clutched to my chest, pages warped with the heat, the words blurred by the weight of time.

I dream of a voice I barely remember. It's faint, like the echo of a name whispered in a dream you've already forgotten.

Sometimes, I think I hear Lysander in the wind. The sound brushes against me like the lightest of touches, fleeting, elusive. But when I turn to chase it, it's gone. It's always gone.

By twenty-three, my reflection is a stranger.

I look into the glass, the dark surface of the water, or the faint shimmer of light on metal, and there's someone looking back, but it's not quite me. My hair is longer, darker, the strands tangled like the wild vines that snake through the underbrush. My hands are calloused, hardened by the work of the years, the constant mending and building and planting. I don't recognize the lines on my face, the soft hollows under my eyes. They speak of something I've lived through, something I've endured, but they also speak of something I've let go of, something lost to the passage of time. My eyes, once bright and sharp, are duller now. The world has worn me down in ways I didn't expect, and though I am still here, still moving, still breathing, I don't know if I'm the same person who once dreamed of something more.

By twenty-four, I no longer think of leaving.

Not because I've healed, not because I've moved on, but because I don't know who I'd be if I did. The forest has wrapped itself around my bones. The silence has settled into my skin. I have become part of the land, as much as the trees and the rivers, the earth beneath my feet. The forest knows my name now, the way the night knows the stars. It breathes with me, and I with it. It speaks to me in its own way, through the rustle of leaves, the sway of branches, the songs of birds that no one else can hear.

The nights are no longer cruel in their loneliness, but mine, shaped by years of solitude, shaped by my need to be still, to listen, to wait. The fire no longer feels like a distraction, but a companion; the hearth is the center of my world, its flickering light the only constant I've come to trust.

Still, deep in some part of me that refuses to die, I wonder:

Did he make it?

Did he forget me?

Or is he out there, waiting too?

Waiting in a place I can never reach, waiting like I am, buried beneath the same weight of time, the same unanswered questions?

I wonder sometimes if I would even recognize him if I saw him again. If he would recognize me. Would the person I've become, the woman the forest has shaped, be the same one he once knew?

Or would we stand on opposite sides of a river, staring at each other, lost in the space that's grown between us?

The space has been growing for years, for so long now, I don't even know if we could find our way back.

THE FIRE REKINDLED

ONE BRITTLE WINTER MORNING, I do something strange. I write a thesis.

It begins the way most revolutions do, not with fire, but with a whisper: a crack in the dam, a question scratched in the margins of an approved text, unnoticed by everyone but me.

The cold has settled in deep, clinging to the bones of the cabin like an unwelcome guest, and yet I sit there, staring at a blank sheet of parchment, my quill hovering above it. The ink trembles, caught in the grip of hesitation.

I could write nothing. I could leave it empty, as I have done with so many other things, but the words come, slowly at first, tentatively. They don't feel like my own. They feel like something ancient, something untamed, clawing its way out from where it's been buried for far too long.

I suggest... I propose... I believe...

In the end, I write not as a scholar but as something else; something older, something that's been living under the earth for years, forgotten, gathering strength in the dark. I write as a child of the forest, as someone who has watched the seasons turn and the world slip through my fingers, piece by piece.

I suggest the academy reconsider its curriculum, that they teach the old myths again: the legends, the half-sung songs passed down long before the war bled into our bones. I propose that children should hear stories where monsters weren't always evil, and heroes didn't always pray to Light. I believe that memory is more than numbers on parchment, that the truths of the past cannot be measured, only remembered. I believe that there is more to this world than what is taught in sterile halls and sanctified texts.

I sign it with my name, a name I haven't written in seven years. The ink of it feels foreign on my fingers, like it belongs to a ghost, a version of myself I thought I had forgotten. The paper is folded and sealed, no fanfare, no return address; just the quiet motion of sending it off into the world, into a place I'll never truly belong again.

By the time spring unfurls in the underbrush, I've already forgotten I sent it. There are birds to listen to, firewood to chop, silence to outlast, and yet, it feels like the forest has swallowed me whole, wrapping itself around me in its timeless way. The days blur together, and I lose myself in the simple rhythm of survival. I live like a creature of the wild, not like a person with dreams of something more.

One dusk-lit evening, Lucien finds me on the porch with a letter in his hand. A real letter, wax-sealed and carrying the scent of pine, citrus, and old parchment.

He doesn't speak. He just holds it out, the faintest of frowns tugging at his lips. I take it from him like it might break if I touch it too hard. The crest on the seal is unmistakable, Umbraxis Academy, the inner sanctum of sanctioned knowledge. The place where I once dreamed I'd walk as a student, where I would have gone, once, before everything crumbled.

Inside, there's a formal notice: a response, an appointment, a position. Educator at Umbraxis Academy, Order of Illumination: pending completion of a Solis Rite, and one term of theological standardization, a course in the Divine Light.

I hold the letter in my hands, staring at the elegant script, and for a suspended moment, I laugh: not politely, not softly.

I laugh like the girl I used to be, the one who climbed rooftops barefoot, kissed the shadows between syllables, and dreamed of a life she could never have. The one who held onto a boy with a wicked grin and hands full of starlight and promises. I laugh like someone who still believes in ghosts, in things that cannot be touched or proved, but only felt in the deepest parts of you.

The laughter fades and I fold the letter carefully, setting it aside. I begin to pack my things.

Lucien watches me, his gaze steady, his face unreadable. He says nothing until I pause to stare at the cabin, my home, the place where I've hidden for so long. The place where every memory I have of the past is tangled, wild and bittersweet.

"I didn't think you'd ever leave," he admits, his tone careful, neutral.

"Neither did I," I reply, voice thick, thick with the weight of everything I'm not saying.

A beat passes, long enough to feel the chill in the air settle deep into my bones. Lucien shifts, but he doesn't move any closer. His voice breaks the silence again. "What changed?"

I hesitate. I think of my thesis, the ink on the page still fresh and how it came out of me like a breath, unbidden and urgent. There is balance and it is time the world remembers. But now, I speak the safer truth. The one he expects, not the one I carry like a spark in my chest.

"What if what I learned as a child was wrong?" I say, my voice barely a whisper. I don't look at him. "What if I was fed lies?"

The thought hangs in the air between us, heavy and unsettling. There's another part of it, a question I don't voice, but that I can't ignore.

What if Lysander lied?

What if he never meant to come back?

What if he left me behind for good, and all my waiting was for nothing?

Lucien's expression doesn't change, but I see the way his jaw shifts, the way his hands curl into fists, and I know that he's heard the question in my voice. He doesn't answer, but I don't need him to.

The answer is already out there, somewhere; in the places we've both left behind.

The Solis Rite is held in a temple hall at the heart of campus. The air smells of incense and old stone, the weight of history hangs like a shroud around me. I kneel as I'm supposed to. I speak the words they've polished over the years.

"May the Light reveal my path. May it cleanse Shadow, but not erase it. May truth and devotion be my guide."

The words taste of ash in my mouth. I try to swallow them, but they stick there, coating my tongue, turning sour as they leave my lips.

I pass.

I've been preparing for this. I've learned how to wear the mask: how to recite the rituals, how to stand in front of the Order, how to be everything they want me to be.

The course is worse.

It's two months of honeyed sermons and doctrine dressed as dialogue. I read every page, memorize every word. I trace each diagram of Light-based theory, even the ones that contradict the last, the ones that change when no one's looking. When they ask questions, I answer them perfectly. I know the answers, even when I don't believe them.

On the morning of commencement, I am given a sash: gold-threaded, dignified, hideous. I pin it to my chest. I smile when Lucien welcomes me, and I sign my name in the Educator's Ledger.

Sylvaine Nox, Order of Illumination, Educator of Sacred Narratives, Umbraxis Academy.

When they ask me how I became so familiar with mythology, I say, "I was raised in the forest. Out there, we remember old things."

They nod politely, their eyes glazed with the contentment of a world that believes in its own illusions. They don't ask for more. They don't want the truth. They want the performance of it, but I know better.

The forest remembers. It always has.

The onboarding dinner is cold, but not in temperature, though the hall is drafty. My new robes, formal and starched, do little to keep the chill out. It's something deeper, though, something buried in the bones of the place.

There is a hollowness beneath the gleaming, gold-leaf glamour, a coldness that creeps into your skin, settles in your chest, and refuses to leave. The architecture is magnificent, but it feels like it's been built to distance, to separate, to make you feel small beneath its weight. It is like a grand stage designed to house performances rather than people.

The dining hall at Umbraxis Academy is a marvel of precision; every line, every surface crafted with exacting care. Arches etched with Light-bound script, their meaning just beyond the edge of comprehension, whispers of power in unreadable symbols. Chandeliers hang like galaxies overhead, every bulb an engineered imitation of a star, suspended in the air as though gravity itself could be bent by design.

The table stretches on, impossibly long. It is covered in an endless stretch of white linen and polished silver and flanked by chairs upholstered in bone-white velvet. The chairs feel more like thrones, they are not made for comfort, but for the rigid posture of formality.

There is no music, only the soft rustle of etiquette, the polite shuffle of cloth and silverware: napkins adjusted with meticulous care, knives placed precisely, voices rising just enough to be heard, but never lingering. Everything gleams. Everything is silent.

I sit at the far end, alone.

No one speaks to me directly, not more than polite nods, anyway. Someone tries small talk, something about the lunar texts in the south tower. I reply in as few syllables as possible, sip from a glass of white wine that tastes like chalk and snowmelt. The wine is thin, unremarkable, just like the conversation. I chew through the food without tasting it: a paper-thin carpaccio with gold flakes, a chilled aspic in the shape of a swan, bread rolls dusted with rose salt, as delicate as the dead. Everything is elegant. Everything is tasteless. I chew, I swallow, I wish I hadn't come.

The room hums with polite indifference, every voice a faint murmur against the hiss of candle flames. I feel like an observer, a shadow cast across an image I can never touch. The buzz of conversation is an endless drone, words without meaning, faceless exchanges with nothing behind them. No one wants to truly know anyone else here, not really. No one wants to be seen, and I... I don't want to be seen, either.

Just as I start to lose myself in the rhythm of my own unease, I see Lucien.

He is at the far end of the table, at the head of the table. He is cloaked in ceremony, draped in the sleek white-and-gold of the divine, his form a perfect image of authority. There are pins on his collar now, pins I don't recognize: ranks, honors, distinctions.

Beacon of the Light, divine ruler of the realm, Light Warden, ruler of the academy; he is everything I never thought I'd see him become. He has been lying about his role with the Light, just as I've been lying about my intentions.

He does not look young anymore. He doesn't look old, either, but there is something in the sharpness of his features, the way his body has become a perfect silhouette, speaks of years of discipline. He has been carved into this shape by something more than time, more than the academy's teachings. He looks... dangerous now: efficient, sharpened, like a blade that has been honed too long and too hard.

His face is thinner. His hair, once wild, is now perfectly combed back, every strand in place, like it has been forbidden to rebel. The relaxed man I once knew is gone, buried under layers of this new skin.

His smile, when it comes, is slow, calculated, perfect for the occasion. There's nothing genuine about it. He holds just the right amount of light in his eyes to make it seem like something human still exists beneath the rigid formality. He raises his glass in perfect synchrony with a toast from a scholar near him.

"To unity," they say. "To order. To the illumination of all minds."

Lucien drinks, but his eyes, sharp as broken glass, find mine across the river of flickering candles and untouched food. He holds my gaze for a single second, a frozen moment, and everything around us falls away: the chatter fades, the hum of the room becomes a distant thing, blurred, like a dream that can't reach us.

I don't wave. He doesn't nod. The moment passes like a needle through silk, seamless and gone before I can truly hold onto it, but it was real. Later,

I wonder if I imagined it, the flicker of recognition, the silent weight that passed between us. But I didn't imagine it.

He saw me; he looked straight into my eyes and he looked away first.

His hands, steady as stone for the toast, tremble once when he sets his glass down, just a twitch, barely noticeable, but I see it.

His voice, when he answers a question from a patron beside him, is clear: commanding, brittle. There is something hollow underneath it, something fragile masked by articulation and dogma. Something that might shatter if anyone dared to speak too softly to him, too close. Something that could crack under the weight of its own self-importance.

The dinner continues in its sterile, unfeeling march. The room around us is full, but somehow, it is empty. The taste of food is gone, replaced by a dull, aching silence. We are all part of a grand performance, a dance we've all learned too well. But somewhere, hidden beneath all of it, in the shadows of the room, something feels off, something feels like it might break.

I wonder if he feels it too.

That night, I move into my new housing.

They call it a cabin, but it's little more than a glorified groundskeeping shed. The walls are whitewashed, the bed freshly made, so crisp it looks as if it's been pressed by a hundred ironed hands. There's a desk, some mismatched furniture and a closet of uniform robes, all neatly folded, each one as sterile and blank as the walls around me.

The key they gave me is smooth and gold, an object of perfect crafts-manship. It gleams in my hand, but it doesn't feel like mine. It's too polished, too unmarked, too clean. Like something meant for someone else, someone who belongs here. It doesn't fit me and the worst part is, I'm not sure I want it to.

My boots leave grey ash on the pristine floor, the faintest trace of the forest still clinging to them, a ghost of a place I once called home. The floor, so carefully scrubbed, swallows the dust with a quiet, efficient hunger, and I don't bother wiping it away. It feels wrong to make this place cleaner, to smooth over the edges of the mess that is me. Instead, I let the ashes stay, let them mark my presence, if only for a moment.

I sit at the edge of the bed, the thin mattress pressing into my bones, and stare at the wall for a long time. The silence in the room thickens, the air heavy with the weight of being alone in this hollow place. My pack is still at my feet, unopened, untouched. The contents of it, half-forgotten and half-resentful, seem like something from a different life.

I could leave.

Tonight, I could walk right out the gate and vanish into the woods again, back to the wildness, back to something real. The Light would barely notice I'd gone. It would simply flicker and burn its way through another set of names and another set of stories. I wouldn't matter, not really, not in this place.

I don't leave.

Despite the taste of doctrine still clinging to my tongue, bitter and dry, despite the heat of Lucien's smile seared into my memory like a brand, and the lies sewn into every corner of this place, every polished corner, every gleaming surface, I came here for something, not to belong, not to convert, not to twist myself into a shape that fits their narrative, but to remember.

I came here because the world is forgetting too fast. Every year, the forest loses more names. More stories drift into the wind, forgotten as quickly as they were spoken. The trees lose their ancient voices. The land's rhythm grows quieter, muted by the constant hum of order and structure. The

Light, the ever-present, ever-demanding Light, is writing over stories it doesn't understand, burning through them with its relentless fire, calling it truth.

But truth is never so simple, is it?

It's never just a blanket of light that smothers everything else. Truth needs Shadows, needs the dark places where stories grow wild and untamed.

So I stay and I unpack every item in my pack as if each piece has to find its own new place in this rigid order, in this house of silence and control. I move through the motions without thinking, folding clothes, placing books on the small shelf, even setting reminders of home on the desk with a care that feels almost sacrilegious. The scent of this place, clean and antiseptic, mixes with the faint memory of the pine-scented air that still clings to my skin.

I begin again with the Light; not because I believe in it, I don't, but because I believe in stories, and someone has to tell them, even here, especially here.

The walls may be whitewashed, but they won't keep out the words.

The doctrine may be written in ink that burns like fire, but they can't erase the things that live in the dark, the things that are whispered in the spaces between words.

The Light may think it's the only truth, but I know better.

I sit for a long moment in the silence, and then I stand. I take a deep breath, and as I walk into the night, the only sound is the quiet scrape of my boots on the gravel. The stars are sharp in the sky. They might be distant, but they haven't forgotten and neither have I.

RETURN TO
THE HOLLOW
PRESENT TIME

"Only those who leave can choose to re-turn. Only those who remember can choose what to become." — The Book of Names (banned)

REUNION

EPILOGUE

I WAKE SLOWLY, NOT with the sharp gasp of a nightmare's end, but like a leaf drifting down from a great height: weightless, unmoored, unsure if I'm still falling or finally coming to rest.

Time feels fluid here, unspooled. My body is a distant shoreline I can't quite reach.

The world comes to me in pieces: warmth, smoke, the scent of damp wood, like a hearth burning in the heart of a forest. The edges of the room bleed into each other, watercolor soft, as if I'm looking through a veil of rain.

Somewhere beneath my ribs, a dull ache pulses in time with my heartbeat. My breath is shallow, brittle. Every inhale feels like a memory I have to relearn.

I don't open my eyes right away. I drift, float. The weight of my limbs is too much to bear.

I hear a cough, soft and uncertain, and a voice, cracked with fatigue but threaded with something gentler: hope, or desperation.

"Sylvaine... you're awake."

He says my name like a question, like a prayer, like the sound of someone trying not to break in half. I try to move toward the voice, but the effort sends a flare of pain through my skull. My eyelids flutter. Light filters in; low and amber, flickering like firelight. Slowly, the room comes into view.

Wooden beams stretch across a slanted ceiling. Embers smolder in a stone hearth across from me, casting gold across the walls. Books and scrolls clutter a nearby table. A pitcher of water glints beside a pair of mugs. Shadows shift in the corners, familiar and strange all at once.

Beside the bed, slouched in a worn, creaking chair, is Lysander.

His posture is tense, like he hasn't moved in hours. Like he's held vigil, afraid to even breathe too loudly. His robes hang in soft, wrinkled folds, dark as ink and dusted with ash at the hem. His hair is shorter than I remember, cropped close at the sides, the top tousled like he's run his hands through it too many times. He looks broader now. His frame filled out by time, by hardship. His shoulders squared with quiet strength.

But it's his eyes that undo me, still silver as moonlight on water. Still too deep, too knowing. They catch the firelight as they settle on me, and for a moment, I forget how to breathe.

He looks older, not just in years, but in the weight he carries. The hollows beneath his eyes are bruised with sleepless nights, with grief that has gone too long unspoken.

He leans forward, breath catching. "You're awake," he says again. This time more certain. More real. His voice is rough, sanded raw.

"I thought..." He stops, swallows hard. "I was afraid you might not come back." His eyes search mine. "You didn't open your eyes. Not once. I started to think..."

Emotion crashes over me in a wave: relief, confusion, grief, longing, rage. It all twists together inside me, too tangled to separate. I blink, my throat dry.

"Where...?" My voice cracks, a whisper broken on the edges.

"You're safe." He says it quickly, as if he knows how little that word means right now. "We're in Velmourn, the hidden city of Umbriel. We are at the Hollow Guard base."

Umbriel, a name I've only heard in whispers, half-legend, half-threat. Fragments stir in the fog: running, fire, power bursting from my hands, wild and untamed, fear curling through my veins like smoke.

"I..." My mouth is dry, the word catching like ash on my tongue. "What happened?"

He nods, slow and careful, as if afraid I'll shatter again. "Your magic... it surged. It overwhelmed you." A pause, like he's reliving it. "You ran straight into the woods, to the Archive. I was there, just back from a mission. It was when I was updating ledgers that I felt it, something rupturing, like the ground itself was holding its breath."

His voice tightens, frays at the edges. "I found you on the threshold. You collapsed before I could reach you, but I..." He swallows hard, his eyes flickering down to his hands. "I caught you before you hit the ground."

Caught me.

The words echo, hollow and thunderous. Memories stir, disjointed flashes behind my eyes: the trees melting into darkness, my knees giving out, the floor of the Archive rising too fast, and then... Shadows, not stone, a gentler fall, warmth in the cold, the faint scent of clove and smoke, a voice saying my name like it meant something.

"Caught me," I whisper, as if tasting the truth will make it real. My eyes lift to his. "You carried me?" The words sound strange in my mouth, soft and unbelieving, like I've stumbled into someone else's story.

His expression flickers, grief and relief warring behind his silver gaze. "Of course I did." The answer is immediate, absolute. "You think I'd leave you there?"

"But I was dangerous." My voice trembles. "I was out of control."

He leans back slightly, arms crossed over his chest, not in anger, but like he's trying to hold something in, or maybe hold himself together. "You were scared, hurt. You didn't lose control, Sylvaine. You were abandoned. You reached for the only thing that answered you back."

His eyes find mine again, steady and unflinching. "You are powerful, not dangerous. There's a difference. The Light never taught you that."

My breath hitches. "Have you been here the whole time?"

His mouth twists. "I didn't want to leave you alone." He hesitates. "I didn't want you to wake up and be alone, not again."

Silence stretches between us, brittle as glass. I turn my head slowly, taking in the room. It's modest, lived-in, safe, if such a thing exists anymore.

A narrow window near the bed lets in pale blue light, the color of pre-dawn. Somewhere outside, I hear the rush of water, maybe a river, or a spring trickling over stone.

Inside, a storm rages, one that's been building for years.

You left me.

The words hover unspoken. I don't say them yet, but the weight of them presses behind my ribs.

"I never stopped thinking about you," he says suddenly, like he heard the words anyway. His voice is quieter this time, thicker. "Not for a day. Not for a breath. I wasn't going to pull you from a life that was keeping you safe, protected. I've been watching over you. I was every Shadow you saw, every breeze you felt. It felt like punishment, being able to see you, hear you, having my Shadows feel you, but not being able to talk to you, to explain."

My throat tightens. I don't know what to do with those words. I don't know how to believe them, or how not to. The silence that follows isn't empty, it's full of things we never said, things we're still afraid to say. It sits between us, heavy and fragile.

I close my eyes, not to shut him out, but to stop the tears threatening to rise, because for a moment, for a breath, I want to believe him.

"How long have I been here?" I ask, though I already know I won't like the answer.

"You've been unconscious for six days," he says. "And in that time, the Light has taken half the northern border and burned the forests to ash. Their soldiers are advancing like wildfire. Too fast, too organized; like they're being driven by something more than strategy."

He meets my gaze, steady and unflinching.

"Something's changed in them, Sylvaine. It's not just zealotry anymore. It's hunger." His voice drops, low and reverent, as if speaking to something older than either of us.

"Lucien is unwell but he is losing control. Elowen is acting in his place." The words hang heavy in the air, colder than the chill that shudders down my spine. Lysander's jaw clenches so tightly I hear the faint grind of teeth. His eyes are distant, almost haunted.

"When you ran," he says slowly, like dragging the memory out hurts, "he went feral. It wasn't just grief or rage. It was... deeper." The last word is bitter on his tongue. He spits it like venom. "The Light called it a purge."

The floor tilts beneath me. My balance sways, not from the wound still healing beneath my ribs but from something far more fractured. "What kind of purge?"

His shoulders draw tight, like bracing against an old wound.

"They started raiding villages, Sylvaine. Not the war outposts but civilian towns, entire communities were burned. They sent raids into neutral territories, borderlands that had stayed out of this war for decades and then he demanded blood. Proof of loyalty, they said."

His voice cracks. Then hardens, mechanical, like he's had to say this before, too many times. "They captured students, any with traces of Shadow in their lineage. Especially those in your classes."

A slow, nauseating twist coils through my stomach.

He continues, quieter now, but the words cut deeper for it. "Many of them were tortured, interrogated. 'To cleanse what was compromised.' That's what Elowen called it. Your name came up in every room, Sylvaine. Over and over again."

"No..." The word slips out, soft and broken. "No, they wouldn't..."

"They did." Lysander's voice sharpens. Not cruel, but final. He needs me to hear it, to understand. "Two are dead. An Educator, Hallen, I think, because he defended your name. And a student, Elswyn. The student claimed to know nothing of your whereabouts or your affiliation with Shadow, despite being in your class. Both of them were used as examples."

The air thins, each breath catches in my throat like shards of glass. My vision tightens to a pinprick.

"If me being gone is what's making the Light worse... then why bring me here? Why not take me back to them?" I ask, my voice breaking on the edges of the words.

His gaze flickers. For the briefest moment, the walls he's built, stone by stone, secret by secret, crack. There's something in his eyes that wasn't there before. A tenderness, yes, but also a quiet devastation; raw, unprotected, like he's been bleeding beneath the surface and just now realized he's still alive.

He leans in, not close enough to touch, not yet, but close enough that I can feel the gravity of him pulling me forward, like the edge of a cliff asking to be stepped over.

"I made the mistake of leaving you once," he says, voice low, tight, a confession carved from regret. "I won't do it again. I wasn't going to uproot you from your life when it was keeping you safe. But you chose the Shadows. I am going to ensure you choose me again, too. Now that you're here, we need to fight this war together. We're stronger together. When it's over... when balance is restored..." He exhales like the words are costing him pieces of himself. "We'll have time to make up for what was lost."

I don't speak, I can't. His words hang there, suspended like a breath we're both afraid to release. I feel the weight of everything he's not saying, looming like something vast and timeless pressing at the edges of the moment. His voice might have said *when*, but what I hear is *if*.

If we survive. *If* we're still the same people at the end of this.

"Do you remember what you heard in the archive? Just before you collapsed?"

I shake my head no, confused because nothing comes back to me.

He pauses. "There's a prophecy. It's the reason the Light is hunting you. The reason the Shadows knew your name, why they whispered to you."

A shiver slips down my spine. The word clangs through me, loud and unmistakable: a prophecy.

Lucien had always called me special, his miracle crafted for the Light; a prodigy, yes, but more than that, a vessel.

But for what?

The question curls in my mouth like smoke, too dense to form. I search Lysander's face, desperate, and all I find are Shadows, unspoken truths buried deep in his eyes.

Still, the questions break free. "What prophecy? What does it say? Why...why me?"

He looks away, the muscle in his jaw twitching.

"I'll explain everything, but not now." His voice is quiet, but it carries the weight of something solemn, a promise laced with danger.

I reach for words, for meaning, for anything to make this make sense, but he cuts me off with a slow shake of his head. "Not yet. You're not strong enough. You need to rest, Sylvaine. You need to heal."

I swallow the stone rising in my throat. The ache of needing answers, of needing control, gnaws at me. But he's right, I'm not ready, not yet.

That doesn't stop the dark presence lingering at the corners of my mind: whispering, watching, waiting.

I swallow hard, the frustration sitting like a stone lodged in my throat, heavy and unmoving. The silence between us stretches, brittle and electric. I can see the weariness carved into his features like lines drawn by time itself, the sag of his shoulders, the flicker of something distant in his eyes.

The way he says it, *later*, lands like a dull blade but something in me softens despite it, the sharp edges of my fear dulling, just a little.

I look at him: past the armor he wears in every breath, past the echoes of everything we've lost and everything we still stand to lose.

Our past hangs between us like smoke, unseen but suffocating and yet, even through the heaviness, there's something else, a thread.

Fragile, yes, but woven through with all the things we never dared hope for, a tether made of promises we never spoke but somehow kept anyway.

His hand finds mine, tentative, hesitant, like he's afraid he'll break me or, worse, that I'll pull away. I don't. His fingers tighten, just slightly, and it feels like something ancient has been returned to the earth, like a relic found after being buried for centuries, still warm to the touch.

For a moment, the chaos fades: the noise, the war, the darkness fringing everything. I rest my head against him, breathing him in, letting the warmth of him sink into my bones.

"We'll end this," I whisper.

It's barely more than breath, but it carries weight. A vow born in the dark, one I haven't dared let myself believe in, until now.

He doesn't answer, not with words, but I feel the sudden stillness in him, the way his grip tightens ever so slightly, as if he senses it too, the chill creeping in around the edges of this moment.

The war isn't done with us yet and something darker stirs beyond the veil, watching, waiting.

In the silence that follows, something inside me twists with a quiet dread I can't name, because I realize then, we may win the war, but we won't both survive it.

THE PROPHECY

When the Mourning Star descends, the sky shall bleed, and from its ash, the buried truths shall seed.

A king unburned, a root unsplit, who once bound flame to what was lit.

He wore no crown but divine thread, no golden helm upon his head.

His voice was hush, his blade was grief, he walked through dreams and held belief.

The king's eye's flare; one silver, sharp as steel, the other amber, like fire trapped in a sealed zeal.

The child divides on two paths wide, one burns with war, a raging tide.

The other, a fragile thread, of peace that dances where fears have fled.

When shadow sings and memory stirs, Earth shall wake beneath old slurs.

Stone will whisper, soil will cry, and bones long lost will rise and fly.

The ground will speak in breaking groans, she walks alone.

She is the key. The hidden flame. Unmarked by blood. Unclaimed by name.

Raised by silence. Cloaked in night. Her heart the blade, her truth the Light.

She bears the wound. She is the thread. The door, the fire, the book unread.

Let sky be shattered on her spine, let Earth split wide along the line.

The orphaned child must choose it all, to rise in flame, or let all fall.

And in the wreck of gods grown cruel, she will bleed, she is the rule.

ACKNOWLEDGEMENTS

As always, my deepest thanks go to my husband. This world and these books would not exist without you. You believed in this story when it was nothing more than a messy idea rattling around in my head, and you believed in me, especially during the moments when I struggled to do so myself. Thank you for your endless patience, your quiet encouragement, the late-night pep talks, and for never once making me feel guilty when I disappeared behind my laptop for hours at a time. Your love carried this story from beginning to end.

To my friends who supported me, encouraged me, and somehow made me feel incredibly cool for being an author, thank you. Your belief and enthusiasm mean more to me than I can say.

And to every reader who picks up this book, thank you. Thank you for giving this story a chance, for stepping into this world, and for letting these characters matter to you. Your time, your imagination, and your heart are what make any of this possible.

ABOUT THE AUTHOR

Jennifer Poliwoda was born in the wrong universe. In her ideal reality, she'd be a whimsical forest dweller living among moss and magic with her jester of a husband and four small but ferocious protectors: her cats. Since interdimensional relocation hasn't been invented yet, she writes immersive novels instead, giving both herself and her readers a chance to escape this world for a while.

As a lifelong reader, Jennifer never actually planned to become an author. Despite earning a degree in Biochemistry from RIT, Jennifer somehow ended up working in government contracting. Her writing journey began with a dream she couldn't shake, one that slowly grew into a story she had to put on paper. Once she started writing, she realized she couldn't stop. Now she is often squeezing in writing sessions between a full 8–5 schedule and the rest of life's chaos.

Jennifer lives in Rochester, New York with her amazingly kind and patient husband and their crazy cats: Diego, Delilah, and Maple. She loves nature, getting lost in good books, and pretending she's much more witchy than she actually is.

You can find her on Instagram @jenn.is.booked.